# Genesis of the Hunter

## Book 1

### By

## Joshua Martyr

Rachel,

It has been wonderful getting to know you these past two months. You are an amazingly gentle, considerate and compassionate person and I truly do cherish and enjoy the time I am able to spend with you. Hope you like the story.

Josh

Damnation Books, LLC.
P.O. Box 3931
Santa Rosa, CA 95402-9998
www.damnationbooks.com


Genesis of the Hunter: Book 1
by Joshua Martyr
Cover Art © 2010 by Ash Arceneaux
Edited by Lisa Jackson
Copyedited by Lisa Jackson
Layout and Book Production by Ally Robertson


Digital ISBN: 978-1-61572-121-4
Print ISBN: 978-1-61572-122-1

*Dedication*


To my parents: Marcellus and Mary Martyr, without whom I could not have achieved all that I have.




*Acknowledgements*


To those friends and loved ones who have been waiting in not so quiet anticipation.
To Leslie Shore, a wonderful, kind-hearted educator who unfailingly inspires renewed love for the English language.

# Book One

# Chapter One
## The Huntsman's Lore

*I*

The wind whispered across the rolling landscape, and where it met the interspersing plots of thicket and forest, a gentle symphony of fluttering flora rose to crescendo. In response, the great stag raised its head, crowned with a spread of antlers, regal and proud. In its ears, the wind spoke without meaning, but to its wet nostrils, which snorted in alert, it disclosed a hidden presence. This place abounded with dangers, and its calm, summer beauty belied a land that had seen much death. The soil of the plains had sopped the rushing blood of the fallen to nourish the same verdant beauty that disguised its history of bereavement.

From the south, the reach of Northumberland stretches its northernmost limits to encompass this aforementioned place. To its north, the Scots sought to regain their ancient homeland. The Holy Roman Empire had all but lost its formidable grip on Germania and, like the tide, was receding to its body of greater dominion. The Ottoman Empire flourished, as would the Prussian, but it would be Scotland and ultimately England that would score the path of this land.

The town of Berwick Upon the Tweed is precariously situated between Scottish and English territories. Berwick lies on the eastern coast of the English-Scottish border, about fifty-four miles southeast of Edinburough. It is aptly named, in that Berwick was constructed upon the north bank of the great river Tweed, a tributary of the North Sea. The precise geographical location of Berwick is one of the foremost reasons why the town was such a prized commodity. A town upon such a coast affords access to docking ships, which in turn allows a degree of import and export, as well as trade with foreign merchants. The Tweed itself generated saw mills, and was an abundant source of salmon. On the south bank of the Tweed, built upon the coast, lies the Tweedmouth. It is the smaller of the two towns and domicile to a seaport to exploit Berwick's economic potential. Such a town as Berwick would be a financial blessing to any king and country that could lay claim to it, because of its great size and various sources of economy. Thus, in the war for dominance upon the great isle, both English and Scot battled for control of this town, its castle, and surrounding lands.

# *II*

The boy gazed upwards at the huntsman, whose tall frame swayed gently above him with each long, smooth stride. The huntsman's grizzled beard and long hair lashed about in the strengthening breeze. The midday sun overhead shone off his great bald crest and illuminated his thin, tawny hair so that it gleamed like hot gold. The huntsman had been speaking in a low whisper, but stopped abruptly and cast his icy, green-eyed stare somewhere off into the forest.

The boy heard nothing at first, but then thought he heard a high-pitched, reedy snort from some distance away. Suddenly, from amidst the trees, a tumultuous crashing of leaves and twigs interrupted the gentle whispering of the wind. His eyes shot to the source of the disturbance, only in time to see a large animal charging through the foliage away from him. At the last, the beast leapt through the air to vault a fallen log, and the boy saw a large stag disappear into the forest, its mighty antlers tearing leaves from the trees and underbrush. The sounds of the vanished stag soon supplicated to the breeze and the singing birds of the forest. The boy looked up and saw Ober Hrothgyld smiling at him. It was difficult to make out his smile under his greying beard and stone-like face, but the wrinkles of his eyes betrayed his amusement. He placed a giant hand upon the boy's shoulder, and they continued through the woods towards the meadow.

Ober was a huntsman under the aristocracy of King Henry VII, and had once serviced the royal hunts directly under Edward the IV. Edward became ill a year after securing Berwick and perished from the ailment in 1483. Ober sought another venue for his vocation through a few turns of the season. Now, a town lord commissioned the huntsman and others to manage and hunt the local game for the gentry and nobles of Berwick Upon the Tweed. This day, however, was one of education for the boy. Ober, perhaps feeling he had become somewhat long of tooth, desired to pass his wisdom to vessels of greater vitality and youth. The boy had been an obvious choice. His body was strong for one who had not yet seen his thirteenth year, and his vision was as remarkable as Ober had ever observed in one so young. It was not any man who could draw the tensile might of the longbow and release with the accuracy required to warrant mastery of the art. It was this ability Ober foresaw in the boy, and so gladly taught him his deadly trade.

Around the outskirts of the town, Ober showed the boy how to make a proportionately sound longbow, and how to make use of the weapon. The boy had darkening bowstring welts on his left arm as proof of this practice. Later on, the huntsman made him a leather sleeve to protect the boy's forearm from the occasional rake of the bowstring. The huntsman also showed him how to craft arrows of varying purpose and the technique of tracking game. Ober had, of late, allowed the boy to test his budding skills by applying his teachings in the wilds beyond Berwick Castle. This was their second foray into the patchwork of woods west of Berwick and the first time the boy had seen the huntsman sidetracked.

The boy had, throughout his limited years, acquired only pieces of accurate historical information regarding Berwick, whose rich history was to him, largely unknown. In lieu of this discovery, the veteran huntsman, who had fought in more than one battle, began to recount what history he knew of Berwick. An old acquaintance of Ober's had been a steward of the keeper of records at Berwick Castle and Ober enjoyed disseminating what he had learned from the old monk.

The fleeing stag had momentarily halted the huntsman's tales as they made their way back east to Berwick. Now, as they cleared a section of forest and entered the meadow hills, the huntsman began once again to thread the yarns of old.

* * * *

Ober explained to the boy how Berwick had been warred over by the English and the Scots for countless years: how it changed hands over a dozen times, how under Edward III, England became a might to be reckoned with in Europe, and how Northumberland, their northernmost English county, had sequestered Berwick from the possession of the Scots following a monumental battle at Halidon Hill in 1333, anno domani. After recounting these tales for some time, the huntsman then spoke of another, grimmer lore.

The boy learned that in 1348, an invader that no army could vanquish had introduced itself to English soil.

The Black Plague spread north through England, weakening the nation's foundations and leaving corpses in its wake for three years. The possession of Berwick was still such a great commodity that the Scots attempted to repossess it in 1355 after the Black Death entered Scotland. England had spread itself too thin in the pursuit of further English conquests, a problem exacerbated by the prolific death tolls left in the wake of the plague. Scotland was successful and reclaimed Berwick. In England, serfs were in short supply, as were various tradesmen. Gentry, nobles, and lords were willing to double and even quadruple payment for services, and the distance between classes curtailed. It was not long before workers banded together, revoking serfdom and demanding an end to the weighty taxation they received under Richard II. A man named Thomas Baker, of Essex, rallied a group of villagers in 1377 and killed the royal tax gatherers of the area. Incidents of this kind led to the peasants' revolt of 1381 and to the right for the peasant class to work and own land. Throughout this grievous period of upheaval, the Scots and the English warred with one another. Berwick changed hands no less than thirteen times until a final and defining English victory in 1482 under Edward IV.

* * * *

A vestige of the midday sun now hovered above the western horizon behind them. Its monarch fire cooled to an amber glow, the world seemed bathed with the essence of Midas. From where the forest opened into moorlands, the huntsman and the boy headed southeast to meet the Tweed and follow its course eastward towards Berwick. As the boy listened to the huntsman's tales, he looked down at the Tweed, which flowed gently off to his right. The water churned, a golden liquescence in the waning sunlight, burbling fondly near the shore. He had heard many stories during their journey home and he held them to memory. He felt as if he possessed the experiences of kinsmen long dead and that to forget their tales would dishonor their teachings and legacy. Though the huntsman endeavored to give the boy a thorough rendition of history, his subsequent tales under the setting sun revolved with greater frequency around his own battles. His deep, grating voice was stoic and his eyes distant as he told the boy which mechanisms of the longbow he employed to introduce death to the enemy.

Berwick Castle loomed overhead as they passed. Their legs were weary and their bellies demanded fodder, but the huntsman ensured their pace was unmitigated. He fell silent as they neared civilization, lest roving Scots or bandits should hear them. These were unlikely, but the huntsman had not lived so long in a life fraught with danger without exercising caution. Ober took the hide flask from his side and drank. After giving some water to the boy as well, he stopped the flask and returned it to his side. In the last hour of light, the boy could see Berwick before him. From the north bank of the river, the land rose in a gradual escarpment, only to level off gently and there become the foundation of the town. They continued their approach from the river, and only when the huntsman turned northeast and began ascending the hill, were they headed on a direct course towards the town gate. The boy could only guess as to why the huntsman had delayed in plotting a more direct course to the town gate after passing Berwick Castle. Perhaps skirting the river till the last allowed them to avoid the scant patches of forest between the castle and the town; perhaps the slope of the land was less from the huntsman's chosen point of ascension. Either way, the boy did not question his motives.

The sun began its final descent into the west and the sky changed. Where the golden globe rested upon the earthen horizon, a deep pink and orange radiance filled the air and infused the very clouds with brilliance. Ober Hrothgyld strode purposefully uphill towards a patch of wood whose leaves were coated with the warm light of a sky nearing dusk. The shadows across the land became as dark as the blackness behind the stars and they absorbed what earthen splendor they could under their black veils. They coalesced into twining shapes under tree and thicket, standing in stark contrast to areas still bathed in soft light. Ober moved through the small cluster of wood, and upon nearing the foot of a massive oak, stopped and turned to the boy. Though adumbrated in the dappled shadows of the woodland flora, the boy could see the stern look in the huntsman's face. Spots of colored light seeped through the darkened arbors above them. One such spot caused one of the huntsman's eyes to gleam fiercely. Ober put a hand to the boy's shoulder, his voice barely audible.

"Of all our travels and doings this day, of this moment you can tell no one. Do you understand, boy?"

The boy nodded.

"Very well. Now, no matter what I say, you will look to my face and my face only. You will remain still and silent till I break gaze and turn from you."

The boy swallowed, his face taut, and he nodded again. The huntsman breathed in, and with a clear voice, spoke.

"Friend...I have been as far west as the forests beyond the meadow hills. There is naught to be seen but bird, beast, and bush. To my reckoning, you have only to watch the waters and the wayward. Be at peace this night."

The boy was baffled by the event unfolding before him. The huntsman's voice had risen from its dry whisper as if he spoke to one other than the boy; yet his eyes remained fixed upon the boy's, and it seemed he spoke meaninglessly to him. The boy was startled from his thoughts by a whisper from somewhere high above.

"I thank you, Ober, for your report and your discretion. But, be at ease friend, no more eyes lurk here than our own. Still, caution is a man's livelihood."

"Aye." The huntsman replied.

The boy dared not look up, for the huntsman still stared into his eyes. His body atwitter with anxiety, he struggled against himself to maintain composure.

"Till tomorrow even then?" The huntsman inquired.

"Of course…I believe I am still owed an ale."

The tone seemed almost jocular. The huntsman's face yielded a mild, if amused grimace. He turned and beckoned the boy with a flick of his massive hand. They passed underneath the great oak, heading uphill towards the town gate, which lay some distance away. Only a meager stretch of woodland and shrubs lay beyond the oak, and beyond these there was naught but grassy plain between the patch of wood and the town walls. The boy reasoned that the voice must have come from the oak itself, though the logic warranted to sustain such musings escaped him. The huntsman continued uphill towards the town, his old, deer-hide tunic swaying in the breeze. The boy followed, but he could not alleviate his thoughts of the whisper from the trees. Questions poured through his mind. Clearly, the huntsman had been required to tend to some task other than his education this day, and he wondered what it had been.

Furthermore, to whom did the voice from the oak belong? And to what did he owe such strange and sudden secrecy? He had been looking up at the oak before the huntsman had halted him, but he had seen nothing out of the ordinary from its southern aspect. He was now only a few paces beyond the tree and wanted desperately to look up into the mysterious canopy. His curiosity superseded his will to heed the huntsman and he turned his head. He did not want his movement to catch the huntsman's eye, so rather than turning about to face the oak he peered surreptitiously over his shoulder, straining to stare from the corners of his eyes.

He saw the thick, knotted trunk of the oak, the large branches, which like giant, crooked arms, rose towards the firmament.

The twining body of the massive oak was obscured by a dense covering of leaves, which, like the rest of the oak, was vaguely silhouetted against the darkening sky. Still, he saw nothing that caught his eye. Then he glimpsed a large wooden structure built upon a spread of large branches, branches that stretched and twisted from the oak like a giant, supine hand, clutching the base of the wooden structure.

Its floor was some twenty feet from the ground and seemed to consist of lumber, chiseled flat on the topside. It was long enough for even the huntsman to lie in, and nearly wide enough as well. Save for the edge built into the central stem of the oak, it was girded along its sides by fitted logs, which were perhaps as high as a man's waist. The boy marveled as to how he had not seen it immediately.

From the other side, the structure was well hidden with other branches and leaves, but from the north it was merely bathed in shadow and only wreathed by leaves and twining limbs. Through this dark vista, he thought he could make out a figure. It was most definitely a man: well built, and in all likelihood seated, for what must have been the dark silhouette's shoulders were barely visible above the wooden railings. The boy's heart quickened as he observed that the man might be looking back at him, and he whipped his head away, returning his sights to the huntsman.

Ober saw the boy quicken his pace and come abreast with him. The boy was looking up at him quite fixedly, as if he wished to spew a deluge of questions.

"You wish to know what took place, eh, boy?"

"Aye, sir."

Ober adjusted the bow and quiver upon his back and then began to speak.

"He is a sentry, the foremost lookout for the town and first defense against attacks upon Berwick. His presence is known only to guardsmen, a few huntsmen, and lords and their confidants. He watches the coast and port for invasion by sea and observes the bank for invaders advancing along the base of the hill. As you know, the town lays upon the hill's plateau, north of where the land descends to the Tweed. The advantage to this, boy, is that Berwick can be defended from the high ground. However, discerning what may lay in wait at the bottom of the hill is made difficult in darkness, or by fog from the Tweed. Even the eyes of yonder guardsmen upon the parapet walk of the town wall may not find the enemy at night."

The boy looked up towards the town. They were close enough that the incline of the slope had lessened significantly, and the boy could see the wall, the figures atop it vague in the distance.

"The sentry's position allows a better view down the Tweed's bank, and a closer one at that. In the event he spots a danger to the town in the night, he keeps with him a large horn, whose bellow alerts the guardsmen of an attack from the bank. One sounding forewarns of a lesser threat. In truth, these types of threats, in the form of bandits, heretics, and such, are the most likely danger that could find their way so near the town undetected. Enemies of greater number would be sighted and reported before reaching such proximity...God willing."

The boy looked back at the oak, its grand presence made increasingly tenebrous by the small trees before it and by the fading daylight. They had put some distance between themselves and the oak, and were over halfway to the town gate. It was true, he thought, he had been able to see further down river from lower on the slope.

"Boy! Are you attentive, or do I speak for my own amusement?"

"Nay, sir, I am listening, you were speaking...speaking about the horn." The huntsman grunted under his beard and allowed himself a wry smile.

"Yes, the horn. Continuous soundings of it relay a significant, ensuing danger to the town. The sentry's position is purposely hidden to catch unawares those who attempt to shed the sight of the guardsmen. That, boy, is why his position must be kept secret, it is for both his safety and that of the town.

# III

The huntsman and the boy strode to the town wall. The earthen ramparts that encompassed the town were not of a staggering height, but the cold, grey stone of the wall rose more than high enough to prevent the attempts of would be intruders. The walls and the parapet walks behind their tops ran nearly uninterrupted about the town, save for entrances like the one before them, which was barred by a thick, cast-iron gate. Upon the walls to either side of the gate stood guards. The boy looked up at them. They were clad in mail, covered with red tunics, and crowned by open sallet helms, whose low brims cast the upper portion of their faces in shadow.

"Ober," one called with a mischievous grin, "what lessons did you teach that young one all alone in the woods without a soul to see? Can't catch the favor of a good woman these days, eh?"

The guard atop the other adjacent rampart looked at his compatriot nervously. He was clearly uncomfortable with the familiar manner with which his fellow guardsman had addressed one so renowned in Berwick as the stone-faced huntsman.

"Nay, Kayleb," the huntsman retorted unruffled. "You speak lies about me without regard, for in truth, I have caught the favor of a woman. Good, I would not deem her though, you are right in this respect, for she is a filthy whore, but she serves my purpose. Indeed, I still have business with your mother this night, so raise the gate whelp and perhaps I'll beget you a brother."

The guard's amusement was cut short, and he simply stared at the huntsman with his mouth slightly agape, as the huntsman regarded him with stoic indifference. A snort burst from the guard atop the adjacent rampart, his fist covering his mouth and his face contorted and reddening. This was accompanied by two bursts of laughter from behind the walls inside the town.

"Well," said the adjacent guard atop the rampart, his face flushed and grinning. "You are fortunate to have come when you did, we were about to barricade the gate for the night. A good even to you, Ober, and give Kayleb's mother a greeting for me as well."

The guard named Kayleb whipped his head to his counterpart, but before he could say a word, raucous laughter erupted from all around him.

"Raise the gate!" the guard managed before bursting into laughter once more.

The iron gate grated and creaked as it rose, and the huntsman passed underneath, dipping his head and tilting to lower the bow and quiver upon his back. The boy followed, and when he was beyond the gate, he spied two guards turning the gate cogs. They were chuckling and sniffling as they regained their composure. To either side of the gate rose steep stone stairways, which reached the parapet walk, one of the few accesses to the walk in the town.

The huntsman and the boy walked into the town; the boisterous sounds of the market had dwindled, and only the occasional voices of the people could be heard. Here and there a chicken would cluck, a goat bleat, or a dog bark in evening calm, and the usual odors of the town hung in the air. They walked past the market area and passed rows of small, quaint homes.

Bolstered by daub, many were wooden dwellings with shingled roofs, and many had a second level built atop the first. The ground levels oft accommodated the owners' trade and supported their sleeping quarters above. The pair walked into an area of the town where the more prosperous tradesmen took residence. Here, the hard, earthen ground and scattered hay transitioned into cobblestone, and led to larger houses. It was one of these that the huntsman approached, and he was about the knock upon the door when the boy spoke.

"He said that you owed him...remember? He said that you owed him ale. Why did he say that?" Ober sighed, his eyes squinting subtly.

"I made a bet with him and lost."

The boy persisted.

"What was the bet? How do you know him? Who..."

"Boy!...boy...it is late...I," Ober sighed again and looked down at the boy, stroking his beard. "I met him some years ago and like myself he is not from Northumberland. In fact, he was raised a Spaniard. His father took his mother as a wife after a Spanish army attacked and overran a small town in southwest France. She had been married off to a wealthy landowner there, but was herself English. The sentry learned our language through her company, but was educated and trained as a Spaniard in the imperial capital of Toledo. His father disagreed with the budding practices of the Inquisition and was denounced, along with his family, as a heretic. His mother was burnt at the stake. He told me his father was a great swordsman, and reaped sickening vengeance before he himself was killed.

"This I believe, for the sentry still carries a broad blade of Spanish steel, and is nigh unrivaled in its art. Our sentry escaped and made his way to England. This, young one, is how I was acquainted with him. After the plague of old, which I spoke of earlier today, England became more accepting of foreigners who were willing to do a good days work. I, a Welshman, skilled with a bow, and he, a fearsome warrior, found each other and our trade through war. We became friends, regardless of the gap between our years. I taught him much as I do now with you. He was an avid learner, and I soon found that he held teachings for me as well. Now, boy, I leave you to your father's keeping."

"Sir, the bet. What about the bet?" the boy whined.

"Christ have mercy, boy, your mind is not large enough to consume all you have heard today." The huntsman's speech quickened. "He and I were in the wood before sundown not long ago. We spotted a deer grazing in a clearing some sixty paces from where we were. In short, he hit from a distance I did not think he could and he is now owed a flagon of ale. Now...to your father."

The huntsman turned towards the door and knocked. The

boy's mother answered, her long dress flapping in the evening air. The huntsman towered above her.

"Even, Ober, my husband has not yet returned. He told me to give you these." She pressed a few shillings into his hand. "Thank you for returning my boy to me safely." The huntsman bowed his head.

"My thanks to you and your husband. The boy is an apt pupil. Goodnight."

As he was about to turn, the boy spoke from his mother's side.

"Are you going to visit Kayleb's mother now?"

The huntsman's eyes widened in alarm. He stared down at the boy in disbelief, chanced a brief glance to his mother and seeing her jaw drop, spun and walked away with a degree of haste in his stride.

# Chapter Two
## The Sentry

## I

He watched the giant figure of Ober move through the tavern throng. It would become more crowded still come dark, but, for the most part, it was most enjoyable at this time. Few were so drunk yet that they would totter about reeking of spirits, or ale and blather in inebriated stupors. Most were comrades sharing tales of old or present gossip, clanging their gourds together, and enjoying each other's company. They sat around coarse, dark wooden tables, atop stools of similar refinement. Still others stood and held palaver away from the copious sitting area. The clatter of gourds and platters, and the grating of stools could be heard all about. The air was heavy with coalescing voices and laughter, which echoed throughout the tavern in undulating murmurs. The air was also stuffy and hot, and he rolled up his linen sleeves hoping to cool himself.

Ober was heads above all in the tavern, and small parties of merrymakers cleared a way in his presence. When he was a few paces from the door, he half turned and gave a parting gesture in the form of a reserved nod. The huntsman pushed open one of the wide tavern doors, and a brilliant beam of golden sunlight rushed into the room. Ober stooped his head under the doorway and walked out of view. The door swung back behind him, returning the tavern to its warm, ochre ambiance.

He looked down at his table. Ober had left his finished gourd upon it. To himself, he had a flagon of ale. It was nearly finished, and he looked down at the scant froth on the surface of his drink. Normally, he would drink not half so much, a gourd at most. This was, however, the prize of their bet, and as it was at the huntsman's expense, he intended to imbibe to the limit of his tolerance.

A few tavern wenches were going about their scullery duties, collecting soiled gourds and platters, and catering to those whose thirsts remained unquenched. They wore burgundy blouses with white frills around the breast. From an anteroom where the dinnerware was washed, another wench emerged, wiping her hands on an apron, which may once have been white. She was strong bodied and fair skinned, and her long, reddish hair fell below her shoulders in thick, flowing waves. He kept his eyes upon her as she lifted an empty gourd from a table and looked up at him. She gave him a subtle smile and approached his table. As she did so, a ragged-looking man barred her way with a knobby hand, gripping her about the waist. He grinned up at her with squinting eyes and broken teeth.

"C'mere, cully. There's not you'll be wantin that ole Cuthbert can't n'er provide I'll warrant. Aye, cully?" The man issued her a wry grin. "A tussle in the furs with someone wise in the ways, what say yer?"

She looked from the withered man to the man seated at the table to which she had been advancing. The wrinkled elder followed her gaze. His most open eye took the man in and then shot down to peer at the massive quiver of arrows beneath his table. His face was clearly discouraged and was nothing short of anxious when his shifty eye fixed itself upon the exquisite guard and scabbard of the long sword at his waist. The man stared back at him, his demeanor as cool and hard as granite.

"Er...off with ye then woman, there'll be girls a plenty yet who'll be wantin fer a taste of his ole dog. Off with ye girl, g'on bout yer business."

He released her waist, and with a nervous half smile to the seated man, turned to his gourd and his table company. The girl smiled and walked to the seated man's side. He looked up at her.

"Hello, Bronwyn," he said calmly.

"Twas much like the day we first met was it not," she replied with sarcastic nostalgia. "Ye, comin te me rescue after some ole fart tries te latch upon me like some starved leech. Such lovely memories." She smiled again. "And where has the ole huntsman gone? Didn't enjoy having his pockets emptied by ye, did he? God, the look on his face when ye said that fer some reason ye had a greater thirst than usual this even. I thought I'd burst, the way he eyed ye. Oh, aye, he's such good man that one, oh heavens."

Bronwyn sighed; her cheeks flushed as she recovered from her little chuckle. He had always loved her Gaelic accent; it seemed to make whatever she said more amusing.

"Ye'll be leavin soon then, too, I'd wager, to guard some noble for the night or whatever it is the lord'll have ye do this night."

He had not told her the specifics of his duty, but given the small armory he carried upon his person, one need only assume.

She subtly slipped her free hand on to his, bent low so that her breasts bulged above the frills, and whispered softly.

"I'll not be here late tomorrow, mayhap ye could keep me company till before the sun sets." She smiled almost mischievously and he took her hand in his own, returning her fond touch. They allowed their hands to part and she giggled quietly. She took the huntsman's empty gourd in her free hand.

"An this time, do'ne spend te much time in speaks with mi'brother, er ye two will gabber till sundown about war and wounds and such nonsense, and I'll be forced te seek company from ole Cuthbert over there."

He shook his head amusedly and watched her turn away towards another table, holding two gourds in the crook of her arm. She snatched up some greasy plates from two young men and made her way back to the anteroom.

He had met Bronwyn soon after the appropriation of Berwick from the Scots. Herself and her brother, Colin, were Scottish themselves, and had been holed up in Colin's smithy during the attack. He had heard from a fellow infantryman that their troops had rammed through the smithy door thinking they might find soldiers in wait and weaponry to be pillaged. What they did find was a naked, pale-skinned, red-headed Scotsman, sitting bare upon an anvil. This, of course, had halted their raucous charge and added an element of confusion to the situation. The infantryman had told this tale to a small party in the tavern some years back and had recited Colin's exact words in the face of fifteen or so swords, pointing directly at him.

"Em...ah...hello there. I suppose ye'll be wonderin what's become of me clothes," Colin had said. "Well, I got te figurin tha ye would storm in here expectin hidden men an weapons an general danger from all about. As ye can see, I've got no weapons on mi'person...well...tha may be a matter of opinion, but none tha ye need worry about anyway. So...I'll be brief, least ye anxious rascals o'the group skewer me naked hide before I finish mi'proposition. I'm a fine blacksmith, and tha you'll be needin sure, te replace broken weapons, horseshoes and the like. I'm more valuable alive than dead and ye'll get ne ransom fer this ole white arse. I'll live under English law as well as any, just leave me and me wee sister to work as we did fer a Scottish Berwick."

He smiled to himself, the gall of that fool. He had come to learn that it was Colin's nature to diffuse tense situations with his comical yet methodical whit. Poor Colin had still taken a heavy beating, all the while stark naked, and had in the end been robbed of a few swords. But he had survived, and Bronwyn, who had hidden on the floor above the smithy, had, for the most part, escaped what could have been a horrid scene of murder and rape. Like other Scots, they had become integrated with the English of Berwick under Northumbrian rule. In fact, Colin was quite popular amongst the townspeople; his metalworking skills were renown, as was his sense of humor. Bronwyn had captured the eyes and hearts of many in the town, including his own, he thought. They had been discreet lovers for some months now, and he had never experienced a woman so sweet as she.

He broke from his musings and brought his flagon to his lips. He finished his remaining ale quickly and reached under the table, hauling up the large quiver by its thick leather strap. He stood and slung it across his back. He then picked up his massive bow, which rested against the far side of the table. The bowstring was securely wound around it to keep from being snagged or misplaced. A few eyes were upon him now, mainly from old Cuthbert's table. They watched him move through the clamoring crowd, push open a tavern door, and walk out into the sunlight.

Though the sun was readying to drop into the west, it was still bright enough that it strained his eyes, which had grown accustom to the dim light of the tavern. He walked towards the town gate, passing the marketplace on the way. The final bustle of the market was beginning to dwindle, as was the enlivened cacophony that sounded from the marketplace throughout the day. Chickens fluttered about in cages and in the hands of buyers as they were passed around, held by their legs. Clothes and linens where draped about and swayed in the wind. Merchant and crop stands were scattered about, their produce nearing depletion and their proprietors urging passers by to partake. As he moved on towards the gate, he spotted a boy walking beside a man whom he presumed was the boy's father. He soon recognized the youngster, and inadvertently fixed his eyes on the boy. The boy looked at him, then away, then back again with a mildly quizzical look.

The boy had looked up from his father's side to see the man staring at him. He was tall, but not nearly so tall as the huntsman. He had long, black hair, which reached his shoulders, and a man's stubble about his face. He was quite striking to behold, for even his brown leather tunic could not hide the powerful muscles underneath. Across his broad back and shoulders was slung a large quiver of arrows, and at his left hip, tethered to his belt, hung a scabbard which holstered a large sword. A thick dagger was sheathed on his right side, and he held a great bow in his left hand, which ran from his head down to the very bottom of his boots. Tightly gripping his left forearm, just below his elbow, was a thick leather sleeve that covered him to the wrist. The man gave a knowing and nearly undetectable half smile and moved on from the marketplace.

He walked onward briskly, and soon found himself at the town gate. As per usual, two guardsmen stood watch from the parapets and two faced in towards the town from the ground on either side of the gate. The guardsmen held menacing pikes and had short swords at their sides. The gate was still raised for the day, but he slowed his pace anyway to address the four guardsmen.

"All quiet on the front today then?" he asked casually. One of the two guardsmen atop the wall turned and was the first to answer him.

"Even friend. Aye, peaceful as usual, praise God. It has been some time since I myself have seen any roving bands of Scots and the like, eh, lads?" One or two guardsmen nodded or grunted in consent. "Seems only fanatical unrest from within occupies us these days, and we are blessed that even these are scant. But outside the town, nay, nothing but what you see now."

He passed underneath the gate, issuing a curt nod to the pike bearers.

"Till next we met then," he exclaimed with a hand raised high. His pace quickened once more and he headed down the steepening slope, deviating slightly to the west.

# *II*

The sky was cloudless, suffused by the deep brilliance of the fading sun. Birds were singing their last songs of the day and a gentle breeze combed the soft grasses at his feet, shivering them as it passed. He always enjoyed these walks during the warmer months, they were calming, and his isolation somehow connected him to the land. He approached the familiar plot of wood. Moving through the scant bush and passing through a sparse assemblage of slim trees, he finally reached the great oak. It towered above the rest, its branches spanning wide. He loosened his bowstring so that, from its attachment to the bottom of his bow, it dragged limply on the ground. He held the other end of the string in his right hand. He braced the bow between his legs and the ground, using the downward force of his left arm to bend it. The wood creaked under the strain, wanting to snap back to a straight position. He attached the loose end of the bowstring to the top of the bow. Now tightly strung, the bow curved gently, and he slung the giant weapon over his shoulder, adjacent to the quiver. He returned his attention to the oak. Inconspicuously wrapped around its bulky, gnarled trunk was a thin rope ladder. This he unraveled until it hung relatively straight from the central stem high above. He gripped the drooping rungs, and without hesitation, the sentry began to climb.

He moved with a practiced balance, easing his ascent now and again by pushing off against the trunk. He climbed through the first spread of branches and leaves in this fashion, careful not to catch his projecting bow and sword on the way up. He looked up to the rudimentary floor of the hide. The timbers on the underside were still layered with bark, and green mosses grew from them. The bark had been left purposely to increase the camouflage of the hide. The rope ladder was attached just above the hide, and the sentry climbed above its base, gripping and stepping upon the enormous branches which supported the construct.

He hauled himself up into one of the large crooks of the tree, letting go of the rope ladder. He stepped up and out from the central stem onto the floor of the hide. Once there, he turned to face the tree again, bending over to grab at the rope ladder. Leaning over the railings of the hide's north side, he quickly reeled the ladder in. Its bottom end moved up into the foliage, as if it were being eaten by the oak itself. A few green oak leaves flittered in their descent under the setting sun, after which, it seemed, there had never been anyone there at all.

Up in the arbor-held loft, the sentry threw the heap of rope to the floor and removed his quiver and bow. He leaned them gently against the log rails to his right. The bow he set on an angle, to better conceal its projecting length in the hide. A small wooden stool had been built into the floor, close enough to the inner edge that his back could lean against the oak itself. Here he sat, and looked at the bow leaning off to his right. He had made it for himself under Ober's guidance. Its tips were recurved as was Ober's. His bow was not so long as Ober's, for his bow matched his height, but it was much thicker and cored with yew. Though still elastic, it made his bow particularly resistant to compression, which when compressed, could release arrows with fearsome force. Still looking off to his right, his eyes then ran along the length of the hide and its rails, whereafter he observed the chest. It was unlocked as he had left it, so that if he were ever hastened by intruders, he need only lift the top and remove the horn therein to sound it.

During his few years at this post, he had developed a near unconscious vigilance. His head and eyes had become so accustom to scouring the land before him that they moved about methodically of their own will. The wilds below and beyond were as recognizable to him as his own reflection, and thus his attuned eyes and ears were sensitive to deviations of the familiar. Any such noise or movement in the range of his senses would tear him from his musings, compelling his complete attention and focus.

He thought about Bronwyn. He pondered what pleasures the following evening might bring. He envisioned her standing before him, a robe dropping slowly from her shoulder, revealing her fair skin and wondrous body. He remembered how at ease he felt with her face nested against his and her body pressed against him.

The leaves rustled in a strange fashion, unlike their easy fluttering influenced by the light breeze. The sentry sat up and leaned slightly, to peer over the stacked log barrier on his right. Over the railings he saw a fox lope through a patch of bush and exit the plot of wood to bound away in the southerly direction of the river. He sat back against the tree. The sun was a languishing orange crescent in the west.

His hand brushed the guard of his sword. He looked down at it. He thought about his father. He remembered Spain and his home in Toledo. His recalled his father speaking to him in Spanish, telling him he had a present for his fourteenth birthday. The present had been his sword. A Tizona blade, fashioned of Spanish steel from Toledo, the finest in the world. He studied the exquisite guard, like a crescent moon made of briars, frozen in silver as they had begun twining upwards from the hilt. The hilt: this brought his father's face to mind again. His father had commissioned a blacksmith in Toledo to extend and balance the dimensions of the Tizona design at the hilt and blade, so that it could be used both as a two handed weapon or a one handed blade if the left hand was otherwise occupied. Not once had the sentry used his sword in such a manner. As a youth, the blade had been weighty for him, even held with both hands. Now strong enough to hold the big blade with one arm, he favored laying waste to his enemies with the maneuverability and brutal force afforded by gripping the weapon firmly in both of his capable hands. Perhaps if he had fought then as he could now, if fear had not checked his resolve to disobey his father's vehement order to flee, perhaps then he could have saved him, and his mother as well. He had watched both of them die in the respective twilights of morning and evening on the same day.

The air cooled and he rolled down his sleeves. He thought of his mother as the sun vanished in west, leaving only a vestigial pink glow in its wake. He remembered his mother's strength and her kindness. He remembered the morning that zealots of the growing Inquisition burst into his large home in Toledo before his father returned from his enterprises. He and his mother had been forced to flee to the upper floor, where he quickly snatched his scabbard and sword. He helped his mother through the window onto the roof, and barely had time enough to throw himself through it before a sword shattered the frame above him.

He was able to keep them at bay for some while, but he could only obstruct one possible access to the roof at a time. He and his mother were soon inundated on the small section of roof. They wasted no time and nor did he. Deadly slashes were exchanged and parried. His longer, heavier sword helped fend the Spaniards off, but their lighter Jinetas were wielded with greater speed in single hands. He was forced to retreat little by little to maintain his sword's length away from them. He saw his mother caught and dragged back inside through a window. On the verge of madness, he fought like a cornered dog, his mother his only concern. In the end, he lost his footing at the edge of the roof and fell, crashing onto the top of a carriage below and rolling bloodied and scratched onto the ground.

The sentry looked at a small scar on his wrist, one he received from the fall. He looked around. The night air was soothing and nearly quiet. Sovereign and bold next to the dense mist of stars that shone like brilliant pin pricks in a sheet of night, a full moon hung in the blackness above. The loft became invisible, and he with it. Thickly blanketed in darkness he saw all and was seen by none. His mind wandered again and he lapsed back into thought.

He remembered rising slowly, in time to see two men in the distance dragging the beaten figure of his mother into the woods behind the house. He had gathered his sword and given chase, but realized that the remaining Spaniards had seen him, and he was in turn pursued. As fleet of foot as he was, he hoped to reach the two men holding his mother and dispatch them before they could do further damage to her. He prayed he could accomplish this feat before their fellows reached the fray from behind him. No sooner did he breach the edge of the wood, than he was upon them, and they drew their blades. They had begun to tie his half conscious mother to an isolated tree, under which they had piled all sorts of dry woodland litter. Understanding their intent, he engaged them with an animal's wrath; yet, skilled youth that he was, he was only able to maim one of them before the others entered the melee. He was forced away from his mother by three advancing villains and he scrambled to the nearest hill in the wood. Only when he had gained higher ground did he turn to face the onslaught. Through the trees and fallen leaves, they harried him backwards and uphill.

As he fought, the remaining Spaniards secured his mother to the tree and began dousing her, and the pile beneath her, with a liquid from their swollen flasks. She had become coherent and was screaming, begging for mercy. From an increasing distance, he saw one man sparking flint onto a patch of tinder wedged into the woodpile. He remembered how the fiery sparks had danced ominously atop their fuel. He was red in the face and roaring with desperation, tears streaming down his cheeks. In his fervor, he took a step downhill to heave wildly with his sword. He managed to clip the side of the middle man's head. The man's temple and brow ruptured in a spray of blood. The man's body flew back limply, his sword leaving his hand. The weighty blow he had dealt the man left him somewhat unbalanced, and his vulnerable leg received a painful slash below the knee which nearly buckled him. He slashed back at his attacker, regained his footing, and defended his position.

His mother's screams had intensified then, for the tinder had given wisps of smoke and then a small flame. He turned to see his mother once more. She was soaked, disheveled, and beaten, and flames began to lap about the pile. The fuel must then have caught, for black smoke spiraled about her, and great tongues of flame hungrily engulfed her with a sound like the last breath of the dying. Her body writhed and strained against its bonds, a moving conflagration. Her piercing, rasping screams were choked with flames, and the air blackened with char-scented smoke.

He recalled the image of the tree and his mother both burning in the dim morning light. With despair in his heart, he had abandoned his fight, turned tail, and ran. The last glimpse he had of his mother had been her burning body as it fell forward then snapped back towards the tree in a tangle of half-charred ropes. Embers and sparks scattered into the air as her dangling body swung through the pile at the foot of the tree like a fiery angel fallen from grace.

He did not know if the makeshift immolation had killed her, or if his mother had finally been finished by the stroke of a Jineta. What he did understand was that she was beyond saving, and with a crushed spirit and spent tears he turned from his assailants and fled up into the forest. They followed as best they could, but he knew the forest and his own stamina. He remembered their faces and the noise of their pursuit fading in the distance. He remembered being alone in the forest, gasping for breath against a tree, his wounded leg stinging and throbbing horribly. Fearing for his father, he moved through the forest to where it neared the road, and there he lay in wait to intercept his father's journey home.

He felt then as he did now, safely concealed in a womb of the earth, watching the often wicked world of men pass him by. He adjusted his position and breathed in the cool air. Crickets began to chirp here and there, and a few trees creaked almost imperceptibly as they supplicated to a brief gust of wind. He stared down the length of the hill to the river. The moon cast a rippling white glow on the Tweed, and where it opened into the North Sea, docked boats rocked gently near the seaport. He leaned his head over the railing, straining his head to the right to look around his oak throne. As he suspected, the banks and surrounding land were tranquil. A light vapor began to rise from the Tweed. Moved by the gentle breeze, it crawled just beyond the river bank towards him, after which, it dissipated into the night air.

From time to time, the sentry would stand. He would move slowly and quietly, stretching his muscles, feeling the flow of his blood quickening. He strove to delay his fatigue, which if left to nature's design, would soon attempt to lull his body and senses. He sat again, his head tilted up momentarily, resting against the bark to ease the muscles on the back of his neck.

His ears detected some change around him. It was the crickets, something about them had changed. He still heard their wet chirps all around the landscape, but somehow the symphony was not as it had been. He heard them in the distance and from his left towards the town, but the strident chorus beyond the hide to his right, fringing his plot of wood, had fallen silent. Still seated, he stiffened against the tree, becoming part of the oak under its shadows. He straightened his back as much as he could and, ever so slowly, leaned somewhat, stopping in a position that allowed him to peer over the coarse railings.

He scoured the wood below, analyzing the shadows between the trees and shrubbery. Argent moonbeams glowed amidst the trees, seeping through the twisted apertures in the leafy canopy and between the staggered trunks. Still, he saw nothing. His exhalations slowed as he further silenced his breathing, his focus full and sharp. He thought he heard a noise, the sound of something brushing against flora as it passed. His eyes shot to the general area and held there. This time he heard a definitive brushing of foliage, and saw a momentary disturbance of moonlight between the trees: a quick flicker of movement. His eyes intuited from whence the movement had come, and fixed themselves. He was sure he saw a hunched shadowy form move over the woodland floor behind the scant trees. He noticed it was drawing closer as it wound through the trees and bush, quietly caressing the leaves upon occasion as it passed. No more than fifteen paces away, the sounds of faint footfalls were barely audible from his loft. He felt and heard his heart hasten in beat, pounding louder and stronger in his chest.

This was no animal which passed by happenstance. This was

the gait of a man who crept in the night. Indeed, as the figure wound closer and moved through spots of moonlight, the sentry observed a man stealing swiftly in a deep crouch. The man wore some kind of old, tattered, open shirt, his lower half still entirely obscured in darkness. Though the sentry could not clearly see his face, there was something about the man's shadowy visage that troubled him. He was so focused on the man's aspect, that he nearly missed the second figure, which trailed close behind the first in a similar fashion. The sentry struggled to watch both interlopers as they made their way towards his position. The first was now only a few paces beyond the hide, but it was the action of the second that caught his eye.

A fallen birch lay over a patch of thorny hedge, spotlighted by unfiltered moonlight that shone through a large opening in the canopy above. The figure, perhaps seeking to traverse the thorns by moving across the fallen tree, leaped up onto it with an odd agility, alighting in a crouch on the birch. What the sentry saw caused his breath to freeze in his chest, and an icy wave to twist his gut. It was man, and yet most assuredly not. It did not face him, yet from what he could see of its profile, it bore the strong face of a man; but the facial bones seemed somewhat overly distinct, and its brow was hairless and menacingly furrowed. The brow was not so much pronounced as it was thick and heavily muscled: a feral excrescence, which joined to the bridge of the nose like a predatory beast's.

When its head turned to glance at the other, the sentry stared on disquietedly, shaken to the core of his being by its lurid, yellow eyes, which seemed to pierce the darkness. The man-thing paused briefly, and it tilted back its head. Its horrible eyes appeared to stare vapidly into nothingness, and it looked as if it were subtly sniffing the air. Its mouth relaxed and opened slightly, and the sentry was sure he saw the tips of strange pointed teeth on either side of its upper jaw.

His mind raced to explain what he saw before him, but could reason nothing at all. It felt as though he were dreaming, for in the world he knew, such as these could not exist. His mind shook free of its denial and he observed the thing further.

The only clothing this one wore was a filthy rag that might once have been pants, torn and hanging in shreds at the knees. Thick, bristle-like hair hung ragged and raven-black at its shoulders, an almost leonine mane that stood in stark contrast to the skin of its body, which was as pale as the illuminating moonlight. The coarse mane ran unnaturally low upon its back, the shaggy tangle tapering where the nape and spine met, somewhat akin to a wild boar's. The body itself was built with a lithe musculature, so pronounced from beneath its white flesh, that it seemed to have been deeply chiseled out of chalk. It clutched the fallen timber with bony hands and feet that found purchase with solid, blackened nails, which tapered into points so feral they were no less than claws.

With a quick movement that was part scuttle and part bound, it moved across a portion of the fallen birch on all fours, and then dropped out of the moonlight to the leafy floor of the wood, crouched in the shadows as before. The movement sent another chilling wave through the sentry. He had ceased to understand these creatures as men in his mind, he simply could not. The thudding beat of his heart was now resounding throughout his body, and beads of sweat had formed above his brow. Still peering over the log railings, he craned his neck to look below him and saw the first of these horrid things disappearing from sight directly under his wooden hide. Losing sight of it stirred greater anxiety in him.

He was only more troubled when the other crept through the wood in his direction as well, and vanished from view in the same manner. He could hear movement below him, but the rustling began to subside and finally ceased. In the dead silence, his eyes closed and his heart nearly stopped. He wondered if the one atop the fallen tree had actually caught his scent, and if perhaps both were now climbing the oak towards him as he sat motionless in the hide therein. It was an eerie thought, and he attempted to clear it from his mind.

Beginning to recover from the shock of the situation, his

courage began to steel itself, as it always had in the past. He turned slowly to look over the railings to his left, half expecting to find himself face to face with a horrid leering countenance. Instead, he found them poised some distance away near the edge of the wood, their backs to him. Their torsos swayed gently now and then, their heads slowly cocking to one side, like a village dog, or cat. They stared through the darkness, uphill towards the town. They watched the distant town with a disturbing interest, or at least seemed to watch it, as though they had found what they had been searching for. This realization steeled his fortitude even further. They intended to enter Berwick. For what hellish purpose he knew not, but he would be damned if he would wait to discover it. He thought of the sleeping babes of Berwick, of the boy, of Bronwyn, of mothers and fathers. A small flame sparked within him, charging him to perform his duty as a sentry, his duty to protect the town.

* * * *

He could see them quite clearly now, for where they crouched, the land transitioned to the short grasses which spanned most of the landscape. The few slender saplings which stood near them did not allow the same concealment as the larger, more densely grown trees deeper within the wood, and the brilliant moon at their backs gave them away to the sentry's eye. He noticed that the unclothed one was somewhat smaller than the other, and that, by his estimation, neither were larger than he. This observation gave him little comfort, however, for their inherent predatory quality sparked in him a deep, primordial fear.

So hellish in nature, yet so near the state of man, surely they must be escaped demons of the pit, twisted angels who fell with the Morning Star. He knew not how these demons came to be here, nor why, nor from whence they had prowled in the night to reach so near to Berwick. Perhaps they had, by scent or sight, stalked the paths of the few huntsmen who passed him by before heading to the town gate. Perhaps their presence this night was merely a chance misfortune. Whatever the means, the fact remained that these fiendish creatures had found their way to Northumberland, and now, in so far as he could tell, sought to skulk forth unto his town of Berwick.

A feeling of contempt hardened his heart and made clear his purpose. If he sounded the horn he would give away his position and perhaps send these hellish things scurrying back into the night. What then would stop them from returning once more along a different path, upon another night? His only course was to strike them down here and now, and God help him if he failed.

For the first time in what seemed ages, he allowed his body to stir. His breath was slow and silent, as was his movement. With his right hand, he reached for the great yew bow, reluctant to let his eyes leave their marks. He gripped the weapon and hunched forward, gradually moving off the stool to take a knee on the floor of the hide. He switched the bow to his left hand in a smooth silent motion, and held the bow parallel to the floor under cover of the railings. Forced to break sight for a brief moment, he turned his head to the right and peered down at his quiver, which was propped against the wooden railing off to that side.

A forest of white plums stood erect within it, and in the midst of them were nestled a scant clutch of black feathered arrows. Of these, he slowly drew two. These were his bodkin arrows, tipped with substantial spikes, and able to pierce armor. He slipped one halfway into his left boot tip down, and held the other bodkin arrow in the fingers of his right hand. He lifted his eyes, and training them upon the demonic pair once again, he realized, to his horror, that they had risen from their haunches, and had begun their advance towards the town.

Slowly, he raised the great bow and tilted it lengthwise in the fashion of a crossbow, careful not to scrape the tips of the bow against the floor or railing. Delicate and meticulous, he knocked the arrow. His heart began to pound high in his chest once more, and he forced his breath to ease in and out of his lungs. He rose to his feet steadily and noiselessly, simultaneously lifting the bow above the wooden rails and leaning his bow arm out beyond the wooden barrier. He began to supinate his left forearm in the slightest, so that the bow yawed to the ready. He swayed forward at the waist to gain the bow further distance from the wooden fortifications, so that he was better able to aim down upon the lurking demons. Thoughts of making the slightest sound in the near dead silence threatened to unnerve him, while the hope of victory was nostrum to compel him.

The creatures had cleared the edge of the wood by only a meager distance, their movement slower and more circumspect. They moved only a couple paces apart, nearly in file, hunched and bent forward at the waist, their clawed hands swaying at their knees. He would have to take the closest first, and hope to hit the other before whatever cognizance it possessed dawned upon it.

His bow arm stretched out to the fullest. He stared beyond the knocked bodkin, his face hardening with concentration. He was statue-like in his stance and, thus poised, his muscles tensed, as his right hand began to draw the great yew bow. He pulled the bowstring past his rigid bow arm, and slowly across his chest. The bow groaned a quiet, fibrous tone under the mounting strain. He prayed to God that neither of the stalking creatures would turn in alert, and neither did. Perhaps it was God, or perhaps the choruses of crickets that played to the night sky which had saved him once again. He drew the string past his face and locked his pulling hand into position behind his right ear. The strain was now incredible, but his muscles stiffened to the purpose, the bowstring digging into his fingertips; yet only the sweat-dampened wisps of hair, which quivered vaguely near his brow, betrayed any sign of his Herculean effort.

He closed his left eye, and with the right, which stared unblinkingly down the shaft of the arrow beneath it, took aim. He inhaled deeply and caged the breath within his chest, the bow and arrow now unwavering. He saw before him the rippling bulk and pale skin upon the back of the closest demon; then, he saw only the muscle-laden spine, to which his eye locked with baleful focus. He hesitated only briefly, and then unleashed the terrible force he had held captive with a relaxed exhalation and a quick release of his right hand. The bow leaped back to form with a marked rush of air, loosing the arrow. The arrow streaked through the moonlit night, prompting a hushed whistle of malevolence, its flight barely visible in the darkness.

It seemed then, that time slowed, as if all motion were made laggard by this one moment, a moment that could never be regained, and which fortune would bless or curse upon a frivolous whim. The sentry held the posture of his release, gazing wide-eyed at the path of the bodkin as it snaked forth to its mark. With maddening anticipation, he watched the movements of both the interlopers and the arrow simultaneously, though his true focus remained on his chosen target. At the sound of the releasing bow, its body had tensed and moved impossibly fast. It spun round into a deep crouch: its arms spread wide, its blackened claws at the ready, and its head tilted upwards to stare in the direction of the sound. It stared starry eyed, with its bestial brow furrowed in a silent snarl, and its fangs bared threateningly.

The moment was drawing to a close, for even having turned to face the noise, it seemed the arrow might still strike the demon's breast, high and to the left, but before it did, the thing appeared to catch sight of the bodkin as it flew. The thing twisted with inconceivable speed and agility, continuing in the same direction it had initially spun. The sentry felt a cold chill wash over him, and his heart sunk. He watched in horror as the demon moved aside and arched backwards, coming to rest on a single hand outstretched behind it. Its face was hatefully contorted, and its amber eyes were fixed upon the arrow in flight. Its head turned as it followed the path of the bodkin, even as the arrow whisked by just above it.

Eyes still forward, the sentry moved to snatch the second bodkin from his boot. He was about to break his gaze when he noticed a swift movement behind his target. It seemed the lead demon had reacted a fraction slower to the broken silence. It appeared to have pivoted in a manner opposite to the other. Where his target had turned and inadvertently deviated somewhat from the bodkin's track, this one whipped around, blundering into its path. Perhaps with the other twisting about and masking its line of sight, it did not see the flight of the arrow. Though the leader had swiveled into a lower crouch than the other, it was positioned higher upon the slope, so that the wayward arrow found a purpose once more. With wicked speed, the bodkin struck the thing's skull with such force that its head jolted back with an audible wet crack.

The sentry froze in surprise. He watched the furthest of the demons reel back with the arrow jutting out sideways from its head, close to one of its eyes. A brief, grating screech escaped the demon's open maw as it toppled to the grass. The other demon had righted itself after having followed the arrow into the face of the lead demon. Now it stood rotated at the torso, looking back at its fallen companion over its pale shoulder, unwilling to entirely turn its back to the sentry's general direction. The fallen demon convulsed and shivered, dark blood welled in its ruptured eye socket and streamed down its face. A rasping moan issued from it, as one yellow eye stared about blankly in the direction of the wood.

The sentry's eyes flashed back to the other as he registered movement from it. In a rage, the demon faced him again, this time its eyes glowered into his. The moonlight in its eyes caused them to glow like a cat's by a fire. Its effect was harrowing, as if he now faced a wrathful specter, or death itself. It curled its upper lip, revealing the fangs once more, and like a village dog, issued forth a low growl.

With alarming speed, the demon leapt into motion. No longer concerned with stealth, it darted back into the plot of wood and rushed towards the oak at a terrific rate. Its startling movement towards his position shook the sentry from his stupor. He saw that its eyes were still glaring and fixed upon him as it tore through the underbrush, and he realized it intended to come right to him. Fearing his time was short, he quickly bent towards the chest and threw the top open. He snatched up the horn and placed it to his lips. He sounded the thing and it bellowed into the night sky, the deep timbre of the long note resounding across the land.

\* \* \* \*

From above the town gate, the guardsmen shot glances downhill into the patchwork of forested darkness. The eldest of them, a scar faced archer atop the wall, was the first to speak. Turning to look down at the pikemen inside the wall, he yelled anxiously.

"Raise the gate and rally us our men."

Already, patrolling guards who had heard the horn were running towards the gate. At the gate, before assisting his fellow in raising it, the shorter of the two pikemen sounded a shrill trumpet to assemble any patrolling guards who may have somehow missed the sounding of the horn. It did not take them long to rally, for with so few guardsmen patrolling the town, they tended to keep in and around the area of the gate. The trumpet was also an echo for the sentry, to confirm that they had recognized his initial alarm, and that a party was on its way.

\* \* \* \*

The sentry dropped the horn and snatched up the arrow from his boot, placing it across his mouth where he held it with his teeth. He looked down in time to see the onrushing creature vault a briar patch and, at speed, disappear from his view under the hide. Still holding his bow, he took a quick step towards the central stem of the tree. Franticly, he jumped up from the wooden floor of the loft onto a large branch, and hauled himself against the oak with his free hand. There, in one of the oak's great crooks, he knelt with his back to the tree and faced out towards his abandoned hide.

He swiped the arrow from his mouth with his right hand, and maneuvered it dexterously. Once more, he raised his bow and knocked a bodkin upon it. As he drew the bow, he heard the pitch of a trumpet in the distance, almost masking the swift crashing of foliage that rose from somewhere below. The wood of the thick bow groaned violently as he yanked the bowstring back to the ready, and his rigid body tremored once more under the strain. Suddenly, the ruckus in the underbrush ceased, allowing a brief instant of quiet.

With a thud, the leaves of a small tree beyond the hide shook tempestuously, owed to an impact somewhere below on its trunk. He heard a brisk scratch of bark from the darkness below, and then another instant of silence chilled him once more. He could not control the wild beating of his heart, nor his erratic breaths, as he stared expectantly at the hide. He held his position in the crook of the oak, his drawn bow and arrow trained on the hide. His eyes, however, shot involuntarily to the tree most proximal to the hide, which, following another thud, erupted in a fury of shaking, shadowy leaves. More audible now, he heard a powerful scrape upon the tree bark, this time higher up and accompanied by a bestial exhalation.

From somewhere within, fear compelled him to turn and flee. With an intractable will, he checked himself and grimaced with exertion, as he forcefully drew the great yew bow beyond what one should. Wide-eyed, with beads of sweat rolling from his brow, he shifted his gaze to the far side of the hide, where a sudden movement caught his focus. His heart stopped, and time seemed to slow afresh, as flailing, bristling tendrils of raven-black hair rose from beyond the hide. The windswept mane was followed by a daunting, ashen visage, which was followed in turn by a pale, sinewy musculature.

Having leapt from the nearby tree, the demon lifted into the air as though it were weightless, and its fearsome, white form soared above the far rails of the hide. Its arms wide spread and shanks coiled, it appeared before him like some wild apparition, as it seemed to float through the air above him, its malevolent expression searching and intent. In the moment before it would alight in the hide, he saw its ember eyes flash from the empty hide to his position in the crook. In this mortal moment, he unleashed the second arrow with a stinging hate. From his range, the arrow found its mark in an instant. The bodkin thumped into the thing's chest, a hair's breadth below the breastbone. A rumbling breath was forced from its mouth, which hung agape, it eyes staring wildly: vapidly. It landed stiffly on the floor of the hide clutching its impaled chest, and then tilted its head upwards to stare at him vengefully, its maw curling into a silent, chilling snarl.

He wasted no time. No sooner had he loosed the bodkin, than he dropped the bow to draw his sword. The blade unsheathed, he held the Tizona in both hands and leapt forth from the crook of the oak branch, hefting the blade to strike. Even so grievously wounded, the thing moved with frightening speed. He had scarcely begun to swing his sword when it sprung forward to meet him in the air. With a roar that bore the quality of both man and beast, it slipped below the path of the sword and bashed into his ribs. The blow was so solid and so powerful, that his body folded over the thing's shoulder, and his breath was forced from his lungs. He felt his teeth click together, and watched his sword hurtle to the far side of the loft, to clang against the wooden rails. He was slammed back against the oak, the thing's shoulder still driving into his gut. As he began to collapse down the rough bark, he gathered his feet beneath him and braced himself against the oak in an awkward crouch.

The thing held him fast at the waist, its painful grip unbreakable. He noticed that with his left hand, he had grabbed a tuft of the thing's thick black hair, which felt as coarse as a horse's mane. With all his might, he held the demon's head down while his other hand moved to the hilt of his dagger. Regardless of its lesser size, the strength the thing could summon was immense. A savage sound resonated from it, which was so reminiscent of a man it harrowed his soul. The veiny muscles of its neck and back pulsed as its head began to rear against his full weight and strength. The arrow shaft lodged in its chest snapped, catching under his thigh as the thing rose. He watched in horror as searing yellow eyes turned up at him, knowing full well that the yawning, fanged maw would follow.

As the head rose inexorably to meet his, he swung his right arm round in a tight arc, homing his dagger into the side of its neck, just below one of its strange, pointed ears. A chalky blur shot across his chest - the demon's clawed hand. It caught his forearm below the wrist, but not before the blade was driven more than halfway into the greyish-white flesh. The thing's face twisted with loathing and pain, and it emitted a gurgling yowl, a light spatter of blood spraying from its mouth. He felt streaks of hot pain along his forearm, and saw that before the hard talon had gripped him solidly enough to stop the blow, it had slashed his sleeve and skin open against the resisting claws.

The thing's rearing force ebbed, and though it held him with a grip so excruciating and crushing that he could barely hold his weapon, he still forced the blade with all he could muster. Its neck and torso curled to trap his blade between its jaw and shoulder, and it shied to one side, away from the pressing dagger. Still grasping its mane for dear life and driving with his dagger, he pushed off the oak at his back in the direction to which the demon had faltered. Locked together, they spun out towards the side of the loft. He drove the thing into the rails, which cracked and creaked under the force of their combined weight, showering splinters of wood over the underbrush. The demon's back arched over the rails, the sentry impelling it with the dagger, trying to twist the blade. They leaned dangerously over the edge of the hide, rivulets of dark blood rushing from the thing's neck to wet the roots of the oak far below.

The hushed grating of his blade against the underside of the thing's jaw and skull was overpowered by its throaty growl. Shivering with effort, pain, and rage, it stared at him wide-eyed beyond its dreadful maw. All at once, it repositioned its clutch to grip his hand, crushing his fingers against the hilt of his dagger. A noise escaped the thing as the blade drove deeper in that instant. It was then he realized he could hold the demon down no longer. Controlling his hand, it forced the blade out of its gullet and wrenched his hand with such strength that he felt a crunching in his wrist, and the dagger dropped down into the darkness below. Abruptly, its free hand seized his face with a jarring force.

His eyes covered by its rough palm, he felt his neck snap back with a series of crackles, and he sensed his feet leaving the ground as the demon thrust his head violently with its clawed hand. Toppling over backwards, he crashed into the opposite rails at an angle. With a loud crack, his shoulders broke off the uppermost railing. Still attached at a point near the oak, it swung out to hang over the darkness, bent and splintered. The sentry jounced from the wooden barrier to sprawl into a heap against the far rail of the hide.

As he raised his head, blood trickled from his nose and from the puncture wounds around his face. His was disoriented, but made out his sword laying beside him, and he took hold of the hilt. His head was throbbing, his body ached, and his breaths pained him, but he forced himself up. As he rose, he looked to the demon and expected to be mauled to death before even coming close to reaching his feet. Instead, he saw that it held one hand to its neck, while the other clasped the broken shaft, which still projected from its chest. Blood seeped through the fingers of both hands, letting small reddish droplets over the wooden floor. It leaned off the railing, standing to face him. It cocked its head and its face wrinkled in agony. With a grim ululation, it tore the bodkin from its chest. It snarled and glared at him as its body shuddered, a rush of blood pulsing from the open wound.

Sensing weakness had finally found the demon, the sentry hefted his sword with renewed strength. This time it was he who roared, leaping forward again to swing the blade. The thing slipped away from his sword once more, staggering back against the broken rail on the opposite side of the loft. The damaged rail cracked yet again and hung limply over the side. The sentry carried the momentum of his first strike up into a second and slashed down upon the thing, which was braced upon the weakened rails. With another unbelievably fast movement, it swiveled and recoiled from the attack. The blade rushed by its head and shoulder, but its trailing arm could not escape the blow.

The sword hewed the demon's left hand below the wrist, accompanied by a damp, crunching sound and a spattering of deep crimson blood. Gathering himself from the last heave, he looked over his shoulder to see the thing. Its black mane was matted with gore on the left side, the milky flesh of its neck and chest glistening with shadowy ichor. It stared at him like a caged beast, its yellow eyes torrid with hate as it roared feverishly, forcing reddish trickles to course down either side of its mouth. Its left arm was languid by its side, and the pulverized hand hung limp, held to the forearm by a ruptured, bleeding carnality.

Before he could pivot to face the demon, it charged him with a wild fervor. He had only enough time to lift the guard of his sword to protect his head before the demon hammered into his side with such force that it took him from his feet. His breath left him a second time. He heard a muffled snap sound from within him, and a sharp pain at his side intimated a broken rib. The demon bashed him against the north barrier so vigorously that the barrier splintered from its nails. The blow flooded the sentry's chest with pain. The sword jolted from his hands and spun overtop of him into the bushes below. With a thunderous crack, the rails began to fall, and the two combatants followed.

As he slid over the edge, he caught sight of the rope ladder, a portion of it falling over the verge with him amidst the chaos. He snatched at it desperately. Finding purchase, he was surprised when his fall stopped abruptly, only a couple of feet below the floor of the hide. One of the rope rungs had been snagged on a jutting post left by the broken rails so that he hung from a small loop of rope ladder below the hide. What was more shocking was the crushing grip that clasped him near the elbow and ripped into his skin. His body jerked violently into an angled cruciform, and his clenched intercostal muscles gripped his injured side agonizingly. He grunted between gritted teeth, his face a pained grimace. He looked down to see a white talon clutching his arm with blackened claws, his linen twisted and frayed under its clutch.

From below, the demon's ghostly face stared up at him, its maimed arm hanging uselessly at its side. Abhorrence still lingered on its face, but some of the hellish fire had left it eyes. They hung in a brief stalemate, oscillating to and fro. He winced as he felt the grip tighten somehow, and he saw the demon quiver, its muscles twitching with exertion. Panic arrested him as the demon raised itself steadily with one quaking arm. Its head came level with his forearm, and its animal eyes shifted to stare at it.

Horrified, and able to do nothing, he watched its mouth open and neck strain forward as it bit down. Its jaws compressed his arm painfully, and he could feel the sharp pressure of its fangs. He cried out.

Though excruciating, its teeth had not been able to penetrate his leather sleeve. It gnawed and gnashed desperately, as though its life depended on exacting vengeance upon his arm. It looked up at him once more and growled loudly, a possessed look in its desolate eyes. It began to rise again, its body quaking notably with the undertaking. He began to feel the demon's labored breaths upon his face as he watched the wide, glaring eyes draw ever nearer. Its ascension halted a mere hand's breadth from his face. Its heaving chest brought level to its hand, and its elbow locked to its side, it could no longer haul itself up towards him. Perhaps from the strain, or perhaps from growing infirmity, its body began to shake with further vigor. Its lips curled and, teeth clenched, it breathed franticly in harsh, snarling gasps, staring blankly into his eyes.

The agony in his chest and the tearing pressure, which ruled his body, made his vision spotty. His grip on the rope ladder was failing and he contemplated simply letting go. He would most likely survive the fall, and just as likely cripple himself for the rest of his days. It seemed any fate would best the sheer evil that glared at him from a breath away. Their locked forms swayed together, a beam of moonlight flickering between them. He saw the demon raise its legs as a hawk would when snatching prey from the sky. He felt the demon's clawed feet grip him above the ankle. With this new leverage its head rose once more. Just above his shoulder, the demon's mouth opened eagerly, the crescent-shaped fangs of its upper jaw gleaming like pearls. He felt despair take him as he stared into the maw, waiting for death's touch to take him.

There was a sound of tearing cloth as the demon's head dropped from his face. The sentry's linen had given way under the clutching hand, and the demon's claws slid under the leather sleeve. It pulled the leather down and inside out, leaving his left arm bare, but not unscathed. His forearm was streaked with long lacerations down to his wrist where the linen and leather had bunched together. Here the demon regained its grip. It stared intently at his bare arm, and looked as though it intended to haul itself up again when he heard a loud snap. Suddenly, he was falling. The snagged stump had succumbed to their weights, and the rope ladder slipped out over the broken edge of the hide. The demon's grip slackened, and he tore his arm free of the vestiges of his clothing. With both hands, he held on to the rope for dear life.

The rope ladder went taut and swung in towards the oak. The demon attempted to clutch his ankle with its talon-like feet, which only raked the sides of his boot and caused it to plummet headlong to the ground below. The sentry swung feet first into the oak at a manageable pace, and then placed his feet on the supple rungs as the rope ladder swayed. He heard a loud thud on the ground below him, and was suddenly aware of another noise. He heard faints shouts, and the clinking of mail at a run. New hope entered him, and he began to descend the ladder hastily, facing towards the town, hoping to see the men approaching. As he did, something just outside the wood stole his attention. Even given what he had just experienced, he still could not believe what he saw.

The other demon was struggling to its feet. Its body still convulsing horribly, it staggered about as though drunken. Its head jittering about involuntarily, it tried to gaze out in the direction of the sounds. This done, it floundered around to face him. Its head tilted upwards, tremoring, and it looked down over its nose with one bleary eye. The other eye was obscured by gore, and evidently deformed by the bodkin, which still jutted from the ruptured socket at an angle. Its mouth hanging agape, it reached up and pulled the arrow from deep within its skull. He watched it drop the bodkin and look shakily over its shoulder to the closing soldiers of Berwick. Holding its cavernous wound, it staggered into the brush to the west. It slipped between the trees to vanish into the night, the noise of its escape drowned by the shouts of men. He could see them clearly now, moving at a solid pace down the slope.

As he descended, he looked to the shadowy ground below him. Sprawled over the bulky roots of the oak, he made out the pale form of the demon, which stirred weakly. The bloody thing seemed incapable of accepting death, and following this thought his face sagged disconsolately. In his heart, he knew that the demon would rise again, and that he could not afford to allow it any respite. He was close enough to the bottom now that he released the rope to land painfully on the ground. He winced as his damaged rib moved in his side, the pain a necessary sacrifice.

The moonlight shone dimly off his sword, which had fallen only a few feet from him. He took it up in time to see the maimed demon rising sluggishly from amidst the twining roots of the oak. Fresh blood trickled from somewhere upon its scalp, and it turned slowly to gaze upon him. Ignoring his body's pain, the sentry advanced upon the demon, stepping between it and the oak. It took a few diffident steps backwards, scowling and bearing its teeth in warning. It turned abruptly to see the small preponderance of armed men closing in from the grassy plain beyond the wood. With the demon thus distracted, he pressed the attack, swinging methodically with the sword. Anticipating it would somehow evade him if he struck high, he changed the path of the blade to swing low.

As he predicted, the thing sprang back and spun from the blow with stunning speed. Yet the blade cleaved one of its knees as it leapt aside, and the demon buckled as it tried to alight back on the ground. It scuttled to one side awkwardly upon its good arm and leg, and then faced him anew. It stared at him as it mantled over the ground in a decrepit crouch. Seeming to understand it could not longer evade him, the demon attempted to leap at him once more. The pounce was ungainly, but still fast enough to catch him off guard as he stepped forward to attack the demon. With his sword already raised over his shoulder, he did not have time to hew the demon with his blade; but he managed to whip the hilt about in a tight arc to bash its skull with the ornate, silver pommel.

The demon's head shuddered with the blow, and its body glanced off his side to roll haphazardly on the ground. The blow pained his side and, as he staggered back, he lost his footing on some fallen branches. He fell to the ground stiffly and curled up in pain. Holding his side, he was slow to rise, and before he did, he saw that the demon stood already. They simply stared at each other, both seemingly in disbelief of the other.

Two arrows whistled into their midst. One struck the demon's ribs, the other struck its thigh a split second after. The sentry turned and saw that the guardsmen had entered the plot of wood, and that a meager line of archers took aim from its fringe. The two pikemen, and others armed with swords, crashed through the foliage towards him. To his eyes, in that moment, they were the embodiment of salvation. With sallet helms and mail shimmering bluish in the moonlight, his warrior brethren rushed to his aid. The demon merely turned to growl feebly in their direction. The sentry gained his feet as a third arrow struck the demon's gut. Two others flew by errantly before another stuck it below the neck.

At these, the demon simply turned its bestial gaze back towards him. It stood doubled over before him, forlorn and shivering faintly. Its eyes did indeed stare at him, but seemed to see nothing, and the baleful fire in its strange, yellow eyes seemed to have dimmed. The sentry lunged at the demon for the final time, his sword hefted high above him, glinting the argent starlight. He feared he could not kill the demon: that it would somehow stand once more to stare into his soul with its icy, golden stare. In a raging voice that surprised even he, he roared one single word, "Die."

The demon barely raised its eyes as he heaved the blade down and across its bloodied neck. He felt the Tizona discharge its full force, and heard a sickening, gristly sound as the demon's head was nearly riven from its body. Blood spattered over his face, and he watched the body seize and slowly crumple to the ground.

The rushing guardsmen silenced their shouts and silently gathered around the sentry. They watched as he straddled over the back of the eerie, white body. They watched him take hold of a tuft of the wretch's bristly, black hair, ignoring the body's strange spasms. Pulling up the head and wrenching brutally with his sword, he hacked the head free of the remaining tissues. The sentry looked disheveled, battered, and half crazed. Blood ran freely from countless wounds on his body, and his hair hung in slicked tendrils of blood and sweat. He raised his head to the moon and stars and the men saw victory in his eyes. They looked on as the sentry raised the strange man's head in his left hand and unleashed a stentorian bellow to the heavens above. Dark blood ran from the base of the severed head, twining about the sentry's forearm. A few of the rivulets coursed over the gaping wounds on his arm, pooling briefly therein to coalesce with his own blood before dripping to the earth as sanguine rain.

*Chapter Three*
*In the Eyes of a Child*

I

He reached over to place his hand on his valise-style schoolbag. He steadied it, and not wanting it to tip from the seat to the floor, he decided to set it to rest on its side. The top end brushed against the beige leather backrest of the seat and the wooden handles clacked together briefly as he set it down. As it was it laid flat, a luminous blur of movement caught his eye. He looked up to see an intensely bright, if somewhat misshapen, image jittering about on the ceiling of the limousine. It reminded him of the impatient, fitful movements of Tinkerbell from a play he had seen about Peter Pan. He would have liked to read the novel as well, but his father shunned the prospect. His father told him that it was wasteful to fill the mind with such nonsensical fancy. Instead, his father force-fed him historical works, praising their relevance and educational value. His mother, however, had lovingly taken him to see the play in secret one day after school. If there was one thing he was learning quickly, it was how to keep a secret. Watching the play, he had reasoned that the shining pixie was a flashlight being moved around from somewhere off stage, but he was still amused by the effect.

He observed the spot of light with almost scientific curiosity. He enjoyed the way the sun played off burnished surfaces, and he looked out the far window to analyze the origin of the projection.

The limousine hummed mechanically as it cruised along, and he studied the world as he passed it by. The sun was a bright gold and filled the limousine with warmth and light. The sun was still quite high in the sky, but angled enough from the west that it shone through the far window and reached his lap on the opposite side. The bag at his side also lay in the path of the sunbeam, and it was the source of the dancing light. The dark leather had a certain sheen to it, but the golden badge attached to its topside shone blindingly, and he squinted against its brilliance. He placed his hand upon his schoolbag and rocked it slowly, watching the luminous patch above sway in correspondence. He could not make out the engraving in the reflected light and looked back to the badge itself to view the artful lettering. His name, Andrew Sinclair, was radiantly lit upon the polished surface.

He lay back in his seat and turned his head towards the window beside him. It was open just a crack, enough to tussle his parted hair gently and allow a cool breeze into the back of the limousine. The sounds of the Virginian suburbs echoed from outside the window as he peered through it dreamily. He became aware of the shrill shrieks and laughter of playing children from beyond the tinted glass, and his focus became devoted to their source. He looked out over a green, grassy park and observed the large playground there, which he passed daily on the way home. On and around it were dozens of children, many his own age, who frolicked about joyously in unworldly bliss. Their clothes and shoes were scuffed with dust, or grass, and he stared after them longingly. He looked down at his black shoes with their silver buckles. His long, grey socks covered his shanks and matched his stiff, grey school shorts. He fidgeted uncomfortably in his black blazer and realized he was stifling in it. The gold cufflinks rattled as he sat up and divested himself. He held the blazer out in front of him and folded it dutifully. He placed it on his schoolbag and saw the cufflinks, in rows of three on each cuff, gleam in the sunlight. The A and S on each button shone just like the engraving on the badge. Watching the other children play so freely made him somewhat uncomfortable in his school uniform.

He loosened his tie, undid the top button of his shirt and then lay back against the seat to gaze out the window once more.

Andrew wondered how different the lives of those children were from his own. He could only guess as to whether the sixth grade was the same at their schools as it was in his own. He knew these children probably went to school and met hundreds of new friends, and played with them without a care in the world. He reasoned that these children at the playground could have met then and there in the park, laughing with each other without distrust, without fear. He bet that they did not have to keep secrets from each other - that they shared all upon frivolous whims. What a wondrous thing that would be. In reality, he was not permitted to fraternize with children, or anyone, for that matter, outside what his father described as their guild. The only children allowed to attend his private school were the children of his father's associates. Even then, though he was allowed to exercise and play with them occasionally, as a precaution, he had been instructed never to divulge any of the secrets he kept. He imagined his schoolmates had been similarly instructed, though they never discussed the matter with one another.

As he understood it, his family had always held great wealth. His father told him certain people would do anything to acquire even a fraction of it, that human greed knew no bounds. He also understood that his father and his associates were all important to the state somehow. A few of them, like his father, were affiliated with organizations of national security. For these reasons he could not mingle with the general public. Even contact with extended family, who were not amongst his father's ranks, was by and large prohibited. He was constantly reminded that it took only one chance meeting with the wrong person to be taken hostage and held for ransom. His father even warned of communist, Soviet spies using him as a bargaining chip to obtain sensitive intelligence. Andrew knew his father's patriotic position on coercion all too well, and what it would ultimately mean for him if he were held hostage.

It was hard to imagine that those jubilant children romping

about the playground could pose a threat to himself and his family, but he knew they could. To insure he understood this concept, his father compared contact with the public to touching a hanging branch in a forest. Still gazing out the window expressionlessly, he recalled the gist of his father's lesson and imagined himself reaching for a leafy limb from a forest floor. The branch he touched grew from a larger branch. The larger branch could support many others upon it. It would also connect to the central portion of the tree that could bear many branches, and those, in turn, could carry hundreds themselves. His father stressed that by touching a small part of a tree, he was unknowingly touching a large system, which joined along different offshoots from bottom to top. Even the limbs of other trees could touch and intertwine, joining at levels unseen. It was the last part of the analogy that truly opened his eyes. His father spoke to him of a black widow, employing his aversion to them to emphasize the point. This aforementioned spider could travel to the tree he touched from an adjacent one, or from others further still. It could wind through the systems above and make its way down towards him to bite his unsuspecting hand.

Andrew pictured the innocent face of a playmate he might meet at the park. In all likelihood this little friend would be of no danger to him, but the circle in which he traveled could be. The danger could lurk somewhere within the boy's network of relations, in the most unexpected places: perhaps a disgruntled father desperate for money, or a greedy daycare worker at a youth center. The threat could manifest itself in the form of a cousin's friend, or a friend's cousin; there were so many possible connections, so many systems, and within any of these the spider could lay.

The road curved gently and he felt his shoulder pressing delicately against the door as the limousine followed the bend. This gradual bend in the road was a landmark to him, signifying he was nearly home. He faced front and took a casual interest in the back of Roger's head. Flowing from under his navy-blue cap, Roger's white hair stood in stark contrast to his dark uniform, as did his white-gloved hands, which were both holding the wheel. He had known Roger as long as he could remember and had actually grown quite fond of him. Roger was always punctual, cordial, and ever so professional. His latter virtue was probably the reason his father held such appreciation for his services. He wondered what Roger knew of his father's enterprises, if anything noteworthy at all. After all, if his father trusted Roger with his safety in transit, then perhaps he entrusted him with a few secrets as well. Given Roger's age, he would at least know some interesting tidbit of his family history. He leaned forward and rolled down the partition window.

"Roger, how long have you known my father?"

Roger's head turned briefly, revealing a profile of his bushy, white mustache and cheerful wrinkles. Roger's sparkling blues eyes gave him a quick glance from their corners before returning to the road.

"Ah, hello, young sir. I thought you were about to doze off."

"No, I was just thinking about things," Andrew replied.

The old man eyed him occasionally through the rear view mirror.

"Well, there's nothing wrong with that. Only natural for an inquisitive youngster such as yourself to think about things... about the world." He apparently noticed the puzzled look on Andrew's face in the mirror. "Oh...inquisitive. Means to ask lots of questions." He paused. "So, you wanna know how long I've known your pappy, eh? Jeepers, not sure that I can rightly recall, though I am sure it was before the war. See, it was your grandpappy I was acquainted with first, and your pappy was just a young man then." He looked to the mirror. "Do you know... acquainted?"

Andrew nodded with a self contented smile.

"Holy Jiminy, wouldn't you know it, looks like that school of yours is paying off," Roger chuckled. "Anyway, I was basically as responsible for your pappy as I am for you now. Similar duties as well. Course that were over twenty years ago now."

"Are you and my father good friends?" Andrew asked

innocently.

"I suppose. As much as two men in our relative positions could be at any rate. There's something more you wanna ask me, and seeing as it might be a bit of a dandy, seems as though you don't wanna let fly with it. What's turning those cogs of yours, huh?"

"I don't know. I just…does my dad tell you things?" he inquired with some trepidation. "I mean, do you know things about what he does for his job, or why some things have to be so secret even from people he trusts?"

Andrew paused, hoping he had not said too much, or unknowingly revealed something he should not have. He was put at ease when Roger answered him.

"Now, you know sure as I do that your father does important work for the government and that he can't just go ahead and tell people how his day went. Your pappy doesn't work in a factory from morning till night, I can tell you that much. His work is private and not to be spoken of to anyone. Now—"

"I know," Andrew interrupted pleadingly. "I would never tell anyone anything. I know about the danger, my dad told me. I just figured that if he trusts you to do the things you do for our family, then it wouldn't be bad to ask you."

Andrew noticed Roger's smile under his thick moustache.

"I know you know, but the risks are high and one slip up is all it takes. We all have to be careful, that's all I'm saying."

"Roger," Andrew's voice was faint in the silence. "Don't tell my dad I said anything, okay?"

"It'll be our little secret," Roger assured.

Andrew sat back against the seat again, staring out the window and listening to the hum of the limousine engine.

* * * *

Andrew noticed they were approaching home and watched as the limousine neared the large, cast iron gates of the estate. Roger waved at the gatekeeper as they approached, and with an audible creaking, the exquisite gate opened slowly. As the limousine coursed the entranceway, he watched the green lawn and lavish gardens passing him by. He looked back to see the gates closing behind him, thinking how safe he felt at home. Roger turned the limousine into the roundabout in front of the mansion.

"Here we are, young sir," said Roger as he exited the limousine.

He left the engine running as he approached the door and opened it for Andrew. Roger gathered Andrew's schoolbag and blazer, carrying them as he walked him up the stairs towards the immense, wooden front door. It opened invitingly, and the butler stepped out onto the patio, holding the door open with one hand. Roger nodded a greeting to the butler and handed him Andrew's effects. Andrew passed through the doorway and waved Roger a cheery goodbye from behind the butler, who had followed him in. The mansion was dim in comparison to the brilliance outside, but his eyes quickly adjusted. The sound of the closing door echoed somewhat in the large foyer, as did the butler's reserved voice. As the butler spoke, Andrew took off his shoes and put on his house slippers, which had been placed on the doormat for him.

"You will find supper ready for you in the dinning room. Of course, your mother will attempt to join you, but your father is otherwise occupied in his study for the moment." Andrew acknowledged the butler and headed for the dining room. "Ah, I would advise changing from your school clothes before dining, young sir," suggested the butler.

"Oh, I forgot. Thank you."

Andrew walked towards the giant staircase and made his way up its winding length, followed by the butler. From his position on the staircase, he could see the door of his father's study along the hallway below. A faint light glowed from beneath it. He turned and continued his ascent. He reached his room on the upper floor and opened the door. The heavy, tasseled drapes were open, and the room was pleasantly warmed and colored by the sun. Amber rays phased through the white, silken sheers over the window, and shone in from the skylight above. The butler placed Andrew's schoolbag in the corner of his closet and turned to him.

"Would you like to have the drapes closed?"

"No, thank you," Andrew replied, turning his attention from

the window.

"Very well then, bon appétit."

The butler turned on his heels, his coattails trailing gracefully behind him. He crossed the threshold and closed the door behind him. The butler left with Andrew's blazer still draped over the crook of one arm, so that, as per usual, it would be pressed for him some time later in the evening. Andrew changed into a more casual ensemble of shirt and shorts. When he was presentable, he left his room, closing the door behind him. From the top of the stairs, he bent over the banister to look down the main hallway. Once more, he observed the study door and its alluring glow.

As far back as he could remember, his life had always been full of secrets and hidden dangers. In fact, when it came to secrets, his family held more from him than he kept for his family. He knew there were some things he would probably never know. The details of his father's job, for one, could never be revealed to him, as they involved national security. However, there were other secrets nesting in his home, which he yearned to uncover. The doors…he felt he needed to know what lay beyond the doors.

The family mansion had many levels and many rooms, most of which he could explore at his leisure. There were five rooms, however, that were always locked. No one but his father had keys for these rooms, not even his mother. Three of these were found on the main floor, and he had actually been permitted brief glimpses into each. His father's study was the room to which he had had the most access. Those instances had always been in the company of his father, and were very brief. It always seemed too tidy when he had been allowed to enter, as if the real work his father did in the study had been stowed elsewhere for his transitory visits.

He yearned for the knowledge withheld from him. Conceivably, he would learn the family secrets when he was older, and then join his father in his important work, just as the five did. He had seen the five many times, yet could barely remember their faces. He had entitled them as 'The Five' in his mind, a necessary moniker, given that he had never actually been introduced to them.

With a general greeting from his father such as 'Gentlemen,

welcome', the five would step through the doorway. They always wore suits and were often cloaked with long coats, open and flowing. Their hats were unfailingly positioned so the brims would obscure their aspects, and they would walk briskly into the boardroom with his father. This was another of the locked rooms, and his father had only once allowed him entry into it. The room was extravagant and had an old, distinguished feel to it. Warm light shone off the many burnished, mahogany furnishings and the speckled grey, marble floor. Two large, white banners with archaic-looking emblems upon them hung on a section of the wall. Coat of arms was the term that came to his mind and seemed to best describe the emblems he saw. Most prominent in both his mind and the room, was the great round table situated in the center of the boardroom. It too was a glossed mahogany, but it bore an odd symbol on its surface. Outlined in half-inch gold trim, was a star of six points. Each point reached the very edge of the table, and at each point, a chair was pulled up next to the table. Six points and six chairs for six men.

In the heart of the star, similarly outlined in gold, had been an emotionless, staring eye. The symbol was strange to him, because he had recently learned that this specific star was the insignia for those of Jewish faith. However, he could recall one of his school lessons in which he learned that the star was originally Egyptian. He believed the eye was as well. His school seemed to focus on history and meaning with the same emphasis it gave business and economy. He wondered if he and the other children were learning the things they did for a specific reason, or if the lessons were meant to occupy them until they were old enough to learn the secrets of their fathers. Either way, his family was devout Christians, and his father would certainly not suffer the offense of an icon denoting the Jewish religion in the home. Yet, Andrew had seen it clear as day in that room. It was simply another mystery, another secret.

\* \* \* \*

Andrew made his way down the stairs, still deep in thought.

He struggled to remember what he could of the large room in the east wing of the mansion. It was the last of the locked rooms to which he had been allowed access. He knew it functioned as some kind of lecture or assembly hall. In truth, it was never really used. His father and the community of associates had some kind of remote lodge they met at, and he could not recall them ever convening at the mansion. He was quite certain his father and the five headed the organization, and perhaps his father had taken the responsibility of hosting an alternative meeting place as a fallback.

Andrew had seen this room a scant few times, and even then, his father had merely permitted him to peer through the door. He remembered the capacious look of the room. At one end was a large podium, ornately adorned with a golden image his mind could not readily configure for his reminiscing thoughts. All he remembered of it was that it had reminded him of a compass. Beside the podium was a large wooden table. Behind the podium were two large, white banners, replicas of those in the boardroom. The podium faced smooth rows of exquisite desks and seats that nearly encircled the podium, giving the room the look of a scholarly amphitheatre. Along the walls, other banners with other designs hung proudly from brass flagpoles. He wondered what proceedings transpired therein.

The last two locked doors were found in the basement level. These were more like giant, bolted vaults than doors, and he had no idea what lay behind them. As much as he tried, he could not reason what aspect of his father's government work would necessitate his having these vaults in the basement. Such important articles should be locked up in some place crawling with soldiers, like the pentagon, or something similar. Regardless of his father's rank, it did not make sense to him that his father was safekeeping things of national importance in their home.

Still deep in thought, he entered the dining room, and the smell of a sumptuous dinner roused him from his ruminations. His mother was absent and he assumed she was with the doctor again in one of the rooms along the main hall. His mother had been complaining increasingly of intense pains near her stomach. She was soon due to add a little brother or sister to the family, but certain complications had arisen. Lately, she had been missing meals, and spent much of her time resting. He took his seat at the long wooden table. It was intricately and organically designed. To Andrew, it looked as if the table were alive and might walk off at any moment. On the table was a spread of serving dishes with round metal covers. A maid entered from the kitchen and smiled at him.

"Hello, back from another long day at school I see. You look like you are ready for supper, yes?"

Andrew smiled and nodded. She removed the metal covers and rivulets of steam rose from the platters.

"Thank you very much," he stated politely, and he began to eat as soon as she had finished serving him.

He was nearly finished his meal when he heard a shriek of agony. He recognized the cry as his mother's and ran from the dining room to the hallway. As he suspected, the sound had come from the clinical room in the west wing. It was not only he who had heard her, for the door of the study flew open and his father rushed out some distance in front of him. The butler appeared further down the main hallway as well, from which room, Andrew had not seen. He was more focused on his father, who did not even notice him as he left the study. Even before he cleared the doorway, his father was already facing down the hall towards the west wing.

His demeanor was anxious and concerned, and he moved hurriedly through the corridor. The butler paused briefly to allow his father to come abreast with him, and the two of them moved briskly towards his mother, whose moaning had subsided to spasmodic whimpers. Andrew began to move towards his ailing mother as well, but a gentle glow on the right side of the hallway distracted him. In his haste, his father had either not closed the study door completely, or had forgotten to lock it altogether. His heart felt as though it had skipped a beat and his eyes widened. He glanced in the direction of his father and the butler in time to see them slip into the room near the end of the hall. He stared at the study door once more, ajar and inviting. He felt he should be running to see his mother, but another feeling gripped him with greater conviction. After all, did his father's work not take precedent over all things, even family? As he understood it, no sacrifice was too great for whatever secret government works lay beyond the locked doors. Besides, he could do nothing for his mother but sit and watch her hold herself in pain, and an opportunity like this would not soon present itself again. He rationalized that when his curiosity was satisfied, he would go to her directly.

His body was stiff with the horrid sensation he would be caught. His throat was dry and his breaths were shaky. He fought himself, stepped forward, and opened the study door.

The study seemed smaller than he remembered, about half the size of his room. He closed the door most of the way behind him, careful not to make any noise. He turned his attention back to the study. He took it all in, the shelves of books to the left, cabinets to the right, and the massive desk against the wall opposite the book shelves. He forced the details of the room to become perfect memory and then approached the desk. The large wooden chair had been shoved away from the desk hastily. The seat and backrest, which were fixed with red cushions, now faced out towards the door. The desk was made of a deep umber wood, and was covered with papers and a few books. Behind these papers, nearly touching the wall, two lamps rested on either side of desk, filling the windowless room with a rich, beige effulgence.

Another such lamp provided the same service from its place on one of the bookshelves. Most of the papers were stacked within files on the left side of the desk. A few sheets, however, were strewn on the center of the desk. Of these, he picked one up gingerly, his trembling hands quivering the paper as he brought it to eye level. He noticed the date, May 24, 1958, the day before last. The document was typewritten, and bore a seal on the top right corner, stamped in red ink. He skimmed the sheet briefly, finding the terminology and jargon of the subject matter difficult to follow. It seemed to be a catalogue of little importance, a report of some kind perhaps, and he placed it back on the desk. As he did so, he noticed a large ring, which had been hidden under the report.

He picked the ring up to examine it. The topside was beset with a large ovular stone, deep red in color. The annulus itself was gold, as was the embroidery overtop of the flat, polished surface of the stone. The gold design overlaying the stone was as strange as it was intricate and beautiful. Covering most of the glazed stone was a golden pyramid. The apex was somewhat segregated from the rest of the pyramid, giving the tip the appearance of a hovering triangular segment. Inside the triangle, was an open eye, similar to the one he had seen on the boardroom table. In fact, an inverted triangle surrounded the eye as well, which formed the very same six-pointed star as he had seen on the table.

In effect, the pyramid was topped with the star, the uppermost point of which being the peak of the pyramid. Behind the eye in the star, an abstract of a sun in splendor emanated golden rays. He immediately recognized a version of this image from the dollar bill. From what he remembered, the inscriptions were exactly the same as well. The first of these formed a semicircle above the star and rays. Also in gold, it read, 'ANNUIT COEPTIS'. He identified the language as Latin, for he studied it in school. He did not however, understand the meaning of these particular words. Beneath the pyramid and parallel to its base was a second inscription, which read, 'NOVUS ORDO SECLORUM.' Of these words, he recognized two. 'Novus', meaning 'new' and 'ordo', meaning 'order'.

However, the golden pyramid differed from the image on the bill in a marked way. Inside the pyramid, also intricately fashioned in gold, was a captivating design. What at first looked like two angels, stood on either side of a large shield, their innermost wings raised above the shield, their pinions like a roof overtop of it. After further inspection, he noticed that their wings took the place of arms, and their lower halves were those of a satyr. Atop the shield, under the creatures' wings, was the arc of the covenant. He recognized the arc immediately, for the little angels on either side of the holy chest were iconic.

The shield itself was bordered by lions, so minute they were barely distinguishable as such. The right side of the shield bore three tiny castles, which looked like the rooks on his chessboard. In their midst, was a compass. Though he knew it was in some way much simpler than the image on the podium, he did not fancy the similarity as passing coincidence. The left side of the shield exhibited four images of lengthy beasts he could not identify with certainty. One was perhaps another lion, another a bull or stag, and another a phoenix or dragon; he simply could not make them out. A third inscription, so small it was nearly illegible, spanned the underside of the strange emblem within the pyramid. It read 'AVDI VIDI TACE.' These words he understood completely, and he whispered the translation aloud to himself.

"See, hear, and be silent."

His father's very ring ordered the keeping of secrets. To an extent, he was not entirely surprised. He did, however, find it very strange. Once more, he felt that his father's job, however top secret it was, did not warrant such oddity. Remembering where he was and how short his time would be, he dismissed the thought. He put the ring back on the desk, positioning it exactly as he had found it. He noticed a small, peculiar book lying on the desk that had also been previously covered by the report. The pages were so old and stained they were nearing a shade of brown, and the leather bound cover was tattered and mangy-looking. His eyes skimmed the exposed pages quickly. The penmanship was strange to him and hindered his imperative endeavor of a brief perusal. The language was indeed English, but was also strange and archaic. He realized that it was not a book. It was a journal. The entry he read was apparently an account of some voyage, or at least a stage of it. Curious about the date, he reached out and delicately turned back a few pages, keeping the page mark with a forefinger. Having arrived at the beginning of the entry, he simply stared in disbelief. His eyes focused on the written year, 1399. Deep in thought, he froze for a moment, staring blankly at nothing in particular. Gently, he flipped the few pages forward again to leave the journal open where he found it. A larger notebook, clearly his father's, also lay open on the desk. He recognized his father's writing, but took greater interest in the heading scribbled in the open book. Below the current date was written, 'From the journal of Henry De St. Clair.'

His head whipped around towards the door as he heard resounding footfalls in the hallway. He placed the report back over everything he had examined and moved towards the door, prepared to hide behind it if need be. The sound came closer and closer, until finally a maid rushed by the study. He watched her hurry on into the kitchen, presumably to fetch something otherwise unavailable in the clinical room. He decided he had tempted fate long enough and readied himself to leave the study. He poked his head out into the hallway. He heard commotion, but the hallway was barren for the moment, an opportunity which he seized promptly. He left the door as he found it, no more or no less ajar. He realized he had been holding his breath as a pent exhalation escaped his lips. He simply stood there in the main hallway, stalk still and gazing in the direction of the west wing. He began to move down the hall when he heard an urgent voice from behind him. He turned around to see the maid returning from the kitchen, a pail of water swaying in her right hand.

"Master Andrew! Where are you going, dear?"

"To see my mother, it doesn't sound like she's feeling well."

"No dear, no, she is not. I think it would be best if you gave her some time to rest. I don't think she is ready to see anybody just yet and her rest is very important."

"But I heard her, and..."

"She is resting now, dear," confirmed the maid. "Best leave her be for a while. Why don't you do your school work, then wash up and get ready to turn in."

She placed her free hand on his shoulder comfortingly and hurried off towards the west wing. He stared after her for an instant and then headed towards the foyer. He climbed the staircase slowly, went into his room, and pulled out his schoolwork.

# II

The rest of the evening passed quite quickly. He had been wrapped up in his thoughts, and when he was not, he invested time into his studies. He had taken the maids advice and washed up after finishing his schoolwork. He was preparing for bed when he heard the doorknocker rap loudly from downstairs. He wondered who had come calling at such an hour. The answer he gave himself sparked his curiosity. On a whim, he left his room and stood hidden at the top of the stairs near the banister. He heard his father's voice from somewhere in the hallway.

"Thank you, Geoffry, I've got it."

The butler, who must have informed his father that company had arrived, moved in, then out of his line of sight. His suspicions were thus far confirmed. His father entered the foyer and answered the door himself.

"Good evening, gentlemen," he exclaimed, and stepped to the side, allowing five men wearing suits and hats to enter the mansion. They shook hands with purposeful brevity and disappeared from view in the direction of the boardroom. It was just as he had thought. His curiosity satisfied, at least in this regard, Andrew walked back to his room and prepared for bed.

\* \* \* \*

Without reason, he woke from a deep and most satisfying sleep. He stretched slightly under the thick white quilt. His mouth felt both sticky and dry, and he debated getting up for a glass of water. One hand was resting against the big wooden headboard, and he let his finger trace a spiraling furrow in the lavish carpentry. He was still sprawled out on his back, which, as he recalled, was the last position he had assumed. He had simply been thinking about things again, and picked up where he left off. As he did, he looked about the room aimlessly. It was still dark, and he guessed it was past midnight, perhaps nearing two o'clock at most. Through the diaphanous sheers, he saw a conjoined mass of shadow swaying some distance away outside the window to his right. His somnolent mind was slow to interpret the black mass as the very same tree line he observed every night from his window.

Vibrant moonlight filtered through the silken sheers, just as the sun had hours earlier. The window was large, allowing a cascade of moonlight into his room, which spotlighted a section of the floor and the lower half of his bed. An ethereal glow poured in from the skylight as well, lighting his room like a winter night with snow blanketing the ground. He gazed across the room drowsily. His closet door was open, like a black nexus to another world. He thought he saw a dark figure within it and for a fleeting moment was quite disturbed. He realized, of course, that it could be no such thing, and easily identified the would-be monster as his school blazer, which the butler must have slipped into the closet at some point.

A breeze whistled soothingly outside, and his eyes grew heavy once more. The swaying trees cast dancing shadows that he observed expressionlessly, as he felt sleep wanting to take him once more.

A momentary and muffled scuffling noise from somewhere above caught his waning attention. He listened for the sound, but heard only the wind. No sooner did he dismiss the noise, than he heard it again, this time more clearly and from almost directly above him. He felt quite awake and attentive now, his roused brain attempting to rationalize the noise, which had to be coming from outside, on the roof. He reasoned that it could be a raccoon, but he figured it was more likely a squirrel. Yes, most definitely a squirrel. How many times had he heard alarmingly audible bumpings and scratchings from a squirrel scurrying around the eaves' troughs?

He looked to the skylight expectantly, thinking the little

animal might investigate, or cross it. Some moments passed. The wind blew and the trees threshed about out on the estate. He watched the skylight all the while, and finally heard the slightest scratch issue from it. The source of the noise must have been its metal frame, for he could not yet see anything through the skylight itself. Suddenly, he could see something. Ever so slowly, so gracefully and silently, its body appeared near the edge of the skylight. He thought it must be a grey squirrel, for its smooth body appeared white in the moonlight. Staring at the thing with greater scrutiny, he realized it was not a squirrel at all.

He felt a burning chill percolate through his insides, and his breath froze in his lungs. His heart began to pound, for what he saw was a large, white hand. Dark, hard-looking nails clicked the frame gently as the hand braced itself on the edge of the skylight. No sooner was this done, than the profile of a pale face slowly crept into view.

His mind was a frenzy of thought, as he desperately sought to find some logical explanation for what he saw before him. The shifting dark mass had been swaying trees, the monster in the closet had been his blazer, but what could possibly explain what he was seeing beyond the glass? Was it some trick? After all, other than the pale color and darkish nails, he felt the apparition had a look that was not entirely unfamiliar to the countenance of men. He lay still as stone in his bed, the covers clenched tightly in his fists. A surreal feeling came over him, his mind attempting to assure him that what he saw was a figment of the imagination. He felt as though he were not really in his room, that he must be watching this ghostly spectacle from somewhere far away. With one movement, the ghost-man caused these desperate hopes to vanish. Still clutching his sheets, he watched in sickening terror as the white face turned and looked directly at him.

Its breath left a trace of fog on the glass, assuring him that the ghost-man was indeed real. Irrespective of the evident humanity he witnessed in its face, some element of its aspect kindled in him, a deep primordial fear. It was as if he stared simultaneously into the face of his fellow man and the very face of evil. He felt tears welling in his eyes, and his own breaths became shaky and convulsive. That one moment was a horrifying eternity, and he could do nothing but gaze vacantly into the ghost-man's eyes. Its eyes were unlike anything he had ever seen. They were piercing and bore into him with a frightening stare. They burned like hot gold from the milky face, like the spectral aspect of an arctic wolf.

It was not the eyes alone which mimicked some lupine quality, for barely visible in its mouth, which opened slightly as it breathed, were the ivory tips of fangs. The white face moved closer to the glass, its eyes still staring into his and its breath steaming against the glass. In a sudden motion, both smooth and unbelievably fast, it vanished from sight. As it did, Andrew saw the tendrils of a great black mane, which he had not noticed against the darkness, lash wildly as the ghost-man disappeared into the night.

He lay in his bed, still staring at the skylight. He could still see the face beyond the glass as though it had never left. He knew the fearsome image was seared into his mind forever, another of the world's secrets that had been kept from him, another hidden danger. Now, he felt unsafe in his own home; now, a spider had found him. He hugged his quilt against his body and began to cry, his gaze fixed on the skylight, his mouth agape and quivering. He lay there as if enduring some debilitating onset of psychosis, gazing up into the stars through the skylight, trembling and waiting for the light of dawn.

# Chapter Four
## The Man in Black

# I

The Haitians' place had the look of a small, double-floored warehouse. It was poorly maintained and dirty. The areas that had been painted were peeling in tatters, and an assortment of scrap and old broken crates were strewn about the property. Most of the windows were intact, but many were boarded up and even some of these had begun to weather. A small transport truck belonging to the Haitians was parked in the tight alleyway between the warehouse and a neighboring building. A couple of other diminutive structures shared the same locality, and were kept in a similar condition. In fact, much of this section of the city had the same dilapidated look.

The general area was a haphazard assortment of small blocks, some so small, that they were more like large, undeveloped lots. On the majority of these lots, much of the space was occupied by tightly packed, two-story structures. A few were quite barren, however, and had the appearance of unfinished construction sites. These properties were unpaved and seemed to be storage grounds, given the amount of vehicles, old machinery, and debris littering them. Considering its function, the area was not so wretched as to warrant any kind of city plan for intervention or rehabilitation, it was simply not the type of area that would attract any kind of attention. Quite the opposite, it was the kind of place one would pass and tend to ignore entirely.

\* \* \* \*

The sniper had been maintaining diligent surveillance of the Haitians' warehouse. He routinely swept the windows of both floors, his eye keen to movements within. He would occasionally survey the rooftop and the perimeter of the premises, but until further notice, his focus was the inside of the warehouse. The few boarded windows made observation all the more difficult, but he was still able to see enough to relay intelligence reports over his head set.

The sniper raised his head from the scope to allow his eye a brief respite from its strain. To his right, and not a few feet behind him, Wilkinson was still scanning the warehouse with binoculars. As one of the deployed sniper teams, they were the eyes for the rest of the unit, and responsible for constant surveillance. The sniper stretched his back, and a sequence of muffled cracks escaped from it. They had both been in position for hours on end, and discomfort and fatigue had set in some time ago. His rifle, a Barrett M95, was propped on a table near the open window. They had lowered the blind near three quarters of the way, and were operating in the dark to maximize their concealment. Wilkinson lowered the binoculars, but his eyes remained on the warehouse.

"This delay takes any longer, we're gonna have to go to night vision," he stated in a somber tone. He was a senior officer and the designated spotter. The sniper looked out the window to see the sun had dropped significantly since he had last seen it. The setting sun flooded the skyline fiery orange and pink, vaguely silhouetting the highways and buildings in the west.

"I'd say we got about twenty...twenty-five minutes tops, sir," he responded.

Operating during daylight hours was easier and more efficient, though the fading light did provide better cover. His weapon had been equipped with night vision and inspected before being issued into the field, but he had checked the function anyhow a quarter of an hour earlier. Having given consideration to the hours they had already waited, he had anticipated that he and Wilkinson might be holed up until nightfall and wanted to insure he could manage in the dark if need be.

A high-pitched whirr had sounded from the augmented scope of the M95, indicating the night vision function had been successfully engaged, and he had not bothered with any further examination. The sniper looked back out over Fifty-fourth Road at the Haitians' warehouse. He and Wilkinson had taken their final firing position on the second floor of a building on the other side of the road. Though they faced the warehouse from the lot fronting it, they and the Haitians' were situated on opposite corners. This angle put over two hundred meters between them. From their corner position they were well hidden and could also watch the approach route of the rest of the SWAT team from the northwest.

The ground team was divided in two, and were staking out the area from inside two large vans near the corner of Fifty-third Road and Forty-fourth Street. To move in, the team need only travel south on Forty-fourth to reach Fifty-fourth, a total transit time of just over ten seconds. A second marksman unit watched the team's back from a building off Fifty-third Street, just south of the Brooklyn Queens Expressway, still north of the team and the Haitians' warehouse.

Additional unmarked support units were lying in wait just outside the team's area of operation. These units belonged to their affiliate, the NYPD, in specific, the hundred and eighth precinct from Queens. One of their undercover officers, Jermain Godfrey, was an inside man, and had been in deep cover for three months. Jermain's father was African-American, but his mother was a Haitian immigrant. He spoke a passable amount of his mother's French Creole tongue, and was thus a perfect candidate to infiltrate the growing Haitian drug syndicate.

The Haitians trafficked contraband into Miami, where they had initially established themselves. Their principal substance was cocaine, though they also moved small shipments of marijuana. They were aggressive, unconscionable, and most dangerous - a desperate, new faction on the streets. Though moderately successful in Miami, they had imposed themselves on the established territories of pioneer traffickers, namely the Columbians and Mexicans.

These drug tycoons limited buyer options and presented a constant threat; the former problem being the most pressing for them. Consequently, the Haitians expanded north, though it was unknown if they changed their trafficking point from Miami to correspond to their new areas of operation. In New York, they established relations with Slavic buyers who were believed to be connected to the growing Russian mafia. It was when the Haitians reached upper Brooklyn that Jermain Godfrey had worked his way into their ranks.

Initially, the infiltration process had been orchestrated using information from a snitch belonging to a Blood sect called the Nine Trey Gangstas. The Blood had been arrested and charged with multiple felonies. He was connected to the rising syndicate through a Haitian cousin, whom he was all too eager to give up rather than snitch on his fellow Bloods, lest he meet some of the Nine Trey in jail, or on the outside. A deal was struck between himself and the police wherein he would give up information on the Haitians in exchange for a reduction in his incarceration sentence.

\* \* \* \*

Officer Sebastian Klyne sat motionlessly in the back of the van, his Kevlar helmet now heavy and hot on his head. The bodies of the other SWAT officers huddled in the van added to the heat, as did his nomex coveralls and HMPE-layered Kevlar vest. Though the air conditioning was running and the sun had nearly set, a slightly humid heat still lingered inside the van. In the dim light, Officer Klyne stared down at the floor between his combat boots. The team had been lying in wait for some time and he had become somewhat introspective. With his assault rifle resting on its butt at his side, he rehearsed their entry procedure and all possible scenarios thereafter. Simultaneously, he listened to the team leader confirming intel over a head set from some second party, probably one of the marksmen or the NYPD. Aside from occasional whispers amongst themselves, and updates from the team leader, the team sat in relative silence.

* * * *

The sniper lowered his head back to the level of his weapon, his cheek almost touching it and his right eye in line with the scope. His gaze swept the little warehouse slowly, from window to window. Their inside man had reported nine hostiles within. From his prior briefing, he had learned that the Haitians usually carried out their transactions in fractions of their present rank, with each small group making sales with different buyers in various locations. Clearly, this current deal was of some significance. Jermain's reported number seemed accurate to the sniper as he estimated the size of the Haitian party from his vantage point.

He observed various areas on the main floor through the windows. A few men had mangy-looking dreadlocks, others shaven heads or colorful hats. Some were playing at dominoes with evident ruckus, and others conversed emphatically with one another, drinking what appeared to be bottles of malt beer, though he was not sure. He caught glimpses of others moving about on the main floor, including Godfrey. Godfrey was tall, sported a lengthy goatee, and his finely braided hair was pulled back into a ponytail. Like many of the Haitians, their inside man wore a loose, lengthy, Carib shirt and baggy pants. His weapon, again like the Haitians, was concealed under his capacious robes, though a small number of them socialized with automatic weapons slung nonchalantly at their sides.

"We've got movement on the roof," he heard Wilkinson announce from beside him. The sniper raised his sights and panned the roof. He saw one of the Haitians close a rooftop door and take a few steps out onto the roof itself. His facial hair was well groomed, and he wore a large, thick-looking cargo vest with a satchel slung overtop it, and greenish fatigues to match the vest.

His bare arms were muscular, and he held an automatic weapon in his right hand, almost unmistakably an Uziel submachine gun. He looked to the horizon and raised his other hand to his mouth, taking a long drag on a thick blunt, the bluish smoke of which wreathed his dreadlock mane. He remained in the shadow of the raised brick structure that housed the doorway, though the darkening world around him was increasingly concealing on its own.

# *II*

Jermain Godfrey leaned against the wall. The room was completely unfurnished save for the few chairs and the single table they had brought with them for the day. Because most of the bulbs in the place had burnt out, they had brought a couple of old lamps with them as well. These bathed and sectioned the main floor into regions of mellow light. Jermain and a few others were listening to one of Etien's stories from back home. Grinning widely and speaking in Creole, Etien regaled his audience with his devious sexual exploits. His short dreads quivered as he gesticulated, and his strangely pitched voice added all the more humor to his tale. Now and again Jermain smiled and laughed, feigning interest in Etien's tale. He usually found Etien to be a genuine riot, but given the situation, he was justifiably distracted.

The real reason he had joined the conversation, was that Etien and Sol had been amid the group. Sol was functionally the leader of the Haitian syndicate. It was he who had originally founded their enterprise in Haiti with Etien, and it was he who organized their business. Jermain had positioned himself equidistant between the two so that his radio transmitter could clearly register what was being said. The bug was made to look like one of the large black buttons on his shirt, the second from the top. He knew the NYPD would be recording everything, and wanted to insure he could give them as many incriminating confessions as possible. However, Etien had changed the serious nature of the conversation, and just as Etien had begun his sordid tale, Sol left abruptly and headed upstairs.

"…So befor she husban come home, mi and mi boy run battry on dis t'hick girl…," Etien had switched from Creole to his accented English for a section of the story, but was interrupted by indiscreet, jeering shouts from the domino table. Jean-Jacques had raised himself from where he sat and was taunting the other two who still sat at the table. They voiced their displeasure, but not so forcefully or audibly as Jean goaded them.

"What! What! Eh, what yo know bout dis? You con andle dis!"

Jean's voluminous gloats dominated the main floor and Jermain, Etien, and a few others turned to face him.

"De hell wrong wit dis man?" Etien queried to no one in particular. "Ey! Jean-Jacques yo'idiot. Yo wan to attract some garcons we don wan to dis'ouse?" Etien admonished.

"A'right, chill broda...mi'don yell no more," said Jean raising his hands apologetically. "Mi'don wit dese beitches anyhow."

Grinning and gloating almost inaudibly, he grabbed his winnings and left the table. Still seated at the domino table, the other two Haitians sucked their teeth, swore under their breath after him, and began collecting the dominoes. Jean plucked a cigarette from a pack he had in his pants pocket. He put the cigarette to his lips and then lit it with a lighter he had pulled from the same pocket. Jean let smoke swirl upwards from his nostrils as he turned to face Etien.

"When dis damn ting goin down Etien? Wher Sol at?"

"I tol yo bout de delay, so juss relax. Dem white-boy dealas gonna com collect ouwa product sameway," Etien assured confidently.

Jermain knew the Russians had been delayed, as did the rest of the Haitians, but that was all he knew. He and some of the newer members of the syndicate were entrusted with the complete concept of their affairs, if not the complete details, and to inquire needlessly about minute particulars would raise suspicions. In fact, Sol and Etien did not usually disclose unnecessary details to anyone readily. Still, Jermain knew enough that the department had sanctioned their sting, which he hoped would run as smoothly as planned.

Etien was still talking to Jean, and both had reverted to Creole. Etien took Jean aside, engaging him in private and ostensive discourse. Someone opposite Jermain had begun to speak in

Etien's absence and Jermain turned to face him, giving further pretence of his attention. When he glanced back at the secretive conversation, Jean was nodding in confirmation to something Etien had said. Jean turned and headed across the room towards the stairs while Etien stared out a window momentarily and then looked at his watch.

Shortly thereafter, Etien's cellphone rang. He put the phone to his ear and answered the caller with a curt greeting. His attitude and aspect became quite serious, and after an abrupt but respectful compliance, he snapped the phone shut and looked out over the large open room. His expression was humorless and almost anxious.

"A'right!" he yelled urgently. "De Russians comin now. Get up y'all and get pre'pard."

It seemed that the posse did not move with enough haste for Etien's liking, and he exhorted them with a redoubled fervor.

"Les go, mon! Dis ain't no damn game. Dis shit real, it happenin now, so grab yo guns and get pre'pared."

The somewhat jocular atmosphere transitioned into a near hostile solemnity as the Haitians readied for the deal. Jermain had made sure to face Etien, and had even taken a few steps towards him to insure the contents of Etien's message were clearly communicated to his units.

\* \* \* \*

The sniper had been scouring the warehouse when, from over his right shoulder, he heard Wilkinson report with some earnestness in his voice.

"Our man on the roof is receiving a call."

The sniper had sighted the Haitian in time to see him stare searchingly down Fifty-fourth Road and nod his head as he confirmed something or the other with the speaker on his cellphone. The Haitian ended the call and subsequently proceeded to make a call of his own. The sniper's initial inference was that whoever had been on the other end of the first call, was associated with the party that his team was expecting to arrive at the warehouse. Wilkinson confirmed his premonition.

"See the way he looked off down the street? That might have been the buyers. Pan the windows so's we can find out if he's makin a quick call to his men inside. If he is, probably means this is gonna go down pretty soon."

The sniper panned the windows on the main floor with methodical scrutiny. The Haitians were still milling around. The domino table was one short of what it had been, and he was sure he had seen the missing player with the lengthy beard pass one of the windows. Through another window, he saw a Haitian with short dreadlocks holding a cellphone to his ear. He seemed to be listening rather than talking.

"Is the guy on the roof doing any talking?" inquired the sniper.

"Yeah," Wilkinson replied as he squinted into his binoculars.

"Cause the guy with the short dreads in the third window on the right looks to be doin some listening."

No sooner had the sniper made this observation, than the man in the window snapped his phone closed.

The sniper watched the man with the short dreads. He seemed to be yelling at his crew. The sniper assumed they were now in the process of preparing for the incipient deal. Verification of his assumption came to him promptly over his headset. He raised his head from the scope momentarily, focusing on the details he was receiving. He glanced at Wilkinson who had lowered his binoculars and was holding his headset gently with his other hand. Wilkinson's face was frozen in concentration, as he was clearly receiving the same intelligence. An NYPD dispatch informed them that the buyers were on approach. As previously determined, their objective now included identification of the inbound vehicle or vehicles, and a relay of the direction from which it, or they, approached. Wilkinson shot a glance at him.

"You copy that?"

The sniper gave him a quick nod of his head and responded.

"Yes, sir."

\* \* \* \*

Officer Klyne looked up from the van floor to the team leader, who was in the process of addressing him and the other officers. Though the team leader maintained a cool professionalism, there was an urgent quality to his demeanor. Officer Klyne sensed that the ball was in motion, and felt a renewed rush of adrenalin course through him.

"Okay, ladies, we're hot. We just received confirmation that the second party is inbound. No changes to our game plan. Other than the wait, everything is proceeding as anticipated. We move in and infiltrate as planned. Make sure your gear is ready."

The team leader turned from them and moved back to the front of the van, readjusting his headset and conversing quietly with the driver.

\* \* \* \*

Wilkinson had already raised his binoculars to his eyes, and was gazing down
Fifty-fourth Road in the direction the Haitian on the roof had been looking during his call. The sniper lowered his head to the scope once more. The rifle moved slightly as he pressed his shoulder against the butt for stability. He recognized the slight alteration of its sight, for the scope now displayed a nondescript area on the roof, the targeting reticle hovering somewhat above the rooftop. Before his eye had completely focused through the scope to properly observe the magnified image within, he registered movement coming towards him from the extreme right of the scope's periphery. It happened so abruptly that he scarcely had time to discern the moving thing; nonetheless, he had the sense that something had leaped from the small building just behind the warehouse towards the warehouse itself.

Though half of the moving thing was outside the sight of the scope as it traveled through the air, he was able to register moving limbs, flailing clothing, and a portion of a face. His instantaneous impression from the fleeting glimpse was that is was a man, covered all in black. He jerked the scope to the right with as fast a reaction as he was capable, but even as he neared the area of the roof where the figure might have landed, it dropped from view, vanishing beyond the rooftop.

The whole thing had occurred so quickly that the sniper was not certain of what he believed he had seen. It could have been a man, but if so, the man's presence there made no sense to him. The only solo operative working with the team was their inside man, and it had most assuredly not been Jermain Godfrey. Given the brevity of his sighting and the increasingly tenebrous dusk, it could very well have been a large garbage bag being tossed about in the wind. Just as brief as his glimpse of the apparition, was the time he had to ruminate upon it. The bark of Wilkinson's voice regained his attention and, for the moment, emptied his mind of its deductive speculations.

"Possible target from the east on Fifty-fourth! Vehicle is a royal blue… Cadillac. Driver and passenger are Caucasian males."

Now fully focused, the sniper turned his weapon so he could aim down the street. He sighted the Cadillac quickly in his scope, and confirmed his acquisition of the target to Wilkinson.

"Roger that, I see it."

The Cadillac had tinted windows and was exquisitely maintained. It seemed out of place in the area, and the sniper watched with growing anticipation as it approached.

# *III*

Fleet of foot, he sprinted across the verge of the roof to circumvent treading upon the rooftop gravel, which might have alerted the man atop the opposite building to his presence. His long black coat billowed out behind him as he sped forward, and wind rushed over his face and through his hair, whistling as it raced past his attuned ears. He had spotted the man on the roof well before he had reached the building whose edge he now coursed. The scent of burning cannabis had met him equally as long ago, and he focused on the man as he raced onward with notable stealth. He approached at a distance from which experience told him the man would soon hear his ever-nearing footfalls.

Barely breaking stride, he leaped from his position on the adjacent rooftop. His body rose into the air, and the dark chasm between the two buildings began to rush past underneath him as he sailed across. To have cleared the gap and landed upon the opposite rooftop was easily done, but that was not his intention. The man on the roof held an automatic weapon, and would most assuredly hear him land upon the noisy gravel, no matter how softly he alighted. He would still be able to dispatch him, but not before the man could pull the trigger. The staccato discharge of the weapon would function as well as any alarm, attracting the others, and these vermin were no doubt similarly armed. Instead, he intended to enter the building through a window on the upper floor.

He began to drop from the height of his leap, sinking down through the night air towards one of the windows, and as he descended below the level of the rooftop, his arms and legs extended slowly to brace against the impending impact. His legs absorbed the brunt of the force as they thumped against the outer wall of the warehouse, and his hands impacted upon and then clasped the windowsill.

On the rooftop, Sol turned his head, certain he had heard something from somewhere behind him. He brushed a few lengthy dreadlocks from his face, careful not to brush them with the embers of his blunt. He squinted into the growing darkness, but saw nothing. He turned away to face down the street once more, and noticed a car on the road. He brought the blunt to his lips and drew in deeply, breathing out a plume of thick smoke.

He hung from the sill effortlessly, even as he outstretched one of his hands towards the planks, which had been nailed in place to board the window. These planks were the reason he had chosen this entry point, being quite certain he could remove them without disclosing his presence. Before he had set upon the building, he had observed that the main floor was occupied, while the second floor was left unlit and seemingly empty. The window had been boarded with two planks from the inside, making purchase from the outside impossible. Knowingly, he placed his palm on the bottommost plank, and began to press against it with graduated increments of force. The plank creaked quietly under the mounting strain.

Staring expectantly at the plank, he patiently increased the strength of his effort so that the nails slid gradually from their holes. With a slight grating sound and a modest snap, the bottom plank gave way, as did much of the top plank. It seemed they had been joined at their tops for support by another piece of timber. Still attached above by a few stubborn nails that were now somewhat dislocated and markedly twisted, the board opened inwards like a pet door. Using it as such, he gently pushed it further inward. Careful not to snag himself on protruding nails, the man in black slipped into the dark room.

Under the now pitch-black shadow of the brick structure housing the rooftop door, Sol watched the approaching car. He was quite sure it was his buyers, though it was difficult to tell. The scant streetlights in the area had only just begun to turn on and glowed dully as they did so. He was just about to head back inside, when once again he heard a noise come from somewhere behind him. This time, he turned around completely. Again, he perceived nothing in his immediate area, nor anything that would warrant his attention. He took a few steps in the direction he believed the sound had come from. Still unable to detect anything that aroused his suspicions, he turned towards to the door, but not before stealing one last puzzled glance over his shoulder. Hesitating, he looked out over his surroundings once more.

\* \* \* \*

Jean-Jacques had paused briefly at the top of the stairs to count his winnings. Leafing through the bills and nodding approvingly, his face held an exulted expression that was both frown and grin, his cigarette dangling precariously from one corner of his mouth. He was distracted by yelling from below and recognized the voice as Etien's. Shoving the bills into his pocket, he listened where he was until Etien had finished shouting, and then walked out onto the upper floor to meet up with Sol and carry the cases of cocaine back downstairs. He flicked on the sole hallway light.

The bare bulb flickered, buzzed and then shone. Like the main floor, much of the upper floor was open space, however, a section of it was compartmentalized into various rooms, most of these having once been used as offices. The stairwell faced the hallway from which these office rooms could be accessed. To one side of the hallway were the offices, a window allotted to each. On the other side of the hallway were a few windowless rooms that had been used for storage.

Jean-Jacques heard a noise from somewhere ahead, something akin to furniture being moved. He glanced out of an open doorway into the spacious section on the upper floor, but he was certain the noise had come from a room near the end of the hall. He faced forward once more and began to walk down the hallway, the thud of his boots audible, and the wooden floor creaking under his weight. He took a long drag of his cigarette and then removed it from his mouth, holding it between his middle finger and forefinger. Being some distance from the light, the end of the hall was somewhat dark, and he called out down the hallway.

"Sol! Ey Sol! What you doin der, mon?"

\* \* \* \*

The sniper watched the blue Cadillac pull into the Haitians' warehouse lot. Four of the Haitians, including the man with the short dreads, came out to receive their visitors. The passenger exited the vehicle first. He wore a steel grey suit and was of impressive physical stature. The significant bulge at his side under his suit jacket suggested he likely possessed a formidable handgun. He acknowledged the Haitians, seemingly exchanging what pleasantries one could possibly expect in such a situation.

He seemed to be explaining something to them, after which he pulled a device from his pocket that looked very much like a walkie-talkie. He was pointing to the silver device, which for some reason caused the Haitian with short dreads evident frustration. They appeared to argue for a few moments before the Haitian threw up his hands in acquiescence. The man in the grey suit nodded to the other Russians in the Cadillac.

Followed by the other Haitians, the man with the short dreads led the statuesque Russian into the warehouse. As he did so, four other men, including the driver, opened the doors of the Cadillac and left the car. One of them carried a large metal briefcase, secured to his left wrist with handcuffs. The sniper panned to the man with the grey suit. He had already entered the warehouse and the sniper watched him through a window. The big Russian was moving the device near one of the Haitians, sweeping it up and down. The sniper's eyes widened with alarm.

"Awww Christ! The Russian inside's gotta freakin bug detector. This guy could make Godfrey any minute."

Wilkinson zeroed in on the man with the grey suit with his binoculars and cursed. The sniper heard Wilkinson relaying the troubling new intelligence over his headset. The sniper watched and waited.

\* \* \* \*

Though he waited in anticipation, no reply greeted his ear in response to his inquiry. Still moving down the darkening hallway, Jean-Jacques became increasingly perplexed by the oddity of Sol's behavior. He placed his cigarette to his lips once more, squinting through the rising twines of smoke. Most of the old office room doors were unlocked and open, as no one used them for anything anymore. Jean-Jacques and Etien had left the cases of cocaine in one of the rooms, but it seemed Sol was not to be found there either. As Jean-Jacques neared the last few rooms at the end of the hall, something caught his eye through one of the doors. He approached the doorway, affording himself a clearer view of the near-pitch-dark room. It was the boarded window in the room that had caught his eye.

The light of dusk, somber and pastel, entered the room from a fissure beneath the planks. The two planks which made up the boarding were still fixed together, but both were displaced near the bottom. The boarding hung limp from a few meager, bent nails still attached above to the window frame. A gentle breeze whistled softly through the gap between the planks and the window, rocking the boarding almost imperceptibly. Sensing something was amiss, he reached under his shirt and pulled his handgun from his belt.

There was an unnerving quiet in the room, which was interrupted by the falls of his boots, and the creak of the floorboards as he slowly entered the doorway. Inches across the threshold, he stopped as he heard the wooden floor creak under a moving weight that was not his. Before he could even turn to face the source of the sound, something struck and clutched him with staggering force about the neck. His cigarette was flung from his lips and fell to the floor beneath a few wooden oddments. Stricken from the blow, he was scarcely aware of his body being driven backward. He perceived a large, dark blur moving in front of him, but before he could focus his muddled senses, his head and back thudded forcefully against the inside of the doorframe.

He struggled to remain conscious as his eyes rolled obliviously in his head. His own body seemed distant from him, heavy and inanimate. A low, quiet growl, like that of a large dog's, rumbled so close to him that it filled his entire being with dread. His eyes began to focus themselves through the spotty obscurity that had been his vision, revealing a terrifying face louring before him. The face was pale as death, the terrible eyes like golden sapphires. A powerful arm pinned him to the doorway by his throat, the pain-dealing hand of which crushed his flesh and windpipe like a vice. The pressure building behind his eyes made them redden with twining, rupturing vesicles, and it felt as though his eyes would dislodge from their sockets.

Another kind of pain made itself known from his gun hand, and he made an unsuccessful attempt to glance down at it. It no longer held his gun, and was contorted painfully in his attacker's other hand. He was sure he heard little snaps and the shearing of bone from his deformed wrist. He was all but paralyzed with fear, shock, pain, infirmity, and disorientation. In one quick motion, the hand at his throat slid up under his jaw, awkwardly twisting his head to one side, so that the white palm cracked the left side of his face against the doorframe. Again the hand pinned him, this time with the hefty palm pressing against his face, straining the very integrity of his skull. He felt faint, and his knees began to buckle.

The harrowing growling had ceased, leaving a silence almost as horrid. Straining to stare through his attacker's fingers, he saw the gold sapphire eyes shift their torrid gaze from his face to an area below it. He saw the mouth open ever so slightly, partially revealing a horror more terrifying than the strange eyes. The face moved towards him, not swiftly, nor slowly, but steadily and purposefully. He could no longer see the face, but he felt its presence. Hot breath at his neck sent chills down his spine. Agony followed, as powerful jaws collapsed the cartilaginous structures of his neck, and two hot points of pain punctured his flesh, forcing themselves deep into his throat. His body was limp; if not for the powerful arm of his attacker, he would collapse to the floor.

Strangely, the pain began to subside somewhat and a lethargic sensation like somnolence, took hold of him. He heard the rhythmic beating of his heart and a sound like water churning in an inland brook back home, or was it…he simply did not know. His vision hazed; first a veil with lights dancing over it, then clouded and grey, and lastly, darkness.

One of the Haitians grabbed the domino table and dragged it further into the center of the room in preparation for the product cases. The rest of the Russians had entered the warehouse, and Jermain watched with mounting anxiety as the big Russian in the grey suit performed a second bug check. Etien looked at the table for a moment and spoke softly to one of the Haitians beside him.

"Ey. I don know what Jean and Sol is doin, but dey takin too long. Go get dem, tell dem dat de Russians is in he're wit us if de somehow diden realize."

Jermain watched Odett, a lithe man with a shaven head, converse with Etien. Odett had been nicknamed SoNoir because he was so much darker than the rest of them, his skin like the color of actual ebony. Jermain saw Odett walk to the stairs and head to the floor above.

The man in black heard footsteps emanating from the stairs across the hall. They were not altogether hasty, but seemed motivated in some way. He took what he could from the limp body he held, before pulling it with sudden force into the dark room and casting it silently into a blackened corner of the room behind a pile of old, dusty oddments. Anticipating the approaching man, he slipped into another unlit office.

Sol tarried on the roof for longer than he realized, and the sound of a slamming car door and voices from below had shaken him from his rooftop vigil. Aware that the Russians had arrived, he took his last few drags on the smoldering blunt and then let it drop from his hand. After grinding it into the gravel under his boot, he headed for the door. He made his way down the rooftop stairwell to the upper floor. He saw Odett step into the hall. Spotting him, Odett tossed him a quick nod.

"Yo know de Russians is he're, eh, Sol? What takin yo and Jean so long?" Sol gave him a stern, quizzical look.

"What yo talking about, SoNoir? Jean-Jacques not wit me."

Sol's face took on a dour expression and he entered the hallway, facing the far end. He called Jean's name, but not a sound issued in reply. He noticed Odett glance at him from his right.

"He is not down wit de rest, an he diden pass mi on de stair."

Sol continued to stare down the hall, giving no sign that he had acknowledged Odett. He was staring at the doorway of one of rooms close to the end of the hall. In particular, he was staring at an area to one side of the doorway, only inches beyond the foot of the doorframe. There, a gun, which he was sure was Jean's, lay on its side. Sol could not escape the feeling that something odd was transpiring, but could not yet justify his concerns.

He raised his Uzi and, speaking in Creole to Odett, pointed at the fallen gun. Odett drew a hefty handgun of his own from somewhere under his shirt at the belt line. A few more quiet words were exchanged before they both began to move down the hallway, one closely following the other, their alignment somewhat staggered. They walked cautiously, their steps creaking in the disquieting silence. The better part of Sol's attention was attuned to the dark, foreboding room the gun lay beside. Though his eyes briefly searched the rooms he passed, they quickly regained their prior fixity. Behind him, Odett paused for a moment to look over his shoulder, and then continued onward. Odett paused once more when he thought he heard a faint creak of floorboards.

Sol approached the gun and peered through the doorway. The most evident disturbance to the room was the window, the boarding of which seemed to have been torn from the window frame. The distinct odor of smoke wafted from the room, and dim, stale light slipped in from beyond the dislodged timber, scarcely lighting the room at all. Still staring uneasily at the boarding, he knelt to retrieve Jean's gun. Had he glanced behind him in that instant, had he not been so preoccupied, he would have witnessed the large, fleeting form of a man erupt from one of the unlit offices. He would have glimpsed a ghostly face and flailing black vestments whip across the hallway behind Odett in a blur of motion. He would have seen Odett's skull shudder under a sudden, violent impact, and his assailant then disappear into one of the old storage rooms.

The heavy blow caused Odett to seize momentarily before his body went lax. As his forearms and hands clenched, his right forefinger pulled on the trigger and his gun blasted an errant shot into the base of the wall. A shower of debris spilled from the gaping hole, and white dust drifted around it.

Sol heard something move behind him and began to turn round. As he did so, he heard a sound like bone striking bone and the clicking of teeth in a slack jaw. This was immediately succeeded by a startling gunshot. He spun round with a look of utter shock on his face, in time to see Odett's limp body pitch forward and thud against the floor in a prone heap. Believing that Odett had been shot, he slunk into the doorway and frantically peered out from within the doorway at both ends of the hall. He raised his Uzi and Jean's handgun, pointed them at opposite ends of the hall, and fired a few reckless shots.

They ripped through the walls, leaving clouds of dust in their wake. His eyes darted from one end of the hall to the other, but his goading shots had prompted no retaliation, nor any reaction of any kind. He heard a tumult of voices from the floor below and steeled himself, knowing his brothers would not leave the sound of gunfire uninvestigated. He spied Odett's body and noticed the bullet hole at the base of the wall, but could see nothing else. He leaned out from the doorway and shouted into the air, addressing the incorporeal assailant in his fervor. Twisted memories of Haiti haunted his mind. He remembered entranced masses under the influence of voodoo, their eyes rolling in their skulls, some writhing about on the dusty ground. He recalled the spattered blood from beheaded roosters and goats, and the old Obeah men casting their hexes of malice, sending black spirits after those they despised. Lastly, and most vividly, he remembered the accusing eyes of the old witch doctor he had killed years ago. He cursed in Creole and then shouted in broken English.

"Who der?...Who der!? If yo a mon, den yo a dead mon! If yo

Obeah, mi'no let yo take mi soul, mi'kill yo same way! Mi'know all about de black art, and mi'no scare of some fockin voodoo magic!"

Downstairs, Etien had been waiting impatiently. He was both annoyed by the Russian with the bug detector and with Sol's nonchalant neglect of their business proceedings. One of the other Russians was inquiring about something, when a gunshot sounded from above them. A barrage of shots followed the first in rapid succession.

Jermain Godfrey, who had been plotting how he would avoid the detector, was as stunned as the rest. The SWAT team's attack plan had been communicated to him, and this random discharge of weapons had certainly not been it. Around him, the throng was catapulted into a frenzy. Weapons were cocked and readied, heads looked about skittishly and voices raised. The Russian, with the metal case fettered to his wrist, turned and began to move backwards towards the door. In doing so, he inadvertently swung the heavy case about and knocked over one of the lamps. The lamp cracked and the bulb shattered, its light snuffed after a brief flicker. The Russians drew together ready to defend themselves, evidently suspecting a double cross.

Etien's voice gradually boomed over the rest. He turned to the Russians, his arms raised in a reassuring gesture. He pleadingly instructed them to wait a moment for him to return so they could close their deal. He beckoned the three Haitians closest to him, and they ran up the stairs, craning their necks to see as much of the upper floor as possible as they ascended. Jermain could hear Sol yelling maniacally as they did so, and he looked over at the Russians, who had apparently chosen to disregard Etien's proposition. No sooner were the three Haitians upstairs, than the Russians made their exit, despite aggressive protests from the two Haitians alongside Jermain.

* * * *

The Russian in the grey suit had moved away from the window so that the sniper had no visual on the Russian or Officer

Godfrey. He and Wilkinson sat in silence, a palpable tension rising as distressing seconds passed. The other Russians had left the car and joined the man in the grey suit in the warehouse. The sniper watched as one of them conversed with the short, dreadlocked man. As he watched the two parties interact, a brisk popping sound reached his ear. He recognized the sound as the report of a gun from some distance. He froze momentarily.

"Did you...," before he could finish, he heard the subsequent reports of submachine gun and pistol fire. Through the scope, the gathering in the little warehouse moved about with evident agitation, and in the section of the building where most were gathered, a light went out. He shot a glance at Wilkinson, who returned his gaze with a face burdened with concern, in which he recognized his own morbid inference. Wilkinson turned to face the warehouse once more, saw the Russians retreating from the warehouse, and began to shout over his headset.

"Shots fired! Shots fired! All units move in! Move in!"

\* \* \* \*

The van's engine roared to life as the team leader barked orders.

"We're live! The other van will neutralize the second party, we breach and enter as planned!"

The officers were poised to rush from the back of the van. Officer Klyne held his assault rifle close to him and licked his lips, which had all at once gone dry. The team stared at the back door anticipatively, like thoroughbreds at the gates. Officer Klyne felt his heart beating in his chest, and felt the van accelerating; the vehicle tremored as it flew down Forty-fourth Street. The van turned sharply and he strained to keep his balance. The van rocked about as it traveled over an uneven surface, and he knew they were now in front of the warehouse. He heard the reports of assault rifles outside, a sign that the other van had begun its neutralization of the second party. His own van came to a grinding halt, and the officers closest to the rear of the van threw the back doors open. Of these two, one officer carried a large, rectangular, bulletproof shield and was the first to emerge from the van. Peering through an eye-slit in the black SWAT shield, the officer raised a pistol with his free hand, aiming towards the warehouse entrance. The other officers proceeded to fall in behind the shield bearer. The team deployed with striking efficiency, and rushed through the swirling dust towards the front door in linear formation behind the shield bearer.

When they reached the door, they pressed themselves against the wall facing the entrance, still behind the shield bearer. Through the surrounding cacophony, Officer Klyne heard three shots fired from inside. He saw McKormann, the team breacher, step hurriedly towards the door holding a one-man battering ram. McKormann rocked the metal ram back and drove it forward, the flat square head bashing the door near the knob. The door splintered, caved, and swung open. They flooded in through the entrance, which was quite dark in comparison to the far end of the large room. When Officer Klyne cleared the door, his assault rifle raised and ready, he spotted Officer Godfrey standing in the middle of the room with his arms raised.

Though he knew Godfrey was aware that the SWAT team had been made familiar with his face and attire, it appeared Godfrey was insuring he was recognized as a friendly. Two corpses lay sprawled on the ground in the room with him: one a few meters from him, and the other near a window. The window had a hole in it, from which spiraling cracks wound their way towards the frame. Officer Godfrey was gesturing with a hand and flicked his head towards the stairs, indicating the rest were on the floor above.

\* \* \* \*

He watched the two SWAT vans speed in from Forty-fourth Street and careen onto the warehouse lot. The first had pulled in front of the Cadillac, so that its length blocked the possibility of escape. The Russians, who were not yet all in the vehicle, drew their guns, save the man with the metal case who dove into the back seat. With the Russians in his sights, the sniper had received a command licensing him to exercise extreme force if necessary to assist in the neutralization of both parties.

The big Russian in the grey suit made a move towards the SWAT driver with his pistol raised. The big Russian had not even taken a second step when, with a bang and the sound of a bullet ripping through the air, the sniper dropped him with a shot that tore into his chest and exited with a spatter from a gaping hole in his back. Wilkinson confirmed the kill. The first van deployed, barking orders to submit. The majority of the stricken party dropped their weapons and cowed, preparing to drop to the ground with their arms raised.

One Russian, who had not realized a sniper was trained on them, leapt behind the Cadillac for cover, provoking a flurry of bullets from the officers' assault rifles. Bullets twanged as they struck the car, riddling the metal and glass. Observing the submission of his compatriots and appreciating the threat of an advancing SWAT team, the Russian tossed his weapon and threw himself down, face first and arms out, onto the dusty ground.

Seeing the threat had been neutralized, the sniper moved his sights to the second team. They were preparing to breach the entrance, and the sniper panned left to scan the windows. In the first window, which had gone dark, he saw a figure moving quite close to the glass. His features were greatly obscured, but the sniper was sure that the man was a Haitian, and that he had a gun raised towards the warehouse entrance. The Haitian wore a white shirt with dark embroidery, and a hat which covered a seemingly shaven head. Evidently, the man was not Officer Godfrey and in the penultimate moment before the figure passed the window, the sniper took the shot.

* * * *

Jermain Godfrey and the two Haitians who had remained on the main floor had watched the Russians take their leave at some distance. As they backed out of the warehouse towards their vehicle, three of the Russians had kept guns pointed at Jermain and the other Haitians, lest they attempt to impede their withdrawal. Soon after they closed the door, the sound of heavy vehicles became audible from outside. Gunfire followed and echoed from the lot. Jermain had backed well away of the door, his face a pretence of concern to maintain his cover. One of the Haitians ran towards the door, locked it, and retreated from it, his gun raised and ready. Jermain raised his gun as well, as the other Haitian peered out one of the windows, strained to catch a glimpse of the front of the lot, and then turned to face the door.

Something whacked one of the windows, and was simultaneously accompanied by the tinkling sound of glass bursting into tiny shards. The Haitian near the window closest the door keeled over, clutching himself just below the neck. Jermain knew that if one of the snipers was using lethal force, then the team would be through the door in seconds.

As the other Haitian stared at his fallen comrade in momentary disbelief, Jermain fired three shots into the man's upper back, and watched him clench violently and topple onto his side. Jermain rushed forward and kicked the man's gun from his dying hand. The man simply stared at him accusingly, blood trickling from the corner of his mouth. Jermain watched the two men gasping their last breaths on the floor, and watched the movements of their bodies subside. As he stared at them, a strong feeling of guilt brewed within him.

These were men with whom he had shared stories, lived with and been trusted by. He knew their sins all to well, but, somehow, he could not help feeling the way he did. His contemplative gaze was broken by a thunderous boom from the door, and he dropped his weapon and raised his hands as the SWAT team came through.

* * * *

"Sol! What yo doin? What happen to SoNoir?" Etien had asked when his eyes caught sight of Odett's fallen body and witnessed Sol standing half hidden in the doorway of one of the far offices, "De Russians is down der mon. Dey gon leave if dey tink owa business no good an yo know dat! What yo gon—"

"Somebody he'ar. Mi'tink somebody from home send de Obeah to us," Sol had interjected, his eyes searching the hallway. "So mi gon kill some fokin Obeah man today....yo he're me? Me gon kill yo, Obeah man!"

Etien, and the men alongside him, turned to the stairwell behind them as they heard the muffled discharge of automatic weapons from somewhere outside. They froze for a moment, before one of them approached the stairwell. Suddenly, three gunshots blared from the floor below, compelling most of the Haitians to put their backs to one side of the hallway. Valmont, the Haitian closest to the stairs, peered down the stairwell, keeping tight to the wall. A single, resounding boom erupted from the main floor. Valmont jerked back behind the wall at the sudden sound. When he peered into the stairwell again, he was staring into the barrel of a handgun held by a uniform with a shield who was ascending the stairs followed by a rushing host of armed men. He spun away from the wall wide-eyed and shouted a warning to rest of the posse.

"Police'la! Allez enden en chamb!"

Etien, Valmont, and the two others, Andre and Wiltord, scattered and took refuge in the closest rooms, while Sol backed further into his. Sol reached into his satchel, pulled out a hand grenade, and yelled a warning to his men in Creole, insuring his intentions were made clear to them.

In a dark office only two doors away from the stairs, Etien and Valmont exchanged disconsolate looks. Etien whispered to Valmont resolutely.

"Sol done loss he damn mind. Mi'no gon sit he're to get ex'plode, an den shot'up by dem flics."

Valmont nodded in agreement. While Valmont covered the doorway, Etien used the butt of his weapon to shatter the window out into the alleyway below. The shards clattered off the hood of their transport truck, and fragmented over the pavement. He peered out through the broken window at the hood below.

"Eh eh...mi'too damn ole fa dis mad mon tings," he muttered before turning to Valmont behind him. "Ey, Val!"

In the stairwell, the SWAT team paused momentarily to allow the entire squad to fall in on the stairs. Officer Klyne stood behind the team leader with his back to the wall and his eyes attuned to the leader's signals. After a quick scope of the environment, and a few brief hand gestures from the team leader, they advanced to the upper floor, preparing to secure the floor room by room. A sudden silence gripped the area, making the creaks of the wooden floor under their boots painfully audible. In a slight crouch behind the team leader and the shield bearer, Officer Klyne stared down the hallway as he moved forward.

There was an acrid odor of burning materials on the upper floor, but he could not yet see any smoke in the relative dark. He was troubled by the concealing gloom at the other end of the hall, knowing full well how visible he and the team were under the exposed bulb, which shone from above just behind him. They approached the first room, which he and the team leader secured. He moved into the room while the team leader held the threshold and the shield bearer kept the other officers covered in the hallway. Officer Klyne heard a muffled shout from somewhere in the hall. A slight movement caught his eye, and he turned towards the doorway. He saw something fly through the air, over the team leader's head, and into the room. The object issued a metallic clank as it thudded against the wall closest to the stairs. The room was sufficiently lit from the hall light, so that he identified the projectile even as it struck the wall.

Shrouded in his coat and in the darkness around him, the man in black waited patiently for an opportune moment. He heard footfalls from the stairs, and a creaking of floorboards as those in the hallway scuttled about.

To his ears, the hallway sounded as though it had been deserted, and he assumed the prior assemblage had taken refuge in the rooms nearby. From the room almost adjacent to his hiding spot, he heard the man from the roof shout emphatically. The heavy scent of smoke emanated from the room, and he assumed that one of the wooden oddments had caught fire.

Sticking to the shadows, he moved into the mouth of the

doorway in time to see the man step halfway into the hall, swing back his arm, and lob what he understood to be a grenade. The man's eyes were focused on their intended target, and his arm had only just begun to descend from the throw. The man had switched his gun to his non-dominant hand, which swung languidly at his side. The man in black sought to withdraw from the window he had breached, and knew that the moment had come.

Had Sol been staring directly and intently at the open storage room across the hall, he might have seen something move ever so slightly in the darkened doorway. He might have seen a ghostly face, barely distinguishable as such in the darkness; he might have seen yellow eyes glint almost indiscernibly from therein.

The attack came without warning, as hard and fast as the ambush of a leopard. Sol left his feet as his body succumbed to the force of his attacker, and they moved as one towards the unlit room. Where in one instant their two bodies met in the hall, in the next, they were gone, vanished into the dark, smokey room.

\* \* \* \*

"Grenade!!"

Even as the word escaped the shield bearer's mouth, Officer Klyne had already begun to fall back from the thing. After striking the wall, the grenade dropped near the doorway between himself and his team, and began to wobble and roll in his direction. The other officers leaped away from the doorway and back into the stairwell. Forced in the opposite direction, and searching desperately for a way to escape the imminent blast as he moved, he saw nothing behind which he could seek cover, nor overturn for efficient protection. His eyes shot to the window on the far wall. Though he knew a fall from it would grievously injure him, it was his last and only hope. Already moving rapidly, he aligned himself with the window. The moment seemed to drag on, and he half expected the grenade to go off before he could get clear. He dropped his shoulder and tucked his weapon tightly into his chest.

His teeth clenched and his eyes shut tight as he launched his body headlong into the window. His helmet clacked against the window before the brunt of his weight and force were channeled through his shoulder, which hammered the glass as he traveled through the air. The window shattered, the glass exploding outwards as his body crashed through. The blow jarred him, but he remained cognizant of the fact he had cleared the window and was now descending.

He opened his eyes as much as he dared with the amount of broken glass cascading down with him. Looking for the ground and attempting to right himself in the air, he almost did not register the grenade detonating above. The force of the blast propelled all sorts of rubble from the window, as well as a wicked spray of shrapnel. Before he could even attempt to right himself, his body struck a hard, white surface. He landed on his back, and despite the pain and his muddled bearings, he had the sense to roll prone and cover as debris from the blast showered down on him from above. He coughed as he breathed in some of the swirling dust. He shook dust and debris from his head, and opened his eyes.

He realized he had landed on what appeared to be the trailer of a small transport truck that was parked in the alleyway between the warehouse and a building of similar size. Squinting, he looked up at the demolished window from which he had fallen. As he did, he witnessed something that utterly shocked him. Laying there on the truck and looking up at the dark, deeply-colored sky, he saw a man streak into view over the verge of the rooftop above, and, at speed, leap from the edge. A long black coat trailed out behind him, and his face, from what he saw of its underside, was starkly pale in contrast with his dark garments. With a low rush of air, the man soared across the alleyway directly above him to land on the adjacent rooftop and disappear beyond it.

\* \* \* \*

From his angled position in the corner building, the sniper panned feverishly to secure another target, hoping to take out another hostile. To him, it seemed he had scoured the area for an eternity, not knowing whether the situation inside had been contained or if it had become untenable. Police cars began to close around the warehouse with sirens blaring and lights flashing with chaotic effulgence. As he surveyed the area, a movement in the upper periphery of the scope brought his sights to the rooftop once more. This time he was sure of what his eyes relayed to him. It was most definitely the figure of a man, running across the rooftop of the building behind the warehouse. The man turned sharply near the far edge of the rooftop so that the sniper caught a glimpse of his profile. As the man in black retreated into obscurity with striking athleticism, the sniper was left with the impression of a pale face and a flowing black coat.

# *IV*

Officer Klyne propped himself on his elbows, gingerly raising himself from the shards of glass which lay on the truck with him. As he did so, he noticed two men running through the alleyway towards the back of the warehouse lot. Despite the faint light and the approximate fifty feet between he and them, he saw that both men were carrying automatic weapons of some kind. Considering their appearances, firearms, evident haste, and immediate location, he reasoned the chance that these were not escaping Haitians was quite slim. He bolted upright, shaking the remaining glass and debris from his uniform. He ran the length of the truck's trailer in small steps, attempting to make as little noise as possible.

He dropped from the trailer to the roof of the truck and slid down the windshield. He rolled off the hood tactfully, landing firmly on his feet. The two Haitians had not turned to face him, and he assumed the cacophony of sirens, vehicles, and yells, had drowned out his approach. He moved to one side of the alleyway and continued his approach in the darkest stretch of shadow between the two buildings.

The two Haitians were just about to clear the alley when an unmarked police car burst into view, lights flashing wildly from the dashboard. It careened off Fifty-third to cut off the Haitian's escape. Having seen the approaching car, the two Haitians momentarily sought cover, each propping their backs against a building at the mouth of the alley. Officer Klyne dropped to one knee behind a dumpster and raised his assault rifle. Before he could take aim, the Haitians suddenly rushed out from the alley with their weapons drawn.

He did not know if the officers in the cruiser had seen the type of weapons the Haitians were carrying, for the cruiser had come to a stop far too close to hostiles carrying that kind of armament. Before the officers could escape the vehicle and take cover behind it, the two Haitians opened fire. They did not stop advancing, nor did they cease firing. Glass shattered, lights winked out, and metallic twangs filled the streets as a deluge of bullets tore into the cruiser. Sparks flew as the cruiser was made porous by the incessant fire. Before the two officers sank below the dashboard, he had seen both their bodies twitching and writhing violently under the onslaught.

Officer Klyne leapt out from behind the dumpster, and at a full sprint, he raised his weapon, preparing to fire a spread of bullets. As he did, he saw the body of the Haitian with short dreadlocks give an abrupt convulsion and reel back. An exit wound had burst open high on the Haitian's back and the man clutched his chest as he collapsed. It seemed the sniper guarding the rear of the warehouse off Fifty-third had zeroed in on the situation. No sooner did the man fall, than the other Haitian raced off to the right, away from the warehouse and out of Officer Klyne's view from the alley. Still running at full tilt, Officer Klyne rushed out from the alley in pursuit of the fleeing Haitian. He took one brief look into the mangled cruiser and the grizzly scene within told him all he needed to know.

The Haitian passed the building and dashed into a small, shadowy maze of crates and other yard rubbish. As he weaved through the grounds, the corner on one of the crates burst into a cloud of splinters, indicating the sniper was still tracking the perpetrator in his scope. Officer Klyne ran through the lot along a different route, keeping the Haitian in his vision as he maneuvered through the oddments. The Haitian was not yet aware of his presence and he did not intend to reveal himself until a more favorable circumstance presented itself.

The Haitian cleared the lot, sprinted across Forty-sixth Street, and darted behind the few scattered structures on the adjacent block, safe from the sniper's sights. As Officer Klyne followed, he realized that in killing the two officers and taking flight in this direction, the Haitian had unwittingly created a chink in the police perimeter that had closed in. Doubtless, the sniper or his spotter would have reported what they had seen, and a unit would soon be dispatched, but they might be delayed securing the warehouse. Officer Klyne had to insure the thug did not escape. He reached the plot of buildings and peered behind the first just in time to see the Haitian cutting across the area towards the next block. Breathing heavily, he cursed and rushed after him, beginning to feel the weight of his uniform and equipment.

Valmont glanced over his shoulder as he ran. A painful cramp was stabbing in his side, but he forced himself onward. He had put a considerable distance between himself and the warehouse, and seemed to have evaded the police. For a short while, he stopped behind an old shed to look for police cars. He was about to move again when he saw an unmarked cruiser pass nearby with two officers inside. For a moment, he thought the officer at the wheel had seen him, but she looked away just as he was readying to bolt in the opposite direction. With the danger passed, he hunched over and leaned against the shed, breathing forcibly. Seeing no immediate threats, he dashed across the street. He slipped into another alleyway, fortuitously stumbling upon the means by which he would assure his escape. Panting heavily, he raised his weapon.

"Get!...get out de damn car!...an...giv mi de fockin keys... Now!"

For a few distressing moments, Officer Klyne lost sight of the Haitian. To his relief, he promptly reacquired sight of the Haitian as he crossed yet another street. The distance between them had decreased markedly, and he guessed the Haitian had taken a quick breather somewhere. He watched him pass into the next block and enter another alleyway. Evaluating his proximity to the Haitian, Officer Klyne altered his gait to diminish the sound of his approach. As he neared the alleyway, a loud voice, which was indubitably the Haitian's, rang out from its depth. As the voice rose to a desperate yell, he peered into the alley, his shoulder pressed against the wall. He spied the Haitian standing with his gun leveled at the head of an elderly gentleman, who sat quite discontentedly in the driver's seat of a lengthy black car. The Haitian clacked the barrel of his gun against the window.

"Mi'say get out de fockin car!"

To Officer Klyne's surprise, the man did not comply with the Haitian's demands. Instead, he abruptly twisted the key in the ignition as though he intended to simply drive off. Anticipating the Haitian's reaction to such blatant disregard, Officer Klyne took one quick step forward into the mouth of the alley and raised his assault rifle. As he did, the Haitian responded just as he feared. His gun still leveled at the man's head, the Haitian unloaded automatic fire into the driver's side window at point blank range. Bullets smacked into the glass, while Officer Klyne, cursing his timing, pulled his own trigger.

In his haste, not having wanted to inadvertently hit the man in the car, the first of his bullets tore through only the clothing and flesh of the Haitian's left arm. The Haitian recoiled in pain, his mouth and eyes opened wide in panic. The Haitian's dead arm flailed as his body spun under the impact of the bullets and he began to fall backwards. As the Haitian sank, his right arm came about with the weapon still firing. Officer Klyne trained his assault rifle with increased accuracy, his bullets riddling inwards from the Haitian's arm into his chest. The Haitian's mangled body twisted violently as it keeled towards the ground.

Yet, even as the Haitian collapsed, the man continued to fire, whipping a wild arc of bullets across the mouth of the alley. Officer Klyne saw that the gun had swung towards him and leaped back from the mouth of the alley. Before he could take complete cover behind the wall, he was struck by a spread of bullets that tore across his body. His thigh was struck first, then his abdomen, his chest twice, and finally his neck. The wall beside him was alive with small bursts of debris as the final spread of the bullets rattled into it. He was stunned by how quickly it had all happened, and his body clenched as it registered an excruciating array of pain.

Bracing himself against the wall, he managed a glance into the alley. The Haitian was still moving, but his activities were solely the unconscious spasms of a dying body. Officer Klyne allowed himself a brief glance at the car window, expecting to see another body slumped against the seat. What he did see was the elderly man staring back at him, a look of worry and dismay dominating the man's face. Officer Klyne realized that the glass was still intact, and that the bullets had done nothing but leave behind whitish scuffs and tiny cracks; the elderly man was sitting behind a window of bulletproof glass.

Pain overtook Officer Klyne's body and senses, and he staggered backwards. His legs buckled, and he tumbled, rolling off the wall and falling away from the alleyway. His mind raced with thoughts: what he might have done differently, his own mortality, the man who had shot him. The few bullets that had struck his torso had been obstructed by his Kevlar vest, though he still felt throbbing pain from where the bullets had bored in. His most prominent agonies were the gaping holes in his thigh and neck. Greater in severity than the one on his thigh, the wound at his neck was bleeding profusely, and he clutched at it with his hand, pressing his palm against the opening. Blood poured out from between his fingers, and he gritted his teeth as he attempted to cope with each painful pulse from his neck.

A gentle hand gripped him by the shoulder and he heard a friendly voice with a British accent from above him.

"Oh! Oh, dear God...you require medical treatment. Can...can you stand?"

Officer Klyne looked up to see the elderly man from the car crouching over him, a dark, hazy, bluish-grey sky looming beyond the man's stooped form, a sky streaked violet over the horizon. The elderly man's face was caring and concentrated while he seemed to assess the wounds. He had calm, blue eyes and a long, gentle face. He was almost bald over the top of his head, while grey-white tufts of hair puffed out almost comically from around the sides and back. He was clean-shaven, and wore a white shirt, grey pants, and an unbuttoned, beige, woolen cardigan. Officer Klyne stared up unresponsively at the man, his body and mind in a state of shock.

"Poor chap, don't worry to answer. Come, let's just get you out of here, shall we."

Officer Klyne saw the man look about nervously before moving behind him and hooking his arms underneath his armpits. Officer Klyne was incapacitated with pain, but understood the man's intentions, and the mortal urgency of the situation.

"I am going to help lift you. Try to use your good leg to help if you can. All right then…on three. One…two…three!"

Officer Klyne groaned in agony, but still placed his good leg underneath him to assist the man hauling him to his feet. The man ducked his head under Officer Klyne's arm, insuring his damaged leg bore no weight. Blood smeared over the man's clothes, and Officer Klyne could hear him laboring under his weight. They moved through the alley together, towards the passenger side door of the car.

The elderly man opened the door with his free hand, rested the injured officer against the seat, and closed the door after him. The man hurried around to the driver's side and entered the car. The car was already running, and without delay, the man drove out of the alley. He did not turn on his headlights, as though he was attempting to keep a low profile. The elderly man turned to the officer beside him, whose eyes were tightly shut, his face twisted into a grimace. He was losing a copious amount of blood, which coated the hand the officer held to his neck, and ran down his uniform. The officer opened his eyes and looked at him. He attempted to speak, his voice frail and dry.

"Wh…who…are…you?"

The man looked at him with a piteous compassion.

"Shh, shh…don't speak, please. You'll induce more pressure around the injury, and since you may have a ruptured carotid artery and accruing turgor pressure from inflammation in surrounding tissues, speech will only result in discomfort and increased blood loss, which of course we are needing to prevent at this time. Not to worry, you are in the best care around, I assure you. You could say you were both fortunate and unfortunate to have crossed paths with me tonight. I am a doctor…ahm…I just realized I have not yet introduced myself. My apologies, I am Dr. Nigel Canterberry."

"S...S...Sebastian," offered the officer, "S...Sebastian Kly....,"

"I believe I was quite clear about the repercussions of speech," the doctor interrupted concernedly. "Now...Sebastian...if you will kindly follow my instruction, we'll have you right as rain in no time."

He gave the officer a half smile, hoping the young man could not detect how unsettled he was by the gravity of his wounds.

They had only neared the on-ramp to the Long Island Expressway when Dr. Canterberry pulled over into a small side street and came to a stop. His head moved about searchingly as he peered into all the mirrors on the car and out the windows. He reached over into his glove compartment and pulled out a first aid kit. He closed it quickly, unsure if the officer had seen the gun inside. He pulled out gauze wrap, rummaged through the kit, and pulled out a wad of cotton, placing both on his lap. He then unwrapped a large Band-Aid and a wet towelette, holding one in each hand. Dr. Canterberry noticed he was being watched and regarded the wounded man with a pleasant smile.

"I am going to go about this as gently as possible, I assure you. Right...let's have a look, shall we? If you would remove your hand from...yes, thank you."

A gory, dark hole was revealed as the officer complied, and fresh blood oozed from it. The doctor gave the site a moderate cleaning with the towelette before attaching the bandage. He immediately placed the wad of cotton over it, and began wrapping gauze around the officer's neck. He secured the swath with the remains of a roll of athletic tape.

"There. That should hold you until we get to the clinic."

The officer gave him a weak nod, his tired eyes staring out through the windshield. Dr. Canterberry reached for a sweater that had been lying in the back seat and wrapped it around the officer's injured thigh.

"There you are. Keep pressure on the quadriceps yourself. It will keep you awake for the ride."

Dr. Canterberry started the engine and turned back onto the main street. Sebastian Klyne stared through the window as the elderly doctor pulled out. The pain in his neck was intense and he had begun to see spots in his vision. He pressed the sweater against the bullet wound on his thigh and wondered if he might be dying. A cellphone rang beside him; the ringtone was a piece by Mozart. Though he continued to stare forward, he heard Dr. Canterberry take the call. A hard, commanding voice was audible over phone's speakers. In a somber tone, both calm and somewhat deep, a man spoke.

# Chapter Five
## Requiem

## I

His head was heavy with thought and exhaustion. He stared down at the soft grasses beneath him, as nightmarish visions plagued his mind. The sun had not yet risen, but the birds had already begun to stir and warble their first songs of the infant day. He found that their cheerful nocturnes infused him with something like purity and gaiety, which helped distract him from the visions in his mind. Though night maintained sovereignty over the surrounding lands, the east was becoming an increasingly luminous grey-blue, preliminary to the birth of the morning sun. He walked stiffly, slowly, and gingerly, fearing the pain any sudden or supple movement would bring. Breathing alone caused him discomfort at times and his body ached throughout. His mangled left arm had been wrapped in the torn sleeves of his own shirt, and he held it across his waist, clasped by his other hand, which was swollen at the wrist. Blood began to seep through the makeshift dressing, and the lacerations coursing his forearm underneath burned wickedly. To either side of him, a guardsman kept his measured pace, escorting their sentry back to Berwick Upon the Tweed.

The sentry had not spoken a single word since they left the wood. He simply gazed into the earth as if languorously transfixed, instinctually making his way home like an old mule. The guardsmen both eyed him warily now and again, seemingly disturbed by the harrowing scene they witnessed only hours ago. Though they both harbored questions relating to the night's preternatural transpirations, recollections of the sentry's crazed ferocity dissuaded their queries.

He appeared to have distanced himself from the world around him during their journey home, cognizant only of his pain, and of thoughts spawned in the deepest recesses of his mind. A desolate, yet calming, silence hung about them, interrupted only by songbirds, the gentle whispers of the wind in the grass, and the soft clinks of the guardsmen's mail. One of the guardsmen repositioned the sentry's bow, which he had slung over his own shoulder and back. In fact, save his dagger, they carried all of the sentry's effects between the two of them in order to ease his burden and pain. It had taken some time to retrieve the weapons, for they had fallen into the shadowy underbrush below the loft, but the sentry had insisted that he would not leave without them. One of the guardsmen had even climbed the now tattered loft to fetch the sentry's quiver and fallen arrows. The other soldiers who had been part of the relief assemblage had already made their way back to the town, and had no doubt been obliged to calm a gaggle of townspeople, who in their panic, would have likely broken curfew.

The sentry raised his head for the first time in what seemed hours. Atop the grassy knoll spanned the town wall - a most inviting and welcome sight. His mind began to clear itself of his dark thoughts and the air was suddenly sweeter and the sky brighter. The three men approached the gate, around which the other guardsmen had reclaimed their stations. The scarred archer regarded the sentry with a look of concern and deference. He wasted no words, and turned to the two guardsmen inside the wall.

"Raise the gate, lads!"

As the gate lifted from the cobblestone beneath, the scarred archer turned his head back towards the sentry. He issued a slight nod and the sentry returned the gesture, concomitant with the faintest hint of a grateful smile. The noise of the raising gate ceased, and the three men entered the town. They passed the barren marketplace and a section of peasant homes; they were small, made with wattle and daub, and roofed with crude, wooden shingles. The sentry led the two guardsmen onwards to a single level stone home. It also bore a shingled roof, and had small windows with wooden shutters. The sentry stopped a short distance from the dwelling and turned to the guardsmen.

"My thanks, friends, for easing my pain all this way. You are both due ales when next we cross paths in the tavern." He extended his right arm. "I can carry my own weapons this meager distance. Return to your posts...I've been coddled too long already."

As the guardsmen returned his effects, one of them offered jovial counsel.

"Have that woman of yours give you some lookin after. I'll reckon she'll know how to cure what ails you, eh?"

The other guardsman smiled, as did the sentry, while he collected his weapons in his free arm. They exchanged parting gestures and the sentry turned towards his stone domicile. As he did, he heard one of the guardsmen speak up from behind him, and he turned slowly to peer at him over his shoulder.

"That wild man in the wood...his...his look was...strange to my eyes from where I stood. Perhaps it was the darkness. Of what people was he, then? Norseman? Or of some rogue hill folk? His...his flesh was—"

"I know not," the sentry offered both softly and abruptly. "In truth...I know not." He turned away from them, and with a guarded yet steady gait, made his way home.

Immediately after he opened the door and crossed the threshold, he dropped his weaponry to the floor in the nearest corner of the single, open room that was his home. The room was rather dark, even with the door having been left open. Built into the far wall was the hearth, and he traversed the room towards it. The knobby, wooden floor beneath him amplified the sound of his footfalls and creaked under his weight. Bare ground surrounded the hearth where floorboards had not been laid, lest sparks and burning ash ignite the dry timber.

A large woven basket lay on the ground near the hearth, brimming with an assortment of tinder. The hearth itself was but mere darkened embers, and the sentry stooped gingerly to salvage the fire. He tossed dried grasses over the embers and laid long pieces of the bark over it. He then leaned a series of firewood together over the kindling. He blew on the embers and pain ignited in his side as readily as the embers did in the hearth. He winced and stood.

The grasses burned quickly and small flames leaped from them to the strips of bark, lapping against and adhering to their sides. The room became luminous with a warm, ambulating glow, and the sentry turned from the hearth. He lowered himself onto his bed and the wooden frame groaned. The soft straw wrapped in linens gave invitingly underneath him, and placing an arm against the rough wall for support and grimacing with pain, he lay down on his back. The straw rustled as he searched for a position that did not cause him discomfort. He stared up at the wooden underside of the roof, watching the firelight flicker about. He felt a weight over his eyelids and his breathing began to slow. Shortly thereafter, he fell into a deep and much needed sleep.

* * * *

When he awoke, sunlight was leaking through the tiny cracks between the shutters and the wall. The hearth cradled a blackened, smoldering heap, upon which, small, fading flames flickered here and there. Though subdued by the stone walls, he could hear the clamor of a bright Berwick day from his bed. He was also met with immediate pains, a reminder that the night's events, which were so like the remnants of a horrid dream in his mind, had indeed occurred. Groaning, he righted himself to a seated position on the bed. His shoulder and back cracked as he moved and the wrist of his right hand ached unforgivingly.

His side was no better, but his bruises no longer throbbed; his cuts did not sting as they had, and his body felt renewed from his slumber. His hair hung in stale, salty locks, where sweat had dried and adhered to it.

Still wary of his movements, he walked towards the door and opened it. The afternoon radiance illuminated the room and caused his eyes to squint so severely they nearly shut. The now unrestricted noises of the town found his ears with greater amplification and the sentry stepped out into the sun towards them.

As per his tacit promise to meet with Bronwyn, he would make his way to Colin's smithy early on in the evening. For the moment however, other matters required his immediate attention, most pressing of which was his need for a bath. With that done, he sent word to his lord to insure one of the archers acted as sentry in his stead, as his injuries prevented him from performing his duties with even a modicum of competence.

He prayed his body would mend quickly, for he would not receive payment from his lord for laying about in bed. He completed a few other errands before the onset of evening, impatient with how great a hindrance his paining body was to his travel - his side in particular. After eating a small meal of bread and cheese, and allowing his body further respite, he made his way to the smithy.

He skirted the marketplace, for Colin's smithy was only a short walk from it. Once again, the throngs of the market waned in the wake of evening, and he paused for an instant, watching the spectacle of the marketplace with a newfound appreciation for humanity. How wondrous man was in contrast to the baser beasts, how like a god in nature.

He turned from the milling throng and continued on towards the smithy. The smithy was one of largest structures in its vicinity, due mostly to the large section on the ground floor that housed the smithy itself. During its hours of operation, two enormous wooden doors remained open, occasionally even in the dead of winter. The forge raised the temperature within to such a degree that a winter breeze was sometimes welcome. In mid summer, especially at noon, the smithy was excruciatingly hot, testing the limits of any blacksmith's tolerance. However, in seasons of growing warmth, as at present, evenings at the smithy were most comfortable.

The sentry passed the large wooden doors, which had been closed for the evening. The shutters on either side of the smithy were open and golden firelight spilled out from within. He heard Colin's voice and the reserved, deep chuckle of another. He approached the stone house to which the smithy was conjoined and knocked on the door. He heard the scuffle of some wooden furnishing and Colin's voice nearing the door. Colin opened the door and scratched at the disheveled shock of bright orange-red hair beyond his brow.

"Em...I'm hearin all sorts o'tales bout why the town guard sounded a call te arms last night. I've heard...Jesus, wha happened te yer arm? Wha the bloody hell happened oot ther, ye...would ye look at me manners then. Christ, come in, come in. Ye came at a perfect time, Ober happened te drop by only a while ago."

They moved through the stone house, which was dimly lit by the hearth, and exited it through the open, stone doorway into the smithy. Colin kept the smithy as tidy as could be expected and had evidently cleaned up for the day. To one side of the spacious smithy, a collection of metal tools were tucked away in an old shelf. Fetters, blades, chains, and other metal works hung from hook and nail about the place. The forging station lay off to the right and two cauldrons, one filled with water, sat on the packed-dirt floor. A table had been prepared for company just beyond the threshold of the stone doorway that led into the smithy. Ober sat upon a wooden chair, his elbows resting on the table. A few candles had been placed upon it, which when assisted by the dim glow of the cooling forge, lit the room pleasantly. A clay flagon and mugs were present on the table, one of which Ober held gently in one of his massive hands. He regarded the sentry with a look of slight consternation and the sentry addressed him reassuringly.

"It's all right, my wounds are nothing mortal. I probably look worse off than I am."

"Sit down here," Colin directed, gesturing towards the backed chair opposite Ober, which had evidently been his, prior to answering the door. The sentry nodded his head in thanks and wincing, eased himself down into the chair.

"Well, at least you come back to us alive," Ober remarked, observing the sentry with some concern. Colin pulled up a stool to the head of the table from elsewhere in the smithy. He sat, and resting his forearms upon the table, he eyed the sentry expectantly.

"So...em, any time ye'd like te let us hear the truth o'the matter."

The sentry looked at Colin, then to Ober. Both stared back at him with fixed eyes, and both seemed to have leaned closer in anticipation. He sighed, his side nagging him as he did. Colin pressed him.

"How many wer ther?"

The sentry stared at him for a moment, then answered him.

"There were two of them."

While Ober sat motionlessly before him, Colin leaned further forward, his interest more keen than before.

"Two men attacked ye? How'd they manage that then? Crept up on ye through the brush I guess, and found yer wee wooden box in'tha tree."

The sentry put his hand to his mouth and exhaled, briefly closing his eyes. Ober grunted impatiently.

"Colin! Can you not govern your trap for but a few moments?"

Colin faced Ober, his face soured as though he had been somehow victimized.

"Well, I can'ne know the full truth o'this tale if I do'ne know every little part." He returned his attention to the sentry. "I'm sorry fer the big lummox's interruption. Please...continue."

Unsure if Colin was jesting, the sentry simply stared at him for moment while Ober issued a derisive snort. Colin reciprocated the sentry's gaze with an expectant, solemn stare, and the sentry could do naught in the sudden silence but continue.

"At any rate…where do I even begin now?…No, they did not find me unawares, though one of them did attack me. I was…" Colin's green eyes widened.

"Wait a moment. Yer saying te me tha one man did all this te ye?" Colin eyed the sentry's battered body, then met his gaze once more. "Wha was he, some sort'o giant then? Some barbarian, or the like? I mean, I've seen…" he glanced at Ober who was staring at him quite discontentedly, "…we've seen the way ye can use a sword. Christ, I'd be leary o'tha sword alone. Ye do'ne mean te tell me tha some nomadic rogue or roving madman got the better of our war-hardened Spaniard do ye?"

The sentry stared at Colin incredulously, unable to fill the fleeting void of silence before Colin spoke anew.

"Tha…tha's it isn't it? Ye were taken off guard by some commoner, a hunch back even, and ye feel shamed by it. Listen, ye have nothing te be ashamed of. We've all seen ye fight before, and Lord knows every dog has his—"

Ober pounded the table with a large fist.

"That is not what happened, you idiot! Hunch back!? Are you entirely without sense! He has not answered you because your babbling flap has disallowed him any opportunity, and because he was in all likelihood, contemplating striking your fool skull with something of significant weight to silence you! Now, for the love of God would you—"

Interrupting Ober's tirade, Colin raised his hands apologetically.

"A'right! Okay! Jesus Christ!" He faced the sentry once more, "Just make sure ye do'ne leave anythin oot."

The sentry smiled despite himself. As he collected his thoughts, his demeanor became somber, and he began to unfold his harrowing tale. The two men listened, intent and spellbound. When finally he had finished, they merely stared at him, wearing expressions of worry and disbelief. Colin shook his head, as if his mind refused to give credence to the existence of such evils.

"Yer sure tha they weren't a pair o'derelict highlanders, like in the tales ye might have heard as a lad about Celts and Picts. I remember hearin tha they wore few clothes, wantin te look as wild and fearsome as they could. I know ye said tha they were pale as death itself, but perhaps...I mean, in the moonlight I am ne exactly lookin like a Moor me'self."

The sentry, who had been staring down at the wooden tabletop as he considered Colin's speculation, raised his head slowly, meeting Colin's baffled gaze.

"I wish that they had been men, but they could not have been. No race of men could yield those hellish beings. No grip of madness, nor any amount of drink, or affective herb could give men such power. These creatures were fast and nimble as stags. The one that assailed me in my loft was no larger in height or girth than you Colin, yet even clutching a tuft of its hair and straining with all my might, I could not even stop it from raising it cursed head. Underneath its white flesh, I felt muscle that moved about like shreds of living iron. And what of the mortal punishment they endured? What man could resist death in such a fashion as these did after suffering such fatal wounds? I tell you, these things were not born of this world...they...they were surely demons of the pit...I can find no other explanation."

Ober, who sat contemplative and stolid, broke the ensuing silence.

"What of the guardsmen? Do any of them return home with tales of similar woe? For from those to whom I speak, I have not heard tales of things so passing strange."

"When they arrived," the sentry explained, "the thing was already weakened and bloodied. It was dark, and the archers struck it with arrows from beyond the fringe of the wood. A few would have noticed it looked odd, as I did at first, but none saw it as I did. I...it stared into my very soul with its demon eyes. It was so close to me that I shared its breath. Locked in combat with it, I felt that I began to understand its very essence and nature...I have no other words to...it was as though I could not—"

The sound of footsteps from the wooden stairs, which led to the slate-shingled sleeping quarters above, halted the sentry's tale. From the smithy, he peered through the open doorway of the adjoined stone house to find the source of the footfalls, though he already knew to whom they belonged. Bronwyn appeared in the doorway, one hand gently brushing a wavy lock of auburn hair from her face. She wore a simple, short-sleeved dress made of cream-colored linens, which bore a neckline flattering to her body. She smiled at the grim-looking trio.

"Well, why are ye all so glum this even then? Did someone—" she took note of the sentry's mangled appearance and her jaw dropped, her face ripe with concern. Colin tossed his head back and looked up towards the heavens as if pleading assistance.

"Ack! Here we go! Bronwyn, he's fine, he just—"

But it seemed his attempt to make light of the sentry's injuries was an effort in vain.

"Oh, me God! Wha' happened te ye? Yer a bleedin mess. ye are. How long have ye had tha bandage on yer wounds? Tis likely time te redress it. I will ne let infection spread as a result o'negligence an the pride o'ye foolish men."

"Bronwyn, would ye go'way, er not be a bother for just a while longer. We were discussin…well…things, and besides, I've been holdin in a gem of a tale te tell these two fe..."

Ober and the sentry exchanged amused grins at the siblings' persistent, Scot-accented squabble, while Bronwyn huffed and interjected.

"Are ye sayin tha I can'ne be privy te this tale on account o'the fact tha I am a woman?"

Colin raised his hands effusively, his tone betraying a growing impatience.

"Wha'ever, just sit down and do'ne make a pest o'yerself fer the time being."

The sentry braced himself and was about to rise when Ober's long arm extended towards him, his giant hand holding him down from the shoulder. Ober stood, his great height looming over the table, and he then stepped away from his chair. With a gesture, he offered the chair to Bronwyn.

"Sit here, lass."

Bronwyn smiled at him affectionately, gave her brother a playful glare, and seated herself at the table. Ober sat himself upon a nearby anvil, clearing his throat as he eased himself down. Stroking his lengthy, grizzled beard, Ober looked to Colin.

"Well...let us hear this gem of a tale you purport to have."

In the moments that followed, the wry blacksmith's disposition transformed from a state of mild annoyance, to a bubbling humor. A smile crept across his face, and it seemed as if he were struggling to restrain his laughter. The sentry smiled to himself as he observed Colin's mischievous face. He reached out towards the flagon, and with some discomfort, lifted it and its contents, and poured himself a mug of water. Unable to withhold the occasional chuckle, Colin had begun his tale.

"Right...Lord, but this is a good one. Anyway, ye remember ole William Millar who has tha flock o'really woolly sheep?" he stifled a snicker. "Well...some do'ne know it, but he has two large pigs o'prized stock. One a boar, the other a sow. He breeds 'em and sells the piglets, sometimes keepin one or two te rear fer his family te eat at some festive occasion. So...ole Millar's got tha youngest daugh'er Rianin, whose about te wed some tailor's lad named Brian or Biron...Beorn?...I can'ne recall...let's call the lad Biron, it makes fer greater sport tha way. So Biron has been assistin ole Millar with chores around the place...ye know, te keep good relations and the like. Young Biron handles the chores and cares fer the bleetin beasties quite well, but Millar notices tha he behaves kinna strange around pigs, especially the sow. When the two o'them set out te the sty together, ole Millar always catches the lad eye'n the sow in a most earnest and...secret fashion."

Colin burst out laughing and then regained his composure. The others wore anticipatory grins as they began to understand the story's tilt.

"Biron had an especially keen eye fer the prize sow when her back was te him. Millar told me tha whenever Biron would pour the slop and the pigs would crowd 'im, he'd make space fer himself by gently pushing the sow, and only the sow, away with a hand te her backside, starin a'it from the corner o'his eyes."

"Oh God, Colin! Ye canna be serious," Bronwyn exclaimed laughingly. Colin shot glances at the three of them, his eyes wide, and he himself laughing.

"I swear...I swear ne a word o'what I tell ye is a lie or stretch o'the truth. Now one day, one o'the gates in the sty either broke er was ne properly closed, and the sow along with two of her piglets got loose before Millar could close the thing. Ole Millar told me tha he thinks Biron let 'em escape, but either way, Millar starts yellin 'Get the pigs! Get the pigs!' So Biron sprints off without a moment's hesitation...now which one de ye think he went after?"

Ober, Bronwyn and the sentry were now laughing quite heartily. The sentry's side issued sharp pains in response, but he could not help his laughter.

"Tha is correct friends...the lad tackles the fleein sow and wrestles the swine te the ground. Millar notices tha he's taken her down from behind, and now tha he's got her, he's still thrashin and wrigglin about, as though the ole sow is given 'im the fight o'his life and ne just lyin there like the fat sow she is. Ole Millar slips a noose around the sow's neck and tells the lad te go get the other two, but when Biron gets up to take after 'em...again I swear it's the truth...Millar sees the boy is as hard in the pants as a ram ready fer the rut."

"Jesus!" Ober uttered through his rumbling guffaw. Holding his belly and laughing, Colin paused briefly to catch his breath, his reddened face almost tearing.

"So then, the boy runs off te fetch the piglets with his prick swayin about as if he were a jouster ready fer the tilt!"

They were all laughing uncontrollably now, and it took a few moments for the jovial party to compose themselves. Tears now freely rolling down his red face, Colin continued.

"Tha's ne the worst of it, if ye can believe it. So needless te say, ole Millar start'ed keepin a watchful eye out on his sow whenever Biron was around. One night...this was only a few days ago, before he told me all this...Millar notices wha' looks like light coming from the sty. Naturally, he goes te investigate its source. Unsure of wha he would find...I believe he may have been worried tha bandits were after his stock o'pigs, as I recall... ne matter. Anyway, he opens the wooden door slowly, as ne te draw any attention te his presence, and enters the sty."

Ober was shaking his bald-crowned head and smiling, having forecast the goings on in the sty.

"Ole Millar did'ne find any bandits, though wha he did find was young Biron, pants about the ankles, rumpin the sow with every once of strength and every inch o'his manhood."

"How did the sow take to young Biron's engagement?" the sentry asked jokingly through his painful snickers.

"Tha is exactly wha I asked!" Colin laughed, "Apparently the lad was havin quite a good go, fer the sow was content te stay put and receive all he had te give."

"What did old Millar do?" Ober inquired, chortling through his beard.

"He chased the lad oot the sty with his pants still down, brandishin a pitchfork after him. I do'ne know if there'll be a weddin, but I do know tha I am grateful te that Biron lad fer makin this fine tale possible."

They chuckled in disbelief, some wiping tears from their eyes, others holding areas that pained from excessive laughter. Bronwyn rose and skirted round the table until she stood next to the sentry.

"A'right, time te take care o'those wounds o'yours."

The sentry smiled in consent and rose, evidently in some discomfort. He bid Ober and Colin a friendly farewell and allowed Bronwyn to lead him by the arm back through the open doorway, into the house. Colin looked after them as Ober reclaimed his seat at the table. With a somewhat disturbed look upon his face, Colin turned back to see Ober smiling knowingly at him, an almost prankish twinkle in his green eyes.

"I swear, ye old stinkwind, one word and I'll be pullin tha mangy beard from yer face...I'm serious."

Ober's smile grew under his great beard. Grunting his displeasure, Colin turned away from him, rolling his eyes and shaking his head.

# II

With his hand in hers, Bronwyn led the sentry to the flight of wooden stairs that led to the sleeping quarters. They moved slowly for the sentry's sake, the stairs creaking sharply beneath them as the pair ascended. The upper floor was dark, but Bronwyn needed no light to guide her within her own home. She led the sentry to her quarters, and they passed underneath the thick hide flap that hung from above the stone doorframe to the floor and covered the entire doorway. The lengthy flap served to allow her privacy, without the expense of a door. Inside her quarters, she released his hand to move around her bed and throw open the large, wooden shutters. Moonlight streamed into the room, coating the bed, walls, and floorboards like an ubiquitous, glowing, argent veil.

A gentle breeze stirred Bronwyn's dress and flowing hair. She stood by the window, the moonlight lambent over the fringes of her body and twining locks, casting a lean shadow over the foot of her bed. Gazing fondly at the sentry, she bent forward and patted the bed suggestively. The sentry approached the bed and wincing, lowered himself upon it. He made a move to reach for his boots, but the sharp pain from his side halted him. He attempted to remove his boots by pushing near the heel with the opposite foot, but Bronwyn had already come back around the bed to kneel at his side.

"Come now, I can see yer in pain. I'll remove yer boots fer ye."

Before he could object, she had taken the heel of one boot in her hand. As she slid off his boots, she regarded him worriedly.

"God...ye were ne pierced were ye?"

"No. It was only a hard blow. There is some form of damage, though nothing serious, I promise you."

"I suppose tha'is a blessin in itself. Te bad the same can'ne be said fer yer arm," she noted as she rose from the ground to stand over the sentry. "It looks te have takin a heavy bit o'slashin." She paused. "Well, are ye goin te tell me wha happened then?"

The sentry took her hand, issuing her a half smile.

"Ahh...not tonight Bronwyn. The tale is...unpleasant and somewhat lengthy, and I have already prattled on about it at great length tonight with Ober and your brother. Another night though."

She observed him for a moment, playfully exaggerating her disappointment.

"Fine, but I'll hold ye te those words."

She helped him reposition himself in such a way that his back was able to rest against the wall at the head of the bed. Kneeling at the side of the bed once more, she took his left arm gently, and carefully began to remove his old dressings. As she unveiled the five deep lacerations that had been raked along his arm, she winced empathetically.

"Hold yer arm there. I'm going te get ye water and a washcloth. Do'ne move."

With that, she rose and hurriedly left the room. The sentry observed his wounds, and noticed that none of the slashes had begun to scab in the least. In fact, other than the fact that they were not bleeding, they showed no real sign of healing at all. He was still gazing at his forearm when Bronwyn returned with a clay pot, which contained the water and a washcloth. She also carried a bundle of fabric under her arm. She knelt again and placed the pot on the floor beside her, laying the fabric on the bed. Reaching into the pot, she snatched up the dripping washcloth. She wrung out some of the water from it over the pot, and proceeded to rid the sentry's wounds of the gore and pieces of debris that had accumulated in and around them.

The sensation on his arm was irritating, but the sentry was more attentive to Bronwyn herself. He watched her as she worked. She was so gentle: so focused, so compassionate. Her green eyes lifted to meet his and she smiled humbly before returning her focus to his wounds. Having cleaned the wound, she dropped the bloodied washcloth back in the clay pot and then picked up the length of fabric from the bed. With this, she swathed his forearm, tying the cloth off securely.

"Thank you," he said softly while reaching across towards the bedside with his right hand to take her gently about the arm. He pulled her towards him more suggestively than forcefully, and from where she knelt at the bedside, she leaned forward and ran a hand through a few hanging wisps of his dark hair. She rose steadily, lifting her leg so that she sat astride him on the bed. She leaned forward slowly, hands gently clasping either side of his head under his locks. He wrapped his arm around her as she neared, and felt the heat of her body as her lips met his.

Her kiss was long and delicate and sweet. She leaned back and brushed her wild auburn mane from her face, then reached towards her sleeve, pulling gently and exposing one of her strong, smooth shoulders. The sentry caressed her bare shoulder and, ever so gracefully, she swayed free of her linen, the top of her dress sliding to her waist like a cowl. He caressed her smooth skin, his hands massaging her bare back and sliding forward from her shoulders and neck to rest at her soft, ample bosom. She leaned forward again, her kiss more passionate, more needful than the last. With their lips inches apart and her forehead resting upon his, the sentry whispered to her.

"Be gentle with me tonight fiery Scotswoman."

She smiled and they embraced in the moonlight. Heeding his words, she moved gently upon him, undulating to and fro under the eyes of the moon and shining stars.

\* \* \* \*

When he awoke, it was sunlight and not moonlight, which shone in splendor about the room. He realized it had not been the morning sun itself that had woken him, but the strident call to rise of some boisterous cock. It crowed a few times more before its cries ceased, leaving the common sounds of a bustling, waking Berwick in its stead. He wondered what the hour was, for Bronwyn had left her chambers. Guardedly, he rose from the bed, but was stricken by a wave of dizziness as he did. A greyish haze clouded his vision, and spots danced about therein. As in a dream, his awareness of his body dulled and became distant. He was vaguely aware that he was falling, yet still maintained the presence of mind to understand he would simply fall back onto the bed. He landed in a sitting position on the bed, but the impact was surprisingly abrupt and jarring, and he realized he had not been as cognizant of his body as he thought he had been. His teeth clicked, and as his daze passed, he was increasingly aware of the agonizing complaints from his side.

He sat for a while, holding his side and breathing. Cautiously, he rose once more, and feeling no ensuing faintness, made his way from Bronwyn's chambers to the main floor. As he set foot on the wooden floor, he spied Bronwyn near the hearth, adding logs to the dwindling flames. She wore her burgundy tavern dress, and much of her hair was tied back on the top of her head. She must have heard him descend, for she began to speak to him before she had turned to face him.

"Mornin, mi'lover. I did'ne want te wake ye, but I was going te anyway. I was ne going te leave fer the tavern without tasten yer lips one last time fer the day."

As she approached him, a wailing voice from the smithy made the sentry aware of a clamor of movement and metal from therein.

"Christ! I mean…I'm right here, ye know!" The sentry peered through the doorway into the smithy.

"Um…morning, Colin."

Colin met his gaze with a look that forced a smile on the sentry's face. Colin smirked back at him, shaking his head.

"Aye, aye…morning te ye, ye wretched Sodomite."

Having reached the sentry's side, Bronwyn then turned to face her brother through the doorway.

"Colin! Honestly, sometimes ye are so very crude."

She faced the sentry and kissed him upon the cheek with some vivacity. In the smithy, Colin had thrown up his arms in repulsion, a hammer in his right hand.

"I'm off te the tavern. I'll see ye soon, then?"

The sentry smiled and watched her walk to the door, a playful look in her green eyes as she left. He called out to Colin, the effort nagging his injured side.

"Take care, Colin. I'll be seeing you."

A harsh, yet jocular voice emanated from the smithy.

"Kiss mi arse, sister stealer!"

The sentry chuckled and left Colin to his work.

# III

The sentry spent much of the day in bed. Though he desired to be up and about, he did not want to aggravate his injuries, and thus forced himself to be as restful as possible. He feared losing favor with the town lord and consequently the source of his wages. That night, as he changed garbs for bed, he was afflicted by another dizzy spell. Anticipating the result, he lowered himself to a knee, lest he fall from his full standing height. A dark haze and speckled points of light obstructed his vision once more. The room seemed to spin and shift alignment, so that he was confused as to which direction was up or down. Collapsing on all fours, he attempted to steady the infirmity of his limbs and the entropy of his senses. He was unaware of his surroundings, of the wind outside, of the dancing light of the fire from the hearth. His breathing became erratic and beads of sweat formed at his brow. His extremities began to feel increasingly distant until he was unaware of them altogether. His mind clouded entirely, and he crumpled to the wooden floor, oblivious of anything.

His other senses returned to him before his vision. He became aware of the feel of rough wood on his bare chest and arms, and a stabbing pain at his side. He opened his eyes to see dust billowing before him from the floor under influence of his breaths. Moaning with pain, and still somewhat out of sorts, he picked himself up from the floor. Most perplexed, he sat upon his bed and rested his head in his hands. Some time passed before he eased himself into his bed, and more time still before sleep finally took him.

\* \* \* \*

Over the few days that followed, such sudden lapses in function become more frequent and more severe in effect. The spells were increasingly difficult to combat, and the time it took him to wake from them lengthened. He noticed that his appetite was not what it had been, and when he did eat, his stomach felt increasingly heavy and bloated. He found that drinking greater amounts of water during the day, and with meals, eased the plight of his gut, but never remedied it. He also observed that the wounds on his forearm were still raw, and that his side still pained him, as if his body refused to mend itself.

His condition deteriorated rapidly. His strength had begun to leave him and his body had lost some of its bulk. He had begun to disgorge the contents of his stomach after any substantial meal, and his guts now ailed him regularly. He felt faint equally as regularly and his fainting spells had worsened as well. He suffered a general feeling of malaise and fatigue, causing him to sleep more often and remain within the walls of his home. He feared he had contracted some strange sickness and wrote to Colin, promising a young boy from the town a few pence if he ran the message to the smithy for him. In the letter, he explained his symptoms and asked Colin to inform Ober and Bronwyn of his condition so that they would understand his recent absence from them.

That night, Colin paid the sentry a visit. The sentry had left the door unlocked and Colin opened it, finding the sentry lying in bed with a pelt overtop of him. The sentry sat up with some effort.

"Colin…please…no closer. I know not what this sickness is, nor if it can travel like the black plague itself. I…"

Colin gave him a friendly smile.

"Oh, come now, ye look none the worse fer wear. I've seen ye fight off brutes more threatnen te yer life than any sickness could be. As fer the plague, I know its signs well, and ye do'ne have anything the like, friend. Those ailed with plague grow putrid black sores over their bodies and cough blood from their lungs. Whatever ails ye, tis ne plague. God can'ne take ye yet, I will ne let Him."

Colin passed the bed and piled a few more logs on the hearth.

He grabbed an old wooden stool from the corner of the room and pulled it near the sentry's bedside. They talked for a time, light from the hearth playing gently over their hunkered forms and gilding the stone walls with fluttering gold. Colin regaled him with a few of his youthful misadventures and updated him on the latest news in town. That done, he paused for a moment before speaking afresh.

"I have ne spoken te Bronwyn or Ober yet, but ye have mi'word tha I will. I'll have Bronwyn bring ye some bread, cheese, and dry meat in the mornins, along with a pail o'water…ne a word from ye…I know full well ye can'ne have tha much coin left and yer ne well enough te be headed te the market an back. Ye need rest friend, and ye shall have it. Ye can repay me in ales when yer up and about and we're back in the tavern or mi'smithy, laughin our guts oot."

The sentry gave Colin a wavering smile. Colin rose from the stool and headed to the door.

"Are ye goin te lock it after me?" Colin asked.

"No. The way I've been sleeping lately, I might not wake from an early knock on the door. Besides, I am familiar with my neighbors, and of all the houses in the vicinity…"

"Why would a would-be thief choose the one harbor'n a fearsome war monger like yerself?" Colin interrupted exuberantly.

The sentry allowed himself a dry chuckle. Colin bid him goodnight and left, closing the door securely behind him. Colin left the sentry bearing an amicable smile, but upon closing the door, his face took on a solemn expression of concern. He bowed his head, ran a hand through his hair, and made his way home.

\* \* \* \*

The morning air was cooler than it had been the past few days, but was refreshing in its own way. The sun still shone through the sailing assemblage of white clouds in the sky, slowly heating the day as it beat upon the earth with warming rays. Bronwyn moved through the town hurriedly. In one sturdy hand, she held a small pail of water, in the crook of the other arm, she carried a tawny sack that contained a loaf of bread, a wedge of cheese, and a few strips of cured meat. Already suited in her tavern attire, she intended to head there straight away after her visit. She had begun to tear the previous night when Colin had told her of her lover's illness. Colin had seemed so grave, so unlike his unwaveringly jovial self, that his tone betrayed the severity of the ailment.

She made her way to the stone home that had become so familiar to her. She knocked on the thick wooden door, but no response met her ear. She gave the door a push and it opened with a creak. He lay asleep in the bed, as thinned and weakened as Colin had said. His pallor seemed overly pale and sweat glistened on his forehead, matting the hair rooted near his brow. She left the door ajar to allow some light in and placed the pail near the head of his bed. She lay the sack on the floor beside the bed and uncovered the foodstuffs. She then rose and opened the shutters to allow the light of day into the room. Eager sunbeams streaked through each open shutter, partially illuminating the sentry's sleeping form and overpowering the firelight's claim on the room.

Not wanting to create too great a draft, she moved to close the door. As she did, she heard a tortured moan issue from behind her. She turned to see the sentry grimacing in his sleep, his eyes clenched together so tightly, that his face had become a mass of wrinkling furrows. His head turned from the source of the light and he seemed to wake from his sleep. He twisted his entire body away from the sunlight and, uttering a louder groan, clutched at his eyes with both hands. He curled into himself as would a child, and lifted his thick pelt overtop of his head with a quivering hand. He clutched the pelt with excessive force, pinning it to the bed with his fist as though he were trying desperately to keep warm, or to shut out the day. His groans became the beginnings of words.

"Wh...wha...what is...my ey...eyes."

"Wha is it? Wha is wrong? Tell mi, please!...oh Lord," Bronwyn interrupted his feverish babble, recoiling her hand and placing it before her mouth in growing alarm. A dry, muffled voice answered her from under the pelt.

"The...the light...it hurts my eyes."

Breaking loose from her initial shock, Bronwyn promptly dropped and locked all the shutters, returning the room to its amber, firelit glow. She watched the sentry's hand relax, and then release the pelt. His breaths had calmed, as if he slumbered anew, his body exhibiting similar lethargy. He did not turn to face her, but muttered to her, his eyes partially open, as though he spoke to her in his sleep.

"Br...Bronwyn?"

She approached the bed and knelt beside it. She noticed his temples and forehead were damp with perspiration as Colin had described, and when she reached out with a hand to touch him, his skin was almost clammy to the touch.

"I'm here, lover. We need te change yer bandages again, and ye need te try te eat someth..."

"N...No. I can't eat just yet. My stomach...f...feels as though it has been tied in knots." He turned slowly so he could look at her. "And these wounds on my arm have not changed since...since you cleaned them last. I'll...attend to these things when I wake."

His lids began to slide heavily over his eyes and he lay flat out once more. Bronwyn saw that even the little scrapes about his face and shoulders, which had been healing, had ceased their mend. She stroked his dampened locks and shimmering, liquescent buds of tears formed slowly at the corners of her eyes, before rolling down her flushed cheeks.

"A'right, I'll see ye later then, mi'lover."

She rose from his bedside and headed towards the door. She turned back to look at him. He appeared to have given to sleep once more, and she slipped out the door, pulling it shut behind her. She sniffled a few times, wiped the tears from her eyes, and hurried on to the tavern.

* * * *

Spanning the period of a further three days, the sentry's

health worsened further still. He ceased to partake of any kind of nourishment but water, and his body had become increasingly frail and withered as a result. His waking hours were few, as he was most often discovered in states of deep unresponsive sleep. He moved very little and his body would tremor now and again. His eyes rarely opened, and when they did, he could see little through the dark haze to which his vision had been reduced. Ober saw him twice, and Colin twice after his first visit. Both were increasingly unable to communicate with him, as if his mind were losing touch with the world around him. Bronwyn saw him each morning and to her heart's utter dismay, was met with the same result.

Strangely enough, it seemed there was hope. On the morning of the sentry's eighth day of disease, Bronwyn had visited the sentry to re-dress the wounds on his forearm and attempt to pour some water into his mouth so that he might drink. She had been careful not to open the door too wide upon entering the stone dwelling and had immediately shut the door behind her as not to torture his sensitive eyes. Though he remained generally unresponsive, his eyelids would flutter rapidly, and his eyes would roll back into his head when the room became overly luminous. His breaths had been ever so slow and carried a slight rasp. His eyelids fluttered now and again, but he never opened his eyes.

Fighting her tears, she had pulled his limp arm towards her and began to unravel the bandages when, to her outright shock, she discovered that his wounds had healed completely. Where only the morning prior there had remained the five deep, raw gashes that had been scored into the length of his forearm, only the vaguest hints of scars remained, the flesh smoother and thicker in appearance than the surrounding skin. Even his small nicks and cuts had smoothed over with revitalized substance. Inwardly, she had rejoiced, knowing her beloved was healing and would soon stand to take her in his powerful arms once again.

Still crouching at his bedside, she looked from the fresh scars to his face and back again - the slightest hint of a smile on her face. She tried to rouse him gently from his staying slumber, but to no avail. Her attempts to persuade his limp mouth to drink were equally futile. Having rested his head back on the bed, she brushed the matted wisps of hair from his face and kissed him fondly upon the brow. Holding his hand, which had begun to quiver along with his other extremities, she stared at him for a long while before leaving him, as ever, with tears in her eyes.

* * * *

Bronwyn awoke with the first rays of morning warming her face through her open shutter. She opened her eyes, yawned, and sat up in her bed, brushing her hair from her face. She had told Colin about her lover's incredible healing when she returned from the tavern. Like herself, Colin was hopeful yet confused; the duality of the sentry's recovery being justifiably baffling. While his wounds had healed miraculously, his body seemed to be a fading husk, from which his soul was severing its ties.

Bronwyn left her bed and dressed herself in her tavern attire. Colin was still asleep, but she let him be, for by the color of the sky it was early to rise. She left the house and headed directly to her beloved. A whirlwind of thoughts rushed through her mind, a spectrum of emotions took hold of her senses. She reached the stone house without memory of how she arrived and with hope and dread warring within her, she opened the door.

He lay in his bed so peacefully, his arms at his sides, and his bare chest half covered with the great fur pelt. With the door closed behind her, the firelight danced and flickered, boasting its vitality over the sentry's supine form and along the grey, stone walls. Slowly, nervously, an ocean of sorrow welling within her, she approached the bed. She dropped to her knees and reached out to him with both hands. She gripped his closest hand with one and placed the other over his face, feeling for some sign of life. Feeling none, she dragged her hands over his body, trying desperately to rouse him while tender sounds of lament escaped her. She looked over his motionless length, fresh tears rolling down her cheeks. She clasped the hair at her temples and, shaking her head in utter horror, she collapsed upon him, crying into his pallid chest. She took one of his limp hands in hers, interlocked her fingers with his, and wept over his lifeless body.

# IV

The evening sun had not yet set, suffusing the world with a rich, bold luster. Bronwyn, Ober, Colin, and a handful of townspeople and guards, stood solemnly over the great mound of earth and the shadowy grave alongside it. A stone cross rested at its head, another in a row of gravestones of similar size. Wooden markers were not uncommon in the area allotted for the dead of the impoverished, which did not detract from the macabre beauty of the surrounding works of stone. Around them, the cemetery stretched for some distance, a forest of gravestones, monuments, and cramped plots of small, exquisite tombs and sepulchers, into which more wealthy households interred their dead. Berwick Castle loomed in the distance, and closer still was the town wall to the east. The sun played beautifully off the little chapel and its stained glass windows. Built next to the graveyard, it stood like a holy beacon of hope amidst death and suffering, like a diamond in the rough.

To one side of the grave, a priest was concluding prayers, a moving litany which he had sung in Latin. Inside the grave, the sentry lay shrouded in white linens, his noble face composed and peaceable within the cowl. A rosary made of black beads wreathed his neck and lay over his chest.

Having completed his service, the priest gave his blessings and with his attendants, left the gravesite. The wind issued the faintest of sounds in the ensuing silence. Ober moved towards the mound, his long hair and beard swaying in the wind. His face was burdened with grief, the furrows of his brow nearly reaching the bald crest of his head. Reaching the mound, he crouched and snatched up a shovel. Leaving his grieving sister's side, Colin walked towards the mound and picked up a shovel as well. In the deathly silence, under the eyes of his loved ones, they blanketed the sentry with soil from the mound, interring him into the cold, dark earth.

*Chapter Six*
*Haven*

*I*

The engine rumbled softly as they traveled, the noise of its moving parts subdued enough that he could hear the man's voice through the ambient hum. The man's words were both statement and question, his temper composed and humorless. The solemn voice was just audible over the cellphone, and from his position in the passenger seat, Sebastian Klyne was able to discern the man's every word.

"I assume that transportation, as per our arrangement, has been altered," the voice said dispassionately. The doctor had recognized the voice instantly, for upon hearing it, he had appeared to have become momentarily unnerved. Clasping the phone to his ear, his posture tense, the doctor was briefly at a loss for words, and he stared forward through the windshield vapidly as he regained his composure. He glanced at Sebastian and saw that the officer was reeling from the severity of his hemorrhaging.

"Ah...yes...ahm...well, about that. I was going to call you shortly, as disingenuous as that sounds, I was just about in the process. Em...a bit of a situation, well more accurately, a complication, has arisen." The man awaited further detail, as denoted by the expectant silence on the line, which the doctor quickly filled. "I have an officer next to me in the car. He has received critical injury and lost vast amounts of blood...I have no other course but to take him—"

A garbled noise interjected from over the phone, a sound which was conceivably a disapproving growl.

"Well… at least you're keeping your compassion and humanity about you," Dr. Canterberry retorted with churlish sarcasm, his initial diffidence seemingly shaken. "Look here, I recognize the danger in taking him back. I know policy, but it is imperative that I get him to the ward immediately. A minute's delay could be the difference between life and death, and this man risked his own to save mine. I could not in all conscience leave him where he was shot, and I cannot simply drop him off at the nearest hospital without drawing more unwanted attention, especially knowing that he can receive no more expert care for his particular circumstance than I can provide. Now, I am quite sure that my being some clandestine, evening chauffer was not in my initial job description that I can recall. I am also reasonably certain that I could guess the cause of that eruption of gunfire from a few blocks down, which consequently led to this unfortunate outcome. Given that, I believe it would be prudent to—"

The now grave voice quelled the doctor's loquacious protest. "Turn left into the alleyway ahead."

"Ahm…beg pardon? Are you close enough for a pickup or—"

"You are being followed. Turn into the alleyway."

Dr. Canterberry glanced into the rear view mirror to see an unmarked police car closing in from some distance behind, its dashboard lights flashing threateningly. His demeanor had become somewhat anxious, and he let out a frustrated sigh.

"Right then. What do I do after I turn in?"

"Pass through and get back en route to the expressway as fast as possible."

Dr. Canterberry looked into the rear view mirror once more to glance at his pursuer and then regarded the half conscious officer to his right.

"And yourself?"

The man's response was dry and cold. "We'll talk later."

Eyes widening, Dr. Canterberry paused for a moment, moved

the phone from his ear and stared at it.

"Oh, dear," he muttered to himself.

\* \* \* \*

To Officer Tilman, the situation in the Haitian's warehouse and its surrounding area had seemed to be under control. She and her partner had been lying in wait outside the area of operation on Forty-eighth Street, just north of the Long Island Expressway. She had moved in as ordered from her position when the call was given to all the involved police units, and had stationed her vehicle at Forty-eighth Street and Fifty-fourth Avenue to secure the northeast corner of the perimeter. Herself and her partner had been holding their zone without issue before they received the call to intercept a fleeing felon. An urgent relay originating from the marksman team covering the north aspect of the warehouse confirmed that there had been a breach in the perimeter by two felons on foot, and that one of their unmarked cruisers had taken heavy fire. The sniper had been able to neutralize one of the two escapees, and reported that one of the SWAT officers had given pursuit to the remaining felon on foot in an easterly direction.

Moving west on Fifty-fourth Avenue from Forty-eighth Street, Officer Tilman and her partner searched the darkened streets for movement. They eventually came upon the ruin of the unmarked cruiser that had taken fire. Officer Tilman noticed the alleyway next to the mangled cruiser and had pulled up to it so that her high beams shone into the alley, thus eliminating the possibility of being ambushed by the remaining felon should he have doubled back. Her partner had left their cruiser to check on the condition of the officers inside the other vehicle. He returned with a grim look on his face and they had to leave the bodies for the ambulance en route while they combed the area for the escaped felon.

Officer Tilman turned south on Forty-sixth Street, and proceeded east on Fifty-Fourth Road, knowing the felon could not be any further west than the wrecked cruiser. She drove at measured pace, at which she and her partner could properly search the passing properties, but not so slow as to afford the felon a significant window of escape. She turned north on Forty-eighth Street and proceeded to loop around back west on Fifty-fourth Avenue. Neither she nor her partner had spotted anything whatsoever. They were approaching the ruined cruiser once more, when her partner twisted in his seat and began to yell.

"Susie, behind us! Behind us! Pullin outta that lot down there! I almost missed the damn thing with its lights off."

Officer Tilman shot a glance to her rearview mirror and spotted an older-modeled, black car heading east behind them. She heard her partner's urgent voice once more.

"You think that's him? Why would he have a car stowed down there? Unless he…jacked it or something."

"I don't know, but we can't afford not to check it out." She initiated a violent u-turn. "One car, pulling out of a lot in this area, at this time, with the headlights off…too much of a coincidence for my liking."

She accelerated towards the black car and activated her dashboard lights.

\* \* \* \*

"Oh, bloody hell!"

Dr. Canterberry made a sharp turn into the alley, not necessarily because he was trying to evade the unmarked cruiser, but because he had only spotted the alley at the last moment. He turned frantically, cursing to himself, the tires screeching briefly as the car wheeled into the alley.

Though weakened and approaching a state of stupor, Sebastian winced with pain from the swerving vehicle, though he said nothing. The alley was really only an incidental pathway between two lengthy buildings, and could be coursed to reach Fifty-third Avenue. Dust swirled about in the alley, kicked up by the tires as their treads dug into the dirt- and gravel-covered ground. The underside of the car reverberated with the strikes of loose stones propelled upward by the wheels as they sought traction on the unpaved alley. To either side, the fringes of the alley where littered with yard rubbish and various oddments.

Dr. Canterberry was forced to turn on his headlights as he tore through the alley, barely slowing even as he slipped by a garbage dumpster which protruded into the already tight alley. As he neared the end of the alley, with Fifty-third Avenue well in view, vibrant light burst from the mouth of the alley behind him, tearing through and illuminating the dust clouds left in his wake. The cruiser's high beams nearly blinded him as he glanced into the rearview mirror, and the flashing dashboard lights flooded the lane with an eerie, dancing luminosity.

\* \* \* \*

The black car ahead showed no sign of stopping, in fact, it accelerated as Officer Tilman had drawn near. Her partner snatched up the radio and began communications while she gave hot pursuit. The black car made a sudden turn into a passageway between two lengthy, double-storied structures. Officer Tilman did not slow until she approached the buildings, and without a moment's hesitation, cleanly steered the cruiser into the passage. Shallow billows of dust wafted over the ground, making her navigation through the passage more difficult, but not impossible. Ahead of her, she saw the black car nearing the end of the passage, its headlights now engaged. Her partner halted his dispatch and eyed the approaching garbage dumpster with some perturbation. He impulsively placed a hand on the dashboard to brace for an impact.

"Susie, watch out of for that dumpster, huh?"

She stared forward unblinkingly; her face the picture of focus and composure.

"Don't worry, I see it."

She was in the process of easing the cruiser to one side to circumvent the dumpster, when something large, squarish, and metallic fell into her view from above. The weighty object landed on the base of the hood, striking the cruiser with such force that the back end bucked. The hood caved into the engine, and the windshield, though intact, fractured into an opaque, silvery canvas of multitudinous, spiraling cracks, completely obstructing the officers' view.

They were jarred by the impact, and the metallic object rolled back into the windshield so that the demolished glass bowed inwards towards the shaken officers. Officer Tilman lost control of the cruiser and it crashed into the dumpster, prompting an eruptive shower of splintered glass, sparks, and rubbish. The dumpster was pitched aside and the cruiser jounced off it. Though battered, Officer Tilman was somehow able to gather wits enough to force her foot to the brake as the vehicle screeched to a grinding halt against the wall opposite the dumpster.

The cruiser was suddenly silent and static. Officer Tilman fingered a small wound on the side of her head as she turned to inspect her partner's condition.

"You okay, Chun?"

Her partner was holding his hand to his mouth and grimacing. He removed his hand and stared at the smear of blood on his palm, then wiped at his nose.

"Umm...yeah."

Through the broken windows, she heard the black car peel out of the alley onto Fifty-third Avenue. A slight burning smell entered her nose, as faint amounts of smoke drifted from the cruiser. She opened the driver side door, which creaked and groaned. She exited the wreckage and noticed the squarish object lying on the ground a few meters beyond the crushed bumper. One headlight still shone brightly, as did most of the dashboard lights, so that she could still make out its form through the disturbed dust. She squinted.

"What the?"

Her partner was exiting through the driver side door as well, for the passenger side door was jammed against the wall. He stared at the object over the open door and she turned to him as he did.

"I...I think it's an old air conditioning unit."

He turned to face her and she looked up at the verges of both roofs, seeing nothing but the darkened sky beyond.

\* \* \* \*

Upon clearing the alley, he turned off the headlights. With only the scant streetlights to occasionally distinguish the car from the darkness, Dr. Canterberry was able to speed onto the Long Island Expressway with considerable stealth. He had expected to see another burst of light from behind him as the chasing cruiser exited the alley, but it never came. As he raced over the expressway, Dr. Canterberry would inspect the condition of his passenger here and again, unsuccessfully attempting occasional conversation to keep him conscious. The city lights spanned before them and the highway lights blurred overhead as they sped by.

Sebastian Klyne gritted against the pain the car's movements caused him. The pain from his thigh was agonizing, but the bullet wound at his neck was nothing short of torturous. He felt the pain intensifying as the area began to swell. His breaths were miniscule and weak, and his blurred vision had worsened. White sparks floated in his field of vision and the world seemed to consist solely of grey shades. He felt horribly cold, and a strange sense of detachment had crept between his mind and body. He was occasionally aware of the doctor's gentle voice, and he focused on it when he could. His senses began to dull, and with an imperceptible transition, his mind slipped from its faintest ties to the world around him.

Dr. Canterberry weaved through the thin traffic on the expressway. Certain that he had eluded any pursuers, he turned on his headlights once again, as not to arouse further suspicion as he traveled across the expressway. He passed Junction Boulevard and Grande Central Parkway, later still he crossed the Van Wych Expressway and finally exited onto Main Street, heading north off the ramp. As his concerns of somehow being apprehended diminished, a new distress took hold of him. The young officer beside him had lost consciousness some time ago. Though he was still breathing, his vital signs were weak from what the doctor could gather. The young man had lost a great deal of blood and Dr. Canterberry could only hope that he might administer his practiced procedures in time.

Successions of buildings varying in size whisked by, the city lights and limitless cityscape a testimony of high economy and high-density living. The doctor finally slowed the car from its ambitious pace and pulled up to a private, three-story building, encompassed by a wrought iron fence, the stakes of which rose to a height of over ten feet at the front gates. The building's windows were darkly tinted, and it had no kind of discernable front door to speak of. Dr. Canterberry stopped alongside an intercom that stood next to the lengthy driveway he had turned onto, which, beyond the gates, led to a sizable, metal door.

The intercom speaker was deeply set in its casing to protect it from the elements. Below the speaker was a large red activation button and next to the speaker, was a conventionally arranged entrance keypad, upon which the gate code could be inputted. Dr. Canterberry's driver side window slid down, making a slight mechanical whirring as it descended. The scoffs and scores on the glass, made by his attacker's bullets, chaffed against the rubber sheath while it dropped. Dr. Canterberry reached out to the device, which was mere feet from the window, and his hand seemed to disappear into the recess created by the casing design. To prying eyes, it was impossible to observe the entrance code, a second function of the deeply set intercom. Dr. Canterberry did not use the intercom, but entered the gate code directly, and then replaced his hand on the steering wheel. The giant, wrought-iron gates issued a grating creak as they slowly opened outwards.

The black car rolled past the gates and came to stop a few meters from the metal door, while the gate closed behind it. The door's contiguous, horizontal segments were illuminated by the car's headlights and its lower sections reflected the glare. A few feet from the doctor's open window was another intercom system. He inputted another code and raised the driver side window when he was finished. With a dull scraping sound and the rumbling of a motor from inside the structure, the big door lifted, its segments folding as the door slid up into a track that was fixed to the ceiling. Dr. Canterberry had picked up his cellphone, and was speaking to someone inside the building.

"Yes…I'll be in front of the elevator. Meet me there with a gurney on the double…right…good."

The rising door revealed a descending tunnel, lit by a series of lights on either side, which made the smooth concrete walls and floor appear to have an amber hue. The doctor drove down the shaft, which opened into a small underground parking garage. He passed a few rows of cars, with each car parked in numerically designated spots. He turned into another section of the garage and came to a halt next to an elevator. After removing the keys from the ignition, he exited the car and briskly moved around to the passenger side. He was outwardly distraught by the sight of the bloodied officer and with some haste, opened the passenger side door and crouched by the unresponsive officer to check his vitals.

As he did, he heard the descent of the elevator behind him and the resounding ping, which heralded its arrival. From his place at the officer's side, he turned round to see the elevator doors slide apart. A man in uniform stepped out from the elevator pushing a gurney. Another man followed him out. Both wore navy blue, military-looking uniforms with bulletproof vests and guns holstered at their hips. On the front and back of the uniforms, the word *security* was printed in white letters. Dr. Canterberry rose and made room for the gurney to be brought next to the officer.

"Right then, let's get him on there as gently and quickly as possible. I will be attending to him personally."

One security guard nodded in affirmation, wheeled the gurney next to the car, and positioned himself to remove the officer from it. The other took a position near the officer's legs while Dr. Canterberry waited near the head of the limp body, looking to secure the neck and injury site where possible.

# II

He felt a tingling sensation over a few areas of his body, mainly the furthest reaches of his extremities. To him, the world felt as though it was slowly upending, and his eyes felt heavy and strained. Struggling against the infirmity of his body, his breaths shallow and painful, Sebastian Klyne opened his eyes. The room he was in was not overly bright, but his tired eyes still took a few moments to adjust. A subtle, incremental beeping noise sounded from some source beside him and he endeavored to examine it. He found that he could not move his head, as his neck was held firm with bandages and some sort of padded neck brace.

Squinting, he looked down over the length of his body, which was covered by a blue sheet, and saw a mound protruding from his injured leg beneath the sheet. He surmised that the good doctor had redressed his gunshot wounds. He realized he was in a hospital bed and was suddenly curious as to where exactly he was, though his presently muddled senses did not allow him the best possible inductive abilities. He stirred, and was suddenly aware of a pinching sensation on the distal portion of his left forearm. He peered down as much as he could and raised his arm.

A cannula had been inserted into his forearm and the intravenous tube that inserted into it originated from somewhere near the bedside. A red, slightly viscous liquid, which undoubtedly blood, coursed through the tube, traversed the cannula and flowed into his forearm. He observed the process for a few moments, the details of the spectacle somewhat blurred in his bleary eyes. He noticed that a few electrodes had been stuck to his body and Sebastian became attentive to the nearby beeping once again, recognizing that he had been hooked up to an electrocardiogram. He was aware of an intense throbbing from his wounded thigh and a debilitating pain at his throat. To his right, by the bed, he noticed a plastic bottle of water with a squeeze top sitting on a table. He contemplated having some water to wet his mouth and throat, but he sensed it would pain him greatly to swallow.

He scanned the room slowly, observing an array of sophisticated equipment around the room, most of whose function he could only guess at. He was alone in the room, though a few bedded gurneys had been placed in a row on the far end of the room. Almost directly in front of him, beyond his feet on the adjacent wall, was a sturdy-looking door. He observed that the room had no windows and was investigating other details of the room when the sound of a sliding bolt drew his attention to the door, which opened, revealing the doctor. He was now wearing a common, white, doctor's robe and had a stethoscope hanging about his neck. He gave Sebastian a smile of relief, and leaving the door ajar, approached the bed.

"Welcome back, Sebastian. How are you feeling? Never mind, don't answer that. Let's not place further strain on that already suffering throat of yours, shall we. Now, I implore that you do not touch anything that is attached to you at the moment, as these devices are vital to your convalescence. You lost a significant amount of blood from your wounds, and you are now receiving a homologous transfusion of five hundred milliliters. The process takes four hours, nearly three of which you remained unconscious for. The electrodes...obviously...allow me to monitor your heart and such, and I'll skip the details, which I am sure you have been versed in somewhat, given your background."

Sebastian looked as though he were about to attempt some form of communication, but Dr. Canterberry raised his index finger and shook his head.

"For God's sake, man, you seem to be incapable of remaining silent. You know, I have been told I have a tendency to gabber on, but if I received a bullet wound to my neck I would have the good sense not to prattle unless I absolutely had to. Speaking of bullets, the one that struck your neck passed straight through the tissue, as did the one on your thigh. I stitched the wounds while you were unconscious. I did not want to use any anesthetics on your body when you were in such a fragile state anyway—"

A distant, muffled, barely audible reverberation sounded from the hallway beyond the door and cut the doctor's recount short. Sebastian was not sure what it had been, but it sounded like the tortured wail of a man. Yet there had been something irregular about the grim ululation, something definitively harsh and savage. Dr. Canterberry spun round to face the door, a fretful look upon his face. He turned back to Sebastian, a dutiful smile forced over his mouth.

"One...ahm...one of my other patients. He has a most horrid, bacterially-induced gastrointestinal disease brought on by a breech of his transverse colon. Ahm...a very painful ailment as you can...well...as you heard. I'd best be tending to him. I'll see you in while."

The doctor slipped out of the room and closed the door. Sebastian was about to sit up, but was halted by an immediate pain from his neck and a staggering wave of dizziness. Through it all, he was aware of the sound of a large bolt being slid into place outside the door. He felt himself becoming faint again and closed his eyes.

# Chapter Seven
## Advent

# I

A raven circled above, its deep, throaty caw echoing across the clouded night sky. Its descent was labored, its black feathers dampened and heavy from the incessant downpour. As it neared the ground, its wings beat rapidly to combat the speed of its stoop. A cloud of droplets and mist erupted from its fluttering pinions, and the raven seemed to halt in the air for a moment, before alighting venerably on the muddy ground. Beside it, another raven was already clawing and pecking at the loose soil, in hopes of catching the large worms surfacing from their feasts in the churned earth below.

* * * *

When first he stirred, he was not truly conscious of anything. Gradually, he became aware of a distant sound: constant and soothing, a multitudinous percussion from above. A floating memory, drifting through his addled mind, recognized it as the subdued sound of rain, falling and pelting from beyond the darkness. Darkness…he was aware of utter darkness, before him and all round him. The darkness had substance: cool and dense, pulpy and burdensome, bleeding water from throughout its bulk. He was aware of his heart - a slow infrequent beat, which reached his ears from within him. He was suddenly aware of an unsettling feeling germinating in his gut, a sense of being surrounded: of being crushed and trapped where he lay. Accompanying his climbing anxiety was an equally intensifying desire to move, to break free and escape. His heart pounded with a notably greater urgency and with it, a need to open his eyes and fill his lungs with breath. The encompassing darkness restricted this endeavor and as this frightening realization dawned upon him, he twisted his head about, carving a meager pocket in the choking pitch in an attempt to draw breath, the scent of earth ripe in his nostrils. Panic gripped him and where he lay on his back, he strained against his earthen prison. As he moved, he felt that some unseen sheath clung tightly about him. He attempted to free himself with such force that his muscles and joints began to shear under the exertion. With an audible tearing of fabric, his right arm ripped free of the cloth that bound him, but it was still pressed to his chest by the mass of soil atop him. Cramped as he was, he clawed desperately at the dirt, his hand tearing through it - slowly, agonizingly, making its way up to his face as he pawed lumps of dirt down into the space his arm left in its wake.

As his hand approached his face, he began to dig upwards feverishly, while pushing and boring forward with his feet, so as to worm himself higher up into the space he was eking out above. He began to writhe again, forcing soil downwards, frantically attempting to create some modicum of space around him. Whilst he twisted about, his left hand came free, which he clawed towards his face as he had done with the other. With both hands curled up near his chest, he tore at the soil above, moving the loosened earth down with his body and packing it underneath his feet. His legs began to slide free of the shroud in which he had been wrapped and he clawed into the earth with his toes, forcing himself along his augered path.

His heart pounded in his chest and pulsed in his head. He filled his lungs with what little air he could, the maddening sound of his relentless burrowing pervading his senses. Soil and muddied water fell over his face, and his desire, his need to free himself, tortured his mind pinned as he was; yet he tore into the black earth above with redoubled fervor, his tireless hands gouging through the soil with unrelenting strength. His breaths were strange, frantic, and sporadic, as hope and despair clashed like ocean currents within him.

Through it all, the drumming of falling rain sounded nearer and clearer, and he envisioned the open sky of the world above. Sensing his salvation was nigh, a feeling like hate burned inside him, directed outwardly at the earthen cocoon around him, as though the soil were a living, ensnaring, murderous thing. He bore through the earth with crazed purpose, clawing himself upwards, towards the sound of falling rain.

\* \* \* \*

Here and again, the ravens squawked at one another as they scrabbled the wet soil. One raven ruffled its feathers and shook itself, sending a spray of droplets in every which direction. The effort seemed fruitless, as rain continued to beat down upon it from the black firmament above. The raven was drawn to a plot of muddied earth, at which it cocked its head to and fro, its black eyes blinking expressionlessly as it listened intently to something unseen. It prodded the soil with its ebony beak, searching for its rising quarry. The raven raised its head abruptly, cocking its head to a side once more, as if the soil had yielded something unfamiliar. It studied the ground before it, while the rain pattered against the earth. The raven squawked and hopped back with a brief flutter of wings.

A short distance from where it had been, a small portion of the soil seemed to undulate, almost imperceptibly so. The raven stared on incredulously with its watchful eyes as the soil began to roll like a rippled sea, then to heave and fall, causing the surface of the damp earth to fold and crumble. A sudden collapse of the topsoil, created a minute, yet marked depression in the dirt. Rainwater streamed into it, welling momentarily before draining into some unseen hollow beneath it. The raven looked on, issuing another nervous squawk. From the depression, something broke the surface of the soil, clutching and raking into the earth before hauling itself back beneath the surface. The raven cawed in alarm and took to the sky. The other raven looked about anxiously, reciprocated the harsh cry, and then joined its companion in flight.

The small sinkhole in the soil deepened and the area of undulating earth began to expand. Once again, a hand sprung forth from the heart of the depression. Caked with mire, the trembling thing latched onto the soil and tore free a dampened lump as it slid back into the earth. The hand rose from the soil and vanished into it again and again, clawing and tearing at the rain-soaked ground. Abruptly, the hand ceased its emergences, and the soil at the base of the depression slowly forced upward, as the entire plot of bare earth began to swell into a writhing mound. As it lifted, large, muck-filled cracks twisted over the tumulus surface, which had begun to quake violently as though the earth were being assailed from within. The movement ceased, leaving an eerie stillness and silence, an effect somehow unadulterated despite the falling rain. Suddenly, the hand lurched up through the earth again, rising higher than before, exposing a bare wrist and forearm. The hand came to rest on the ground, clutching and bracing under some exertion.

Another hand pushed through the soil beside the other and the two mired limbs began to twist about frantically, forcing up the earth around them in bulging hunks, churning and breaking the topsoil. The elbow of one arm breached the soil and its grime-coated forearm and hand splayed over the ground, bracing once again for an imminent strain. The splayed hand clasped the soil and the forearm seized with effort as another mass of earth was forced up from the ground. The mass began to fissure and crumble, and muddied rain coursed through the rifts while bits of earth tumbled from the rising mound. Both hands and forearms were now braced against the earth, shaking with their staggering effort. The mound rose pronouncedly, large slabs of earth peeling away and falling from it, exposing patches of mud-stained, glistening flesh.

The top of the mound began to split apart, like a seed ruptured by the germinal sprout within. The crown of a head appeared from the opened soil, followed by naked shoulders and the beginnings of a straining, taught chest. Long, black locks hung in quivering, mud-slicked tendrils about the head, casting the downturned face in shadow. Pitiable, strange moans and throaty pants ranged just above the sound of the spattering deluge. Hands and arms braced against the soil once again, and slowly, the length of a mud-streaked body slid free from the dank earth.

The forlorn figure knelt sprawled and hunched on all fours, chest heaving with deep inspirations, head hanging limp between arms that seemed anchored to the ground. From where it had encircled the neck, a great rosary of black beads slid down towards the hanging head and slipped from it to the ground. The raindrops burst into tiny spatters over the broad, arched back, running in rivulets down the sinewy body and trickling from the hanging locks to meet the soil below. Slowly, the head began to rise and the back to straighten, so that the figure knelt upright, staring about with a vapid, overwhelmed expression. Using muddied arms to balance, the figure shifted unsteadily to a knee, planting the bare foot of one leg firmly on the ground. Reaching out to his cruciform gravestone and clasping it for support, the sentry rose from the earth.

\* \* \* \*

His gait was precarious. He could take but a few tottery steps at a time before coming to a standstill, whereupon his legs would waver under his weight. The rain beat down upon him as he struggled to keep his feet and it streamed down his body, seeping into the soaked, linen undergarment below his waist. The filthy, mud-ridden cloth clung to his wet flesh, dripping soil-stained water down his bare shanks. Disorientation plagued him and his mind reeled so that the world seemed to sway to and fro. He felt strangely distant from his own body, as if its function were unknown to him. He attempted another series of steps, but his legs buckled underneath him and he lost his footing. Like a newly birthed calf, he stumbled to the ground, landing awkwardly on knees and hands. Muddied water was thrown upwards as he came to ground and the fingers of his splayed hands slid forward, burying themselves in the mire.

He was slow to move before he eased himself onto his haunches. Kneeling under the night sky, he closed his eyes and breathed deeply, waiting for the world to steady. The chaos of his senses slowly quelled as he sat motionless under the downpour. His pounding heart found a measured rhythm and he opened his eyes for what seemed the first time, as he began to experience the world like never before.

He simply stared at the ground, observing the rain attentively as it struck the muddy soil. He was alarmed by the detail he perceived in each cascading drop and the crystalline clarity of each as they burst and splashed against the ground, shattering into tiny, shimmering globules, which seemed to dance through the air. Even in the darkness, under the meager glow of the moon through the blackened rainclouds, he could see the myriad of liquid eruptions below him with stunning precision. It was as though the faintest light could illumine the world for him and naught but the deepest pits of shadow could keep from him what their utter darkness concealed.

As clearly as he could see the raindrops fall, he heard them brush past the blades of grasses in their surrounding patches and drum against the bare earth like the hoof falls of a charging warhorse. He stared about expressionlessly, his head cocking from side to side as he took in the score of sounds around him. As his head moved, he caught wind of familiar scents. They invaded his nostrils with extraordinary potency: the smell of rain, of moisture in the air, of trees and plants carried on the wind, and of dampened soil wafting from below him. His senses disclosed the intricacies of the world around him with profound sensitivity and he was almost overwhelmed by it.

The night seemed infused and alive with nuances that had never before revealed themselves to him. From where he knelt, his eyes surveyed his surroundings through the shimmering veil of rain. He observed the surface details of the stone monuments about him, the course texture of each gravestone, statue, and tomb. His eyes flitted to other rows of gravestones in the distance. His straining eyes focused with an abrupt and shocking acuity. From a distance where, during the day, the very form of a stag would blur as he knocked his bow, he now made out the epitaphs engraved in the gravestones beyond.

Even as he began to grow attuned to the strange nature and capacity of his senses, he became painfully aware of a new sensation that had been intensifying within him and which now seemed to possess the entirety of his being. It was a feeling like yearning or hunger, but so compelling and so far removed from rational thought, that it could only be called instinct. He knew not how, nor why he was so stricken, or for what purpose, but he somehow understood that he must rise to his feet once more. His hands trembled ever so slightly and his heart began to speed its beat by minute degrees. His body felt sluggish and weakened, yet in a way, stronger than ever before. He took in a deep breath of the night air and stood. Staring longingly into the darkness, he began to move without any inkling as to why. This time, his gait did not falter in the slightest, and his pace quickened.

He took no notice of the field of grave markers as he whisked by them. He weaved amidst the headstones without a thought, driven onward by the consuming compulsion that gripped him body and mind. Rain whipped into his bare flesh as he slipped through the night, his eyes scouring the surrounding blackness. He was unaware of what they sought, though some part of him, deep within, understood the purpose of his search. He was unaffected by the cool of the night and the chill of the rain, though his senses imbibed the night air in a heightened state of arousal. As he moved, a faint scent entered his nostrils, and he came to a sudden halt, his bare feet digging into the soil.

His head moved slowly from side to side, his eyes half shut and languid as he sniffed the air to find the scent afresh. The wind carried it to him and cautiously, quietly, he moved into it. The scent seemed somehow tied to the instinct that urged him forward, somehow familiar, but maddening to savor. As he pressed on, the wind brought the tantalizing scent to him with greater regularity. He paused next to a large stone monument, a great Celtic cross, and he rested a hand on it as he tasted the air. As he did, his ears detected the faintest of sounds from somewhere nearby, obscured by the pelting rain.

He peered around the stone carving, his eyes fossicking the cemetery for his quarry. At first, he saw nothing, save the scattered tributes to the resting dead. His eyes suddenly fixed themselves on something half hidden by a large, intricate gravestone. It was huddled on the ground a short distance away from the stone slab, unmoving and dismal in the rain. Even in the darkness, he perceived the slightest hints of color on the drab, tawny shawl and brown robe, which clung waterlogged and wrinkled to a kneeling, despondent form.

Instinctively, he stalked forward in a low crouch, moving through the gravestones and circling further behind the kneeling figure. His movement was purposeful and deathly silent, his eyes unwaveringly fixed on his quarry. Suddenly, the figure stirred, its robes shifting about the rotund corpulence beneath, suggesting a movement of the arms.

He froze in his tracks, his stone stillness making him nearly indiscernible in the shadows. His burning compulsion drove him forward once more and his circling berth became a direct approach, his stance more stooped and coiled than before. From where he closed towards the genuflecting form, he caught the barest glimpse of a face under the shawl, a woman's face. She knelt with her hands seemingly clasped before her, staring crestfallen and distrait at the tombstone before her. A part of him wanted to pity her, but the thought was consumed by the unrelenting urge that drew him to her.

His face appeared distraught, even confused, as he moved within paces of her. His eyes were boring and unblinking, his mind a whirlwind of strange thoughts and promptings. He wanted her in some way, needed her, though he felt ⌐ stirring within him. He had drawn so near to her ⸌ go no further, his eyes louring over her from where her back. Slowly, he lowered his head to hers, his face a mere hand's breadth from the base of her skull. His eyes looked over her shawl-covered head and neck, and down her stout body. Then his eyes darted back up to her nape, with a cold, malevolent stare. He heard her sniffle over the clamor of the downpour, and she wiped both rain and tears from her face with a shivering hand. Unsuspecting of the looming presence at her back, she returned her hand to her bosom to clasp the other.

He was half crazed by the mortal compulsion that gripped him. The understanding that she would somehow quench his burning need catapulted his compulsion to a state of inner frenzy. A humor that was nothing short of aggression seized him and the urge to clutch her violently inundated his very thoughts. His body tensed and his breaths became somewhat shallow. It may have been that some faint exhalation reached the kneeling woman's ears, for she suddenly turned round, her eyes locking with his.

Her face was flushed, which betrayed her prior weeping, and tears ringed her reddened eyes, merging with the rainwater that trickled down her cheeks. Her eyes widened with what seemed like terror as she came face to face with him. Her mouth opened and hung agape, her bottom lip quivering with fright. As she turned, he saw that she held a silver necklace in her clasped hands, and from it dangled a large, silver cross. He stared at it and looked back to her face, which had paled considerably. She recoiled from him and her stiffened body toppled backward, so that she fell against the gravestone, her back pressed against the epitaph.

Her hands trembling, she raised and outstretched them, holding up the silver cross to his face. Staring dumbfounded into his eyes, she stammered and babbled, iterating the names of the Savior and the Lord in vain, blinking rapidly as the rain met her bare face. He spied her throat under the soaked shawl. The muscles were taut with her fright, the flesh pulsing from the blood rushing underneath. The sight drove him wild and he moved in towards her, brushing past the silver crucifix towards her throat. His body seemed to tingle in anticipation. He clasped the crown of her skull in one hand and clutched her shoulder with the other. She emitted a shrill cry and whimpered shakily in his grasp. Her hands still held the gleaming cross, though her arms had fallen limp in her lap. No thoughts ran through his mind, his body acted on instinct alone. The terrifying instinct screamed for appeasement within him and he dipped his head towards the woman's heaving throat.

He stopped himself abruptly, some remnant of his buried humanity irking the back of his mind, allowing him a moment's thought. His eyes moved to the woman's petrified face. Under his palm, she was staring blankly into the night sky, her eyes half closed and shimmering with fresh tears. Her breaths were erratic gasps and her knuckles had gone white around the silver cross. Though he still felt the potent inclination of his base instinct, the savage delirium that had governed him began to dissipate, allowing his mind to be reclaimed by the reason of his thoughts.

He looked to the woman's face once more, his own aspect seemingly tortured and confused. He saw before him the picture of abject fear and suffering, the plight of an innocent. A distant memory flashed to the surface of his thoughts, and he saw his mother screaming under the fury of swirling flames. A feeling of rising shame and guilt flooded his emotions and he opened his hands gently, releasing the woman from his grasp. He recoiled from her and took a few tentative steps back. She simply stared at him from where she had come to rest against the gravestone, trembling uncontrollably, still clasping the silver cross tightly between her shaking hands.

His actions were unconscionable to his restored reason, and the woman's sniveling form, shivering in the rain, compounded his regret. He slunk away from the woman, gazing at her in utter disbelief, a sorrowful look on his face. He turned suddenly from the woman's chilling stare and darted away into the blackness from whence he had come.

The stricken woman lay in the muck where she had fallen, propped by the gravestone at her back. She stared off into the vacant dark, where the harrowing apparition had once been. She became aware of a sharp pain from her fingers, and realized she was gripping her husband's silver cross astringently, the crucifix still upright, its gleaming surface beaded with drops and running rivulets of rain. She looked from the dark to the cross and to the dark again. Her breaths like gasps, she began to weep, holding the cross to her chest and gazing bleary eyed into the darkened heavens above.

# *II*

His mind was a chamber of chaos, a hectic swarm of memories and thoughts, which flitted in and out of his conscious mind. They preoccupied his attention to the world around him, so that he ran blindly through the night, racing amidst the grave markers. He thought of Bronwyn and the softness of her voice from his bedside. He envisioned his life in Spain and his hunts with Ober. Images of death and brutality ran through his mind as well, and he could not help but see the haunting face of the kneeling woman, feeling once again the terrible desire that had driven him to her. He grimaced at the thought, his eyes half shutting as he tried to shake the image from his mind. As he tore through the darkness, his head turned towards the night sky pleadingly, hoping to the heavens that his madness were some feverish dream.

His lungs heaved as he ran, though he felt not the slightest breathlessness. His sinew, however, seemed leaden: his limbs increasingly cumbersome, his body crying out for something to sustain it. The yearning plagued him and his eyes became little more than slits as his face tensed under the rain, his lips curling back in revulsion of his thoughts. Hopelessness played across his face and rage boiled within him. So consumed was he in his self-loathing and wrath as he streaked over the muddied graveyard, that he did not see a small tombstone in his path.

His shanks jounced against the stone tablet, hurtling him headlong to the ground. His body thudded into the earth, sliding sideways through the mud and grass until his back struck the headstone of another grave with jolting force. Though he felt no real pain, he lay still on his side for a moment, his face grimacing desolately. His head hung low to the muddied earth. He rolled slowly onto his belly and dragged his knees up underneath him.

His black locks were splayed over the mud, and resting on his elbows, he clutched a tuft of hair on each temple with a shaking hand. His body was quivering with rage, and as it possessed him throughout, a strange, low guttural noise rumbled in his throat.

Save his quaking body, he sat motionlessly on the soil, a grim, hunched spectacle in the pouring rain. He did not shake with cold, but from the growing infirmity of his body. Unmoving and silent as he was on the outside, his mind and body were entropic - a turbulent storm of affliction. The relentless craving of his body pervaded him, and he felt as though he would die as sickly waves of enfeeblement assailed his body. From where he sat, he became aware of a subtle sound that his anguish had obstructed from his ears. It was a reoccurring, grating sound, not harsh or resounding.

Slowly, he raised his head and lifted his arms from the ground, peering in the direction of the sound to locate its source. His eyes pierced the darkness, and near the fringe of the graveyard, he spotted a figure in tattered cloths - a man, toiling over an ornate tomb. Once again, instinct began to overwhelm his reason and his face hardened, dour and emotionless. He stared at the figure intently and rose to his feet.

Moving without thought, he closed on the man deftly, barely making a sound as he stole through the darkness. Using a shovel, the man was digging into the ground frantically; this being the source of the noises. Now and again the man would look about anxiously, before returning to his task. He was a filthy, toothless wretch and undoubtedly a grave robber. As he excavated the gravesite for the trinkets he hoped to pilfer from the noble's tomb, the presence of the form stalking at his back remained unknown to him.

His weathered face squinted as rain ran down his visage. The man looked about furtively, wary of being caught in the act by the grave keeper or some passing mourner. As the man's eyes searched the graveyard, the crouching form, that was not a tensome of paces from him, went stalk still. The man turned back to his digging and no sooner than he did, a piece of the night that had appeared to be a shadow cast bit of stone and earth, moved towards him from amidst the tombstones.

He felt nothing for the wretch, for it was not pity, but purpose that commanded his reason. His mind was a single, driving thought, spurred by instinct alone. He crept forward a little ways then stopped, his muscles coiling underneath him. His eyes were wide, staring coldly with morbid anticipation. In a sudden and frightfully fast movement, he lunged forward and pounced upon the unsuspecting graverobber. His body struck his quarry with a shuddering impact and he clung to the body of the other with a fearsome tenacity. He clutched the wretch by the head and shoulder, and as he did, his own head plunged down reflexively to the side of the wretch's neck.

The power of his leap took the wretch from his feet and their bodies twisted about as they toppled through the air. As they spun, he became aware that his mouth had clamped to the wretch's throat and he felt a strange contraction and distention on either side of his upper jaw. Instinctively, he bit down. A gristly sound issued from the wretch's throat. He heard breath being forced from the throat and felt the give of flesh around the side teeth of his upper jaw.

Their falling bodies met the mud, yet he remained unshakably latched to his quarry, even as they rolled and slid across the wet ground. He came to rest atop the back of the wretch, still biting into the soft of the throat, pinning his quarry's belly in the mire. The wretch squirmed underneath him and he hauled the writhing body backward, so that his quarry was hoisted from the ground, awkwardly arched, belly up and barely mobile. Quite suddenly, the writhing and squirming diminished to mere spasms and then to a deathly stillness. Weak breaths and subdued heartbeats kept life within the wretch, yet the quarry lay limp and unmoving in his embrace. He loosened the hold of his jaws around his quarry's throat and a surge of warmth flooded into his mouth. He stared forward blankly and unblinking, as though he were in a trance. Without a thought, he took in the elixir his body had cried for.

The two figures were as statues in the dark, the only movement between them the undulation of the sentry's throat as he drew life into his body. Some time passed as he knelt in the mud, holding his quarry's limp body to him. He felt his stomach swell and become heavy with fodder. His heartbeats slowed and became incredibly strong, and he felt a tingling spreading throughout his body, coursing through his vessels. His muscles felt infused with renewed strength and vitality, becoming more turgid and full, and his insides felt warm and nourished.

His gaunt appearance began to fade over time, a nearly imperceptible transition. The rain began to ebb, then ceased to fall, and his position remained fixed all the while. Any infirmity had left him entirely, and when his body seemed to have reaped all it could, his mind was suddenly returned to him, and he shifted for the first time in what had seemed ages. He withdrew his mouth from the man's throat and released the man's twisted head and shoulder. The exsanguinated body dropped lifelessly before him, the skin pale and drained, and a horrid-looking wound upon the neck. The flesh was discolored and twisted, and two, raw holes were starkly visible against the annular imprint about the wound.

He stared at the man's body as though he knew not what to make of it, as though what had come to pass was some surreal untruth. A sense of revulsion worked its way into him again, accompanied by a trace of regret. He wondered why he had done this horrible thing and he wondered what had become of him. He ruminated over why he had awakened in the bowels of the earth, and why such a twist of fate should have befallen him.

In the peaceful lucidity that followed the departure of the rain, he looked at his hands, as if they could give him some answer as to who he was. Genuflecting in the mire, he raised them upturned almost piously to his face. What he saw in the half-light of the moon chilled his very soul. His hands were pale as the moon itself and his nails were thickened and blackened, so that his hands appeared as horrible clutching talons to his eyes. Looking over his body, he found that it too was sheathed in a taut, whitish flesh.

The association in his mind was immediate, and visions of the ghastly creatures that he had encountered flooded his mind with nightmarish effect. He began to gasp despairingly, and he collapsed to his hands and knees. Beside him, a large puddle of rainwater shimmered as his hands struck the mud, catching his eye. He stared at it for a moment; then, apprehensively, he crawled towards it, unsure of what he would see. Upon the stilled, gleaming surface of the water, he saw the darkness of the sky and the lonely patch of moonlight that shone through the dark clouds. The image was clear, but vaguely distorted by the tiny, glistening pool.

As he leaned forward, the cusp of his head appeared, his black hair hanging limp and wet from it. His heart skipped as he saw a pale brow appear, and then the entirety of a ghostly face. The face upon the water was saddened and anguished; still, the aspect was frightful, a haunting sight. Piercing, yellow eyes stared back at him from the pool, hard and fiery in nature. Still staring inanimately into its meager depth, he drew a hand to his face, running his fingertips along a cheek, the ghostly image reenacting his movements in the water below. Short breaths that were both moan and sob escaped him and a look of utter despair twisted over the face in the pool. Choked with grief, he averted his eyes from the pool, and closed them as if in disbelief of what he had seen. Slowly, he opened his lupine eyes once more, and gazed back into the pool.

As he lowered his face closer to the pool, he recalled the lurid image of the demon's snarling aspect, which was branded in his mind. In his mind, he saw the rage of the thing, its strength, and he remembered the daunting maw that had sought his bare flesh. Staring tormentedly at the image before him, he began to open his mouth slowly. In the little pool, the quivering image lowered its jaw, displaying a yawing mouth. The lips curled back, and to his horror, revealed two fearsome fangs. His mouth still wide, he stared at the strange teeth, sobbing breaths escaping his open maw.

His face tensed with horror, and as it did, he felt the same contraction and distention as he had some moments earlier. He saw something move in the mouth of the floating face in the pool and observed an odd ripple from some musculature in the gums above the gleaming fangs. Even as the contraction occurred, the two fangs extended alarmingly, revealing a greater length, which had been housed in the flesh above. Startled, he uttered a breathy cry and recoiled from his reflection, witnessing the two teeth slide back into their sheaths as he did.

Looming over the pool, high on his knees, he stared down at his reflection, dejected and overcome with loathing. He slashed out at the dark glassy surface: something like a growl involuntarily sounding from him as he did. Water and mud splashed up, and out, over the surrounding soil, and he fell back on his haunches, his head tilted towards the sky: his eyes closed. With a sound that was both man and beast, he roared at the heavens above.

\* \* \* \*

He wept soundlessly as he wandered aimlessly about the graveyard, not knowing where to go, or what to do. He happened upon a great stone monument - a towering, stone angel holding a spear, and he saw that he was near the little chapel. He regarded the chapel with a golden-eyed stare from where he stood, and as he did, a deep, resonating sound shattered the silence of the night. The sound was booming to his ears, and he recognized the distant ring of a bell from its tower: a sound of majesty, of the church, a call to the people and to God. As the bell rang, he looked back to the looming angel. He stretched his hand towards it hesitantly, as if ashamed to touch its holy surface. As his palm came to rest upon it, he closed his eyes, and a soothing calm passed over him.

He stepped forward and rested his head against the stone, his pale arms and hands embracing the stone as though it were a living thing. Tears welled in his eyes, which somehow made him feel of man again, and he delicately touched a rolling tear with his hand and regarded it. He stepped back from the stone and looked up at the angel once more. He dropped to his knees and as the bell echoed throughout the night sky, he put his hands together and prayed.

Like an obeisant, ivory statue, he knelt unmoving through the night, rapt in prayer. Even as the east was suffused with the beauteous colors that heralded the sunrise, he remained in numinous commune with the heavens. The sun began to lift radiantly from beyond the eastern horizon and he opened his eyes, rejoicing at the thought of being bathed in the splendor of the sun after the night's tribulations. He was suddenly uncomfortable with the infant light, which had begun to bleed its essence into the fading dark. His eyes squinted such that they were nearly shut and he was soon placing a hand at his brow to shade his eyes from the sun.

He leaped to his feet with the dismaying conviction that he must seek shelter from the sun. He was instantly compelled to dig into the safety of the earth, an inclination elicited by another self-preserving instinct from within; but having been buried beneath the soil such a short time ago, he darted deeper into the graveyard to seek some alternate refuge. The passing dawn was so brilliant to his eyes that the world around him seemed to have washed over with a painful, white haze. Panic welled within him, fueling the pressing, almost irrational impulse to retreat from the light of day. Frantically, he searched his surroundings, observing what obscured little he could through his paining, squinting eyes. He seemed to be amidst lavish stone gravesites, no doubt an area for the affluent.

He moved amongst the great stone works, increasingly guided more by the touch of his outstretched hands than his tormented eyes. As he staggered about, his waist struck something hard and unyielding, and he lurched forward, his arms and chest sprawling out atop a large, flat, slab of stone. He knew it to be the cover of a tomb, a fashioned length of rock that rested over the portion of the small burial chamber that did not lie beneath earth. At that moment, he wished to be nowhere else than underneath the cool stone, hidden within the tomb from the growing cruelty of the sun. Still hunched over the tomb, he spread his arms wide so that they spanned its width, his hands grasping the edges of the stone slab with some urgency. Experience forewarned him that any attempt to shift such a mass of stone would be fruitless, and would leave him naught but stabbing aches and pains for his effort.

Yet, he felt as though his perception of the slab's weight and the strain it would bring him, had changed somehow. Some inexplicable reassurance reached his mind through his dubious, scattered thoughts, undermining the rationale of his experience. His hands held the edges of the stone with a vice-like grip and he braced his bare feet against the ground, his stance wide and crouched. Out of sheer desperation, he strained against the stone slab, and to his surprise, a low grating noise sounded briefly from beneath it as the slab moved ever so slightly from its resting position. With renewed aspiration, he closed his eyes and heaved the stone with all his strength. From underneath his ashen skin, hard, sinuous muscles raised as they seized with effort, giving his body the appearance of carved marble. His musculature tremored as he strained to slide the stone slab from where it lay over the mouth of the tomb.

The low grating sound became increasingly audible as the stone shifted from its place over the tomb. Dust and powdered stone spilled to the ground as one side of the slab was forced across the mouth of the tomb with incredible force. Stale air wafted from below the slab and it began to slide more readily. A large opening yawed before him, exposing a shallow, columnar, burial chamber below. He lowered his head into the opening to shield his eyes from the sun, and still grimacing, forced his eyes open to peer down into the burial chamber. Below, its edges almost contiguous with the narrow chamber, lay a great wooden coffin. The site of the dark chamber relieved him, and in some strange way appealed to him and invited him against his better judgment.

Nevertheless, he pitched himself forward over the lip of the burial chamber. With a quick, spontaneous movement, he twisted cat-like as he fell, righting himself in the air so that he landed atop the coffin with a thud, crouched on all fours. He rose immediately, standing to his full height upon the coffin. Reaching up, he placed his palms on the underside of the stone slab and began to move the thing once more. Dust fell about him as he slid the slab back into place, the harsh grating sound ringing throughout the narrow chamber. The chamber darkened even further and was finally plunged into blackness. He let his arms drop to his sides and expired a breath he had unintentionally pent in his lungs.

The utter darkness and silence elicited a certain tranquility and he remained standing for some time basking in it. He sank to his haunches and a most sedate sensation slowly permeated his body throughout. Shortly after, he lay down upon the coffin to pass the hours, knowing full well he must wait out the sun. Lying on his back, he stared upwards into the pitch dark. He felt an urge to sleep, to pass the day dreaming, and so avoid the troubling thoughts which were already creeping into his mind. As though his body were responding to his desire for slumber, a definite torpidity spread through him.

He felt as though he were sinking away from the world, disconnected from the sensations of his own body. His eyes closed and he became so distant, it was as though he were nothing but a disembodied mind, floating in the darkness. His heart slowed its beat such that it seemed an age passed between each pulse. His breaths became so infrequent, and his chest rose so imperceptibly, that he seemed lifeless. There, upon the coffin, he fell into a death-like sleep, unmoving and serene in the darkness.

# Chapter Eight
## Disclosure

## I

A familiar beeping registered in his ears, and he opened his eyes. At first, he was confused as to where he was, for his surroundings seemed unfamiliar; but as his waking mind began to shed its drowsiness, he remembered the room. He strained against his braced, aching neck to look over at the beeping electrocardiogram. From the corner of his eye, he glanced at the hanging blood bag at his bedside. The plastic had creased and wrinkled after releasing the majority of its content. Sebastian gazed up at the ceiling, looking at nothing in particular. Rather, his attention was focused on his physical condition and he was quite certain he did not feel so weakened and frail as he had before. His brain still somewhat sluggish, he glanced back at the blood-bag lethargically and stared at it, purposelessly estimating how much longer it would be until the entire transfusion was complete. Tiring of the endeavor, he relaxed himself and let his eyes wander about the room once more.

Upon a spontaneous provocation, he became curious as to whether the good doctor had removed or changed his clothes and lifted the blue sheet with his right hand. He was still in his SWAT uniform, though his vest had been removed and the pant leg of his wounded thigh had been snipped above the site of the injury. The sleeve of his left arm had also been cut off, evidently for his transfusion, and his feet were bare. He began to think about the rest of his SWAT team, which triggered the night's events to unfold in his mind. Certain memories seemed especially vivid: waiting in the van, entering the warehouse, crashing through the window and falling with the shards in an escape born of desperation, Dr. Canterberry, the Haitians, and strangest of all, the man in the long, black coat who had leapt across the rooftops overtop of him.

He was still deep in thought when he heard a metallic thump, which he immediately recognized as the bolt on the door being shifted. He abandoned his thoughts and stared at the door. Dr. Canterberry opened the door and stepped into the room, closing the door behind him.

"Hello again, chap. Feeling any better? Just give a slight nod of your head."

Sebastian gave a measured nod.

"Ah, good!"

Dr. Canterberry walked over to the electrocardiogram, bent forward, and observed it studiously. Murmuring approvingly, he straightened and put a hand to the dangling blood-bag, scrutinizing it as he had the electrocardiogram. Regarding the doctor, Sebastian spoke in a voice that was no more than a whisper.

"H...How is your other patient?" Dr. Canterberry turned towards him, his face the picture of concern and disapproval. "Its...okay," Sebastian informed him with a half smile, his right hand raised to halt the doctor's reprimand. "It doesn't hurt too much when I whisper."

Dr. Canterberry sighed audibly with exaggerated exasperation and became his amicable self once more.

"Quite well, all things considered, though bouts of pain can reoccur quite at random with such an ailment. Well now, I am going to check a few things, only to be safe mind you. I am quite certain you have nothing to be concerned about at this stage."

Dr. Canterberry walked around to the other side of the bed and picked up a stool that had been resting behind the bedside table. He placed it next to the bed and sat down, then removed a few instruments from a small shelf affixed to the wall. He began to examine Sebastian, beginning with his eyes and pupil response. He assessed the young officer's blood pressure, and then, using the stethoscope, assessed his breathing, once again murmuring approvingly as he completed his analyses.

"Thanks for doing all this for me," Sebastian offered. "I would h...have bled out on the street if you hadn't..."

Dr. Canterberry removed the stethoscope from his ears and scoffed in jest.

"Oh come now, it was the very least I could do. I am absolutely sure you would have done the same for me were the situation reversed, and if you recall, it was you who came to my aid first. That was the night's true act of heroism and selflessness. Heavens sake, what I did was just plain decent if you ask me."

With a hospitable smile, he replaced the instrument to his ears, and had just recommenced his examinations, when the wounded officer tilted his head towards him.

"Dr. Canterberry," Sebastian whispered. "Why is my door b... being bolted shut?"

The doctor seemed to hesitate for a moment, his face momentarily robbed of its cheer. He was quick to compose himself however, and showed no signs of discomfort in answering the question.

"We...ahm...we cater to a variety of patients here, prospectively at any rate. Some of these patients may suffer from aliments that could eventually affect their minds, leading to dementia and general mental instability, potentially driving them to any number of behaviors dangerous to themselves and other patients. So...ahm...ergo the bolted doors."

"So...what kind of hospital is this exactly?"

In answering Sebastian's second question, Dr. Canterberry did not hesitate, nor did he so much as blink before responding.

"This place is not a hospital at all, it is a research facility. Though this institution does admit certain patients, it is infrequent and only in exceptional cases, usually involving anomalous or particularly unmanageable immunological, virological, or hematological pathologies, so that we can collect data for their respective treatments."

Feeling his response had been satisfactory, the doctor offered Sebastian a contented smile, only to observe an unsatisfied and expectant look on the face of the young officer.

"Yes...well...you see this is not an institute of conventional practice, but the research hub for a private enterprise, which, in general, creates and sells treatments, and, God willing, cures for the aforementioned pathologies."

Dr. Canterberry observed Sebastian, who seemed satisfied with the information given. However, the officer did not stay silent for long,, his weak, hoarse voice, barely reaching the doctor's ears.

"Sounds pretty interesting. What made you choose this side of medicine? You know...the private research thing. The money or..."

Sebastian trailed off as he saw the old doctor's cheerful blue eyes betray a certain sorrow and lower to stare pensively at the floor. The wrinkles on his face seemed more apparent somehow and his lips were faintly pursed. His eyes flicked back up and he gave his patient a tired smile.

"Partly, I suppose," Dr. Canterberry conceded. He cleared his throat.

"I am afraid that the more...ahm...significant factors that led me to this specific occupation would make for quite miserable conversation."

"I don't mind if you don't, honestly...but I don't want to pry. I mean if it like...bothers you to talk about whatever...then don't worry about—"

"It was years ago lad," the doctor interjected with a cordial smile. "A lifetime ago, maybe two. My emotional wounds were healed before gravity claimed the queen mother's breasts, it is your wounds I am concerned with at the moment, and I suppose it would be prudent to get to know each other a little better, all things considered." The doctor straightened on the stool and drew in a deep breath. "I used to have wife, a daughter, even a cat, which I must say I detested vehemently. I was an immunologist, but I had a strong background in hematology. I was considered one of the foremost minds in my field and began climbing the ladder, so to speak, quite early on. I was in my early thirties then, not bad for a young upstart I must say." Dr. Canterberry chuckled to himself, shaking his head as he reminisced.

"I had secured a position as a research head, in my field of course, at a university of some prestige here in the States. I left England with my family and began working for the university straight away. It was time-consuming business that, but I enjoyed it, and my wife supported me in all that I did. She was a nurse, a wonderful woman, filled with a zest for life, just like our daughter...Maggie." The doctor's eyes were fond and far off as he spoke his daughter's name. "Soon after I acquired my position, my daughter fell ill. She developed an autoimmune disease... systemic lupus. Not necessarily a common affliction, but it is known to manifest in young children.

"My Maggie was about six when she became ill. The irony of it...my daughter having an autoimmune disease, and there I was, a head immunologist, helpless to cure her. I treated her to the best of my ability. I used corticosteroids and all other such conventional treatments. I went so far as to develop new treatments, toiling obsessively to ease my daughter's suffering. I spent long hours at the university, working through the night, using...well...abusing really...the resources at my disposal. I neglected my duties...my wife...my health. I cut corners, breached ethical, even empirical procedures, and kept my findings to myself.

"Still, it is quite amazing what one can accomplish with the will and the means. In the end, I was in fact able to create a highly effective treatment for Maggie's disorder, the details of which I will spare you...ahm...no offense, but even medical minds in my field would be hard pressed to follow."

"None taken." Said Sebastian with a weak smile. The doctor returned his smile, nodded and continued.

"Now, the problem with autoimmune diseases is that they

leave the body vulnerable to other diseases. As much as I did for Maggie, I could not entirely cure her, and she developed cancer as a result of the susceptibility to which her disease left her. Well…once more I became a recluse at the university, seeking desperately to discover new treatments besides the ones she was receiving at the time. Unfortunately, my new research lasted a couple of weeks at most. I had, as I said, been remiss in my duties, and was relieved of my position at the university, along with access to the laboratories.

"My daughter passed away in the following year and soon after, my wife, whom I had pushed away by that time, left me. In the end, to look at each other was to see what we had lost. We were a constant reminder to each other of our greatest sorrow. It seemed as though it all came down upon me at once, the loss of my job, wife, and daughter. I turned to the bottle, as one does when one is English and in the depths of despair, and began to squander all that I had, not caring in the slightest.

"I published a few of the findings from my work, but they had been arrived at with such unregulated methodology that they were discarded and deemed improper science. My good name somewhat sullied, I could not find a position: a plight exacerbated by my newfound alcoholism and blatant disregard for life. I am sad to say that I developed an increasing distaste for the doldrums of my existence, miserable enough to believe that life was not worth the effort of living."

Moved and rapt by the doctor's story, Sebastian regarded him piteously with his brow furrowed, his gaze fixed upon the doctor's friendly, blue eyes.

"It was then that my current employer sought me out and found me. Apparently, some of my publications reached this institution. My unconventional methodology was overlooked in light of my results and I was offered a position in spite of what I had become. My employer offered me a second chance at life and I accepted, and as cliché as it is to say it, I haven't looked back since."

"…Ah…wow." Sebastian managed. Dr. Canterberry clapped

his hands together and leaned closer to Sebastian from where he sat on the stool.

"And what about yourself then? Here I am spouting the chronicle of my life and I don't know a thing about the man who risked his life to save this old bloke's."

"Well...I dunno...I guess–"

"On second thought, lad, I believe I have let you exercise your voice enough for one day. I don't mean to be rude mind you; I am sincerely interested in what you have to say. Given your line of work, who bloody hell wouldn't be? You know, as a boy I often played with the idea of a life of the rough and tumble, running about with guns and the like. I used to be something of an athlete myself, you know."

Remembering the bulletproof glass on the doctor's car, and recalling what he could of the covert nature of their withdrawal from that same site, Sebastian wondered if the pleasant, old gentleman before him was not involved in a little bit of the rough and tumble.

"But, as you now know, it was to be a scholar's life for me. I would have been hard pressed to avoid that path having a father as rigid, strict, and adoptive of the old British schooling as mine was. But I suppose life can...life has a way of throwing a wrench in even the most seemingly preordained paths. How often have y–"

Once again, a distant, obscure cry found its way to the two men's ears from somewhere beyond the door. Sebastian listened to the sound intently, confirming to himself that the wails were indeed as unusual and harsh as he thought he had heard them the first time. Dr. Canterberry's head immediately turned towards the door, a look of complete surprise, and what may have even been panic, on his face. Sebastian observed the doctor quizzically.

"Your patient, right? Doesn't sound like he's doing so well."

The doctor rose from the stool, still staring at the door intently.

"Ahm...no...it doesn't." He broke from his stupor and was already making his way to the door when he turned to face Sebastian. "I need to check on him immediately...let's call it a night shall we? It's late anyway, and you need your rest. I'll see you later."

* * * *

The doctor exited the room, having seemingly attempted to disguise his haste and evident anxiety. The doctor had been so preoccupied as he departed, that he did not turn off the lights in the room for the night, nor did Sebastian hear the thump of the bolt being slid into place. Whatever it was that was so pressing, whatever it was that had put the doctor in such a state, had to be more than a patient with stomach pains. A number of questions and postulations raced through Sebastian's mind. If what the doctor had said about the place was true, then why would a patient with an intestinal affliction have been admitted in the first place?

He reasoned that the affliction might be some side effect of a more significant disease, but he thought it unlikely. Either way, why had the doctor been so stricken by the strange lamentations? Had he not said himself that the patient's pains would return at random? It seemed as though the patient had been present in the ward for some time and the doctor had presumably been treating the patient himself. How then could the harsh cries come as a surprise to the doctor if he had been attending to the patient regularly?

Once again, Sebastian thought back to the unsavory circumstance in which he had first met the doctor, and couldn't help but think there was more to the old man than met the eye. The reality of the situation was that he had lost consciousness in the car and regained it in a strange place, the general location of which he could not even guess at.

Mere seconds had passed since the doctor had left the room and Sebastian stared at the door, contemplating. The distant cry reached him once more and in that instant he made his decision. With his left hand, he pulled off the tape that had been securing the cannula to his right forearm and pulled the feed from his arm. He tied the tube off quickly to obstruct the drip. With both hands, he frantically tore off the electrodes that had been stuck to his body, then flung off the bed sheet. Slowly and gingerly, he slid from the bed foot first, supporting his neck with an arm as not to place any strain on it. His injured leg outstretched, he shifted his weight onto his good leg and rose on it, using the bedside table for support. He dropped the hand at his neck to his side as soon as his body was erect. Once on his feet, he allowed his injured leg to hang as straight and lax as possible, and headed towards the door with an awkward, yet measured limp. Sebastian opened the door as noiselessly as possible.

He stared down the length of a short, dimly lit hallway. To one side, steel double doors stood between himself and another hallway. He was unsure if they were locked, but assumed they were, for a keypad, lit red by a small light above the keys, rested on the wall next to them. The wretched cries sounded now and again from the other end of the hallway, still muffled, but notably clearer. Seeing that the hallway was empty, Sebastian limped in the direction of the erratic moans, bracing himself against a wall with his hand. He passed four rooms, two to either side of the hallway. The doors of each were all windowless and equipped with sliding bolts, as was the door to the room in which he had been. He approached the large, single, steel door, at the end of the hallway.

The sounds seemed to be emanating from somewhere beyond the door and as he neared it, he could hear shuffling and the clamor of metals. Another keypad was fixed to the wall next to this door as well. A tiny green light glowed above the keys and he wondered if this door had not been left open inadvertently as well. His heart had begun to beat quite rapidly as he sensed that things were definitely not what they had seemed, nor were they what he had been made to believe. He felt his pulse throbbing agonizingly in his neck and his injured leg pained with each movement. Still, he limped up to the door and turned the handle; it gave as he suspected. He pulled the door open slowly and as noiselessly as he had the door to the room he had left.

He reasoned that the room beyond the door was nearly

soundproof, for when he had opened the door but a crack, the horrible cries blared from within the room with startling stridency. As he eased the door open, it revealed a room lit even dimmer than the hallway. The room was full of various machines, most of them more complex-looking than those in his room. The majority of the apparatuses were lined against the far wall, a few displaying monitors and active graphs. The doctor stood in the middle of the room, his back to the door, and Sebastian slipped into the room unnoticed. The doctor was standing over a kind of bed, which was securely bolted to the ground. A rounded, somewhat cylindrical cage was mounted overtop of the entire bed, enveloping it. The cage encased the bed sarcophagus-like, no more than a couple of feet above it, even at its highest point along the midline of the cage. It was fastened to the metal underside of the bed, apparently locked on one side of its length and hinged on the other, so that it could open like the lid of a chest if unlocked. Though the doctor stood somewhat between himself and the cage, Sebastian could still make out the atrocity beyond the doctor's white robe.

Inside the cage, strapped to the bed, was a sickly-looking man. What first struck him, was how deathly pale the man's skin was, a near chalky white. The flesh clung tight to an evidently emaciated body, the atrophied musculature of which, projected from the pale skin with unnatural distinction. Yet, the starved muscles still seemed to exert significant force as they strained against their bonds, rippling as the man's body writhed against its restraints. The man was naked save for a plastic codpiece, which covered his privacies, and from which ran two long tubes, one thick and one thin. Each tube attached to two, separate, metal receptacles near the foot of the bed. The tubes traveled through an opening built into the cage at the man's feet, presumably so that it could open without the tubes impeding it. Similarly, a G-tube protruded from the man's stomach, exiting the cage through this same distal opening in the cage. The G-tube was hitched to a device that stood near the foot of the bed against the wall, as were a multitude of electrodes, the wires of which left the cage through the selfsame opening.

The man clutched the mat at his back with hands that ended in hard, blackish nails, and his chest heaved with dry, guttural rasps. Sebastian could not see the man's head, as his view was partially blocked by the doctor. The doctor had been preparing a large hypodermic needle and finally stepped aside to administer its contents into the man's neck. As the doctor moved, Sebastian was taken aback by the greater horror before him. The man's head was tilted back awkwardly, so that Sebastian could see a portion of his face above the inky black tangle of course hair.

The brow was thick, boney, and heavily muscled, more so than that of the heavyset Staffordshire bull terrier a friend of his had once owned. The man was convulsing, his eyes almost entirely rolled back into his head, but from what little of the eyes Sebastian could see, they were nothing short of terrifying. The doctor positioned the needle through the grates such that the tip was pointed at the side of the man's throat. As the needle was driven into the sinewy neck, the lurid eyes stared forward momentarily, and it seemed as though they had gazed piercingly and pleadingly into his own. Sebastian was frozen where he stood, his heart beating in his throat and ears as he peered into the wild, yellow eyes that appeared to hold him in their unnerving stare.

Sebastian felt pressure mounting at his temples and assumed it was a result of the close fit of his padded neck brace. At that moment however, his focus was not on his state, but on the ghastly spectacle before him. He no longer interpreted the sound he was hearing as a wailing, for they were as frenetic yowls and snarls, barely recognizable as the laments of a man. Like a beast, the man had odd, pointed ears and in his gaping, frothing mouth were two savage-looking teeth, which like fangs, projected somewhat noticeably from amidst the row of teeth on the man's upper jaw.

Sebastian gasped and stared wide eyed, his features contorted with bewilderment and horror. Reflexively, he took a step back from the empty, harrowing glare of the thing before him, forgetting the gunshot wound on his thigh. The pain was immediate and he stumbled back against the wall nearest the door. Dr. Canterberry's head whipped about to face him and he straightened, a look of utter shock on his face.

"Sebastian!"

Sebastian limped forward from the wall, staring blankly at the gaunt, pale, figure, his breaths labored and somewhat impeded by the injury to his neck. He stopped as he neared the table and he shot a glance at the doctor, his face searching, demanding an explanation.

Dr. Canterberry simply stared back at him, his mind still floundering from the shock of young officer's presence in the room. The doctor looked down at the caged patient, who had become more sedate, and then glanced back at Sebastian, whereupon he sighed defeatedly.

From behind them, a hard, reserved, questioning voice shattered the sudden quiet that had fallen upon the room.

"Nigel."

\* \* \* \*

Sebastian spun round to see a man clothed entirely in black standing still as stone just inside the room. He was relatively tall, with longish, black hair, and evidently formidable; but what was most notable to Sebastian, was his strange skin, which was as deathly pale as the patient on the bed. Sebastian looked to the man's eyes, and though they were perhaps a hue darker than the patient's, they bore the same burning, lupine, amber quality as they stared coldly and unwaveringly at the speechless doctor. There were differences between the two men, however, differences Sebastian observed immediately. Where the patient bore certain deviations of the human form, some more apparent than others, the man in black did not. Moreover, he had handsome features, a quality marred only by his odd eyes and complexion. Yet there was no doubt in Sebastian's mind that the man in black and the patient shared some sort of relation or commonality, as they shared so many characteristics that were, in his experience, entirely foreign.

A momentary silence followed the single, spoken word of the

man in black, and a palpable tension hung in room. Sebastian looked from the statuesque man to Dr. Canterberry, and watched the doctor close his eyes briefly, exhale despondently, and look up at the man in black with an insincere half-smile. In a subdued, but clear voice, the doctor returned the man's terse address.

"Hello, Gabriel."

Sebastian reverted his gaze to the man in black, who had not yet moved, nor so much as blinked. Sebastian noted the long black coat, looked back up at the fearsome face, and wondered if this were not the very man who had leaped overtop of him earlier that night. His heart pounded harder than ever and he felt a painful and debilitating pressure building in his throat and around the base of his skull. He realized that he was quite light-headed and he experienced a sense of mounting disorientation. As his heart raced, the pressure seemed to build and he felt increasingly woozy. He staggered to one side and placed a hand on a nearby machine to steady himself.

"Um...D...Dr. Canterberry..." Was all he managed before he toppled from the machine, slid off a nearby wall, and collapsed to the ground.

Dr. Canterberry regarded the fallen officer with look of surprise, and then glanced at the man in black, who had still not moved, nor taken his eyes off the doctor. He simply glared at the unnerved doctor with his piercing eyes, expressing his displeasure with a near imperceptible raise of a single brow.

# Chapter Nine
## Neophyte

# I

Thoughts crept into the desolation of his mind and with them the beginnings of awareness. Nonsensical and erratic though these thoughts were, he was aware of them, and aware that it was he who thought them. The substance of his thoughts was increasingly coherent as his mind grew more wakeful and he became conscious of his body as it stirred to life. His breaths grew deeper and his heart began to pound in his chest. Within the still, dark, quiet of the tomb, it seemed as though the deep beatings of his heart were resounding faintly throughout the chamber. Slowly, he opened his eyes, which saw nothing but the utter darkness around him. His body tingled throughout, as his veins surged with substance, forced outward by his quickened pulse. For a few moments, he lay atop the coffin, gazing up into the dark.

He raised his head as his body shed its lassitude, then sat up from where he had lain. He wondered if he had passed the day in slumber, for he had not woken from his sleep, nor lain awake long enough to have gauged the passage of time. He rose to his feet and reached up with both hands in preparation to move the tomb seal once again. He placed his palms flat against the underside of the stone slab above and began to lift. As he lifted the heavy slab, he shifted it to one side and, as before, it grated loudly against the top of the chamber as it moved. A thin beam of richly-colored light entered the tomb, illuminating the cloudy debris that fell from the stone lip of the chamber as the slab was slid out of place from overtop of it. He looked up through the growing opening above, and seeing that the day had passed, continued to slide the stone. More light shone into the tomb and the chamber was soon lit by the subdued radiance of twilight.

When he had shifted the stone slab enough to sufficiently uncover the tomb, he let his hands fall to his sides and lowered himself into a crouch on the coffin. He felt the muscles of his legs coil and tense, and he peered up at the opening above him. He leapt towards it abruptly, seeking to haul himself up and over the edge once he gripped it with his hands. Quite to his surprise, however, he propelled himself from the coffin with such force, that he barely touched the raised lip of the tomb with even one hand, as his body lanced out from the chamber and over the edge of the tomb. As he arced out of the tomb, his eyes widened in alarm and his limbs flailed wildly for a moment in an attempt to stabilize his body, following its unexpectedly rapid ascension. With incredible agility, he twisted his body from its unbalanced, headlong trajectory, and landed in a deep crouch on the ground beside the tomb, with a look of surprise still evident on his face. He straightened, and with some disbelief, turned round to peer back down into the tomb, as if to assure himself of the depth from which he had just leapt.

Composing himself, he took his eyes from the tomb and looked about to see if there was anyone nearby, but the graveyard was barren and quiet, save for a gentle, whistling wind and the songs of birds and crickets. He turned his attention back to the tomb. He stooped down, grasped the great stone slab on either side of the displaced end and prepared his muscles for the effort of lifting and sliding the heavy stone back into place. He took a deep breath and adjusted his grip on the thick sides of the slab. His grip tightened and his muscles extruded from under his pale skin as he strained against the stone.

Unlike the previous night, he hoisted the stone with relative ease, and found himself holding one end of the long slab at chest level, nearly an arm's length above the mouth of the tomb. He looked at the slab and then cocked his head to peer underneath it, so that he could confirm to himself how high it had been hefted. His face took on a somewhat incredulous expression and he stared at his arms, first at one, then the other. With them, he held up the massive stone with barely a shudder and he saw that the musculature over each was remarkably delineated and protuberant.

A feat though it was, he felt as though he possessed some unexplored range of strength he had yet to discover, and succumbing to his curiosity, he heaved the slab up higher. His bare back was an ashen canyon of muscular excrescences as he lifted the crushing weight of the stone slab above his head, the other end of which grated forcefully on the far end of the tomb. His body tremored under the strain, but he held the stone up like a pillar, his vigor unwavering. Astonished by the strength he possessed, he gazed up at the great stone questioningly. His curiosity satisfied, he lowered the slab back over the tomb.

He was suddenly lost in thought as he stood still before the tomb, looking down at it inattentively. Slowly, he raised his hands and stared at them, his mind still aflood with his musings. Once more, he noted the milky flesh and darkened talons, and some part of him asserted that what he saw before him could not be. It all seemed so very surreal. It was as though he had woken into the life of another, for the prospect that he could have been met with such a fate seemed impossible; yet his eyes contradicted his reason. As if to verify what had become of him, he curled back his lip and gently put a finger to his mouth. Therein, he felt the dagger points of his fangs and despairingly, withdrew his hand from his mouth. Macabre thoughts consumed his mind afresh and his eyes seemed to glaze over, staring aimlessly out over the graveyard.

Nightmarish images of the demon that had found him appeared in his mind, and he recalled the horror and gore of the creature's passing at his hands. His recollection of the killing surfaced his memory of the thieving wretch and the savage act he had committed. As he relived the horrid moment, he found that the quality of that memory and others from the previous night, were different from any other memories he could summon to mind. Before that night, his memories existed as a collection of instants, or vague impressions of moments in time. But ever since he had clawed his way up from under the soil, all that he had seen with his strange, new eyes, he seemed to remember in vivid detail, so that his memories unfolded almost seamlessly, with striking clarity.

Once more, fearful images of the demon crept into his mind and it appalled him how like the hellish thing he had become. He wondered if in death, the thing had somehow possessed his body in some way and if his very soul had not been tainted, or even consumed, by the curse he evidently now bore. The thought terrified him and he dismissed it immediately. If this was to be his fate, then it, without a doubt, had been ordained by God as part of some divine plan, the workings of which were as of yet unknown to him.

To the west, the sky was afire in pink and orange as the last of the sun sank beyond the earth. In his eyes, the dim glow shone with the splendor of a summer's day; and for a while, he simply stared into the horizon as he walked amidst the gravestones, fascinated by the luminous spectacle before him. He was increasingly aware of his body, the strength and vitality of which seemed to have grown to a level previously unknown to him. The maddening hunger that possessed him the previous night was subdued and quite tolerable at present. Though the thought sickened him, the blood of the thief had nourished him somehow and he had gorged himself upon it. In some way, he felt more alive and whole, and he noted that the very bulk of his body seemed to have filled out while he had reposed through the course of the day. He walked on, calm and observant, his mind increasingly devoid of thought as he became attuned to his body and senses. He was, in some respect, curious about his body, in spite of his revulsion for what had become of him.

He wandered aimlessly, entirely engrossed in the ineffable nature of his acute sensorium. Eventually, he reached the fringe of the graveyard, and there came to a stop. He observed the open land that lay before him, the soft grasses and rolling hills dotted with patchworks of forest. The sky above was a perfect dark, for all trace of the sun had vanished into the west. Looking up at the sky, he saw that it was heavy with brilliant specks of light. To his eyes, it seemed a sparkling mist had been strewn over the black firmament above and he experienced the sight as never before. The stars and moon above bathed the darkened world around him in pale light, the glow of which suggested a near imperceptible hint of blue and silver. His eyes lowered and he gazed over the rolling plain, the night sky looming above the horizon. He took a few steps beyond the graveyard, and then, upon a whim, quickened his pace, so that he broke into a steady run.

He headed inland along the borderlands, leaving the town of Berwick behind him. At first, his path mirrored that of the river Tweed, but in keeping his distance from Berwick Castle, he strayed from its course. Swift and silent, he roamed the open land like a wraith. At no point did he tire or falter in his stride, as though he were bred to run, like a hound for the hunt. His heart beat strongly and steadily, his breaths were smooth and deep, and with each inspiration, his body denied fatigue its claim. He was enthralled by the stamina of his body and by the scents and sounds that met him. He lost all sense of time as he traversed the hilly plains, driven forth not by a compulsion, but of his own desire and will.

# II

A small forest stretched before him, a vast tangle of gnarled trees twining in the darkness, lit here and there by shafts of moonlight that filtered through the black canopy above. He had come to a halt at the fringe of the forest, and, poised where grass plain met forest floor, he cocked his head slowly from side to side, listening and scouring the forest depths. Moving unhurriedly and quietly, he stepped forward and entered the forest. Like a wave opposed by a rocky shore, the breeze that swept over the grassland perished against the flora, so that beyond its rustling fringes, the forest possessed an air of stillness. As he wound his way through the forest, he detected traces of various scents, some more faint than others. A few of the most poignant were vaguely familiar and others were scents unknown.

Where he could, which was most infrequent, he would trace a scent to its source, thereby creating visual representations for the newfound scents that entered his nostrils. One scent he happened upon, as he made his way through the forest, was particularly potent. At first, he would catch the scent briefly, then lose it for a short while before finding it afresh. He found that in crouching low to the ground, he was better able to keep with the scent, and so refined his methods. The scent grew stronger as he neared its source and he moved towards it with an atavistic stealth, stooping as low as possible to the forest floor. The scent was one that he was almost certain he had come across at some point before, though he had never experienced it in such a primeval manner. It was a smell of flesh, of musk and fur, and he drew ever nearer to it.

He passed through a moonbeam, which shone unimpeded through the canopy. Its vivid luminescence detailed the capable musculature underneath his bare, pallid skin, before he slipped from the light, back into the shadows. When it seemed he could be no more than a few arms breadths away from what he sought, he froze, fossicking the darkness and the patches of underbrush with his piercing yellow eyes. No sooner did his sharp eyes fix upon it, than what had at first glance appeared to be a mound of earth, leaped up from where it had hidden with a violent rustling of bush. A sizeable hare darted out from under a shrub and scampered off into the dark wood.

He watched it go and listened as it made its noisy escape through the forest litter. Standing stark still, his head cocked to a side, he was able to attend to the sound of the retreating hare for a remarkable amount of time before the bustling faded into the quiet solace of the forest. He finally turned his attention elsewhere and continued on into the forest. He was becoming quiet adept in the use of his senses, straining his eyes and ears to see and hear great distances, and sniffing the air to catch the fleeting scents of beasts, determining where and how long ago they had passed through the bush. So consumed was he with all, that he gained the furthest reaches of the forest without an inkling as to how much time he had spent within it.

\* \* \* \*

The forest opened into a vast meadowland, which segued into precipitous, rifted terrain beyond. In the distance, the black silhouette of a tree line contoured a portion of the horizon, reaching towards the brilliant moon above. He stepped out from the forest, but did not stray far from it. He walked along the periphery of forest, clinging to the shadows. Gradually, he began to stray from the forest limits and headed towards the meadow. As he did, he heard a faint rustling from the forest. Faint though it was, the nature of the sound suggested an approaching thing: something which, in all likelihood, was relatively large.

He spun round, and standing still as stone, stared deep into the dark bowels of the wood. The vague rustling became a distinctive pattern of soft footfalls, a rhythmic disturbance of leaves and litter as the thing drew near. He thought it most likely a deer, for it sounded as if it traveled on four legs. Yet, deer were notoriously nervy creatures, which would take flight at the drop of a pebble; whatever approached from the forest was not so timid as a deer, for it seemed to be headed straight for him. His eyes caught a sudden movement somewhere within the tenebrous twists of flora. A patch of bramble quivered briefly, betraying the presence of a form that slipped into obscurity beyond it. He tracked its movement, and saw it reemerge from under cover of the forest, closer than it had been before. He was now certain it was no deer, for the coat was heavier than a deer's, the body thicker and closer to the ground. He reasoned it might be a boar and was almost convinced that it was. Neither hurriedly nor laggardly, the beast loped towards him through bush and shadow. He strained his eyes to see it, so that even before it had emerged from the forest gloom, he knew what beast it was.

His eyes widened, his face the picture of astonishment. He took a few slow steps back, for from the darkened wood, strode a large, grizzled wolf. It was said that the last of these beasts had been slain no less than two winters ago; that Northumberland and England itself had been rid of wolves. Yet, here now was one of the ancient hunters, come from night like a ghost of the past. Irrational as it was, for he was surely the fiercer creature, his first impulse was to run, for throughout his life, he had heard gruesome tales of these savage beasts. These were plunderers and killers of children, howling devil-spawn who lived to gorge upon the flesh of the innocent.

He had only once seen a wolf. As a child in Spain, in a forest near the outskirts of his home, he had caught sight of a fearsome, dusky wolf, and watched it disappear amidst the trees. The beast had filled his heart with such terror that he had frozen where he stood, his mind plagued by the many grisly tales of wolves he had been told.

He almost felt as though he were that child again, for he had gone deathly still, and could do naught but stare bleakly into the eyes of the great wolf. It regarded him with serene, ochre eyes. It did not bare its teeth, nor did it growl or show malice. Rather, its aspect was tranquil, its poise and composure seemingly unaffected by his presence. The wolf slowed as it drew near and took a few wary steps forward before it came to a stop, not an arm's breadth from where he stood. He stiffened, but did not tremor in the slightest. Indeed, he did not so much as breathe while the wolf stood before him. Its ears would prick and pivot now and again as it marked the faintest sounds in the night air, but its eyes never left him.

Though fear still quickened his beating heart and petrified his limbs, a part of him could not help but revere the great beast. The moon shone down upon them, and the argent light seemed to lend the wolf some ethereal quality. The wolf seemed almost curious, and took another step forward, and cautiously, even tentatively, leaned in towards him. With its thickly furred neck outstretched, it brought its gracile muzzle so close to the bare flesh of his waist that he felt its whiskers brush against his skin. The wet, black nose sniffed at him, investigating with quivering nostrils. The sound of its forceful inspirations seemed to echo in the silence of the night. It proceeded to sniff his thigh and hand, then took a leisurely step backward and raised it head, ears pricked. The wolf relaxed its jaws and its tongue hung languidly in its mouth as it began to pant, ever so softly. Its aspect seemed peaceable, even amicable, and after eyeing him one last time, the wolf looked out towards the meadow and loped off in the direction of the rocky hills.

He watched the lonely figure of the wolf slink out over the vast plain. Here was not the hellish beast of common lore, but a fascinating creature that had left him in awe. He wondered if this would be the last wolf he would ever see, perhaps even the very last of its kind. He felt a sudden pity for the beast, alone and outcast under the moon and stars, a fate, he thought, not unlike his own. For some inexplicable reason, he found himself calling out to the wolf, in a voice he barely recognized as his own.

"What men…what men have said of you…that your kind are wicked…it is untrue."

Its ears pricking once again, the wolf stopped in its tracks, and with majestic grace, turned its head around to stare back at him.

He stared back at its eyes with a look that was almost apologetic.

"I…I am like you now…destined to be despised and alone."

He faltered, as though he were about to speak again. Instead, he remained silent, still staring at the wolf, who regarded him with renewed curiosity. The wolf turned its head to look over the meadow, then returned its gaze to him. He in turn, stared into the star spangled horizon then glanced back at the wolf. He took a few hesitant steps towards the old wolf, who stood calm and still, watching his movements. It seemed to wait upon his approach, and when he drew near, it turned towards the meadow once more and broke into its tireless lope. He was unsure if it was curiosity or some strange solidarity that prompted what he did next. Regardless, after a brief moment of indecision, he sprang into a run and followed in the path of the wolf.

\* \* \* \*

The unlikely pair had kept a steady pace since leaving the forest behind them. They ranged across the meadow for some time. He watched the open land pass him by while the distant hills drew ever nearer. At first, he trailed the wolf from a respectable distance. As they traveled, the wolf would look back at him from time to time, and seemed quite comfortable with his continued presence. Little by little he closed on the wolf, so that in the end he ran almost abreast with it, some paces off to one side. The once-distant hills now loomed before them, garlanded by small plots of forest around the foothills. The viridescent terrain was increasingly gouged by small gullies and basins, and occasionally dotted by stones and boulders. The wolf came to a sudden stop and lowered its muzzle into the grass below. It sniffed audibly and loped off once again with its head still lowered to the ground. He tasted the air himself and even lowered into a crouch to catch the scent. Finding nothing, he turned his attention to the wolf, which was headed towards a small, sparse wood at the base of a hill.

\* \* \* \*

They entered the wood, both moving silently amidst the trees. He came to a sudden halt as his nostrils caught the faintest scent, which wafted from amidst the trees somewhere beyond a small rise in the wood. The scent was familiar, for he had come across it in the woods earlier, yet he still could not place it, for he had not seen the beast to which the scent belonged.

"I smell it." He whispered to himself under his breath. "What... is it?" He looked to the wolf, not truly expecting an answer. Some distance from him, the wolf had flattened its back and ears and was stalking up the face of the rise, winding stealthily through the trees. He stole forward with equal whid and clambered up the far side of the rise. The scent was suddenly quite strong and he tempered his ascension to a stolid stalk. He saw that the wolf had become motionless, its gaze fixed upon something near the base of the rise, on the opposite side. He came to the crest of the rise himself, behind a briar patch, and peered through it to see what lay beyond. His yellow eyes flitted about, searching amidst the trees and brush below him from behind the briars. He spotted them immediately: two deer. Does. One grazing and the other on alert with ears pricked.

It was to be a hunt and his body reacted to the notion. His breaths became slow and deep and his heart thudded in his breast. He did not hunger for the deer, but for the hunt itself; a chance to catapult his body forward in chase, exploring his furthest limits. Though he was not entirely possessed as he had once been, instinct had begun to influence his reason. He glanced at the wolf as he lay in wait for the incipient ambush that would set him upon the prey. Now both does were looking about nervously with ears pricked, snorting raspingly.

From its deathly stillness, the wolf sprang to life. It bounded down the slope towards the deer, which, startled, leapt away from the grizzled beast. As the wolf reached the slope, he darted out from behind the briars. His legs pounded against the earth and he found himself propelled forward at an unprecedented pace. Upon sighting the wolf, the deer scattered. One of the quarry had unwittingly chosen a path which set it directly ahead of him and the wolf honed in on the animal as though it recognized him as part of the hunt. The other doe peeled away and fled, leaving its hunted compatriot to its own devices.

From the onset of the hunt, it was clear that the wolf could not match the speed and agility of the fleeing deer. He thought that the ambush might have been the desperate act of a starving wolf, for there was a scant chance that a solitary wolf would catch a fleet-footed deer. Yet the wolf was assiduous in its pursuit, its eyes never leaving its prey. The wood rushed at him and by him at an amazing rate, and he weaved through trees at full sprint. The wolf was pressing the opposite flank of the deer a few paces ahead of him, and he noticed he was steadily gaining on the grizzled hunter. The dark blurs of trees and bush whisked between them as they raced through the wood. He returned his sight to the doe, which darted and sprang amidst the trees.

He ducked under a hanging branch, then vaulted over a fallen tree, a low whoosh left in his wake as he knifed through the air. Before he knew it, he had pulled past the wolf and was closing on the doe. He ceased his effort to outflank the deer into the wolf, and instead, moved into a flat out chase. The doe, now acutely aware of its second pursuer, redoubled its efforts to distance itself. He was only a short distance from the doe, but it seemed as though he could not close upon it any further. Each step he gained was lost, as the deer would suddenly juke to one side, forcing him to make up the distance. Still, he was enthralled that he could even keep pace with a deer, and he pressed on doggedly. He followed the doe's every twist and turn, and they tore into the earth, kicking up debris as they careened through the wood. For a while it seemed the doe would continue to evade him. As they entered a particularly sparse bit of the woodland, he marked that the doe had slowed in the slightest. He saw that it eyes were wide with fright and its mouth frothed from its exertion.

Though his heart beat madly in his breast, and ears and his chest heaved mightily with breath, he continued to chase with relentless vigor. Sensing weakness, he bore down upon the doe with renewed fervor. It veered and dodged as before, but had lost the vital spring in its stride, and he closed the distance between them to an arm's length. The doe veered in an attempt to shake him, but its weary legs did not carry it to safety. Just as the doe veered, he gathered his legs underneath him, dug his taloned feet into the ground, and pounced upon the exhausted animal.

Arms and body outstretched, he barely caught hold of the doe about the haunches, but clutched what little purchase he had with fearsome tenacity. Locked together by a grim embrace, they rolled and tumbled over the woodland floor, casting leaves, dust, and twigs every which way. The stunned doe kicked and flailed its limbs helplessly and he pinned it down. He could not believe he had actually caught it, and a trace smile crept across his face. With the hunt over, and his competence tested, he was almost at a loss as to what he should do. With bulging, tearing, crazed eyes, the doe keened and rasped horribly underneath him. He watched it, wide eyed.

With a sudden rush of soft, but rapid footfalls, the wolf shot forth from the darkness. He had thought the old wolf had given up the chase, but, evidently, it had been in pursuit, relying on its stamina and cunning rather than its speed. The wolf immediately sought the doe's throat and clamped its jaws down upon it. He sat beside the two beasts, watching the mortal drama unfold with a vacant look upon his face. The doe's struggles ebbed and finally ceased, its gaping eyes staring blankly into the darkness. The wolf began to tear into the bowels of the carcass, gorging its starved body. He watched it feed for a short while. Prompted by curiosity, he outstretched his arm and dipping his hand into the mangled carcass, bathed his middle and forefinger in the doe's blood. He observed his bloodied fingers then brought them to his mouth. He imbibed the scarlet liquid on his fingers and paused, gauging his body's reaction to the variant nourishment. It was not necessarily bad, but there was something about the doe's blood that did not sit well, and he licked his lips with a somewhat discontented look on his face. He looked up at the night sky through the canopy above and then glanced at the wolf, who was still feeding on the carcass with some avidity.

"Who...am I?" he remarked to the wolf in somber whisper. The wolf turned towards him, panting heavily, its pale fur stained red with gore.

"Good hunting," he offered as he rose to his feet and turned from the wolf. He headed back the way he had come, deep in thought as he stole through the wood.

The wolf stared after him for a few moments, then returned its attention to the carcass.

# III

He found himself thinking of Bronwyn as he made his way back through the wood. He yearned to look upon her loving face and hold her in his arms, though he wondered how she would receive him. Presumably, she thought him dead, for had he not clawed his way from the bowels of earth after waking from his slumber? Had it been slumber? He knew not what to call it. Either way, many of the townspeople would know him dead and buried, including all those he held dear. He was contemplating whether or not he should attempt to see Bronwyn, when he met with a most peculiar scent, and his body stiffened and stilled. He was sure the scent was foreign to him, yet it elicited in him, a distinctive sense of foreboding. Something about the scent knotted his gut and sent a shiver down his spine.

Gradually, as he ruminated upon the scent, a petrifying memory manifested itself. He remembered clutching a coarse tuft of black mane and straining against a rearing head. He recalled the face of the risen head: a bestial brow, yellow eyes, ghastly flesh, and a gnashing, fanged maw. He vaguely recalled the smell of its breath and body as it drew itself towards him, terrifying and imposing. His breath caught in his lungs, and his face went taut, for he had caught the scent of a demon, and more than that, it lurked nearby, somewhere in the darkness.

His first thought was flight, but he was too terror-stricken to move. He was afraid to make the slightest rustle of leaves, lest he alert the skulking demon to his presence and draw it to him. Thus, he lowered into a crouch to further conceal himself in the shadows and shrubs, moving only his head and eyes, slowly and searchingly. He remained hidden for a short while, listening intently for the faintest disturbance from the wood. In return, the wood lent him naught but an eerie silence for his efforts and gradually, warily, he rose from the shadows. Employing his reason, he steeled himself against his fear. Though he had been battered and wounded, had he not already dispatched one of these creatures? Indeed, the other had been fortunate to escape before the guardsmen had come to his aid. Somehow, by means of some curse or divine plan, he had become like them, this he could not deny. His body was changed, savage, formidable, and so this demon could not possibly still overwhelm him the way the other had in the loft. He would be afraid no more. He spoke aloud under his breath in a menacing whisper, seemingly directed to the dark wood itself.

"I shall not fear it…it…it shall fear me."

He half shut his eyes and concentrated on the scent, attempting to discern in which direction the fiend traveled. He wound through the wood until it opened into grassland. The scent was infrequent and faint, and its vagueness made him irresolute on the trail. Nonetheless, he stalked along the edge of the wood, following the intermittent scent towards the foothills of the looming range.

He was so engrossed in his efforts to course the path of the demon, that he nearly missed a distant movement on the face of one of the foremost hills. He froze, and his eyes searched the hill where they had first caught movement. The brilliance of the moon lit the verdant hill, and his eyes scoured it with remarkable proficiency. They strained into the distance and his periphery blurred and warped. The area upon which he focused, however, was enhanced, so that it appeared more substantial and clearer than before. With sight beyond sight, he observed scant trees and crags coated by pale moonlight, but no movement save the supplications of leaves to the wind.

Quite abruptly, something that had appeared to be a small, ashen boulder began to rise. A smooth aggregate of muscle under chalky flesh straightened, and he saw the demon before him. Its back was to him as it sniffed the air, its head cocked to one side, yet it was instantly familiar to him. Its torso, once covered by a torn, tattered rag, was now bare and only the mere remnants of its previous garment covered its loins. It suddenly hunkered back down near a small spread of shrubs, preoccupied with something behind them. When it rose again, the shrubs shuddered, and the demon appeared to be dragging something that had been lying behind them. It hauled the body of a man free from the shrubs, the head held firmly at the scalp in the clutch of the demon. Blood matted a tuft of the man's long chestnut hair, as well the man's forehead, beard, and neck.

The man's clothes were tattered and stained, and the body was covered with dust and filth, as though it had been dragged for a great distance. With a single arm outstretched behind it, the demon hauled the limp body up the face of the hill with brutal disregard. The demon ascended at an unwavering pace, pulling the body up over increasingly barren, stony terrain. The body shook and twisted limply, as it was ground against stone and earth at speed. The demon's skin seemed to camouflage against the pale, moonlit rocks, and he lost sight of it for a moment as it moved between two large boulders. He regained sight of the thing in time to see it vanish into a large rocky pass, formed by two overhanging crags. The demon dragged the man's body in after it violently, leaving a few tumbling pebbles and swirling, moonlit dust in its wake.

He stood still for a moment, staring into the vacant pass; he then looked out into the horizon and turned his back on the hills. He believed he now knew for what purpose he had risen from the earth, and thought that he might understand the path ordained for him. He would return to this place again, and he would do so not as man, nor a cursed being, but as an instrument of the Lord in earthly flesh, for surely this is what he had become.

He looked to the night sky once more and saw that it would soon birth the morn. He knew he must reach Berwick before sunrise, for if he were unsheltered ere the break of day, it would not be long before the sun blinded him and overwhelmed him. Swift and silent, he retraced his path through the meadowland and back through the forest, racing against the sun. He burst from the forest and tore across the rolling plains like some grim phantom, unyielding in his pace. He raced along the borderlands near the Tweed, and soon saw Berwick Castle, adumbrated on the horizon.

The east was streaked vermilion as he neared the town. His breaths were heavy as those of a warhorse and his heart pounded fiercely, yet still he did not falter. A forest of headstones and statues cropped up beyond him, and he closed on the graveyard.

When he reached the tomb, the vermillion east had become a vibrant suffusion of color and he blinked under its radiance. He leaned forward and lifted the tombstone, uncovering the chamber underneath. He looked about and without another moment's hesitation, swung his legs over the lip of the tomb and dropped into the chamber. Reaching up from atop the coffin, he replaced the tombstone overtop of the chamber, plunging the tomb into darkness. His breaths became calm and reserved, and he lay down upon the coffin. As he had the morning past, he closed his eyes and willed himself to slumber.

# Chapter Ten
## Revelations

## I

Sebastian's eyelids felt heavy and tired, but he forced them open. He blinked involuntarily at the bright, pellucid blur before him and watched as it took shape. As his vision cleared, he realized he was staring up at a light fixture. Once again, he took note of the steady beeping off to his left, and knew that he was back in the room. He thought he heard something else near his bedside, a faint sound, almost indiscernible. His neck was still throbbing painfully, and the spongy neck brace restricted the movements of his neck and head, but he turned his head as far as he could manage to take a look.

Beside him, Dr. Canterberry was hunched over the electrocardiogram, regarding it with his full attention. Sebastian could not exactly make out what the doctor was doing, for Dr. Canterberry had his back to him, but the doctor had the electrodes Sebastian had previously removed in hand. Glancing at his left forearm, he saw that the doctor had reinserted the intravenous feed. He returned his gaze to the doctor, who was still unaware that he had awakened. He did not know what the doctor intended with him, but he was reasonably certain it was not honest. He reasoned that if he was to uncover the true nature of his predicament, he would have to act quickly, for he would not be capable of much else in his debilitated condition.

As fast as he could manage, he reached out with his left arm and grabbed the back of the doctor's white robe. Grimacing with the pain of his injuries, he yanked the doctor towards him as hard as he could. Dr. Canterberry, obviously caught entirely by surprise, was only able to gasp in alarm as he was lurched backward. The doctor's legs clipped against the bed, so that he toppled, wide-eyed, onto Sebastian, who guided the doctor's fall in towards him with his hold on the robe. As Dr. Canterberry fell, Sebastian swung his right arm across the doctor's neck, securing his forearm under the doctor's chin. He squeezed Dr. Canterberry's head into his upper chest, hard enough to immobilize him, but not with sufficient force to cause the old doctor to black out. He sat back against the bed, hauling the stunned doctor with him.

As he did, he released the doctor's robe and hooked him around the chest with his left arm, pinning the doctor's arms to his sides. The needle in his forearm wriggled about in its vessel as he pressed his left arm across the doctor's chest, sending sharp pains and tingles down towards his fingers. This discomfort, his wounded thigh and the agonizing throbbing from his straining neck, caused him to wince, but his grip did not waver. He felt something slim and hard under his left hand. Glancing down over the doctor's shoulder, he saw that it was a pen that the doctor had tucked into his breast pocket. Sebastian grabbed at it with evident purpose. Freeing the pen from the doctor's pocket, he flicked the top off with his thumb, gripped it tightly, and pressed the tip into the soft of the doctor's neck, just underneath the jawline. The doctor, who had not really been squirming vigorously to begin with, went quite still. Sebastian spoke into his ear in a harsh tone.

"Where the hell am I? The truth this time and if I smell any bullshit I start pushing the pen."

The doctor stammered, then spoke, his voice choked by Sebastian's right forearm.

"Ahm…S…Sebastian, let's…ahm…let's not do anything rash. I…I am not sure what you intend, but you do not need to do this. I assure you, you are in no danger here."

"You're stalling, doctor." Sebastian remarked threateningly.

"I am not…I…ahm…this is unnecessary, Sebastian, please take a moment to think it over. If my concern for your well-being were disingenuous, then I would have left you in the streets. I would not have risked taking you here, which was a greater risk for me, mind you, than you know. I did not bring you here and work into the night to revive you, just so I could…dispose of you, or whatever it is you think I might do."

The doctor's face and eyes were going red, and his voice was hoarse under the pressure of Sebastian's arm.

"L…Listen. Everything I told you about this place, about me, is true…essentially. I simply left out the details you were not supposed to know… privileged information, research and like, that not even the vast majority of the staff here are privy to."

"It's exactly because I've seen too much that I'll be leaving now, with your help."

"How exactly? By using me as a hostage? My dear boy, not to sound condescending but…"

Sebastian tightened his stranglehold, unappreciative of the doctor's temerity. The doctor wheezed and sputtered, and finally got out a few words.

"Tr…trying…to…w…warn…you."

Sebastian allowed the doctor's throat its prior slack and Dr. Canterberry gasped for breath.

"Warn me about what?" Sebastian asked, his throat maddeningly painful.

"The only exits from this facility," continued the doctor after regaining a modicum of composure, "have guards posted by them. These are not your run-of-the-mill mall guards. They are mercenary-issue, mostly former military personnel. They are armed and authorized, by contract to this facility, to use their weapons if need be. Even if in your precarious condition, you were able to…ahm…torture me and obtain the key codes to exit this wing and access the level-three clearance elevator, the facility would go into lock down before you could even reach the ground floor. Steel doors automatically seal the exits…ahm…the facility has inconspicuous video surveillance everywhere, save some of the rooms…ahm…however you might have approached it, there are no windows to escape out of from this floor, it is simply made to look like there are from the outside…not to mention…please trust me, there is no way out."

"Sucks for me. Still doesn't help you very much at the moment though, and you know, I caught on to the fact that nothing about this place was 'run-of-the-mill'; 'cause that naked, albino thing in the other room sure as hell wasn't just some dude with a little problem with his shit tract. What the hell is going on?"

"You…you really would not believe me if I—"

"Try me," Sebastian interrupted, increasing the pressure of the pen against Dr. Canterberry's neck. "Let's start with why an old man was hanging out in a dark alley, in a car with bulletproof glass, just within the area of a police perimeter. Or how about that other freaky, white-skinned guy with the black coat in the other room. I recognized his voice…he called you on your cell; and that dude just happened to be well inside the perimeter as well? In our area of operation even, 'cause I am fairly fuckin sure that that guy jumped over my head, across a gap between two fuckin' buildings."

Sebastian's neck throbbed mercilessly and he felt faint. He blinked rapidly as his vision began to spot and was able shake it off before he passed out again. In the meantime, Dr. Canterberry had begun to speak again.

"The…that man is my…ahm… employer, the one who gave me a second chance after my life had begun to spiral into ruin. He—"

"See, doctor," Sebastian intruded coldly. "This is that smell of bullshit I was talking about. Correct me if I'm wrong, but you were well into your thirties when your so-called employer offered you a job. Problem is, you're probably damn well sixty now, and that man who was in there, his strangeness aside, is in his mid-thirties at max." Sebastian dug the pen into Dr. Canterberry's neck so that it almost drew blood. "So, do you smell that yet? 'Cause I sure do."

Dr. Canterberry groaned and gritted his teeth.

"Wait, please…I am not lying."

Sebastian kept the pen at his throat, but eased the pressure.

"I...oh dear...how do I even begin to...if I am to do any kind of competent job in explaining all this, I am going to have to start at the beginning...ahm...if you and my pen don't mind, that is."

"Where is the surveillance camera in this room?" inquired Sebastian, addressing a new concern as he looked around the top of the room.

"This is one of the rooms without. Why?" The doctor replied worriedly.

"Just want to make sure no one interrupts our little FAQ session." Sebastian looked down at Dr. Canterberry expectantly.

"Ahm...right...well...let's get on with it shall we, though you will simply think me a lunatic when all is said and done." Dr. Canterberry took in a deep breath and sighed, "This whole facility: its surreptitiousness, the guards, all of it...it exists because of the...ahm...'naked albino' you saw on the bed in other room. Incidentally, albinos are blond and often pink-ey—"

"I know what an albino is, thanks."

"Right, of course...ahm...well...that individual in the other room actually belongs to a distinct group of organism, and is not itself an aberrant form. You see...ahm...I think I will approach this from another angle first. Ahm...I wonder if you would be so kind as to release me for the duration of this 'FAQ session'. I promise you, I will do nothing untoward. It's just that I am finding the lack of oxygen and the threatening prod of my pen at my neck, quite distracting."

"Keep talking." Sebastian directed, though he did significantly loosen his lock around the doctor's neck.

"All right...ahm...stories...stories often convey some moral, or speak to us in a way such that we can relate certain of their elements with things we do or experience in our everyday lives. Likewise, mythology, within its fantastical narrative, often holds elements of truth, meager or elaborated as they might be. Consider the story of the flood. This is chronicled in the mythologies of various cultures, namely the ancient Sumerians. We see the same flood story in the Bible as well. Now, each of these myths, or biblical tales as it were, is a different story unto itself...obviously. The one element of interest common to these myths is the account of a great flood, which leads one to believe that these various cultures may have all experienced some great flood at a single, chronologically synchronous point in history.

"However, myths are also retold and changed throughout time as they pass through history, so that similar accounts may actually be variations of the same myth, or recycled mythic themes, which could also explain the striking recurrence of the flood theme. Nevertheless, modern, empirical evidence supports the idea that there was in fact some kind of great flood, though whether it was a cleansing of the earth by God, or the thousand tears of a giant, or a—"

"I get the point."

"Ahm...very good...ahm...well...there are other mythologies that various races and cultures share, and the more cross-cultural accounts there are of these historically endemic events...the more likely the common element is to be true in some way, shape, or form, especially when they seem to have occurred at a specific time, spanning vast geography. Now, historically...well, at least especially historically, there have been a plethora of accounts from countries and cultures around the globe of men and women, or creatures that, in the dead of night, leave their graves and reap the blood of humankind. They are purported to perform this act for various reasons and in various ways, but the point is, what is the one constant: the one element of truth? If one were to examine the evidence—"

"Come on, doc, it sounds like you're talking—"

"I know how it sounds," Dr. Canterberry interjected. "I know what you must be thinking as well, and I told you that you would believe I was off my rocker. I had the same doubts, the same suspicions when I first learned about...all of this, but...after some of the things I have seen..." The doctor trailed off for a moment. "I swear to you, Sebastian, I am telling you the truth. I would swear to God, but with respect to my life experience in the last thirty years or so, I don't think it would be a worthwhile endeavor. I...I swear on my daughter's honor, that everything I say will be the truth."

Sebastian was still somewhat dubious, but he had just seen things with his own eyes that he would not have readily believed. Admittedly, he needed some kind of explanation, if for nothing else than to put his baffled mind at ease. Thus, instead of voicing any kind of displeasure, he left Dr. Canterberry an open silence to fill. The doctor took a deep, cogitative breath.

"These myths and urban legends point to a class of organism known as hematophages, meaning blood eaters. Hematophages can be classified as obligatory or optional, where the former subsist solely on blood and the latter can also ingest other food items. Hematophages are typically quite small, and most, like mosquitoes and leeches, are insects or parasitic worms. However, nature inevitably finds a way to surprise us, and we find an unlikely hematophage, a bat, in the class of mammals. There are well over one thousand species of bat in the world and only three of these have adopted hematophagous feeding practices.

"Why would a small mammal adapt such an uncommon… ahm…at least for mammals…method of feeding? We don't question it, nor find it exceptional, because it has become common knowledge, but it is as marked an adaptation as those of the extremophile organisms that survive on thermal vents, in the deepest, darkest depths of the ocean. Nature, Sebastian, is a limitless exploration of forms, an interaction and trial of its astounding variety. Remember what I said, Sebastian…nature always finds a way to surprise us, no matter how much we think we know." Dr. Canterberry attempted to peer at Sebastian out of the corner of his eye. "How much schooling did you receive in the sciences, specifically biology? Because some of what I am going—"

"I'm not Darwin, but I'm no Jessica Simpson, we're good." Sebastian broke in with some impatience.

"Listen here," came Dr. Canterberry's embittered rebuke. "I feel I have been a compliant hostage up till now, having been nearly asphyxiated, then jabbed at with my own pen. On top of that, you feel it necessary to interrupt my every thought. Can you not, at the very least, engage in conversation with some shred of decency?"

"I apologize," Sebastian offered somewhat sarcastically. "Please continue."

"Thank you," replied Dr. Canterberry, who was seemingly placated. "Right then, now where was I going from...ahm...oh, yes, of course." The doctor cleared his throat, "So...ahm...as I mentioned, accounts of these creatures, varied as they may be, can be found throughout history. From ancient Babylon, we find mythological accounts of creatures called the Lilu, the daughters of the demon Lilith. The Lilu, like a succubus, would drain men of their energies, often until the point of death. Even earlier, ancient Sumerians told of creatures called the Akhkharu, who took children and pregnant women in the night. From Sanskrit folklore in India, come tales of the Vetelas, ghoulish creatures, which inhabited the dead, took people in the night, and could climb and hang upside down in trees. A few stories document the Indian king, Vikramaditya, who tried to hunt these elusive creatures and purge his lands of them. Ahm...there are other such examples from ancient history, but these are the ones I remember at the moment. "

Sebastian's arms were beginning to fatigue holding Dr. Canterberry in check, and they began to tremble under the effort. Waves of pain radiated from the sites of his injuries and he gritted his teeth, trying to disregard his sharp discomfort.

"Anyhow, myths and folklore of this nature persisted in many parts of the world. Then, in the seventeen-hundreds, what had once been folklore became all too real for many who resided in the Slavic nations, particularly in Prussia. Here, documented cases of nocturnal predation created such unrest with local townspeople that corpses were constantly being exhumed from their graves and often mutilated, for fear that they had risen after death to drink the blood of the living. The Slavics called them Strigoi, Upir, and finally the term with which you are familiar, Vampir or Vampire.

"There were such a number of these vampiric accounts, that in 1746, a renowned French theologian...ahm...oh, what is his name...ahm...Dom...Dom Augustine Calmet, compiled a record of these attacks and composed a dissertation on the subject. In it, he claimed it was plausible that the reported attacks were perpetrated by vampires. Panic was so widespread that eventually the monarchy was involved, namely Empress Maria Theresa of Austria, who sent...I believe it was a physician of hers...yes, sent her physician to investigate the alleged vampire outbreak with greater scrutiny. After his investigations, he was of the opinion that the creatures did not exist, and laws were passed to prevent further fear-mongering and exhumation of the deceased. Reports of the undead declined soon after and it likely became somewhat taboo to claim witness to, or to have been attacked by the undead."

Sebastian knew his face was the picture of skepticism and he sighed derisively.

"Dr. Canterberry...you are expecting me to believe in the undead, in vampires. You want me to accept... like... Dracula, and casting no shadow, or showing no reflection, turning into bats—"

"No, of course not, that is all complete rubbish and I apologize for interrupting you...won't happen again." Dr. Canterberry said coolly.

"What? Then what exactly are you trying to accomplish here other than wasting time?"

"I was simply demonstrating that the historical accounts were in fact alluding to some kind of truth. You see, that is the problem with truth where it is woven into the framework of mythos. To begin with, the truth is often marred by misconceptions. Recall that history belongs to those who wrote it. The truth undergoes further perversion as it courses through the ages, succumbing to bias, misinterpretation, and elaboration. Ahm...imagine that the biblical figure Goliath had actually existed, as he very well might have. Now, if he did actually exist, he was surely a large man, perhaps even stricken with acromegaly or something, but he was nowhere near his biblical proportions for the simple reason that the human body does not function past a certain size. So even if there had been some truth to the Goliath legend, it is essentially lost in the narrative."

The pain Sebastian was experiencing was mounting and he could no longer ignore it. He was grimacing again, and trembling more notably.

"So, what are you saying about vampires? What we hear is not the truth, but something like it is true?"

"Precisely." Answered Dr. Canterberry with an air of satisfaction.

"You could have said that in so many words." Sebastian chided.

"Ahm…no. If I am to give an explanation, then it will be a proper one thank you. Besides, I never really get to discuss this information with anyone and I know so damn much on the subject. Somewhat of a release for me, I suppose, quite enjoyable really this…save the awkwardness of our respective positions."

"Yeah, about that…if I let you go, you're not going try anything are you?" asked Sebastian defeatedly.

"Of course not. I will swear to that as well if need be." The doctor offered honestly.

"It's not so much that I trust you entirely, it's more the fact that I think I'm going to pass out again if I strain myself any longer. I…I hope I can trust you."

Sebastian placed the pen back into the doctor's breast pocket and released the doctor's head. Wincing and inspiring quite audibly, he sank back into the bed with his arms at his side, the intravenous tube still attached to his left forearm. Staring up at the ceiling, he gave a sigh of relief, as did the grateful doctor who was evidently relieved to wash his hands of his prior predicament. Sebastian looked down over his nose at the doctor, unsure what to expect.

Dr. Canterberry simply sat up, albeit awkwardly, on the edge of bed, and turned to face the young officer. He half smiled and raised his greying eyebrows.

"Well, I am glad that is over, that position was quite rough on my old back," he said as he put a hand to his low spine. "Not sure how much more I could have taken myself." He laughed to himself, shaking his head. "Took me hostage with my own pen, I'll not forget that. I suppose that is what I get for turning my back on a trained and disgruntled officer."

"It was worse for me, believe me." Sebastian said with a weak smile of his own.

Dr. Canterberry scratched the back of his head and looked down at the floor for a moment before returning his gaze to the weakened officer. The doctor was suddenly quite solemn.

"Sebastian...ahm...I hope you appreciate the gravity of this situation. I need you to understand that you have stumbled upon entirely undisclosed matters, which require the utmost secrecy. What you have seen is beyond classified, because not even the government has been given full disclosure. To them, this is a research facility, and for the moment, all they are concerned with, is that we continue to raise the bar where treatment for human illness is concerned. Now, to a degree, you already know a great deal, but what I am prepared to share with you is momentous. I cannot stress the amount of discretion you must employ in the safekeeping of this information. You should be advised that this knowledge does not come without consequence, and you must be prepared to suffer certain repercussions should you attempt to divulge said information to others, or disregard security protocol while you are here. There is...ahm...one other thing. I...I have aged since my initial employment, and I need some help with the legwork around here. I could give you more than just information. I could offer you a chance to do something that you never believed possible. The question is, given the stipulations, are you ready for what knowledge I have to give?"

Dr. Canterberry regarded Sebastian sternly and questioningly.

"Well...I'm an only child, my parents live out of state, and how could anybody say 'no' after a speech like that. Um...is it worth it?"

"You mean aside from the ridiculously high salary and a touch of the James Bond lifestyle…every bit." The doctor enticed with a far off look in his eyes.

"All right…all right, I'm in. Tell me everything."

# II

Dr. Canterberry brought a laptop into the room and placed it, open, on the bed beside Sebastian. On the slender monitor, an artful screen saver swirled against a black background. The doctor left the room again for a short while and returned, as promised, with a steaming teapot and two teacups on saucers. He carried them in on a quaint tray that also bore some packets of sugar, two spoons, and a small pitcher of cream. As the doctor moved, the tea set and silverware clinked and tinkled musically.

"Earl Grey...hot." He said reverently and with a cheerful smile. "Could you take that bottle of water off the table for me please?"

Sebastian lifted the bottle and laid it on the side of the bed nearest the I.V. equipment. Dr. Canterberry rounded the foot of the bed and gently placed the tray on the side table. That done, he inquired as to Sebastian's preferred amount of cream and sugar, and attended to both their teas. Sebastian thanked him, but refrained from imbibing immediately, leaving the scalding tea to cool on the tray. Tea in hand, Dr. Canterberry took a seat on the wooden stool, which sat where he had left it at the bedside. He took a sip of the steaming tea and regarded Sebastian thoughtfully.

"Sometimes, I simply sit back and think, whoever would have guessed I would be doing what I am now...for a living. When I distance myself from the prospect, it seems entirely surreal, yet here I am, and here you are. You know, I have been studying this species for thirty-some-odd years now. I work to uncover their complete history with what evidences I am presented. I analyze data I extrapolate, as well as the physiology of the couple specimens I was lucky enough to have been provided with. This is the main focus of my efforts, the center of all my research." He let his teacup rest in his lap.

"My employer came to me—"

"That…um…Gabriel?" Sebastian clarified.

"Yes…Gabriel." Dr. Canterberry admitted hesitantly. "He came to me because he believed my proficiency as both an immunologist and hematologist would be vital in furthering his understanding of the species' incredible physiology. He also came to me because I had lost my way in life and had no ties, nothing holding me to the old life that had passed me by. As I told you earlier, I felt that life, for me, was no longer worth living. I am shamed to admit I contemplated suicide many a time. One night, as I stood on the verge of a rooftop with a bottle in hand, overlooking the city lights and contemplating whether I should simply let it all go, I heard a cold voice address me from the shadows. It gave me such a thorough startling, that I near bloody well fell off the roof anyhow. I looked around, but saw nothing, hearing only the imposing, disembodied voice that spoke from the darkness."

The doctor's eyes look upward, as though he were recalling some distant, fond memory.

"I'll never forget what he said to me that night. He began with that first, chilling 'Dr. Nigel Canterberry' and followed with '… in your short life you cannot possibly have met with such that could justify squandering your life, or a mind with so much to offer. What I offer you is a second chance: a chance to do research and derive a fine living from it, a chance to study something you have never seen, nor would ever have imagined possible. An entire world of possibility awaits your discovery, Nigel, and I have need of your skills as a scientist.' Then, he simply said, 'Do you accept?'"

Dr. Canterberry returned his attention to Sebastian.

"How could I refuse? He offered me what I had worked for my whole life, what I thought I could never do again, and he offered it with such allure. I said 'yes', or nodded stupidly…perhaps both. After that, I heard the softest crunching of gravel, the approach of quiet footfalls on the roof. I stared into the shadows where I thought the sound came from. At first, there was nothing but that ominous sound of approach. Then, quite abruptly, I was able to make out what appeared to be a pale face, as it grew increasingly distinguishable within the veil of darkness surrounding it. He emerged from the shadows slowly, extended his hand and said, 'Then please come down from the ledge.' He was quite frightening to look at, and I will admit, I was nothing short of terrified, but I did as he asked."

"Wow." Sebastian followed this exclamation with a wry smile. "So, does every newbie get a cool speech or what? By the way, you completely ripped off that whole, 'I offer you something never before seen,' thing from his speech. Just letting you know that I know."

"But it really is so compelling isn't it? It was an unavoidable conclusion. I simply could not top it." Dr. Canterberry admitted jovially, before taking another sip of tea.

Sebastian looked down over his feet, pondering something. His musings were brief however, and he returned his concentration to the doctor before he could rest the teacup back in his lap.

"So…um…Gabriel and the thing strapped to the bed…they're the same. Both are…um…vampires." Sebastian stated uncertainly.

"No…ahm…to a degree, I suppose, but they are different. Their differentiation is another story in itself and I will explain that shortly. First, however, I think it would be prudent of me to tell you what I know of the actual species, which is what you saw fettered to the bed." Dr. Canterberry took another sip from his teacup before placing it on the tray next to Sebastian's.

"As I mentioned, they are hematophages, however, they are unique in that they are large, predatory hematophages, where others are mostly simplistic parasites. There is no magic to this species I am afraid, only mystery. They are an organism slave to the same dictates of nature as any other, and have lived alongside Homo sapiens since the dawn of our race, preying upon us and evolving with us every step of the way. For every large population of organisms, there is another that preys upon it, and humans are no different, though we have somehow managed to forget this.

"Ahm...remind me if I forget to get back to it, but I have a smashing theory on vampiric origins that points back to a parasitic ancestor. Anyhow, most hematophages are nocturnal and silent, so they do not alert or disturb their potential hosts. Given the size of some host animals, such a mistake would jeopardize a meal, and their lives. Vampires are no different, in that they use the dark and their stealth to get close to their prey, but of course...ahm...they have little to fear should their prey be disturbed. Having considered behavioral reports on the species from Gabriel, along with my own observations, I inferred that the vampire is primarily an ambush predator...ahm...much like a leopard I suppose, pouncing from trees or from behind some sort of cover.

"Like all hematophages, they have specially adapted mouths that are instrumental for phlebotomy, the...ahm...letting of blood from a vessel. The proboscis of a mosquito for instance, is an apt example. In the case of the vampire, finely pointed canine teeth are utilized to press into and puncture major arteries, namely the carotid in the neck. Unlike the rest of its teeth, which are fixed like our own, these canines are extensible. I...ahm...I think this would be a perfect segue to..."

The doctor trailed off as he leaned forward on the stool with a hand outstretched. He brushed the touchpad of the laptop with his fingers and the screen saver vanished, revealing a page with a sizeable window that displayed a blurry close-up of an open mouth, which appeared to be the frozen image of a video file. Dr. Canterberry maximized the window and played the video file. The image came to life and the camera came into focus. Sebastian saw working hands covered by thick, rubber gloves.

The right hand held forceps, and the other was gently gripping and immobilizing a chalky-colored chin. A thin, metallic device held the mouth open, exhibiting a set of pointed fangs along the upper rung of teeth. The file had audio as well, though there was not much in the way of sound to be heard. The hands presumably belonged to Dr. Canterberry, who in the video, clasped one of the jutting canines with the forceps and began to pull slowly. Above the gumline, a fleshy portion of the actual gum undulated, as though something were burrowing underneath the glistening, pinkish sheath. At this, Dr. Canterberry began to speak again.

"Ah…here we go. As you can see, about ninety percent of the tooth is housed inside the gum. What you can't see, is that the housing for the canine extends into a special cavity in the upper jaw."

On the screen, the tooth, though somewhat resistant to manipulation, had been pulled out so far that, even with the mouth held open, the sharp tip reached the bottom canine, displaying an alarmingly lengthy, sabre-like, ivory fang.

"There are actually three inches of canine hidden up there on either side, in addition to the resting protuberance of each upper canine. Of course. this length varies slightly between individuals. Now one would never see this extensile property, because the musculature that is engaged to perform this feat is under voluntary control, and only activated when the mouth is open and biting down on a prey item. There are two of these canine muscles, one for each of the upper canines. This muscle originates to either side of a single canine on the upper jaw, a… ahm…split muscular attachment adhering to the maxilla itself… the maxilla being the upper jawbone.

"The other end of this muscle inserts way up on the pseudo root of the tooth, so that when the muscle contracts, it pulls the insertion end down towards the gum line, and the canine is forced out from its housing. Also attached to the top of the pseudo root, which is why I have called it a pseudo root, is tough, highly elastic, connective tissue, the other end of which attaches to the upper jaw itself from inside the canine cavity. When the tooth is forced down by the contracting canine muscle, the elastic tissue is stretched, so that when the canine muscle is disengaged, the elastic tissue snaps back into place, pulling the canine back into its resting position. This allows the individual to probe deep into the flesh of the throat, or wherever it bites, puncture and tear open an artery, and then retract the its implements from the wound so that it may take in the blood. It is an absolutely brilliant adaptation really.

"Interestingly enough, they have even evolved heat pits in their nostrils, which allow them to detect the warm blood running through major vessels beneath the skin. It is an adaptation common to snakes and a few other animals, though snakes are much more advanced in this regard."

Sebastian's eyes left the screen for a moment, which was still displaying the open mouth.

"What about the idea," Sebastian queried, "that a person who is bitten by a vampire becomes one later on? Is that...I dunno..."

"Ah, yes, the infamous turn by the bite. More nonsense, much like the notion of repulsion by garlic, crosses, and holy water. If the prey of each vampire were to become vampire, then they would be exponentially eliminating the prey species they require to survive and increasing competition for their prey at the same rate. It would be evolutionarily...ahm...even logically, counterproductive. This is not to say their bite is not without effect, because it does actually do quite a number on the human body. First off, vampire saliva contains an incredibly efficient anticoagulant, which causes the blood to flow freely from the puncture site without clotting in the least. The vampire is also somewhat venomous, so that shortly after it bites its prey, the prey undergoes temporary sedation due a barbiturate property of the venom.

"Ahm...it is not actually a venom really, in that it is not usually lethal, simply debilitating. Some people, a slim few, have a tolerance to the toxin, and are eventually able to recover from its effects so long as they have not bled to death, though their subsequent mental and physical conditions can be quite disturbing. I think this must have been the case in the Peter Plogojowitz account. This was one of the more notorious cases of that Slavic vampire epidemic I mentioned, wherein townspeople were returning from the dead. I will give you some historical literature on the subject if you like...might make your recovery time in bed fly by.

"At any rate, the venom also has a succinylcholine-like

property, and causes long lasting skeletal muscle paralysis. The venom glands are activated by stretch receptors imbedded in the elastic tissue connected to the top of the canines. The sedative and paralytic properties of the venom facilitate efficient feeding, in that they make the prey passive and eventually immobile."

Sebastian clapped a hand to his brow and rubbed it down his face.

"Doc, doc...succinyl...what? I'm understanding everything pretty well so far, but you're starting to talk to me like I'm Stephen Hawking."

"Ahm...Stephen Hawking is a quadriplegic astrophysicist." Dr. Canterberry chimed in.

"I know that...you're missing the...never mind. Let's just... um...pick up where you left off."

"Perhaps we should call it a night," Dr. Canterberry remarked as he regarded Sebastian. "This is an ungodly hour to be up at after all."

"Are you kidding me, I won't be able to sleep for a second tonight, especially if you just cut me off now. You stopped after the glands and that. Please continue."

"I suppose...if you are certain you are all right," Dr. Canterberry said with a sigh.

He reached for his tea, took a generous sip, and placed the teacup back on the tray. Sebastian followed suit. Dr. Canterberry leaned towards the laptop again and closed the video file, only to open another, which he maximized as before. He played the video, which appeared to be an abdominal dissection, for the pallid subject's abdominal cavity had been opened like a saloon door from the midline, revealing two strange, thick-looking structures that ran the length of the cavity.

"This is the vampire stomach, or stomachs, to be precise." The doctor announced as he sat back on the stool. "They are not so much organs for digestion, but nutrient-rich reservoirs for blood. You see those two large, cylindrical chambers," asked Dr. Canterberry as he pointed to the screen. "Those are each capable of holding about three liters of blood, which when combined, is close to the blood volume of the average human, about five liters. The esophagus branches into two tubes, which each open into a cylindrical stomach. These stomachs join again, via two similar tubes, at the base of each. This common tube becomes a meager intestinal tract, then a colonic structure, and ends as...well...the anus.

"The most amazing thing about these two chambers is that they produce an electric current. An arrangement of minerals that bridge their bases and tops through the branching tubes, serve as electrodes, and the plasma within the chambers functions as a rudimentary alkaline electrolyte. In effect, the chambers act as a simplistic, organic version of a battery. The lining of each chamber is dense, and the inner lining acts as an insulator, preventing leakage of charge. The electrical output is relatively low mind you, not a surprise given its constitution, but it allows near perpetual reconstitution of energy-yielding molecules for a prolonged amount of time, and that is in addition to the calories they derive from feeding."

Dr. Canterberry pulled back the sleeve of his robe to glance at his watch. He reached for his teacup as he straightened on the stool. He finished his tea while Sebastian took a few sips from his own cup. The doctor placed his cup back on the tray, while Sebastian kept his own on his lap. In the video, the same gloved hands were prodding and manipulating the glistening stomachs with implements.

"Right then, what to next?...ahm...ah! Their sense of hearing and smell is commendable, as is their vision. The species can actually magnify objects in the distance that they are straining to see; this adaptation however is rather limited, especially when compared to...ahm...a bird of prey, for instance. Their eyes are very much like a starlight camera, in that their sensitivity permits them to see in the dark, so long as even the dimmest light source is present. Their eyes are so sensitive, in fact, that any length of exposure to intense sunlight would bleach their vision, making activity during the day impossible for the species."

Casting his gaze to the floor, Dr. Canterberry put his index finger to his mouth, evidently contemplating what he might discuss next. He raised that same index finger in the air when what he sought came to him, and he looked back up at Sebastian.

"Though they are on average smaller than human beings, their muscle density is about twenty-five percent greater than that of the average adult human male, and their bone density exceeds ours by about the same percentage. Their strength output for a given muscle is about three times as much as our own, allowing them to leap distances of about twenty feet from a standstill, and they can, in my estimation, run at approximately sixty-one kilometers per hour...ahm...thirty-eight miles per hour.

"To give you an appreciation of what kind of speed that is, the fastest human runs at about forty-four kilometers per hour, which is twenty-eight miles per hour. A greyhound runs at approximately sixty-three kilometers per hour. That is just over thirty-nine miles per hour."

"Jesus," whispered Sebastian with some amazement. The doctor continued.

"Not only that, but they can maintain their top speed for over a minute, and can keep a pace of just under fifty kilometers for over two hours. This is accomplished by that energy molecule reconstitution I mentioned, as well as effective skin breathing, and an incredible VO2 max...ahm...the capacity for oxygen usage in the tissue. The species can utilize ten percent of the oxygen drawn into their lungs without suffering any kind of free radical damage from that kind oxygen concentration. Again, as a yardstick, human beings utilize about five percent of the oxygen contained in the lung at full capacity. These capabilities allow the vampire to range over vast distances in search of prey and... oh...I will tack this on as well before I forget. They possess eidetic, photographic memory, so that in their minds exist vivid mental maps of their roving, and lucid recollections of the locations and tendencies of various human populations.

"Vampires tend to be solitary creatures, for only one to a few hunt a given population of humans, or at least it was that way until human communities began to grow past a certain size.

Nonetheless, they remain quite solitary even when sharing a prey population, hunting in numbers no greater than a pair...well... at least as far as I know. They tend to keep to a large territory, relatively close to a human population, until of course, they move on in search of...ahm...a mate perhaps, or whatever else may spur them on. Few and scattered as they are, finding one another is a lengthy process. Fortunately for them, they can live as long as two hundred years or more."

"What? Come on," blurted Sebastian.

"It is not so shocking really. Some parrots and lizards can live as long or longer than humans, a few species of tortoise can live to two hundred years, and sturgeons can even live to near three hundred years. Do you recall what I said could always be expected of nature?"

"Yeah. That it...um... can always find a way to surprise us."

"Precisely! And the most fantastic surprise, the most phenomenal aspect of this species, is secreted in the workings of their each and every cell."

Dr. Canterberry's eyes seemed to light up, and enthused, he leaned forward on the stool, occasionally gesticulating explanatorily as he spoke.

"I believe that vampires are the product of an extraordinary evolutionary history. I told you I had a theory that the species stemmed from a parasitic organism...ahm...and of course, you no longer have to remind me to discuss it. Anyhow, during a phase in my research, where I was trying to decipher a physiological explanation for the species' considerable longevity, I, along with a geneticist here at the facility...ahm...Dr. Ling, discovered lengthy sequences of genes, which correlated with those found in the nematode caenorhabditis elegans, or C elegans.

"There was enough similarity to conclude orthology, suggesting C elegans, or its predecessor, was a common ancestor. Oh...ahm...and in case you were wondering, a nematode is a parasitic worm of sorts, and C elegans in particular, possess a few key longevity genes, which we also identified within the sequences of genes from the vampire cell. Now, why would the genes of an organism that might have been something like a nematode, actively exist within the nucleus of a vampire cell?" With a speculative expression, Dr. Canterberry leaned in closer to Sebastian.

"Um…no idea. It doesn't really make sense to me." Answered Sebastian.

"Exactly!" Dr. Canterberry exclaimed as he tossed up his hands, as though reliving some past frustration. "Even more puzzling, was that the nematode-like DNA seemed to have been spliced with genetic information derived from some sort of viron. In fact, the cell behaved much like a virus in many ways and even had glycoprotein peplomers covering its surface, though the cell was without doubt eukaryotic. I also discovered this cell belonged to a particular cell type within the vampire that is genetically dissimilar to the majority of cells comprising the organism. For reasons that will become clearer in a moment, I called these virus-like cells…primordial cells.

"I would place a small collection of these cells in Petri dishes, submitting each sample to some test I deemed relevant, most of which I found were relatively inconsequential, save two. In a common nutrient bath, the primordial cells functioned and flourished as any other eukaryotic cell, dividing until they reached replicative senescence, an endpoint of cell division also know as the Hayflick limit. However, when I introduced human blood into a sample, the primordial cells would literally swallow or envelope all DNA-carrying cells in the blood through a process similar to both endocytosis and pinocytosis. The primordial cells would rupture the blood cells…ahm…they were mostly white blood cells…ahm…they would rupture the membrane and…sort of…filter feed on the cytoplasm and cell bodies before expelling excess substance for neighboring primordial cells to feed on. What was surprising and simply amazing, was what the primordial cell did with the bundle of human DNA in the blood cell nucleus. Now—"

"Doc, sorry to interrupt…um…eukaryotes? It's been a while since my last bio class."

"Not at all. They are simply a classification of more complex cells that belong to the animal, plant, fungi, and protist kingdoms. Ahm...I said that the primordial cells acted like a virus. A virus survives by attacking a host cell...ahm...penetrating it, and using the host cell's replicative machinery to reproduce exact copies of itself. The primordial cell does much the same after attacking the human host cell. However, the primordial cell actually incorporates its own genetic information into the human DNA sequence before replication.

"First, the primordial cell recognizes a portion of the human DNA chain, either by certain promoter regions on the DNA, or by sequence recognition...ahm...I am not exactly sure. The primordial cell then breaks the human DNA chain with an enzyme, just like cutting a rope, and moves much of its own DNA chain, which it severs with the same enzyme, between the break in the human DNA chain. Somehow, it reattaches the human chain onto itself, amplifying the chain with a specific length of its own primordial cell DNA in a process similar to transposition, where the primordial cell DNA acts as an incredibly lengthy transposon. Ahm..."

The doctor took a breath, as if he were going to continue on, but halted abruptly and gave Sebastian a thoughtful, inquiring look.

"Oh...no, I'm actually okay with this, I get it." Sebastian asserted.

Dr. Canterberry nodded.

"I should make it clear where exactly the primordial cell imposes its DNA on the human DNA chain. It does not simply graft itself between sequences that code for the entirety of the human being. Instead, it enters the chain at a point where genetic information ceases to be overtly utilized in the composition of the human form, and which is thus deemed junk DNA. Junk DNA is theorized to be potentially useful genetic information, where supposed vestigial genes can reemerge if selected for, via some beneficial mutation, to redirect an organism on a new evolutionary path.

"Anyhow…ahm…once the primordial cell transposes its own DNA into the human chain, a completely new genetic chain is formed. Like a virus, the primordial cell commandeers the human cell's genetic machinery, namely human enzymes, but proceeds to completely unwind the new DNA helix, split it down the middle and replicate it, as a human cell would naturally do before it divides. The cell does in fact divide, forming two cells of markedly different, and markedly more complex genetic composition to the original primordial cell.

"This new composition codes the cells for the vampire species. The resultant cells are of the cell type I mentioned earlier…ahm… the ones most prevalent in the vampire, and so I named them, quite aptly I would say, vampiric cells. Oh…how silly of me," muttered Dr. Canterberry as the reached for the touch pad on the laptop. "This last visual might help solidify your understanding of what I was blabbering on about."

He closed the video on the vampire stomachs, which had not yet ended, and opened another video file. This third video had been created using time-lapse photography under high magnification, as it displayed a collection of translucent, globular cells that quivered in some fluid matrix. One of the cells, evidently the focus of the video, had begun to engulf and drain another cell of a different type. As the primordial cell, which Sebastian inferred it must be, performed its function on the screen, Dr. Canterberry continued.

"My research has shown that the physiological make up of the vampire is similar to our own. Their muscular and skeletal structures are similar to our own, as well as host of their other organs. Cells belonging to their various organs are, like ours, specialized, and divide until they are no longer able. However, at the heart of each organ, or beneath their underlying tissues, are embedded a mass of primordial cells. These divide as irregularly as possible, as they can only replicate a finite number of times before reaching replicative senescence. They divide only to replace those primordial cells that belong to the most superficial layers of their ranks.

"These superficial primordial cells, closest to the organs' tissues, are those that are directly exposed to the organs source of nourishment....human blood. The blood brings with it human DNA-bearing cells that are attacked by the primordial cells as soon as they are brought into contact with them. Two vampiric cells are consequently produced after the division of each attacking primordial cell, ready to replace the damaged, or senescing, vampiric cells of that particular organ. The newly formed vampiric cells will also divide until their progeny reach replicative senescence. The process is discontinued only when the last of the primordial cells binds with a human cell, or of course, if the organism is killed."

Dr. Canterberry scratched his right temple, ruffling the comical tuft of grey-white hair on that side.

"What tends to be most difficult, is trying to deduce an accurate history of the species...ahm...I mean its evolutionary history in particular. Even the most skilled paleontologists would be hard pressed to find their remains, for aside from their relatively scant numbers, their bodies degenerate quite severely as they approach death, and their bones become so osteoporotic, that they are more fragile than a birds. And even if one were lucky enough to find skeletal fragments, they are so like a human's in proportion, that they could easily be mistaken for an early modern human's. The canine teeth, the most distinguishing features, fall out soon after decomposition, because if you recall, they are not actually rooted in the maxilla, as are the other teeth."

"What about the skull? The thing's forehead seemed somewhat different to me, kind of bony." Sebastian probed.

"That is a definite possibility, however, a deal of that thickness is muscle, and again, the bare skull, if not intact, could be mistaken for a known variety of hominid. Also, if my theory is correct, I would predict that some of the earliest remains are nonexistent and unfossilized. I mean, for a substantial portion of their evolutionary history, they may have bloody well have been soft-bodied parasitic creatures, regardless of how complex they became in comparison to something like C elegans."

"Okay, so how do they go from a worm or related parasite, to something so completely humanoid? I understand that they incorporate human structure, but...I mean, how could that happen?" Sebastian inquired.

"Again, this is mere speculation based on evidence, but the viral genetic information assimilated in the primordial cell suggests that differentiation from a common nematode began after a viral attack on a specific population of the parasitic ancestor. Ahm...these virons may have killed off much of this nemotode population, but perhaps a group with chance mutations survived the virus and carried on with it living within them. Viruses have been known to alter genes when they attack a host cell and perhaps, somehow, the change did not kill off these hosts.

"As has been the case throughout our discussion, this kind of thing is not uncommon in nature. Though it usually takes longer to accomplish, simplistic organisms, which have become symbiotic, can each become part of a single entity. Look at the algae that live inside many marine life forms, or a better example, the mitochondria that power our very cells. Even these are believed to have once been foreign bodies that have become part of our genetic makeup. I believe that a virally-induced change, in a population of prehistoric nematodes, allowed the survivors to acquire an ability to assimilate foreign genetic material into their cells.

"I am sure that in the beginning, the organism's capacity for this ability was meager, able only to recognize and incorporate tiny human transposons. I am also fairly certain that those best able to assimilate more complex genetic material, and thus enhance themselves, were those that survived...well...survived best at any rate.

"Now...ahm...perhaps this population lived in a dank cave, or...or well, somewhere where developing hominids, and pretty well only these hominids, were congregating. In an environment like that...ahm...they would have adapted a greater capacity to utilize a specific type of DNA, and again, those most able to enhance themselves survived. These would have gained greater mobility and intelligence, making it easier to feed upon, and avoid detection from, increasingly intelligent hominids. I imagine they transitioned from a primal nematode, to a larger, larval-looking organism, without pigment. Then perhaps to something like a... like a...naked mole rat perhaps, which might have later become something vaguely simian, though the organism was likely both relatively hairless and small. From there they might have transitioned into something resembling their current form, until they achieve what you have seen today.

"Obviously, as they were able to incorporate greater proportions of the hominid DNA, they would have gradually increased in size and, as I said before, in intelligence and mobility. They would have had to leave the hominid-inhabited caves... or wherever they were...and seek shelter from the sun in other caves or elsewhere. They would have had, especially given their growing size, to have become increasingly predatory rather than parasitic. At some point, they must have reached a stage where they were reconstituting themselves with such a great percentage of the hominid DNA, that some gained a further adaptation. They became able to simply graft a specific portion of their DNA into the hominid chain, as I elaborated upon earlier. So, what had once been nematode-like creatures were: one, evolving as accomplished parasites, two, assimilating the evolutionary advancements of the homininds they fed upon, and three, evolving as complete organisms as well...as vampires.

"This is, of course, a gross generalization, for the evolution of any organism is an intricate series of chance mutations and... ahm...environmental compatibilities, through whose capricious devices an organism's function and form is unwittingly molded. What I am trying to stress however, is that through its rather unique ability to manipulate its genetic structure, the species was able to, in a manner of speaking, fast track their evolution. We took over six and a half million years to become what we are today, from a structurally similar primate form. The vampires transitioned from mere soft-bodied parasites to complex humanoid organisms within that same time frame."

Admittedly, some of what had been said had gone over his head, however, Sebastian decided that he was impressed with Dr. Canterberry's historical overview.

"If that truth isn't the whole truth, but even something like it is true..." Sebastian remarked with a knowing smile, "...damn. By the way, that was...that was all pretty detailed for an estimation of their history." He emphasized *estimation* jokingly. "You really do spend all of your time in this stuff, huh?"

"Oh, I have no life. I can admit it." Dr. Canterberry said amusedly. "Well, at least not in the conventional sense."

The cell culture video had stopped and the screen had become a still, blurred, image of clustered cells. While conversing with Sebastian, Dr. Canterberry had leaned forward, closed the video file, and shut down the laptop. A melodic chiming issued from the laptop as it powered down and the screen went dark. Dr. Canterberry closed the laptop and it shut with a sharp click.

"I can't believe no one else knows about this. I can't believe these things have been living around me and I haven't seen them."

"Well," said Dr. Canterberry reassuringly. "No one has really, especially not on this continent. The species has its beginnings somewhere in Africa, and they spread through the Middle East, Russia, and Europe afterward. Theoretically, those that managed to make it to the Americas might have stowed away on ships, or perhaps a few followed the small, nomadic, human contingents across the Bering Strait." The doctor shrugged with an almost bemused expression. "At this point, I believe anything is plausible."

"What if they built their own ships to sail over here?"

Dr. Canterberry allowed himself a polite, single chuckle.

"Ahm...that, as much as I believe anything is plausible, is impossible."

"Why?" argued Sebastian. "They could have gotten together, built a ship at night and sailed it at night, too."

"Well...ahm...their solitary nature aside, they possess the functional intelligence of a three- or four-year-old child. They are infinitely more intelligent than their parasitic ancestors, but they are not as intelligent as human beings, at least not yet."

"Oh. Then why the hell can't anybody find them if they are so simple minded?"

"They are relatively few in number and they are nocturnal predators, stealth is their livelihood. Even when they are in diapause—" Even before Sebastian could inquire, Dr. Canterberry was explaining the term to him. "Sorry...ahm...diapause is the low metabolic state the species falls into during the daylight hours, it is more like hibernation than sleep really. Anyhow, when they are in diapause, they are often underground, and are always well hidden from human eyes. I am sure, at some level, they are instinctually elusive as well. Ahm...and with regard to their mental capacities, do not be fooled. They are still a highly intelligent organism, and from what I have gleaned from behavioral studies, historical accounts, and relatively recent reports, their cognitive faculties seem to be improving. This is a species that has, for the most part, in secret, hunted the most intelligent beings on the planet for countless nights. They might not score very high on an IQ test, but I assure you, certain of their mental capabilities, though few, function at a level beyond our own."

"What's your IQ, just out of curiosity?"

"Bah. That is such a frivolous assessment of mental ability... around two hundred, give or take." Dr. Canterberry replied casually.

"You know what else I'm curious about?"

"Pray tell."

"Your boss."

"Ah."

"Yeah...um...Gabriel."

"Gabriel." Dr. Canterberry muttered with a drawn out expiration. "Hmm...well, what would you like to know?"

"Aw come on, doc. Whatever you were going to tell me...like... what the hell was he doing in the middle of a SWAT op? What is he? Why and how is he? That kind'a crap."

"Well, Gabriel's presence during your tactical operation was unforeseen, I assure you. We do our best to stay under the radar, not leap headlong above it. Gabriel learned the relative location of a fairly new band of drug traffickers in the area from a street ruffian who he…well…got the information from. Anyhow, it was a matter of sheer coincidence that he happened to find them on the same evening your precinct sanctioned the operation. His powers of observation are usually quite profound, but I suppose with all the vehicles being unmarked and scattered some distance from the actual warehouse, he did not recognize that an operation was in effect…and I obviously had not noted anything either…until that man put a gun to my window."

"So, why was he looking for drug traffickers anyway?" Sebastian inquired with a furrowed brow.

"He….you know what, upon consideration, I believe I will let him tell you himself, tomorrow perhaps. As it is, I have been negligent in my duties in providing proper hospice. Here I am conversing with you into the morning hours, when I should have let you sleep in silence through them."

"Doc!" Sebastian interjected pleadingly and was about to disapprove, when Dr. Canterberry raised a hand firmly.

"Ah ah! It is a finality, I am afraid. Get some rest. Your body desperately needs it. I will be back to check on you tomorrow…or later today, more accurately."

Dr. Canterberry was suddenly quite serious.

"You have been given a wealth of information today, Sebastian, more than enough information to wrap your head about for one day. You will learn all there is to know to the fullest, in time. For now, goodnight."

With that, Dr. Canterberry took the near-empty teacup from Sebastian's hand and placed it on the tray. Then, he picked up the laptop, tucked it under his arm and turned on the stool so that he could lift the tray with both hands. With the tray resting in the palms of his hands, he rose from the stool and made his way to the door. For a moment, he balanced the tray in a single, splayed hand as he opened the door. Dr. Canterberry glanced over his shoulder at Sebastian, though he did not actually look at him.

"The bathroom is the first on your right, make sure you hold your IV firmly as you wheel it over if you need to go."

Dr. Canterberry closed the door behind him. The door was left unbolted, though this time Sebastian knew that it was purposely done.

# Chapter Eleven
## Interloper

## I

As before, he awoke slowly as his body revived from its torpor. Adequately wakeful, he rose in the darkness and reached for the stone slab above. Once his palms were firmly placed against the underside of the slab, he lifted it and slid it aside. He sprung up gracefully from the darkness and half leapt, half hauled himself up onto the stone lip of the uncovered tomb. Perched on hand and foot upon the lip of the tomb, he squinted and blinked for some moments in the twilight brilliance. Once again, as though he were slave to some inescapable design and rhythm, he had risen in time to see the last of the blazing orange sun sinking into the west. His eyes adjusted to the world above the tomb, his pupils contracting into black pinpricks within the golden orbs of his eyes. In one smooth motion, he was off the tomb and standing on the bare, cool earth. Unlike the previous night, during the course of which he had not fed, he felt the beginnings of hunger, or something like hunger, making itself known within him. The sensation, though compelling, was still tolerable, but was definitively more acute than it had been the previous night.

He reminisced upon the previous night, recalling its events with astounding clarity. He looked up into the darkened sky and reflected upon his grim intentions for the night ahead. The night was young and full of possibility, and he wondered how it might end. Time and again he had prayed, to God, to the Savior, to his angels. He had asked them what they expected of him, or intended for him, for he had been certain he was a thread woven into some celestial plan, no matter how cruel and horrid his plight might seem. They did not answer him through words, but by signs, for surely, it was more than mere caprice that had led him to the demon's very doorstep.

He stared out over the graveyard towards Berwick and thought of his home beyond the town wall. He thought about his friends and, as he had been doing more frequently of late, he thought of Bronwyn. He wondered if before he set out to hunt down the demon, he should find his way to Bronwyn. This night might very well be his last, and if he should shun her, for fear that she turn from him in revulsion and fright, he would miss what could be the last chance for him to ever lay eyes upon her again. If she should abhor him, he would simply bid her a final farewell, and over time, should he live so long, let her memory fade from his mind. He turned his attention to the tomb before him. Lowering himself towards it, he gripped the sides of the stone slab. He lifted the hefty stone and began to move it back over the open tomb. The slab ground against the lip of the tomb, disturbing the gentle quiet of the twilight hour. He turned from the tomb and began to distance himself from it at an unhurried yet purposeful pace. Coursing through the graveyard like a pale shadow, the sentry slunk through the growing darkness towards the town of Berwick Upon the Tweed.

\* \* \* \*

With the graveyard behind him, he approached the town wall, and crouched low as he drew nearer. His black hair flitted gently behind his ears as he ran, his footfalls the mere whisper of a presence. Upon the wall, guardsmen patrolled the parapet walk, but each was stationed no less than three stone throws apart from the other. Their sallet helms and mail gleamed dimly in the last light of the day, and when still, they were as silhouetted, protective statues, jutting up from the wall. Their presence upon the wall was unusual. Perhaps the town lord had been unsettled by events yet unknown to him, save, of course, the recent sounding of the horn.

Having chosen a path that, in his estimation, bisected the distance between two guardsmen, the sentry stole directly towards them through the soft, shadowy grasses, which stretched before the town wall.

Even if their sallet helms had not obscured the faint, primeval sounds of the dawning night, they would have been hard pressed to detect the deft footfalls, which slowed into eerily silent steps as what approached transitioned from a prowl to a resolute stalk. The two guardsmen looked out over the darkened expanse before them, though not necessarily with their full attention. Teeth clenched, one guardsman scratched at his scraggly beard. The other, a younger man, was adjusting the position of his crossbow about his shoulders. Perhaps if they had heard the indistinct rustling of something on approach, they might have seen the flimsy, waist high grasses parting and wavering ever so discreetly, ever so quietly, and ever closer. Had they but looked betwixt one another along the wall, they may have seen a large, ghostly form erupt from the darkness and rise through the air, up to the verge of the wall. They would have seen the pale wraith cling to the cold stone for the scarcest of moments with hands and feet, before watching it fling itself over the wall, onto the very parapet walk on which they stood. In the time it takes one to blink, they would have seen it leap from the parapet into the town, alighting and then vanishing into a peaceful and darkened Berwick.

Out of the corner of his eye, the younger of the two guardsmen thought he had seen something disturb the tranquil stillness of the night. It was more a fleeting impression of movement than anything else, and when he turned towards it, there was naught to be found but a barren stretch of the wall. In the distance, atop the wall, he could scarcely make out Malcolm's form, but could not discern what exactly Malcolm was doing. Regardless, it did not seem that he had seen anything either, and he began to wonder if he had actually witnessed something of substance in the first place. He looked behind him into the town and along either side of the wall where his vision was not obstructed from his position. Seeing nothing and feeling somewhat on edge, he began to patrol his length of the parapet walk once more.

# II

The sentry wound his way through the town, skirting along the sides of the small brick and daub dwellings, keeping to their cast shadows and darkened alleyways. Some homes and other larger constructs of stone and wood were lit by flickering lanterns, but most of the town was bathed only by the growing light of the moon and stars. All townsfolk should, by all accounts, have been in their homes or in taverns. However, the patrolling guard was of such a meager number, that they could not possibly monitor all of Berwick. As a result, the earthen streets, though relatively quiet, were not entirely empty, and the sentry was forced, now and again, to sit still in the shadows, as vagrants, drunken merrymakers, and other townsfolk passed him by. He knew the town quite well, and skulked through it judiciously, traveling only through those areas that he was certain would provide him the greatest concealment.

Some atavistic part of him wanted to flee, to escape this place of men and seek solace in the wilds and the dark. His heart however, at least for the most part, rejoiced at being back amongst the people, hearing their voices and laughter as he passed them, unnoticed, in the town's back alleys. He surmised that most of the townsfolk he had passed were headed home for the night from the tavern, for the town was devoid of life and silent. He quickened his pace, loping through the streets in a low crouch: his arms barely swinging, bent at the elbows and balanced near his sides. He stared forward intently with lurid eyes, which upon occasion, broke their fixed gaze as he fossicked his surroundings anxiously.

His attentiveness was rewarded, for as he neared the smithy, he heard and then saw a figure stepping into his path from between two stone domiciles, less than ten paces away. Before the man cleared the stone structures, the sentry had, from his coiled crouch, leapt from the narrow alley. The only evidence that he had ever been there were two, small, indistinct clouds of dust, which swirled, then settled on the dry ground below.

* * * *

After a discreet and intimate visit with the tanner's daughter, the man was making his way home. He had lain with the tanner's daughter longer than he had anticipated, for, evidently, night had fallen upon the town. To avoid possible detection from gossiping neighbors and, though less likely, patrolling guards, he elected to course the tight, winding passages between the town's smaller and unfailingly unlit homes. He left the tanner's house as quietly as he could and walked between it and an adjacent stone dwelling, heading towards his intended course home. He adjusted his brownish, woolen shirt, pridefully recalling his sultry engagement. As he rounded the corner behind the tanner's home, he though he heard a faint rustle. He looked up and saw that the alley was empty.

He stared about for a moment, lest he had missed some hidden bandit, and was relieved when he heard a clucking sound. He watched as stray hen strutted into the alley some distance away and then continued on his way, wondering if he could catch the hen without causing to great a commotion.

Having remained unseen directly above where the man had passed, the pallid sentry rose slowly from the straw of an overhanging, thatched roof. The straw-colored thatch and his skin both seemed a blue-grey-white under the soft glow of the moon. The sentry watched the man depart and then dropped quietly from roof, followed by a few disturbed threads of thatch.

* * * *

He reached the smithy without further encounters. The large wooden smithy itself was quiet and the wooden shutters were all closed for the night. He approached the smithy tentatively, searching the surrounding area for any who might spot him. Seeing and sensing nothing, he eyed one of the four, thick wooden pillars that supported each corner of the smithy. He crept forward, and staring up concentratedly at a single point on the pillar, he crouched and then sprang upwards towards it. His hands and feet clamped onto either side of pillar, their hard, blackened nails holding fast to the wood. Smooth and nimble, with a soft scratching sound like a squirrel scuttling over bark, he began to climb a corner of the smithy. The transverse lengths of wood that comprised the walls jutted out unevenly near the edge of the pillar on either side, and he simply used them to aid his ascent.

As he pulled himself, in silence, onto the roof of the smithy, he wondered if Bronwyn were even there, and what he would say to her even if she was. Bronwyn's quarters overlooked the slate-shingled roof of the smithy, as did Colin's. With this in mind, he had climbed the side of the smithy closest to her window, so that Colin's own was the furthest from his position. The second floor of the stone dwelling rose a little distance above the roof of the smithy, to which it was conjoined. The smithy had been built against the stone home so that the sills of the two large bedroom windows rested only a few hands span above the roof of the smithy. The wooden shutters of Bronwyn's window were wide open, as she usually left them on beautiful summer nights.

Still on hand of foot, he crawled almost noiselessly up the sloped roof towards the open window, which seemed to him both inviting and unnerving. As he drew nearer to the window, he was increasingly able to see into the chamber beyond, and a familiar scent reached his nostrils. His eyes pervaded the darkness and he saw the hide flap that covered Bronwyn's door. He saw the stone walls of her quarters and they were tinted a bluish grey in the faint light that reached them. He saw her bed, similarly illumined at the heart of a pool of moonlight, but brightly so. Kneeling at the bedside, her back to him, and moonbeams filtering through her wavy, auburn locks, was Bronwyn.

His heart fluttered at the sight of her. His gaze unwaveringly fixed upon her, he stole up to the open window, and slowly, silently, crept up onto the windowsill so that he came to rest in the window crouched on all fours, his head bowed in the incommodious opening. His amber eyes peered up from his hanging head and through the black tendrils of hair that hung over his face. He sat in the window for a few moments, tenderly observing Bronwyn's still form, with a mounting feeling that she: her gown, her walls, everything, seemed, in some way, surreal. With a fluent, synchronous movement of both arms, he placed his palms against the insides of the window. Thus braced against the cool stone, he slowly, hesitantly lowered a pale foot to the wooden floor.

Bronwyn had lost herself in prayer, as she often did whilst praying so whole-heartedly. She finished her heavenly commune with a final prayer, and crossed herself slowly, as if prolonging the moment of blessing. She opened her eyes and rose from her knees. As she did so, she observed her shadow, which cast itself over the bed and onto the base of the far wall. It seemed strange to her, large and imposing as though it were another's shadow cast over hers. She had not yet even finished the thought before she heard a voice, low and somber, speak her name in a chilling whisper. She gasped and spun round to see a large figure standing before her, no more than a few arms lengths from where she had risen.

The figure was vaguely silhouetted in the moonlight, but she could make out a grim, half-naked form, with a skin of deathly pallor. She recoiled from the specter, and a choking sound issued from her throat as her breath caught in her chest. Her limbs seemed to lose their strength and her bowels knotted and burned with fear. She wanted to cry out, but she could not, and she simply stared, open-mouthed and wide-eyed at the figure before her. She stumbled backward upon her bed, unable to take her eyes from the shadowy obscurity that was the figure's face, as though she were entranced by her fear. As she fell, the figure took a step towards her and, for an instant, thought she saw two fiery eyes glint within the figure's darkened visage. As the figure moved, the moonlight played over his whitish, muscular form, and his features became increasingly discernable. He outstretched his hand pleadingly as he leaned in towards her, and spoke in a soft voice, both terrifying and soothing, and somehow, oddly familiar.

"Bronwyn, please...do not be afraid, I will not harm you, I would never harm you. It's me...I...I know this is strange and frightening for you...it is for me as well, but...it is me."

At first, Bronwyn could only stare at him from where she had fallen upon the bed. She was nearly still as stone with fear, though her hands and lips trembled noticeably. Her breaths were erratic gasps, which became spastic sobs, and she put a trembling hand to her mouth as her eyes welled and glimmered with tears.

"Please, Bronwyn, do not fear me." He said softly and sorrowfully.

Bronwyn cleared a quivering tangle of auburn hair from her blanched face, upon which, the first of her tears had begun to stream.

"I know how horrid I must appear to you. I...I know how different I am, but look at me Bronwyn...in your heart...you must know it is me."

Her voice was a quavering whimper, nearly lost in her sobs.

"B...but...I...I...saw ye die. I...I...held y...yer dead body in mi'arms and...and I sa...I saw ye buried i'the ground. H...How can ye be here?...How...how can ye be?"

"I do not know myself," he whispered. "Everything is so strange now. I am...changed, but I am no ghost, no spirit. I am flesh and blood like you, like I was."

He sunk to a knee by the bedside, and slowly, fondly, he extended a pale hand towards her, his white palm upturned. She regarded his hand nervously and followed the strange talon with her eyes as he found her hand and took it up gently in his. A few short, quiet sobs escaped her as she looked at the savage hand that held her own so delicately, and she lifted her eyes to gaze upon his face. She could see him quite clearly now, and though his face was pallid, and his eyes like stark, yellow gems, to her he was no less beautiful than he had ever had been.

His piercing eyes searched her face, as if they hoped to gain some insight into her innermost thoughts and feelings. She looked back down at his hand and, somewhat hesitantly, placed her free hand overtop of it. Slowly, tentatively, she ran her hand along his smooth arm and shoulder, and as though in a daze, watched her trembling hand as it slid over his milky skin. She raised the same hand to his face, waved a few strands of black hair from his eyes with her fingers, and placed her hand on his face. She ran the tips of her fingers down one side of his face, staring intently at the smooth skin underneath.

"Somehow...it really is ye, isn't it?" She said softly. "Wha... wha'is this then, some kind'o miracle er something? I...I do'ne understand."

"Miracle?" He looked down at his hand then back up at her. "Perhaps...at least, that is what I have begun to believe."

"Wha'de ye mean? Wha'led ye te feel this way?" She asked with imploring eyes.

"I...well...one night...You recall that night I came here wounded, when Colin and Ober were in the smithy?" She nodded. "The night before that, fiendish...creatures fell upon me in the night, at my post outside the town. They were so...savage, so hellish in nature, that I can find no more fitting a word for them...than demons. In the end, I slew one, though I very nearly died that night myself. The other took flight into the wood upon the approach of the town guard. After that night, I believe some fate intended for me was sealed."

He told her of his rebirth from the earth: of his long night of prayer underneath the stone angel, of omens, and of what he believed God intended for him. Bronwyn watched him as he spoke, watched his lips move and his eyes regarding hers. She listened to his voice and touched his cool, smooth skin, and yet she could barely believe he was truly kneeling before her. When he had finished his tale, she was silent for a time. She slid from her bed, and kneeling at his side, she drew close to him, looking up into his eyes as though the mysteries of the universe were revealed within their golden depths. She ran her hands along his sides to his back, and resting a tear-streaked cheek on his bare chest, she held herself against him in a tender embrace; her touch, her warmth made his heart beat like a destrier's in his chest. He closed his eyes and rested his face in her thick, fiery hair. He wreathed her in his powerful arms, and they held each other for some time in the argent pool of moonlight, as though time itself streamed and roiled around them, as ineffectual as a brook lapping against a rock. Bronwyn listened to his beating heart, and wondered if she were dreaming - if she might soon wake. By and by, she spoke, her voice a tired whisper upon his chest.

"If...if ye are te go te seek tha creature, if ye really must, if it is yer callin as ye say, then...then ye'll be needin yer sword."

She lifted her head from his chest and looked up at him dreamy eyed. He looked down at her fondly.

"You kept my sword?"

"Well...Ober had it, and was going te sell it eventually, but I had ne a thing else te remember ye by, ne like tha. It remined me so much of ye, tha I could'ne bear te let it go."

She sniffled and wiped her tears with a hand. She rose, turned from him, and walked around the foot of the bed to the opposite bedside. He stood as well, and watched as she crouched beside the bed and reached at something with both hands. He heard a scraping sound, that of weighty metal over wood. Bronwyn's arms tensed and she rose once more. In her hands was his sword, the blade firmly sheathed in its scabbard, and hanging from it, still attached to the hide fastenings, was his old leather belt. She held the sword before her, cradled in her upturned palms. She glanced down at the sword, then looked up at him and made her way towards him once more. As she neared him, she extended her arms in offering, holding the great sword out towards him. The sentry reached out with a single hand and clutched the scabbard. Gently, he lifted the blade from Bronwyn's hands and stared at it reverently. He held the sword at his left hip and let it dangle from the leather belt as he grasped the two ends of the belt with either hand, preparing to fasten it around his waist. Bronwyn watched the sentry adorn himself with the sword.

"I still do'ne know what te think er feel. Whether te be afraid, er joyful, er te believe tha'this is some workin o'the Lord, er the blackest o'magics."

The sentry raised his head and looked at her. She was trying to smile as she struggled to restrain the fresh tears welling in her eyes.

"How...how de ye know tha'this was all God's doin?" She asked worriedly.

"I do not," said he. "I can only have faith."

With his sword secured to his side, he stepped towards her and embraced her a final time, kissing her forehead as he held her and relishing her lovely scent. He let his arms slide from her back, and with his hands, held her gently about the shoulders. He stared at her with his piercing eyes, and his gaze caused her breaths to quaver.

"Bronwyn, tell no one I was here, promise me. God knows what people might say."

"O'course...I'll ne tell a soul, but...wha'about Colin, should I tell him ye came, tha'yer alive, about all o'this?"

"Should I survive this night, I will tell him myself in the coming days. For now, I shall be your secret to keep."

He kissed her brow once more, filling his lungs with her scent. He released her shoulders and took a few steps away from her, backing towards the open window. She stood stalk still, trembling ever so subtly and staring at him wide eyed.

"Will I see ye again? Will ye come back te me?" She asked desolately.

"If...If that is what you wish, what you truly wish." He glanced down at his dark-clawed, ghostly hands, then looked upon her once more. "Then, God willing, I will return to you."

He turned from her to face the open window and looked out over town. He reached out with both arms and grasped the sides of the stone window frame, then lifted a leg and placed his bare foot upon the windowsill. Moonlight streamed over his body, lambent over the hard, twisted muscles of his back. He hesitated for a moment, and peered at Bronwyn over his shoulder, yet his eyes never met her teary gaze. He stared back out into the night and pulled himself gracefully into the open window. All was silent, save the scrape of the sentry's sword against cold stone, as he leaped from the open window and plunged into the sleeping town.

Bronwyn took a small step towards the window, one hand at her breast, the other, fingers trembling, she held over her mouth. Tears fell freely from her flushed cheeks as she stared out the open, empty window.

"Goodbye." She whispered to herself, still staring out into the darkness.

\* \* \* \*

After a night of drunken revelry, Colin had fallen into a deep, undignified sleep in his bed. His fiery hair was a strewn mess, and his mouth hung agape, leaking spittle out of one corner. Beside him, her arm across Colin's bare chest, was the wench he had brought home from the tavern to prolong his night's merriment. She had not imbibed nearly so much as Colin had, and her unfamiliar surroundings made her slumber light. She had not been asleep long before she awoke, and lying in bed somewhat restlessly, she pulled the sheets over her nakedness. The wooden shutters over the large window had not been shut, at least, not properly. One side was ajar, and occasionally it would creak and rattle against the other; as restless as she was, the faint noises began to bother her.

She huffed frustratedly and slipped out from underneath the sheets. She strode to the window silently. Streaks of moonlight filtered in from the opening between the shutters, illuminating her strikingly slender, naked form. As she reached out to close and lock the shutters, she thought she heard voices from somewhere on the roof near the Scotsman's sister's window. She covered her chest with one arm, and gently placed her other hand between the shutters. She was quite nervous, but her curiosity compelled her, and widening the opening between the shutters ever so slightly and quietly, she leaned forward and peered through the moonlit slit. She was now certain she heard whispering voices off to the left of the window she peered through, though they did not sound from the roof, but rather from the window of the neighboring room.

From where she peered out over the roof with her beady eyes, she could not see into the other window, for it was built into the face of the same stone wall as the Scotsman's. She was leery of craning her head out the window, lest she be seen by any roving townspeople, or by the occupants within the next room themselves. Thus, she continued to peep through the gap between the shutters. Though she could not see into the open window, she could see that the shutters had been flung wide open, yet the voices which emanated from the opening were still quite indistinct. She was about to return to the warmth of the Scotsman's bed, when a movement in the neighboring window caught her eye. She could not rightly tell what they were, but two pale things, and she reasoned that they were hands, clasped the insides of the window. Before she had ascertained that the strange hands were indeed hands, they were followed by an equally pale foot, which planted itself upon the sill. A face appeared in the window, the profile of which was ghastly in appearance, yet somehow familiar.

Horrified, she withdrew from the window, her breath pent in her chest. She believed she had seen the man before in the tavern, and at odd occasions around the town. She had also heard it told that this same man had perished from illness the previous week, and the thought sent a chill down her spine. From the adjacent window, she heard a sudden, muffled scraping sound, that of metal over stone. Still shaken with fear, she dared to look between the shutters once more, in time to see the man's barebacked, ghostly form leap from the roof and vanish beyond it. She gasped and stepped away from the window. Affrighted, she closed then locked the shutters and crawled back into bed. Under the sheets, she pressed her tremulous body against the sleeping Scotsman's and buried her head into his chest.

# III

The sentry made his way back through the quiet town. It seemed to him that the town was devoid of people, more so than before, and he stole swiftly through his circuitous return route. His left hand clutched the hilt and scabbard of his sword, and he pinned the weapon against his side, so that it did not clatter as he slipped through the darkened alleys. As before, he ran in a low crouch, sprinting silently around corners and over obstacles at an unfaltering pace.

Before he saw anything at all, he heard their chants, like mournful laments, which droned from somewhere nearby. He slowed to a cautious lope, his eyes searching. The warm glow of firelight began to color the maze of passages before him, dancing and flickering upon the surrounding walls. Long shadows began to appear in the mounting effulgence, and he halted his approach, pressing his back to a wall near a juncture of passageways. He leaned forward to peer around the corner of the wall to which he had entrusted his back, and saw that, moving towards his position, was a procession of monks - perhaps a dozen or so. Some held large, burning torches, from which plumes of black smoke spiralled up into the night sky. They were attired in linen robes, some a color that might once have been white, the others an earthy brown. Some were hooded and those not, were as bearded, unkempt mendicants, lacking the clean bald crowns typical of monks. Their chants grew louder as they approached, wailing moans most unbecoming of men of the cloth.

The sentry withdrew from the corner and glanced up at the roof above him, thinking to employ his earlier stratagem. This particular roof however, was higher than the last, for sleeping quarters had been built over the shop. He looked about for structures of lesser height. Instead, his eyes came to rest upon a ruined wagon he spotted behind him, which was lacking one of its large, wooden wheels and was propped against the wall. Without a moment's hesitation he darted towards it and leapt up to its highest point. No sooner did a foot touch the wagon, than he sprang from it with a single, explosive effort, so that he rose through the air towards the roof. He raised his legs out before him like a stooping hawk, his arms spread wide to steady him. He alighted upon the slate shingles on all fours, and they clinked softly underneath him.

Careful to keep his weight on the wooden supports underneath the shingles, he crept to the verge of the slanted rooftop and peered over the shingles that hung near the edge. Below, the procession of robed men was passing directly underneath him. He noticed that all of the men carried lashes, their flailing tails fixed with nails, hooks, or shards of metal. As they walked, they slung their whips over their backs, flogging themselves as they trudged along. The metal bits and implements at the ends of the lashes shredded their robes and slashed their backs, spattering blood over their exposed skins. A baser side of him observed their spilt blood with marked attention. The pain in their sorrowful chants was clearly rooted in their masochism, and he grimaced as he watched the disturbed congregation.

These men of perverse piety were the flagellants, a dying sect of religious zealots whose inception could be credited to the scourge of the black plague. The plague had passed through Northumberland well over a hundred years ago, and though he had heard it said that in distant lands it still took the lives of men, neither he, nor any with whom he had spoken, had ever bore witness to anything of the like. The flagellants believed that mankind was rife with sin and that the ancient plague had been sent by God to cull the sinful from those worthy of His grace. They believed that only by suffering as Christ had, could mankind find salvation and escape the wrath of God.

From his vantage on the roof, he saw one man look to the night sky, raising an empty, crooked hand to the stars. The sentry lowered his head and shoulders closer to the shingles and wondered if the old man had spotted him. But the old man only ranted to the heavens, proclaiming the demise of humanity for their sinful transgressions, and warning of God's wrath: a second coming of the black death.

The flagellants began to file into the darkened passageway below him, their backs to him and their torches lighting the way. He had never felt pity for these wretches, and felt even less for them now. He was suddenly aware of a compelling sensation from his body and his instinct to feed began to grow within him. The compulsion did not possess his reason, nor was the instinct untenable. Quite simply, he saw no reason to restrain himself for the deluded wretches below. As the last few flagellants passed underneath him, he brought himself closer to the edge of the roof.

The way he moved had changed, even the very look of his face. His gaze was piercing, solemn and cold - his movements, purposeful and insidious. His eyes had fixed themselves on the small, bearded man tailing the procession. He was weak, held no torch, and was the last of the congregation by a few paces. He watched as the man flogged himself, and heard him whimper under the lash. The sentry watched as the little man turned his back on him to follow his fellow flagellants. In that moment, the sentry pounced from the roof, his eyes never straying from his quarry. With a soft thud, he landed, cat-like behind the man.

The grim laments of the chanting flagellants carried through the night air, and so masked the subtle sounds of the sleeping town. Behind them, a ghostly form descended upon their congregation from above, alighting upon the dusty ground, only just beyond the last of their brethren.

The small, bearded man thought he heard some indistinct sound behind him that was accompanied by the slightest of tremors underfoot and a faint rush of air, which coolly caressed his searing, bloodied back. Before the man could turn to investigate the disturbance, something seized him with violent force and snatched him from where he had stood.

The sentry lashed out like a striking serpent from behind his quarry. He slung one powerful arm about the flagellant's neck, nearly breaking it, and simultaneously swung his other hand around towards the flagellant's mouth to stifle any sound the man might make. The open palm of his white hand struck the flagellant's face with such force, that the bony bridge of the man's nose splintered under the flesh and blood burst from the man's splayed nostrils. With the same hand, he clutched the face of the half conscious flagellant in a vice-like grip. Even as he grasped the man, he was headed back into the shadows, and so, lunging backward off powerful legs, he hauled the man from his feet by the head and neck, and spirited him in the darkness.

In the briefest moment, where once a man had stood, only a fallen lash remained, its bloodied ends sprawled out over the ground under a whirling cloud of dust.

Behind the robed flagellants, the ghostly form slipped into shadowy obscurity with one of their brethren in its clutches, and finally vanished beyond what might have been an old, broken wagon.

# Chapter Twelve
## Vengeance

## I

A gentle wind had blown in from the coast, forcibly coaxing the grasses and leaves to sway and tremble in its wake. Their susurrations were as a symphony of whispers as they bowed to the breeze. The young guardsman sauntered atop the wall upon the parapet walk, his back to Malcolm, who was barely discernable from where he stood on the wall. Equally vague, and entirely ephemeral, was the abrupt and noiseless reappearance of the grim specter as it passed unseen betwixt them once more. Feeling that he had patrolled the wall a sufficient distant in his current direction, the young guardsman pivoted on a foot and continued his patrol back the opposite way. Neither he nor Malcolm noticed the pale specter as it stole through the tall, dry, moonlit grass, nor witnessed the subtle spectacle of its evanescence into the dark expanse beyond.

\* \* \* \*

The soft tufts of seeds pods, which swayed atop the long grass like a forest of furred pennants, brushed gently against the underside of his chest and neck as he swept through them in a low crouch. Once again, he reviled what he had done, and yet he could not ignore the wondrous vitality that pulsed through his veins. His dichotomous perceptions and emotions wore each other to a stalemate of reason in his mind, and so he thought of Bronwyn instead. As he was rapt in thought, the long grass below him began to transition into a green expanse of short, soft grasses as he distanced himself from the town wall. Having withdrawn into the steppe, beyond the reach of the guardsmen's eyes, he straightened from his skulking crouch to gain ground at a greater pace. He did not pass through the graveyard.

Instead, he made his way towards the Tweed directly, coursing its path inland. As he had before, he strayed from the Tweed to steer clear of Berwick Castle before regaining his westward path along the borderlands. His heart pounded, his breaths were deep and steady. At his side, his sword rattled faintly in its scabbard. He paid it no heed, but simply stared, dour and stone-faced, towards whatever fate lay ahead. His black hair streamed behind him and his legs pounded against the earth in rapid succession, as he raced across the grassy plains.

He reached the forest and without a moment's rest, or hesitation, plunged into its shadowy depths. He weaved amidst the trees, here and there disturbing the perfect shafts of moonlight, which streaked through the black canopy above like giant, ethereal blades from the heavens. The flora sang harsh, susurrant songs in the wake of his passing, as he tore through brush and hanging leaves alike. Through the trees, he could see the moonlit meadow stretching before him as he neared the limits of the forest. He burst out from amongst the trees and shadows and without so much as a break in his stride, raced across the meadowland towards the precipitous, rocky hills, which loomed in the distance. All around him, the chirps and shrill songs of crickets filled the night air, yet he barely heard them, despite his keen ears. He swept across the meadow on a direct path towards the colossal hill, the hill upon which he had seen the demon. The meadow was increasingly dotted with rocks and boulders as he approached the great hillock, and it was not long before he reached the foot of the eminence.

\* \* \* \*

He stood stark still, though his chest heaved with breath as he filled his lungs. He gazed up at the pass between the crags, which he knew he must reach. The pass was not entirely visible from where he stood, but he had kept a sharp eye on the spot even as his perspective became such that the pass itself was hidden. Knowing what lurked high above, made the looming eminence before him imposing and foreboding. The slightest pangs of doubt began to prickle in his gut, but he disregarded them, strode forward, and began his ascension.

He moved slowly and quietly, his left hand clutching the twining, crescent guard of his sword to ensure its silence. His eyes scoured the rise above him, sensitive to the slightest movements. The grass upon the hill was lush and soft underneath his feet, and the trees were scattered and sparse. He was increasingly aware of an ill wind, which moaned eerily in his ears and rustled the leaves of trees and shrubs, which grew ever scarcer as he ascended. The grass itself became drier and thinner, and soon it too grew scarce, as rocks and boulders began to dominate his surroundings. The slope had become steeper as he climbed; so steep, that he found himself using his free hand to help him clamber up the face of the slope. Quite abruptly, the incline flattened out into a somewhat rocky ledge of some width. Beyond the ledge, the hill continued upwards at a more reasonable tilt.

With his arm outstretched and his hand anchoring itself on the flattened rock, he eased himself up onto the ledge. He looked down over his shoulder and saw how high he had actually climbed. It seemed much darker below and he reasoned that the pale rock about him seemed to reciprocate the silvery glow of the moon, whereas the dark grasses below did not. He turned towards the face of the hill once more and noticed a crop of shrubs off to one side. The scene was instantly familiar and he recalled, in vivid detail, his memory of the limp body being dragged from the shrubs by the demon. Small, greyish stones littered the ground beneath him, a score near the shrubs were stained with subtle traces of old, dried blood.

He looked uphill from where he stood and saw that he was

close, for beyond a forest of boulders and rocky outcrops, loured the two, sheer crags that formed the pass. He lowered into a crouch, his eyes wide and frantically searching the face of the hill for any sign of movement. Coiled and ready to spring at any instant, he pressed on, winding his way uphill between the rocks and boulders, concealing himself behind them as best he could as he wound his way to the pass. He saw that his ashen skin was as the surrounding stone under the starlight, but the thought gave him little comfort, for he could not hide indefinitely from the thing he sought. He was careful not to disturb the pebbles and stones at his feet as he crept up the rocky slope, lest their dry grating betray his presence. The tilt of the slope began to level off, and plateaued soon after. Upon the plateau, he reached a rocky outcrop, pressed himself against it, and slowly peered out from behind it. Beyond the mass of rock yawned the darkened pass.

He stared out from the burning gems that were his eyes, observing the twisted length of the pass. From where he crouched behind the rock, he could see naught but the sheer walls of stone to either side of the pass, which doubly cast the way in shadow. He rose from behind the rock and slowly approached the pass.

A whistling wind met him from within the pass, it keened and moaned as it whipped his dark locks about, and brushed coolly against his bare flesh. The pass was about as wide as two persons laying head to foot, though it seemed to narrow further in. Cautiously, he stepped between the two crags and entered the pass. Though the crags seemed to fold overtop of him, he could see the stars through the rift above. The wind echoed within the pass and carried with it a somewhat foul odor. The pass began to meander, and he saw bluish, argent light ahead, which was dimly luminous upon the rocky walls and floor. The pass opened into a clearing, sparsely covered on one side by grasses, brush, and a few scattered trees. Some distance away, off to the right of the clearing, a mountainous boulder rose from the ground. Beyond it, the rocky slope continued its rise towards the summit of the hill and some distance ahead of him, the clearing petered and then dropped into a steep, craggy escarpment.

Crouching low, his right hand gripping the hilt of his sword in preparation to draw, he stole forth into the clearing. He became acutely aware of the foul odor he had been met with earlier, only now it was a more concentrated, fetid reek. He recognized the stench immediately. It was the stench of the dead. The foul scent wafted from beyond the verge of the escarpment and he crept towards it. His eyes were wild and his heart pounded fitfully as he combated a rising desire to flee. He came to the verge of the escarpment and peered down the rocky precipice. Near four fathoms below, a ledge jutted from the stony slope. Dozens of moss-covered boulders and rocks lay upon the ledge and strewn amidst and atop them were the exsanguine, rotted corpses of men, women, and children.

Most were naught but piles of weathered bone: empty, lifeless, grimy skeletons, which stared vapidly from the black holes in their skulls where once eyes had been. However, a nauseating few were still covered in stinking, decomposing flesh, over which droned an army of flies, and within which squirmed their hungry maggots and those of the feasting beetles. Grimacing, he turned from the mephitic decay. As he turned, something caught his eye, something that had remained unseen to him as he passed it moments before. He went deathly still and his breath halted in his chest. Upon the face of the rising slope, near where he stood to the far right of the clearing, just above where the plateau met the slope, lay the lair of the demon.

A short distance from where he stood, the twisted, black mouth of a cave yawned before him, nearly as tall as he at its highest point, and greater still in breadth. The rock encircling the opening was ragged and festooned with tiny weeds and dry patches of crabgrass where dirt and debris had collected between nooks and crannies. A protuberant mass of the rock next to the cave had concealed the opening from him as he left the pass. Now, he stared directly into the pitch-dark maw. Primeval fear pervaded his being, like ice in his veins. The darkness seemed alive somehow, a breathing, palpable nemesis. He was suddenly unsure of himself and the grip of fear held him tighter still. His mouth went dry and his legs became leaden. He turned his head towards the pass and, almost longingly, looked into the crevice through which he might make his escape. He returned his gaze to the cave, and as he did, the darkness within it appeared to move.

His right hand, still gripping his sword, clenched the hilt feverishly. He thought he heard a faint sound issue from within the cave, a whisper of movement over smooth rock. He stared into the cave, wondering if, and hoping that what he saw and heard might have been spawned of the chilling fear that pervaded him. Yet again, he observed some shapeless thing stir within the ominous blackness. As he looked on, horrified, an indistinct form manifested from the shadowy depths, with eyes glinting like dim embers. His heart sank and he was stricken with terror, for the demon was indeed in its lair.

# *II*

Gnarled, whitish fingers slithered from the darkness, heralding a pale, black-clawed hand, which, slow and serpentine, ran along the inside wall of the cave and came to rest upon the outer lip of the rocky maw. Here, the hand, its palm over the outer edge of the opening, clutched the cold rock. Bracing itself against one side of the cave, the demon came forth from the blackness and he caught its scent on the wind. Moonlight bathed the ashen, bestial visage that emerged from the dark and illumined the pale, sinewy shoulders and body that followed thereafter. Its stare was cold, piercing, and lifeless; its fearsome maw hung open without sound.

It stepped forth from the mouth of the cave with a leathery, pallid, bare foot, and lowered its grim head as it passed beneath the hanging rock above. Its lurid eyes never left his, and its harrowing gaze was so daunting, it petrified him where he stood. Crouched low, its near-naked form now clearly visible under the cloudless, starlit sky, the demon watched him intently. It sniffed the air as it observed him and took a few hesitant steps towards him. Its coarse, black mane, like tufts of windswept quills, shivered rigidly in the passing breeze. It cocked its head subtly to one side and regarded him.

In the clearing upon the plateau, less than ten paces apart, they stood facing one another, with only a moaning wind to break the deathly silence between them. The sentry loosed the breath pent in his chest and willed himself to move. He did not break gaze with the demon as, slowly and almost imperceptibly, he began to slide his sword from its scabbard. Ever so faintly, the blade scratched against the scabbard as it came unsheathed, and at this, the demon's eyes shot towards the sword and its bestial aspect twisted with malice. The demon's eyes flitted back up to his, and in those torrid eyes he saw the sheer malevolence of the thing. More than that, somehow, its face seemed almost accusing. Worse still, he had the distinct feeling that there was an intelligence beyond its savage eyes. He froze in mid draw, and once again, fear twined about in his gut like icy tendrils. As he stared into the demon's unforgiving eyes, a feeling that it in some way sensed his dread, worsened his numbing fear.

The demon struck without warning. From where it had stood, still as death, it rushed towards him, its lips curled back in a menacing snarl, and a rising growl in its throat. Still stiff with fright and startled by the thing's sudden rush and harrowing roar, he stumbled backwards awkwardly, even clumsily. Even as he faltered dangerously near the verge of the escarpment, he did not take his eyes from the demon. He managed to scramble away from the verge and, as he regained his footing, he saw that the thing was nearly upon him. In one deft movement, he sprang away from the demon and tore his sword from his scabbard. The blade sang as it was pulled free and in the same motion, as he alighted upon the ground, he hefted the sword up with a single hand, the blade shining in moonlight.

The demon, however, matched his feint with alarming agility, and tearing into the earth with its claws, it redirected its charge and bore down upon him with terrifying speed. The sentry began to swing the great blade downward, but saw that his effort was for naught. The demon struck his open chest like a battering ram, its head and shoulders lowered, and its arms latching about his leg and waist like serpents. The thing met him with such force that he was lifted from his feet and carried through the air. For a single, enduring moment, they floated through the air together. He did not see the tree behind him and was unprepared for the brutal impact.

His spine slammed against the tree and the back of his head cracked audibly against the trunk, rattling his brain in his skull. So forcefully did he strike the tree that the leaves and twigs above shook and rustled clamorously. His limp arms flung wide apart, as his body came to a dead, thunderous stop against the tree. The impact jarred his sword from his hand and the blade spun end over end behind him, amidst the few trees beyond. It came to ground some distance away and, tossing up debris and swirls of dust, it clanged, skipped and wheeled over the ground a short distance more. Specks of light swam in the sentry's eyes and he sagged against the tree trunk; but his legs did not give beneath him and he held himself up against the trunk at his back.

His vision began to clear and he saw the demon's head rise into view from his side. It lashed out at him with a single arm, and he felt its talon clutch his nape, twisting his head in towards its own. With open maw and glinting, ivory fangs, it snapped at his throat like a striking asp. With equal speed, the sentry slung his left arm up at the demon, thrusting the ridge of his forearm into the soft of the demon's throat below its jaw, halting the demon's eager maw a hand's breadth from his neck. A fleeting expression of pain and surprise washed over the demon's face before him. Its pause was brief however, and quivering with effort, it began to pull his throat towards its waiting maw once more.

Wide-eyed with terrible intent, its stare bore into his pulsing throat and he felt the demon's hot, miasmal breath upon his bare flesh. Next to his ear, its growl, now half choked and rasping, was blood curdling. With chilling cunning, it brought its free hand to his forearm and began to pull it downwards, away from its throat. In a panic, the sentry shifted against the tree and forced his empty sword hand across his chest until it found the demon's face. He clasped the demon's skull and, in a brutal act of desperation, drove his clawed thumb into the demon's eye. Like a wounded dog, and yet so like a man, the demon issued a throaty yelp as it reared its head away from his tearing claws. With a sudden fervor, it seized the black locks at the base of his skull with single talon and dug its clawed feet into the ground as it hauled him from the tree trunk.

The demon wrenched his head forward violently and he stumbled towards it headlong. As he lurched towards it, he felt a sharp pain upon his temple as the demon grasped a second tuft of his hair with its other hand, its claws raking his scalp. In one abrupt movement, and with alarming strength, the demon twisted about wildly, heaving him by the head. A menacing growl gurgled in its chest as it flung him towards the center of the clearing. The sentry's bare feet skimmed over the ground as he tried desperately to regain his footing, but the demon had hurled him with such force that he keeled and flew sidelong through the air. He was unaware of the large boulder, which sat anchored in the ground behind him, and hurtled into it with force enough to quake his very bones.

His side bore the brunt of the impact and he jounced against the boulder, falling to his elbows and knees. Wincing, he lifted his head and saw the demon standing where it had thrown him. It snorted forcibly and tossed its head, as would a beast plagued by biting flies. Its eyes opened and came to rest upon him. He noticed a trickle of blood upon its face, which ran from the inner corner of its left eye. Led by a single, dark, rubescent bead, the blood streamed down its face like a crimson tear. The demon's stare was intense and baleful, and it seemed entirely unaware of the blood that welled in its eye and ran down its face.

His pain began to dwindle and the same courage that had seen him through numerous battles burned within him, abating the fear that had knotted his gut. He stared into the demon's eyes with a face that had become stolid, stern, and hard as stone. He placed his hand upon the boulder and rose to his feet. Seemingly prompted by his movement, the demon charged once more, and he watched it come. In an instant, it had covered the ground between them, its growl a hushed rumble in the night air. He saw the whites of its yellow eyes, the sheen of starlight on its fangs, and he watched as the demon pounced at speed, hurling itself towards him, outstretched like a lunging wildcat. He did not so much as move a muscle, nor did his face betray any sign of fear. A certain calm had come over him: the calm prolonged combat begets wherein thought is deposed by honed instinct and action and the chill of fear becomes the heat of rage and the burning desire to survive.

He remained statue still until the penultimate moment, wherein, with wicked speed, he shot forward and stooped below the demon's pounce. He crouched so low to the ground that his fingers skimmed the dust at his feet. The demon cast a shadow upon him as it passed above. It twisted viciously and coiled in the air as it made an attempt to grasp him whilst he swept below its gnarled, clawed hands. He, his swiftness unfettered even as he dodged beneath the thing, propelled himself upwards from the earth with all his might and extended himself into its exposed underbelly. The butt of his shoulder met the demon's gut with a shuddering impact, which forced an airy, grotesque rasp from its lungs.

The sentry felt a jolt run through him as the demon's body folded over his shoulder and the magnitude of the blow lifted the demon skyward. In a single, fluid movement, the sentry straightened, heaving the demon over his back, just as the bulls of his native Spain would toss their victims up over their horns. A growl resonated from somewhere within him as he catapulted the thing into the air, where it spun head over heels like a child's doll and sailed over the great boulder at the sentry's back.

Behind the boulder, the demon plummeted to earth headlong, whilst it struggled to right itself in the air. It struck the rocky ground with a sickening, wet thump, landing awkwardly upon the base of its skull and neck. Its rigid, sinewy body went suddenly limp and then tumbled over upon the ground. Where it lay upon its back, its eyelids fluttered, and then opened, as its body immediately stirred to life.

The sentry turned to face the boulder, and he leapt towards it. He lifted into the air with ease and alighted atop the boulder with arms spread wide as he came to rest upon its crest in perfect balance. His golden eyes were wide and searching, his heart beat wildly in his chest and his entire being seethed with rage. He spied the demon as it rose to its feet a short distance from the boulder. Its eyes met his and it snarled, a posturing of sheer loathing, and yet it seemed in some way leery. The sentry sprang from the boulder, and no sooner did his feet touch the ground, than he charged the demon. He was upon it in an instant and it thrashed out at him like a cornered cat. With a wild, arcing swing, it slashed at his face viciously. He plunged below the whistling swipe of its talon, only narrowly avoiding its claws as they tore through the air above his head. As he swept below the demon's black claws, he clenched his sword hand into a fist and drew it back to such a degree that his arm trailed out behind him like the tail of a comet.

Now, it was he who roared, a mated sound of man and beast, which surprised even he as it echoed throughout the clearing. In his fist was harnessed the force of his charge, and with the added might of his powerful body, he swung his fist upwards, his sinuous muscles rippling beneath his chalky flesh as he unleashed their full force. His fist left a low rush of air in its wake as it hurtled skyward. The blow was heavy and savage, and he felt the demon's jaw and the surrounding flesh of its mouth, yield under the blow, whilst its mane shook with the impact.

He heard the wet, hollow cracking sound of bone and flesh being struck, and watched as the demon's head reeled backward from the staggering force of the blow. A spray of blood erupted from around its mouth as, with arms and legs outstretched, it was lifted into the air for the briefest of moments before toppling backward. He watched the demon's body jolt as its back and skull struck the ground and it rolled once before coming to rest in a swirling cloud of dust. Even before the dust could settle, the demon had already begun to rise. It was shaken however, and it teetered as it attempted to stand. Its mouth hung slightly agape and a portion of its lower lip was raggedly riven, sending twining streams of blood over one side of its jaw. For a moment, its eyes were unfocused, and its head hung off kilter as it fought to keep itself upright.

He had knocked men senseless before and knew the look of one battered to the point of floundering cognition. He thought that here and now he might slay the demon, and chanced a glance over his shoulder in search of his sword. His eyes flitted about as they scoured the clearing for the fallen Tizona. Some distance away, beyond the trees, he spotted something on the dusty ground that gleamed in moonlight. The blade lay on its side, the tip buried in the roots of a bloom of crab grass.

He had only turned from the demon for a moment, yet in that moment, its eyes had lost their glazed appearance and it had shaken itself from its stupor. Had he been more attentive to his foe in that moment, he would have seen a certain awareness return to the thing, as it suddenly stared up at him from below its bestial brow, its face twisted maliciously, and its eyes afire with wrath.

He turned his head in time to see it rushing towards him, startled by the eerie silence with which it struck and by the way its eyes had fixed upon him with such malevolent intent. Once again, with lips curled back in a noiseless snarl, it slashed at him, a wide, arcing swipe. He barely had time to rear his head and torso backward to evade the terrible slash, and the thing's claws whisked by the soft of his exposed throat. He was, however, unable to completely elude the blow, and the demon's claws tore into the flesh of his chest. He stumbled backwards, but kept his eyes upon the demon and watched as the black claws of its other hand swung down upon him like the falling arm of a trebuchet. He managed to raise his right forearm to his face and he rolled with the swipe to diminish the force and effect of the slash.

The demon's claws still bit into his ashen flesh, carving him along the width of his forearm where his gizzard might have been opened in its stead. He regained his footing and took a final, purposeful step backward as the demon slashed at him once more. The claws of its right hand, those that had gashed his chest, whipped towards his face in a blur of movement. With stunning speed and battle-honed skill, he slid the ridge of his left forearm underneath the demon's strike and lifted his wrist level with his brow. Stiff and unyielding, his forearm met the underside of the demon's arm below the elbow, abruptly halting its swipe and suspending the demon's claws above his head.

Even as his arm had risen to parry the blow, he had drawn back his sword hand in preparation for his riposte. With his fist tightly clenched, he hammered the side of the demon's face and its head pitched to one side. The demon staggered, but did not fall, and the sentry lunged towards it, swinging at it savagely with his opposite fist. He struck the demon along the side of its skull and an audible crack filled the air between the two. The demon's head snapped round, and its body followed helplessly, like a banner upon a lance. The thing's head and arms hung limp and it stumbled aside, nearly overset, but still it did not fall. He was upon it in an instant, a deep animal noise in his chest as he continued his onslaught.

He seized the demon violently by the mane, twisting its head and hauling it towards him. The demon seemed to glare at him with, wide, crazed eyes and at the same time, it stared through him seeing nothing at all. He pulled the thing to his right side and dealt it a crushing hit with the elbow of his opposite arm, which he swung deftly across his bleeding chest in a tight arc. Head, body, and limb, the demon bowed under the force of the blow. Droplets of dark blood spattered over its bare, pallid flesh; its head reeled, its eyes seemed lifeless, and still it did not fall. He released the demon's mane, and mustering all his strength, swung his right arm back across his chest like a mace, pummeling its skull with the back of his fist. The demon's head and body twisted backwards and it tried desperately to keep its feet. He half expected the thing to right itself and repay his assault in kind, when finally, after a few brief, awkward, disoriented steps, the demon finally collapsed to the ground on its side.

Even as he strode towards the fallen demon, it attempted to rise, its limbs buckling now and again as it did. With some effort, it managed to prop itself upon its hands and knees, its head hanging limply between its enfeebled arms. Silently, menacingly, he approached the demon from behind, with the poise of an executioner looming over the block. With its remaining strength, the demon rose abruptly to a knee and spun wildly, striking blindly at the sentry with its claws. The sudden attack did not seem to alarm him, nor disturb his eerie, dour calm. He caught the demon's hand at the wrist as though he were snatching a fly from the air. With his left hand, he clutched the demon by the mane and yanked its head backward, so that its yellow eyes gazed into the heavens, defeated and forlorn. Its mouth hung agape and bloodied, as its spine was arched over his thigh.

He then released the demon's arm and raised his fist to the darkened sky, the demon's mane still held firm in his left hand, ensuring the thing was pinned upon its knees. His fist hung in the air, a suspended, ghostly instrument of a fate. The demon's eyes rolled languidly towards him, so that it stared upwards into his own eyes, its face beaten and vapid. In his hand was the power to choose between life or death, a forked road he had traversed many times over. He heard his heart beating steadily within him, and he breathed in deeply. The world around him seemed elsewhere, and all he knew was he and the thing before him, and the spinnings of fate between them. His lips curled, baring his gleaming, ivory fangs, and the muscles of his neck seized and stood out as a roar boomed from his throat.

His bare chest and back were white peaks and canyons of twisted, straining sinew as he brought his fist down upon the demon. Its head jolted with the terrible force of the blow, yet his grip upon its mane did not falter. He raised his fist again and hammered it downwards. He heard a wet, gristly sound, and blood spattered from its nostrils. Again and again he brought his fist down upon the demon, and its body convulsed and shuddered as he rained blows upon it. Its body went limp, yet still he held it aloft by its mane, bashing its skull with a relentless fervor, the sound echoing in his ears like claps of thunder.

Finally, slowly, he let his gore-flecked fist come to rest at his side, and let his fingers hang lax. The body of the battered demon slumped to one side, though its head and shoulders remained suspended above the ground, for he still clasped it by the mane of its crown. He stared at its fallen body, and all was suddenly quiet, save the sound of his breaths and the whisper of the wind. He knew the demon was not yet dead, and that it might not be long before the cursed thing would rise again. He turned his head to where his sword rested upon the ground then returned his gaze to the demon at his feet. Already, a few of its gnarled fingers curled and twitched upon the ground where its drooping limbs were sprawled. He noticed that it eyes flitted sporadically behind its half closed lids and that breath wafted from its hanging jaw.

He did not waste a moment more, and turned towards his sword. His left arm outstretched behind him, he dragged the ghoulish body by the scalp. His strides were pronounced and brisk, and the body of the demon shook and yawed as it was hauled over the ground behind him. He dragged the body across the clearing, past the scattering of trees, and once he had reached where his sword lay, he released the head from his clutches. The rear of its skull thumped against the ground in a most undignified fashion.

He bent, snatched up his sword, and turned to face the fallen demon. It lay helpless on the ground, its eyes barely open and the muscles of its neck hardly able to hold up its head, as, with slow, feeble writhings of its limbs, it began to roll itself to its stomach. He regarded the demon as he straddled its low back and he stood looming over it as it stirred to life. With cold indifference, he seized the demon's coarse mane with his left hand once more, and violently hauled the demon's head to the level of his loins, his left arm outstretched before him. The hard stare of his vivid, amber eyes betrayed his feral state, and the fiery sensation of pending victory that pervaded his being. He inhaled the night air through his nostrils and raised the massive blade above his head.

\* \* \* \*

The sentry walked towards the rocky escarpment as though he were in a trance. His face bore a vacant look, and yet his visage conveyed a certain enmity. The wind caressed him gently and casually tossed the tips of his black locks about his neck. The thin rivulets of blood that had run from the wounds upon his chest and forearm had begun to dry and darken, and the wounds themselves had ceased to bleed. He came to a stop at the verge of the escarpment, and from his vantage upon the great, rocky hill, he looked out over the vast expanse far below. He seemed detached from the world, and not even the miasmal stench of the long dead upon the ledge below could disturb his ruminating mind.

He felt somehow reborn, understanding the simple clarity of his purpose. His eyes lifted to the black firmament, and after a time he let them drop to stare out over the rolling landscape below. Then, as though the world around him were an audience to bare witness to his deed, he outstretched his left arm and lifted it upward. Dangling from his hand was the severed head of the demon, the coarse mane of which he still clasped with a pale fist. As he had done in an instance that seemed a lifetime ago, he raised the head of the demon skyward, as a terrifying bellow was birthed in his chest. The sound echoed throughout the range of hills. His roar was long and loud.

The head tumbled down the rocky escarpment and came to rest amidst the rancid decay and the piles of scattered bones. He turned from the verge of the escarpment and sheathed his sword as he left the gruesome scene behind him. He eyed the mouth of the cave as he passed it, and came to a standstill as he stared into its black depths. It might have been curiosity that drove him to approach the mouth of the cave, or perhaps a need to, in some way, understand the thing he had slain. He regarded the opening for a moment, then ducked his head below the hanging rock as he stepped into the cave. It did not take his eyes long to adjust to the gloom, and he saw that the cave narrowed quite drastically a short distance from the entrance and meandered off to the right. His scabbard scraped along the cave wall as he slipped through the narrow bend. The cave opened into a large, ovular chamber, in which he was able to stand to his full height.

The dimensions of the chamber were larger than the area within his home, or what had once been his home a short time ago. He did not expect what he saw before him, for piled high against the far wall of the chamber, was a horde of treasures and wares. Near the left side of the chamber, he spied the body of a man - a Scotsman by the look of him, his clothes tattered and filthy. The man lay upon his back, and observing his face and clothes, the sentry recognized the man as the very same who had been towed away so brutally in the clutch of the demon. The man's face was battered and horribly scratched, as were most of the areas upon his body where his skin was exposed. The most notable injury was a grievous wound to one side of the man's throat. Upon it, was an annular series of indentations in the flesh where the demon had evidently clamped its maw. The surrounding and underlying tissue was bruised black and blue, and was plainly swollen.

On either side of the circular imprint of the bite were distinct holes wherein the demon had buried its fangs; from these, fresh blood welled over the scabrous crust encircling each wound, to trickle in tiny streams down the side of the man's neck. The sentry knelt beside the body, his eyes searching the battered form for signs of life other than the ebbing pulse, the lifeblood of which leaked from the man's punctured vessel onto the cave floor. The man clung to the most meager thread of life and the sentry knew that in all likelihood the man would expire before the dawn. Though he was satiated, he eyed the trickles of blood with a keen eye. The smell of it drove his mind into a frenzy, and he began to lower himself towards the dying man so that he might lap up the crimson fluid. With sudden revulsion, he turned from the body and rose to his feet.

He walked towards the demon's horde and marveled over the odd assortment of which the trove was comprised. There were pots and vases: small statuettes and trinkets, scattered clothes and segments of armor. Much of the horde was worthless, broken relics; however, to his disbelief, he discovered a small cache of valuables: pouches of coin, pieces of gold, jewels, and jewelry. He wondered what use a demon that had somehow escaped the confines of hell could have had for such a wealth of wares, and why it should care for such things at all. He dismissed the thought, reasoned that the horde was now his, and so took with him a scant few items before he left the cave. From the stash, he took a pouch of coins, though he knew not what use he might put them to: a necklace of gold for Bronwyn, which he hung about his neck, and an ornate dagger to replace the one he had lost, the sheath of which he fastened to his belt, over his right hip.

# *III*

As he left the hills and meadowland behind him, he reminisced upon his harrowing encounter with the demon. He reviewed the whole of his experience without a single lapse and with preternatural vividness. He noticed that the slashes upon his chest and forearm had already knit, bridged by ragged, white scar tissue, and encrusted with dried blood. Upon approaching the town, he found himself excited to see Bronwyn, and anxious to regale her with the tale of his ordeal. As before, he slunk past the wall and the guardsmen, and then made his way to the smithy. When he neared the smithy, he noticed that the front door of the Scots' home was ajar and off kilter, and he was immediately ill at ease. The wood was splintered from the outside, around the level where the bolt would have been slid into place. He approached cautiously, as always, keeping to the shadows. He looked about, but saw no one, and he scampered to the open door.

Gently, he opened the door a little further, and it creaked and groaned upon its damaged hinges. He slipped through the door and moved quietly through the home. Given the general disarray he found therein, he deduced that there had been some sort of struggle. He reached the stairs and heard the faint sounds of someone breathing, a choked, raspy pitiable sound. He was unsure of what to think, of what had happened. Panic seized him and, inwardly, he prayed that Bronwyn and Colin were well. He mounted the stairs into the darkness on the upper floor, following the weak, erratic breaths.

He found Colin lying on his side, just outside the doorway to Bronwyn's room. He rushed towards him and fell to one knee by his side. Colin's eyes were barely open, his bright locks were matted with blood over one side of his head, and his face was scratched and heavily bruised. The sentry noticed two deep wounds on Colin's side and back, most likely the result of a dagger thrust into his flesh. He placed a pale, clawed hand upon Colin's shoulder, his face grimacing in disbelief.

"Colin...Colin!"

Colin did not respond, but continued to rasp as he gasped for air. Colin's shirt was soaked with blood around his wounds and plastered to his skin. With the utmost gentility, the sentry attempted to rouse his fallen comrade - to no avail. A sudden, grim thought crossed his mind, and he lifted his head, looking about maniacally.

"Bronwyn!"

He yelled her name so that it resounded within the stone home. He heard an airy utterance from below him and returned his attention to Colin.

"Colin! What happened here?"

Colin did not move, but the rasp of his breathing changed, and a few, quavery words escaped his mouth in a hushed whisper.

"Th...took...her."

The sentry lowered his head and spoke softly into his friend's ear.

"Where? Where was she taken?"

"M...mm...men...t...took..."

"Where Colin? Please..."

"Th...they...mm...men..."

Seeing that Colin was slipping into delirium and teetering upon the brink of death, the sentry did not waste another word. He ran one arm around the back of Colin's head, then underneath the pit of an arm. He secured his other arm under Colin's legs, along the back of his knees. He scooped Colin up into his arms and straightened, insuring that Colin's head could rest against his chest and his upper arm. He carried Colin down the stairs and paused in the doorway. Once again he looked about for any who might be nearby. With no one in sight, he darted from the smithy with Colin's near-lifeless body in his arms.

\* \* \* \*

The sentry crept to the front door of a neighboring home, one whose proprietors he knew to be well to do, and who had the wherewithal to live in modest comfort. He bent low, and with great care, laid Colin upon the doorstep. He stood and thrice pounded the wooden door with his fist. He raised clamor enough to wake the deepest of sleepers, and the door rattled with each impact. This done, he sank into a low crouch, looked upward, and leapt towards the roof.

Moments later, the sound of a wooden bar being raised could be heard as it scraped against the inside of the door. A balding, middle-aged man opened the door but a crack, peering through with tired, resentful eyes. He was groggy with sleep, and it took him a few moments to spot the red haired man lying on his doorstep.

"Colin? Jesus! Colin!" The man opened the door, revealing his squat, bulky body and the large mallet he held in his right hand. "Its Colin love, he's in a bad way."

A woman, plain in appearance, peeked out from behind the bulky man. Just then a tawny, hide pouch dropped from above and landed at the man's feet. The pouch jangled as the coin within splayed the bag where it came to rest upon the doorstep. Almost simultaneously, the couple heard a dour voice from above.

"Care for him."

"Blimey!" The big man exclaimed as he took a step back. He was not unnerved for long however, and soon strode his great bulk out of doors to stare up at the roof of his home.

"Oy!..Oy! who's there then?"

His inquiry was met with naught but silence, just as his eyes saw naught but the familiar shingles of his roof. The man scratched his head, looked about and cursed.

"Bloody'hell."

His voice was deep and rumbling. He looked to Colin and then regarded his wife, who stared at him dumbfounded. He raised his bushy eyebrows, which caused the deep furrows of his brow to wrinkle together.

"Well!….don't just stand there woman, put some broth to boil!"

She disappeared back into the dwelling as the man squatted beside Colin, pocketing the pouch of coins and preparing to carry the blacksmith into his abode.

* * * *

Having done what he could for Colin, the sentry began to scour the town in search of Bronwyn. He hoped that he might somehow find her before she suffered the cruelties inflicted upon her brother. The town was expansive and with time of the essence, he could ill afford to sneak about through the shadows at his leisure. Keeping to the areas of the town where the dwellings were at their densest, he leapt from roof to roof, and in this fashion made his way through the town. He reasoned that from this vantage, he would be better able to note any sign of Bronwyn or her captors. He soared across the rooftops with unconscious grace and mastery, his eyes nervously searching about for any sign of Bronwyn. He could detect no scent that he might follow, nor discern a single thing to assist him in his hunt. He made a huge leap from a small domicile, to a larger, stone dwelling, alighting and coming to rest in a crouch upon the apex of the roof.

His eyes panned the darkened town, and he wondered what these men Colin had mentioned wanted with Bronwyn. He wondered if the poor girl had succumbed to a brutal rape, and he immediately shook the thought from his mind. As he did, he thought he discerned a scream in the distance. His head cocked to one side and his ears pricked. Now certain that he was hearing screams, he turned his head in the direction from which they ranged. Abruptly, the screaming was stifled then ceased, and in its place he heard the faint commotion of harsh, threatening voices.

In an instant, he had leapt from the far end of the roof and was bounding atop the sleeping townspeople's homes, making his way towards where the screams had sounded. As he traveled through the air, his eyes focused upon the spot from whence he deduced the screams had come. The burning gems that were his eyes pierced through the darkness, and even at some four-hundred paces, he saw men moving about in the distance. A man bearing what seemed to be a thin torch appeared from behind a distant structure. The distant flame began to move, and he saw that the man was walking amidst the others. The man lowered the torch towards a shadowy, jagged mass, and a warm, wavering brilliance flickered to life amidst the gaggle of men. His heart sank at the sight of it. The radiance of the spreading flames illuminated a morbid scene.

He saw men gathered about a large, erected stake, around the base of which were piled the timbers of a pyre, and throughout which, flames had begun to weave. Atop the pyre was a woman, and in seeing her figure and lovely auburn hair, he knew, with rising sorrow, that it was indeed Bronwyn.

His eyes were wide, his face the portrait of disbelief and horror. He tore across the rooftops at breakneck speed, reckless and unwavering. With each leap, the grim spectacle before him drew ever closer. His eyes were fixed upon the tragic scene as he hurtled towards it, forced to look on helplessly, as lapping flames rose within and about the pyre. Bronwyn writhed and shook as fire seared her feet and shanks, her gown ignited by the flames. He saw that her hands had been forced behind her back and around the stake, and there fettered with rope - additional lengths of which held her to the stake about the waist and knees. He was so close to her and yet still so far, and he watched, grief stricken, as her face: scraped and bruised, beaded and dripping with sweat and tears, twisted in agony. Near her brow and temples, her hair was damp with perspiration and was matted to her skin in small tangles of thin, wet tendrils. She could not cry out, for something had been forced into her mouth and there held by a sizeable gag.

The gag, a twisted, grimy rag, ringed her head so tightly that it pulled the corners of her mouth to her rear teeth like a horse's bit. Bronwyn's eyes were tightly shut, and her head thrashed about as she tried in vain to free herself from the stake. The men numbered some seven or eight and were gathered in an open square, encompassed on one side by a distribution of homes. They murmured smugly amongst one another, jeering at Bronwyn, and denouncing her as a witch and heretic as they watched the flames begin to consume her. Her cries were suffocated, but, muffled as they were, he was close enough now to hear the strident, blood-curdling sounds above the clamor of the mob. Some of the men were familiar, others he knew not, and all stood before the stake, perpetrators of the abominable immolation.

The pyre was ablaze with crackling flames, which, coughing smoke and glowing ash into the night sky, enveloped Bronwyn as she thrashed and twisted horribly. He could not help but see his mother in Bronwyn's blistering face and once again, one he loved was tortured before him within the scalding embrace of fire. Bronwyn's frenetic convulsions dwindled to spastic seizings, her cries to quavering moans. Abject despair pervaded him throughout, and tears welled in his eyes as, from aloft, he surged towards her.

Other townsfolk had left their homes to behold the horrid spectacle, and they joined the gaggle of men. The mob stared on at the burning woman, most transfixed with morbid, perverse curiosity. Flame and smoke obscured her form, yet they saw her face and bare arms blister, boil, and blacken with soot, which rose from the burning pyre. The flickering glow of the blaze blanketed all within reach of its flare in a deep, orange, golden luminosity. The warm effulgence played over the dusty ground and danced upon the smooth rotundity of the mob's staring eyes. The fiery color wavered upon their stiffened bodies and upon their cruel, anxious faces. The darkness beyond the reach of the dim radiance seemed absolute and unfathomable to the eye from where they stood near the heart of the glow. It was as if all that existed beyond the touch of the deep glow was blanketed in a veil of perfect black, so that the spectacle of their deed stood stark and lurid before their eyes.

The woman's incessant, violent tossing had begun to ebb as the acrid odor and faint hiss of burning flesh reached their nostrils and ears. Her long hair withered and smoked as her locks caught afire, and her mouth was curled in a horrible grimace over the gag they had forced between her jaws. Her body seemed suddenly limp, and her head hung to a side. Indeed, the only signs that she still lived were the strength with which she kept her eyelids shut and the spasmodic twitches of her dying body.

One of the mob, a young, lithe man, began to look amongst his compatriots, suddenly unsure of the sanctity of their deed. However, he did nothing to halt the immolation, and he stared on in silence as the woman succumbed to the hungry flames. Quite suddenly, a bestial, resounding ululation erupted from the darkness. A harrowing, wild howl of such lament, it drove fear into his heart. Those around him seemed similarly stricken with terror, and they looked about in alarm, but the ubiquitous darkness around them had gone silent once more. The young man felt panic bloom within him as he searched the surrounding blackness and, as it happened, he glimpsed a movement in the dark. Something large had sprung forth from the darkness, but he lost sight of it for a moment as it dropped onto the far side of a nearby rooftop. He heard a heavy, brittle crunch, a sound, he intuited, made by the thing as it landed upon the shingled roof.

Whatever it was, it approached at a tremendous speed, for, through the din of his compatriots, he heard the faint sounds of footfalls, falling in alarmingly rapid succession as they drew nearer upon the roof. Though it must have been the briefest of instants, it seemed an eternity that the thing remained unseen. His heart fluttered and rose to his throat as he stared at the verge of the rooftop nearest the square, apprehensively anticipating the moment when the thing would appear. He did not cry out to alert the others, nor turn his head from the edge of the roof. Uneasy, he simply stared and waited.

His blood ran cold as he witnessed a ghostly form erupt into view atop the verge of roof. As it reached the edge of the rooftop, it leapt into the air. The thing, which looked so like a man, propelled itself forth with unnatural force. It seemed to float as it traveled loftily above the square, leaving the shadows behind as it entered the luminous ambit of the blazing pyre. By firelight, he saw sinuous musculature, a half-bare, pale form colored a deep gold in the rich, flickering glow. He heard a rumble like thunder overhead, and the thing's daunting roar filled his ears. The others glanced upward and fell silent at the sound, watching as the white figure traversed the darkened firmament above, a large, sheathed sword trailing from its side. The grim specter soared towards the conflagration, an impossible leap from where it had lifted into the air.

The young man watched as it extended its limbs like an alighting cat, as it loomed high above the pyre. He watched in awe as, some distance from the flames, it clasped the very top of the stake with its bare hands and feet and there clung to the wood like some arboreal beast. He heard the harsh scraping of claws over wood as the thing strained to keep its hold upon the stake, and indeed, the thing held fast to the stake. The pallid thing pivoted and swung round the top of the wooden shaft so that it came to rest with the towering stake between him and it. Though a portion of the thing's body was hidden behind the stake, the young man was afforded a relatively clear view of the interloper, and he saw that it was a thing of flesh and blood, a pale man with long, black locks.

Indeed, the pale man seemed to be in pain, for as he peered downwards through the swirling smoke, towards the burning woman below, he grimaced and squinted his eyes into narrow slits. The pale man removed one hand from the stake and brought it to his side. Though the stake obscured his vision, the young man saw that the pale man had drawn a dagger. The moment it was unsheathed, the pale man dropped towards the pyre, keeping the palm of a single hand cupped round the shaft of the stake. The pale man's hand skimmed along the coarse length of timber, stabilizing him as he fell, so that he plummeted downwards alongside the massive stake. Dropping towards the flames below, the pale man lifted his right hand to his chest, leveling the point of the dagger towards the stake. As the pale man descended into the rising flames, he drove the blade into the timber, scoring the shaft as he fell.

He landed upon the pyre behind the burning woman and the impact caused an explosion of burning ash and embers, which scattered and swirled through the air within a wafting plum of black smoke. An earsplitting cracking and snapping of cindering wood reverberated from the pyre as the pale man's shanks crashed through and sank into the burning timber, boring knee deep into the pyre. Still, he dragged the blade downward against the stake, unwavering in his purpose. The blade tore into the stake behind the woman, sundering the ropes that, pulled taut against the wood, had bound her hands, waist, and legs. The woman's scorched, shuddering form fell free from the stake and with one outstretched hand, he caught her slumping body beneath the arms and drew her to him. Flinging the dagger aside, he gently cradled her head with his free hand, pressing her nape to his bare chest. Holding her there within the heart of inferno, his head reared, and he wailed in torment, a strange, terrifying animal sound.

In the same instant, he lifted one of his legs from the pyre and pressed the burnt flesh under his foot against the stake. With a single, desperate thrust of this leg, he lunged backwards through the air, hauling the limp body of the burnt woman with him as he toppled away from the blazing pyre. Burning timbers tumbled in their wake, scattering whirling ash and embers afresh. For a moment, the pair traveled headlong through the air, tongues of flame and wisps of smoke trailing from their clasped forms. Together, they fell to ground, dropping out of sight beyond the conflagration.

\* \* \* \*

The sentry held Bronwyn to his chest as he sprang from the flames. His back thudded and skidded upon the dusty ground and he bore the impact of their combined weight. He lay upon the ground wincing with Bronwyn's smoldering body pressed against his own. His feet and shins were agonizingly seared and singed, and his bare torso and arms were badly scalded. He gritted his teeth and tried his best to ignore the hot pain that throbbed over his flesh. He could still feel the intense heat of the fire where he lay upon the ground, and the brilliance of the burning pyre forced his eyelids to tighten over his eyes, so that they were naught but narrow slits. Slowly, he rolled to his side, gently laying Bronwyn upon her back. Her face was covered with soot, and where the skin had not been seared away, horrid, leaking boils glistened in the firelight. Most of her hair had been burnt to the root, and mephitic, deep-grey fumes rose from her charred scalp. Her clothes had been all but consumed by the fire, and he saw her burnt nakedness beneath the smoking remnants.

Over much of her body, her skin had been seared away and the sizzling tissue beneath was damp with translucent fluid. Her feet and shanks were nearly burned to the bone, the flesh blackened and cracked. He rose to his knees and turned his back to the flames, tears welling afresh below his golden sapphire eyes.

"Bronwyn," he whispered. "Bronwyn!" he exclaimed with sorrow in his voice. She did not speak, nor open her scalded eyes. The last of her breath escaped her in faint, erratic gasps, before she lay still and silent. A part of him refused to believe what he saw before him, and her smoldering body seemed somehow surreal. His sorrow was suddenly consumed by a maddening rage and he rose to his feet, his face twisting with malice. He turned towards the pyre and peered through the wall of rising smoke and leaping flames. Beyond the conflagration, the blanched, silent faces of the rabble stared as he rose, and he saw the fear in their guilty eyes. A dead quiet had filled the square, and naught but the snaps and crackles of the burning, scattered pyre could be heard, as the flames consumed it.

He ignored the pain of his seared shanks and singed body, intent on the bloody reprisal he would reap - his eyes sparking like seething slits of ember in the glow of the flames. The sentry brought his right hand to the hilt of his sword, and staring menacingly at the cowering zealots, he rounded the pyre towards them. They stared into his torrid eyes and were harrowed to the very core of their beings. One of the zealots raised his hand aloft and stammered with a quavering voice.

"L...leave this place. This is th...the will of God with which you interfere. By the power of Christ, be...begone unholy—"

His retort was a loud, pervasive growl that stunned and silenced the zealot. The sentry drew his sword and all gazed upon it in despair. His pain fueled his hate. He showed them no mercy and none escaped his wrath.

* * * *

With his fury spent, the sentry stood calm and still in the midst of the carnage. Slowly, he stared at the dead around him, their sundered, gored, bleeding bodies strewn about the square. He sheathed his gore-streaked sword in his scabbard and walked over the fallen bodies as he returned to Bronwyn's side. Pained by the burns he had received, he moved gingerly. He spied his discarded dagger, and grimacing, stooped slowly to retrieve it. He continued on to where Bronwyn lay and winced as he lowered to a knee at her side. With both hands, he reached for the golden necklace he had hung about his neck in the lair of the demon. He lifted the necklace over his black locks and ever so gently, placed it in Bronwyn's blackened palm. Hearing the tumult of voices some distance away and the sound of approaching footfalls, he glanced at Bronwyn's body one last time before he limped off into the shadows.

## *Chapter Thirteen*
### *Dominium Sodalitas*

# *I*

The sniper was well aware that the Haitian operation had not gone as planned. Though all known felons had been accounted for, there had been a breach of the police perimeter, and two police cruisers had been put out of commission during the operation. Worse still, the operation had suffered two officer fatalities and a fire had broken out on the upper floor of the warehouse. The fire had consumed the contraband they were to have confiscated and had nearly consumed half of the structure before firefighters were able to douse the flames. The forensics unit had established that a carelessly discarded cigarette might have started the fire.

As unfortunate as these transpirations were, they had been outside the responsibility of his SWAT team and definitely beyond the charge of himself and his spotter Wilkinson. These incidents were now the problem of the Queens Police Department, specifically the hundred and eighth precinct. Of course, the sudden disappearance of Officer Klyne was a blemish on the SWAT team, but, as he had written in his report, he had no idea why, or how Klyne had gone MIA. Klyne had last been seen by the sniper team covering the north perimeter, which, as was the case with everything else, had nothing to do with him. He wondered why the Director of National Intelligence had found it necessary to request a personal audience with him and pondered why he had been summoned for questioning from his home in

North Brooklyn.

The director was a man who kept direct communication with the president himself, and the sniper had mused over what could have possibly occurred that would prompt the director to question him. As per usual, he and the rest of his team had submitted their personal reports regarding the operation, which had, as far as he knew, been sent to the Criminal Investigations Division's commander for review. If there had been some problem with his report or his performance, he would have heard it from the CIDC. He had been unable to think of any viable reason as to why his specific attendance had been requested in Virginia. Following the Haitian operation, he had received a phone call on his personal cellphone from a member of the Intelligence Community.

He had been told that all matters regarding the operation were now classified and that he would be brought before the Director of National Intelligence at no expense to him. In fact, his time would be compensated for, and his superiors would be notified of his absence. The next day, a man in a black suit, affiliated with the Intelligence Community, had driven him to La Guardia airport and handed him a ticket. He was flown to Norfolk International Airport where another affiliate had met him and driven him into Virginia to meet with the Director of National Intelligence, the head of the Intelligence Community.

The very prospect of the meeting the director had unnerved him, a condition exacerbated by the austere, government edifice into which he had been ushered. From the elevator, he had been led into a large office on the top floor, and there placed before the director, Andrew Sinclair. The meeting, which had seemed to be more of an interrogation, had been somewhat odd. The director had opened with a question or two regarding Officer Klyne, but then proceeded to inquire about the man in black he had seen on the rooftop for the duration of the meeting. A man in a dark suit had been in attendance during the meeting. He had been a man of average size with blondish hair, and from where the man had leaned against the wall off to the right of the director's desk, the man had casually and silently observed him.

Faced with the director's inquiries, the sniper had not been particularly attentive to the blond man's features. The sniper had been quite thorough and detailed in his report, and could not tell the director any more than he had documented for the CIDC. Still, the director had probed him, seemingly testing his memory for chinks, and squeezing every detail he could from him. The blond man had looked on impassively. The director had been unwaveringly attentive to his description of the strange man's features and how he had traveled over the roof. The sniper thought he had even seen a hint of anxiety on the director's face as he recounted the sighting, though he could not be sure.

\* \* \* \*

Director of National Intelligence, Andrew Sinclair, stroked his clean-shaven chin contemplatively, all the while staring incredulously into the eyes of the young sniper sitting in the chair before him. The large office offered a captivating view of Virginia through an expansive window that stretched over most of the south wall. Sunlight poured in from under the drawn shades, causing the glossy finish on Sinclair's fortress of a desk to sheen. He reclined into his high-backed, black, leather chair and rested both elbows on the arms of the chair, clasping his hands in front of his chest.

The sniper eyed the ring on the director's right hand. The annulus was a shiny gold, and was set with a sizeable, deep-red, ovular stone. Upon its flat, burnished surface was a pyramidal design done in golden embroidery. The sniper's eyes lifted back up to met the director's gaze.

"You're certain of all this of course, and you're quite sure you haven't left anything out?" The director finally inquired.

"Yes, sir," the sniper replied. "It happened just like I said...and like I entered in my report."

"All right then. You did well son. Now...you think of anything else regarding this, you call my office, ye'hear? That'll be all Corporal Hayes will see you out and brief you on further protocol regarding this information."

"Thank you sir," the sniper replied confusedly.

The sniper rose from the chair and made his way to the door. A young, dark-skinned man in a brown military suit was waiting for him outside the director's office, and escorted the sniper to the elevator.

Sinclair watched the young sniper leave his office and seemed to stare after him, even after Corporal Hayes closed the door behind them. The young sniper had not been lying, of that he was certain. He had seen the sincerity in his eyes. The youngster had no reason to fabricate such a thing, and moreover, the way he had described the man in black: his appearance, the way he moved, was exactly as Sinclair himself remembered it. He had only ever seen the man twice, once in 1958, and a second sighting in 1977.

However, he had also read the reports submitted by his associate, Kenton Bruce, and his team after they had a run in with the man in 1986. The first of these encounters had been the most haunting experience of his life to date. He had been little more than a boy then, naïve and unburdened by the weight of the world, which like Atlas, he now held upon his shoulders. He closed his eyes as the harrowing image of the man's face crept into his mind, the white face in the window. He ran a hand through his thin, grey hair, rubbed his brow, and opened his eyes. Much had changed since that day, and the memory of it seemed like a nightmare from a lifetime past.

Kenton Bruce approached Sinclair's desk, sunlight limning the fringes of his crew cut, blond hair and emphasizing the hard lines of his face. He raised his eyebrows in an expression that conveyed knowing and concern.

"Thought we'd seen the last of John Smith in San Antonio," Kenton stated solemnly. His voice was calm, granular and somewhat deep, and he had a slight southern drawl.

Sinclair barely acknowledged Kenton, and stared blankly at his desk, evidently deep in thought.

"I suppose he must have survived somehow, and no doubt goes by an alias other than John Smith these days," Kenton continued. "Though I tell ya...I can't conceive how he could have possibly survived that...unbelievable. That was back in what? Eighty-five? Six?"

"Yeah, eighty-six," Sinclair confirmed, still gazing into the glossy finish on his desk with a far-off look in his eyes.

"Hold on then," Kenton mused with a furrowed brow. "As I recall, you said you might have even seen him when you were a kid. That would make John Smith older than both of us, and by now he could be...damn near eighty. It must have been someone else of course; that would be the most rational explanation...but that sniper's description of him...he said the guy looked like a dark-haired albino. That, along with the way he said the guy moved... seems an accurate account. The sniper's report describes a man in his late twenties to mid-thirties, performing what sounded to me to be Olympic feats of athleticism. I told you about that night in San Antonio. He was so goddamn fast I barely had time to track him with my gun before he jumped out the damn window. Now, initially I was aiming to disable, but regardless...assault rifle, full auto, and I still hardly got a piece of him."

As per Sinclair's recommendation over twenty years ago, which Kenton had intended to follow, John Smith was to have been apprehended for interrogation. Kenton had falsely briefed his team to keep the true aim of the operation undisclosed, leading them to believe that their objective was to capture a soviet spy, and thus secure leaks of information pertaining to national security. John Smith had not heeded the team's cries to surrender and had disarmed and then violently dispatched one officer before attempting to escape. The situation had become untenable and John Smith had been fired upon.

"Improbable as it is, sounds as if we're talking about the same person," Kenton continued. "But even if it was our John Smith that sniper saw...what the hell would a senior citizen - cause that's what he would have to be at this point - be doing running around on rooftops in the middle of an op? It's gotta be a physical impossibility at this point....but I mean, even back when we caught up to him in San Antonio, brief as the encounter was, he didn't look a day over thirty or so. And to hear now the possibility that he's still alive? I had the best team I could muster with me, and as fast it happened, we still all saw John Smith hit a good few times as he made a break for the window. He didn't have a shirt on for Christ sake; we saw bullet holes open up in that pasty skin of his. He dropped eight or nine stories..." Kenton pursed his lips and exhaled exasperatedly, "Something isn't right here, something just isn't right. We never found the body, but I mean..." he trailed off.

"I think you're right," Sinclair said as he turned to face Kenton, dropping the subject. "I don't believe that this man the sniper saw was our John Smith, but I don't think their similarities are just a coincidence. Perhaps..." Sinclair paused for a moment, "perhaps we are dealing with an archaic family, as old as either of our own."

"It's plausible, I suppose, but why do you say that? With the resources at our disposal we can certainly trace a familial line, especially if they are of noble descent; but you of all people would know which families are still in existence nowadays, and in what capacity. I would have said this new individual was some kind of copycat, someone following in John Smith's, or whatever the hell his real name is, footsteps. So why is family lineage the first thing that comes to your mind?"

Kenton raised his right hand. Upon it was a gold ring set with a sizable, flat, red stone, a duplicate of the ring upon Sinclair's hand. Kenton tapped the burnished, gold-embroidered surface with the forefinger of his opposite hand.

"Anything you know I should know too," he asserted in a low tone, with one blond eyebrow raised in a suggestive expression.

"I had no reason to disclose this information until now, nor was I obliged. You informed me that John Smith was deceased, and I had no reason to waste further time or resources concerning him," Sinclair adduced curtly. "However, there is something, though it may prove to be irrelevant." Kenton was attentive as Sinclair continued.

# *II*

As preordained by his family, Andrew Sinclair had followed the path of his father. He learned the intricacies of his father's work and had been well prepared for his induction as one of the nation's elites. Following the unfortunate passing of his father, Andrew Sinclair eventually established himself as the director of the CIA. He was well suited for the position, but it had not been this sole attribute that solidified his claim on the position. The powerful and clandestine sway of the secretive fraternity with which his father had been involved, their *'guild'*, as his father had called it, had been the premiere reason for Andrew Sinclair's seat in power. The guild, like the many-headed hydra, had eyes and ears loyal to a single governing body.

Their reach was not illimitable, nonetheless these heads held positions of rank within powerful institutions throughout many states and in the United Kingdom. Of and in their rank were some of the most brilliant minds and wealthiest people in the United States, many of whom were affiliates of some of the most powerful organizations in the Western world. Using their positions of influence, this fraternity was able to manipulate the society in which they were ensconced. They used their respective authorities to keep the nation in economic order, and to maintain the balance of power within the United States – though they were not opposed to using said authority for their self-preservation and personal gain.

With the assistance of five others, Andrew Sinclair's father had led these Illuminati and kept order within their elitist ranks. The fraternity itself was centuries old, continually replenishing its ranks in secret with premiere members the likes of Mark Twain, George Washington, Theodore Roosevelt, and John Blair. With a continuance of this general standard, the fraternity maintained its numbers over countless decades, incorporating persons of similarly distinguished status.

After having assumed a headship in both the CIA and the fraternity, Andrew Sinclair had seen fit to further consolidate the reach and power of the fraternity, and thus extend its influence over the institutions that comprised the core of the American elite. He and his guild achieved this through legitimate means, in the form of a bill concerning national security. Sinclair created the bill himself, and with the assistance of the fraternity, it had been passed along through all the right channels until it reached President Ronald Reagan. The bill recommended the formation of an institution that would incorporate a select group of agencies for the purpose of pooling information and resources to further protect the nation from threats foreign and domestic. The bill resulted in the formation of the Intelligence Community, which was established in 1981 following Executive Order 12333, sanctioned by President Reagan.

With the Intelligence Community in place, the fraternity was able to attend to their hidden and public agendas with greater efficiency – a result of the entrenchment of their members within numerous agencies. Since the executive order, the agencies that comprise the Intelligence Community, and are thus susceptible to the fraternity's sway, include: the Army, Navy, Air Force, Marine Corps, CIA, Defense IA, Department of Homeland Security, DEA, Energy Department, FBI, National Geo-Spatial Agency, National Reconnaissance Office, NSA, State Department, and the United States Coast Guard.

Andrew Sinclair had been born into privilege and not solely because of who his father had been, but who his forefathers had been centuries before; for Andrew Sinclair was of the Lordly line of the High St. Clairs. The appellation had been conceived even before the first of the St. Clairs of Scotland, already Lord of Roslin, traveled to the Holy Land with a descendant of a Rex Deus family, Godfroi De Bouillon, to join the first Crusade in 1095. It was in the Holy Land that the destinies of the St. Clairs, and what would become The Order of the Poor Knights of Christ of the Temple of Solomon, the Knights Templar, became entwined.

# *III*

The Knights Templar was founded in Jerusalem in 1118. Once established in Jerusalem, members became self-proclaimed protectors of Christian pilgrimage routes in the Holy Land, and their numbers grew rapidly. History records that through information divulged by the discreet Rex Deus families, the original nine knights discovered the legendary Stables of Solomon following a grand-scale excavation. It was rumored that they discovered ancient documents and artifacts therein, a wealth of sacred knowledge hidden within the bowels of the earth. In addition, they took into their possession hordes of treasure, spoils of war, and the riches of kings from bygone eras.

The Templars became a powerful order thereafter; a secretive empire unto themselves, with legions abounding. For over two centuries, the Templars were a significant power in the east, wealthy enough to finance the building of cathedrals and castles. They carried such influence that they became the envy of kings and clergymen throughout Europe, even feared for their supremacy.

In 1307, the persecution of the Templars began. Incited by the avarice and envy of King Philippe Le Bel of France, it was decreed that all Templar knights were to be arrested and tried on charges of heresy. The Templars were hunted down, tortured, and forced into hiding. Despite the sudden siege on the order, which found most of the knights captured in France, many Templars were able to escape the slaughter. They commandeered a fleet of eighteen ships belonging to the king himself, and vanished from French shores. They fled to Scotland, which had been placed under papal interdict at the time, and took refuge in the lands of St. Clair and Robert the Bruce.

It is said that in Scotland, families of Templars, and those of immediate Rex Deus lineage, married into the families of the Scots upon whose lands they had sought refuge. One of the St. Clairs, William by name, even built the ever-alluring Rosslyn Chapel in the mid-fourteen-hundreds, a supposed shrine to the Templar knights. The wealth and knowledge of the Templars, which they had obtained from the Holy Land, found its way to the select Scottish clans, namely the St. Clairs, as evidenced by Henry and his grandson, William, the most notable of the St. Clairs.

Henry de St. Clair, the sixth Henry of the St. Clair line, sailed to the New World and back with a small fleet. Henry's first journey to the west began in 1396, from which he returned with goods and tales from the new world. Henry de St. Clair vanished around the year 1400, and it was unknown whether he had been killed, or if had simply embarked for the New World indefinitely. In 1446, his grandson, William de St. Clair, insured that evidence of Henry's voyage was commemorated on the very walls of Rosslyn Chapel. Therein, Templar symbolism abounded. Depicted upon stone engravings were: maize, aloe cactus, sassandras, albidium, trillium grandilorum, and quercus nigra; all were flora from the Americas, plants unknown in Europe at that time. Both Henry and William de St. Clair were men who had been intimately familiar with Templar doctrines, even as their ranks and very order waned.

Following the apparent death of the order of Templars, came the inception of Scottish freemasonry in 1441 – perhaps born of the Rex Deus traditions adopted long ago. The genealogy and accomplishments of the St. Clairs, who eventually became the Sinclairs, were immortalized in history texts and remembered in familial oral traditions. This was a family whose recorded legacy spanned from before the Middle Ages and into the twenty-first century.

# *IV*

Andrew Sinclair turned in his leather chair, swiveling it enough so that he could face Kenton without craning his neck. Kenton stood statue-like next to Sinclair's desk as he waited for him to continue.

"...That same historical document which hinted at the possible locations of cached wealth from the crusades...it is a diary that belonged to Henry de St.Clair from the year 1402. My thrice-great grandad acquired it from the surviving members of the Italian family Henry de St. Clair had voyaged with. Thank God they weren't versed in Old English well enough to decipher its contents for themselves. Anyhow, in the diary, Henry makes reference to a guy he called the interpreter. From what I have gathered, Henry learned of this interpreter through his dealing with Rex Deus families. The interpreter worked for these families in secret. Actually, the way it was worded, I think that only a few individuals from two Rex Deus families knew about him.

"Apparently he had a decent command of more than a few languages, because he would spend much of his time translating old texts, scrolls, maps, and what have you, obtained from the crusade spoils. In fact, it was the sole duty he performed for the Rex Deus families, and eventually the St. Clair family as well. Henry wrote that the interpreter was a recluse, and it was not until the interpreter himself approached Henry one night that he actually saw him. From what I read, I got the sense that there was a good bit of mystery surrounding this interpreter character. A few of the Rex Deus even referred to the interpreter as The Ancient. Not sure what to make of that...I suppose I'm inclined to think that 'The Ancient' might be a moniker for the interpreter's familial line; meaning that perhaps his ancestors had been interpreters for the Rex Deus since the crusades, a family...I guess...whose purpose was, with each passing generation, to learn languages and translate the vast wealth of knowledge the crusaders' descendants had amassed from foreign countries and ancient civilizations.

"I don't know, maybe John Smith and this man the sniper saw are from the same line. If so, then we are dealing with a person, or persons that probably have a great deal of knowledge pertaining to my family's history...hell, they'll know a good deal about quite a few things, and have likely accumulated a substantial wealth. Clearly, they know how to hide, how to keep under the radar, and they seem to be watching us, though I'm not sure what for."

"I tell you one thing," Kenton said after issuing an audible exhalation of disbelief,

"makes a hell of a lot more sense than the original John Smith still being alive and kicking. But...um...what led you to believe there is a familial connection between John Smith, this man in black the sniper saw, and the...um...interpreter?"

"There was one particular entry Henry made that really drew my attention." Sinclair responded with a hand placed contemplatively over his chin and mouth. "He wrote about the first time he actually saw the interpreter. He described him as being frightening in appearance: white, sickly skin, long, ink-black hair, fearsome of body, and most convincing of all, strange, lifeless eyes of a flaxen hue."

"That last description wasn't part of the sniper's report, or any other reports on our John Smith. Why is that so convincing?" Kenton inquired.

"Because I saw his eyes, I saw his face... John Smith's...I saw it, and I remember." Sinclair replied distantly. "I don't know why these people would have this same...um... phenotype after so many generations. Cousin paring was common practice to keep bloodlines pure in the Middle Ages, both our families did it a couple centuries back; perhaps the John Smith line still practices familial incest or something...I don't know. Either way, in John Smith, I witnessed those specific traits of the interpreter that

Henry de St. Clair recorded in his diary. I think you would agree that those traits are somewhat uncommon, and that tells me they have been preserved somehow. That is why I believe we are dealing with a familial line, as old as the Sinclairs, or the Bruces."

"Well, if any of the Smith family is still around, we might be able to find them same as we did our John Smith – follow the sales trail of relevant antiquities and such."

"I doubt he...they...whatever the case, would make the same damn mistake twice, but check it out anyhow, we have to start somewhere. I'll start the search through the proper channels," Sinclair stated resolutely. Kenton glanced at his watch.

"I've got to get back to the Bureau. I'll do my part from there. When we do find this Smith, and we will, just tell me when you want a special ops team put together and I'll send them in."

Kenton gave Sinclair a nod and headed for the office door. Sinclair spoke as he reached for the knob.

"I don't need to tell you this information is more than simply classified."

"Of course," Kenton replied, his face void of emotion. Kenton opened the door, left the office, and closed the door behind him civilly. Sinclair watched him go, stared after him for a moment, and then picked up his desk phone.

# *Chapter Fourteen*
## *Outcast*

# I

The forge was a teeming mass of white-hot, blazing embers that sent billowing flames upwards to consume the layer of ligneous fuel above, which crackled and smoked, inundated by the furious tongues of flame. The brilliant forge cast a wavering, rich, luminosity throughout the smithy. The deep, golden luster played over the old, rustic timbers that constituted the walls; it gave the numerous metal wares a sunset hue, and suffused Colin's glistening, bare back with color. In his left hand, Colin held a long pair of tongs, with which he held a fledgling sword to the face of his anvil. Fresh from the forge, the blade had a vibrant, orange glow and shed lurid sparks as the blacksmith brought his hammer down upon it again and again, perfecting the shape of the blade.

Harsh metallic clangs resounded within the smithy, nearly masking the sound of the forge's fiery consumption. The young apprentice who worked with Colin throughout the day had gone, for night had fallen some time ago; but Colin had been unable to do his work for nearly fourteen days, and thus toiled late into the night to compensate for lost time. Even now, he felt deep, tearing pains where his assailants had gored his side and back. He hefted the hammer gingerly, his movements measured and subdued. The smithy doors were bolted for the night, as was the door o his home. The smithy was sweltering, but Colin had decided he would endure the heat rather than risk depraved men finding their way into his home once more. Sweat dripped from his nose and brow, and ran into the corners of his eyes. His orangey hair was matted to his temples, and his aching muscles added to the pain of his wounds.

Even in the absence of the din within the smithy, Colin would have been hard pressed to hear the approaching presence. He did not hear nor notice the large, hooded form, which silently moved into the doorway between the smithy and the stone walls of his home; a dark-robed figure, whose feet were bare, and whose garb billowed from the waist below a thick drawstring. Within the robe, the figure's aspect was heavily obscured by shadow. For a short time, the figure simply watched Colin as he toiled. Then, in a voice both chilling and familiar, he spoke Colin's name. Colin spun towards the doorway, and seeing the hooded figure he stumbled backwards dropping the tongs, his green eyes wide as saucers. The tongs clanged against the anvil as they fell to the bare ground below, and the sword scratched against it as it slid off the face of the anvil.

"Jesus bloody shite!" Colin cursed in alarm.

Colin raised his blacksmith's hammer over his head ready to strike. Panicked by the figure, he tripped over the pail of water he had been using to cool and temper the blade. He fell to his rump clumsily and collapsed backwards onto his elbows, wincing as the sudden impact prompted a sharp pain to throb from his healing wounds. He saw the hooded figure take a sudden step forward from the doorway, one hand outstretched as if concerned. The figure spoke again.

"Colin…it's…it's me."

The figure slowly drew back the brown, linen hood, revealing a face, which, like the figures voice, was both chilling and familiar.

\* \* \* \*

The sentry took a few, slow steps towards Colin, both hands

outstretched and upturned peaceably.

"Colin…I cannot explain this…I don't know why this is…but it is me."

Still sprawled on the dusty ground, Colin held the shaft of the massive hammer so tightly that the knuckles of his right hand had gone white. Hearing the voice of the man before him, and seeing his face, Colin's grip on the hammer loosened, though his heart still raced in his chest.

"Christ…Jesus Christ…this can'ne be."

"I know," the sentry concurred sympathetically, "but it is."

They stared at one another for moment, a moment that seemed an eternity to each. Colin regarded his friend with a flabbergasted expression, his mind churning to find some explanation as to what he saw before him. The sentry observed Colin with earnest eyes, hoping that his friend could find the faith and courage to believe. Colin sat up, grimacing with pain as he did.

"Tha'night…the night those men came fer mi'self and Bronwyn…they beat me, stuck me, left me fer dead. I remember fallin te the ground, and all the world around me came te be like some strange, hazy dream or the like. I remember hearin yer voice, feelin, knowin tha'ye were close…" Colin paused, his eyes searching the sentry's face, his mind searching for answers.

"I brought you to Argyle's home and left you in the keeping of himself and his wife. I apologize, it was the best I could do given my…circumstance."

The sentry glanced down at his pale hands and curled his fingers into his palms, hiding the short, dark, lanceolate nails at his fingertips. His eyes lifted and he observed Colin once more.

"Aye…aye…Argyle told me of the strange manner by which he found me at his home. Christ…but it really was ye then wasn'it. Ye really were there…ye…ye saved mi'life. I do'ne understand. I was there when ye were put in the ground. I…God…I piled the soil upon ye mi'self. I…I simply do'ne understand."

With slow yet deliberate steps, the sentry rounded the anvil and approached Colin where he sat upon the ground. Standing over him, he extended a pallid hand down towards him.

"I can explain this no more than you, but I am here…it is me, my friend."

Colin stared at the menacing talon, his mouth somewhat agape. He then stared back up into the face of his friend. He looked very much the same, yet definitively different. Even in the warm firelight, his skin was an evident, greyish, milky white, and his eyes seemed to soak the glow of the forge like searing pools of gold. Yet his friend's face was exactly as he had remembered it, even his longish, black hair fell about his face in a most familiar manner.

Colin seemed to have composed himself to some degree. Following a brief hesitation he let go of the hammer, and reaching upwards, took hold of the sentry's hand. The sentry pulled Colin to his feet with the utmost gentility and steadied the blacksmith with his free hand. The sentry was bare-chested beneath the robe, and Colin noted the sinuous musculature around the beginnings of his chest, which had been exposed when he drew back the hood. He also noted the marked rearward protrusion of a sword beneath the capacious, dark-brown robe. Colin looked into the eyes of his friend once more, the mere inkling of a half-smile on his face.

"Well…comin back from the dead certainly has'ne done anything fer yer looks then I suppose…but…tis good te see ye nonetheless."

Despite all that had befallen him, the sentry felt the beginnings of a smile find its way onto his face. It seemed a lifetime ago that he had smiled last. Colin placed his hands upon his hips, closed his eyes, and exhaled violently, his lips loose and fluttering. He lifted his head, and shaking it in apparent disbelief, regarded his friend.

"Ye know, it would have been tryin enough fer me te see ye without ye appearin in me smithy like some sort'o ghost. Could ye ne have used the front door like a normal person?"

Colin received no reply, but the sour look upon his friend's pallid face suggested the answer to his question was self-evident.

"Em…right…well…how did ye get in here anyhow? Never… nevermind, I'm unsettled enough as'it is. Speakin o'which, can I just say yer frightnin as the dickens. Ye might want te consider a change o'clothes er something if yer gonna be around any kind'o descent folk," Colin suggested.

"I am dressed like a priest," the sentry posited dryly. "Besides, I don't plan on spending much time around people."

Colin looked him over from head to foot.

"Oh, Jesus! Ye didn't kill a priest fer this robe did ye?" Colin inquired with some concern and pleading eyes. The sentry sighed.

"No, Colin, I did not kill a priest for this robe."

"Oh, thank God, somethin like tha would'o brought a curse down on ye sure."

The sentry simply stared at Colin, who once again found meaning in his stoic face.

"Well…em…more cursed…than now a least…I suppose… em…" Colin stammered sympathetically. "Yer a good man. Always have been. It can'ne be easy te have gone through wha'ever twas tha'happpened te ye, but wha'ever has passed, I know tis yer soul and yer's only inside ye, yer heart only tha'courses blood through yer veins. I'll be there for ye friend, ye do'ne have te run. Ye have friends here…mi'self, Ober…"

Colin paused, and after staring off into nothingness for the briefest of moments, looked down at the ground. The sentry spoke, his voice hard and full of pain.

"I…couldn't save her Colin. I tried, but I…I couldn't save her. God, I tried."

The sentry's voice quavered with this last remark. Colin raised his head and looked into his friend's tortured eyes, his own eyes shimmering with welling tears. Colin placed a hand on the sentry's shoulder.

"I know ye did, friend…I know ye did. Argyle told me tha'someone sent the lot o'them swine te hell, but tha'none in the town had claimed the deed. Seein ye now, I knew…I knew it must have been ye…and I thank God ye let them damned sons o'whores have a taste o'tha blade o'yours. I hope tha'they burn in the pit ye sent 'em te…burn forever curse 'em." Colin tightened his grip on the sentry's shoulder, breathing shakily, a tear running down his soot stained cheek, "She loved ye, ye know…aye…loved ye with all she had."

"I know," the Sentry replied.

Colin patted his shoulder, a sad smile upon his face. Colin turned from the sentry and sat upon the face of the anvil, wiping his tear streaked cheek.

"We can'ne undo wha'has come te pass…any o'it. Nor can we try te understand God's will. I must accept mi'loss, and ye must accept the new life ye have been given."

"I cannot stay here," the sentry remarked. "Far too many of the townspeople know my face. They'll think me to be a living dead man, summoned by witches, or come from hell, or…regardless, I cannot remain in Berwick."

"Wha'will ye do then?" Colin inquired with a troubled look on his face.

"I will hunt the white demons as God intended, and perhaps learn the source of this curse that has befallen me. I must ask a favor of you before I leave however."

"Wha'is it?"

"I cannot bear the sunlight of late, nor do I dare show my face within these walls for all to see, or else I would have done this myself."

"Think nothing of it friend. Wha'de ye need?"

"Well…most importantly, do not tell a soul of my coming here tonight, of my very existence for that matter. As far as the town is concerned I am a dead man, let us keep it that way."

"I'll ne say a word," Colin assured.

"I also need two horses, both dark as possible in color: saddle blankets and bridles for both, a saddle for one, a good length of rope, and four large sacks of the strongest weave you can find," the sentry listed soberly.

"Em…tha…" Colin stammered with evident dismay on his face, "tha'may prove a difficult set o'errands te attend te…em… referring te the state o'me coin purse o'course. Ne tha'I would'ne sacrifice mi'earnings fer ye, but ye know I simply do'ne have such..."

Colin fell silent as the sentry reached underneath his flowing robe and produced a melon-sized, brown, leather pouch tied with a hide string. He shifted it in his palm so that the mass of coins within jingled quite audibly.

"This will more than cover the expense. Divide what remains between you and Ober...properly, Colin. Ober will be expecting his fair share," added the sentry almost facetiously. "Meet me... fifteen days from now, I suppose: outside the town, at sunset, at the edge of the wood near the Celt stone. Ober will know where it is."

Colin simply stared at the coin pouch, then looked up at the sentry, then observed the pouch a second time, and finally returned his gaze to the sentry.

"Christ!" Colin exclaimed.

"What is it?" The sentry inquired dispassionately.

"Ye did'ne kill someone fer this pouch did ye?"

The sentry sighed impatiently.

"Fifteen days, sunset, the Celt stone. Meet with Ober before you come." The sentry repeated solemnly as he began to move towards the stone doorway into Colin's home.

"Jesus! Ye did, ye did, did'ne ye...ye killed someone fer this pouch. Oh, Lord..."

The sentry turned his head over his shoulder, though he did not actually look back at Colin.

"Colin...I assure you, it was a very bad...person," the sentry reasoned.

"Christ Almighty."

"Goodnight Colin."

"Aye...aye...s...sunset then...fifteen days...Christ!"

The sentry turned towards the doorway and passed through it into Colin's home. Colin marked that his friend had disappeared beyond the doorway in the opposite direction to the door of his home, and thought he might have heard the faint creaking of his wooden stairs. Colin stared at the open doorway and murmured to himself.

"Wha'the? Where's he goin then?"

In the moment of silence that followed, the sentry was gone.

* * * *

Fifteen days thereafter, Colin and Ober left Berwick sometime in the evening. Both sat astride horses. Colin rode a black mare of average size, while Ober rode a large, bay destrier, the bay coat of which was nearly as dark as that of the black mare. The horses were laden with the rest of the sentry's requested effects. They rode staggered, almost one behind the other, for it was Ober who led them from the town gate to the location the sentry had specified. The mare had been tethered to the big bay with a rope from its bridal to the bay's saddle, and complacently allowed itself to be pulled in tow. Though Colin held the reins out of habit, it was entirely unnecessary. As sunset neared, they reached the fringe of the plot of wood that lay beyond the standing stone. Here, they waited patiently atop their mounts, which tossed their heads and snorted from time to time. Both men were wary and anxious, thus their conversation was not as boisterous as it usually was. Nonetheless, Colin entertained Ober with a humorous tale of the tasteless variety, and Ober spoke of battles and hunts long past.

The verdant land about them began to darken and they watched as the sun dipped in the horizon. The sun was a subdued orange orb and, immediately around it, the sky had a rich a fiery hue. Further from its source, this effulgence became a wash of pinks and purples, which merged into the grey-black darkness that pervaded the firmament. Night had begun to stake its claim, its gloom momentarily held at bay by the dying glow from the western horizon. The two men waited – and waited further still as the sun kissed the skyline, beginning its descent into the earth. Presently, Colin and Ober heard a faint rustling of foliage from somewhere along the fringes of the wood before them. It was Ober, with his sharp huntsman's eyes, who first saw the sentry. Ober reached over to Colin with one long arm, rapped Colin's chest to gain his attention and, in stoic silence, pointed to where the sentry approached. Colin followed Ober's lengthy forefinger to the edge of the wood and was surprised see that the sentry was no more than twenty paces from where they sat atop the horses.

The deep brown of the clergyman's robe he still wore made him difficult to spot as he made his way along the limits of the wood. His feet were still bare, and once again, his head was cloaked by the large hood. He stopped a short distance from them, his hooded head slowly turning about, as though he were seeing things unseen. His shadow-cast visage faced forward once more, and he drew back his hood as he entered their midst.

"So I see tha'ye hav'ne taken me'advice then, as yer still stalkin about in tha'priest robe," Colin said as he dismounted. Ober dismounted as well, swinging his long leg over the saddle, and landing upon the ground with his right hand still clutching the small, rounded pommel of the saddle.

"In fact, I have," the sentry said quietly as he approached Colin. "Indeed, it is something I intend to remedy this night." The sentry put his hand on Colin's shoulder, "I am grateful," he said before turning to face Ober, "to both of you."

"It is we who must be grateful to you friend. You've given us the worth of two years' pay between the both of us. If you must go, then take at least some of what you have given us with you," Ober offered sincerely.

"I have found some fortune my friend, at least in that regard. Do not worry about me. Live your lives friends," he remarked, glancing first at Ober then at Colin, "live your lives."

The sentry approached the large, bay horse and took the reins from Ober with one hand. With the other, he reached towards the horse's rounded, muscular cheek. It nuzzled him docilely as he ran his strange talon over the horse so gently, so tenderly, that Colin and Ober could not help but watch him in silence. It was the sentry who finally broke the silence. He turned to Colin and Ober, one hand still holding the bay's reins.

"Fine animals, my thanks again. You two should make your way back to the town. If you leave now, you should reach the gate before it is lowered for the night."

"We shall be fine," Ober asserted warmly.

Momentarily releasing the bay's reins, the sentry walked over to the mare, inspecting her and running a hand over her length. Colin and Ober had bridled both horses and put a saddle blanket over each. However, Ober had decided the single saddle should be placed upon the larger bay. Thus, much of the coil of rope the sentry had requested had been looped around the mare to secure the blanket on its back and to fasten the sacks they had purchased. The rest of the rope had been looped about the base of the mare's neck so that it could be easily accessed. The sentry returned to the bay, and in one effortless motion, slung himself up into the saddle. He took the reins and cast his icy gaze upon Colin and Ober.

"Will we ever see ye again, friend?" Colin asked as he finished securing the mares reins so that they would not fall.

"Perhaps. If I live long enough." The sentry replied with an almost sorrowful tone, "Farewell my friends, your kindness, your company, will never be forgotten."

"Safe journey," Ober replied with sadness in his aged eyes.

Colin forced a smile and gave a weak, despondent wave of his hand. The sentry stared off in the direction of the town and then smiled at his friends as best he could. He pulled the hood back over his head, drowning his face in shadow, though his strange yellow eyes seemed to glint within. He turned from them and kicked the great bay into a brisk trot. Colin and Ober watched as the sentry rode away with the black mare following close behind. Still staring off after his friend, Colin disrupted the silence that had fallen.

"Ye see his teeth just there? Jesus, but he's a frightnin sight!"

"Aye…damn near loosed the dung from me bowels when he came to me in the night," Ober admitted, also staring after the sentry's dwindling form.

"Aye, I felt a bit o'the same mi'self," Colin empathized. "Ye think he'll be a'right, Ober?"

"He will be fine, lad. Besides, we can do naught now but pray." Ober thumped Colin's back with the massive expanse that was his hand. It had the desired effect of jarring Colin from his stupor. "Come," Ober said, "let's away."

The two men turned back in the direction they had come, ascending the grassy hill back to Berwick, as the erstwhile sentry evanesced into the lonely night.

To be concluded in:

*Genesis of the Hunter: Book Two*

Watch for it…Coming Sept 2010 from Damnation Books.

## *About the Author*

Joshua Martyr was born and raised in Toronto Canada. He earned his Specialized Honours degree at York University and received his Bachelor of Education from OISE at the University of Toronto in the disciplines of Physical Education and English.

In addition to being an athlete of some distinction, Joshua is a lover of the world's many animal species and of its untamed wildernesses.

## Phoenix and the Darkness of Wolves
### by Shane Jiraiya Cummings

A dark fantasy novella
$4.50
eBook ISBN: 978-1-61572-055-2
Print ISBN: 978-1-61572-054-5

Australia has been devastated by a supernatural inferno. Damon believes he is the last ash-covered survivor, a man's whose past—and future—is inextricably tied to the magick that caused the conflagration. He tracks a phoenix through this apocalyptic wasteland in the hopes of using its magick to restore his lost family to humanity. His family, in turn, have been condemned to limbo as shadow wolves, emerging for a few fleeting moments every sunset to hunt Damon in the hope his death will free them from their torment. The hunt is on!

http://www.damnationbooks.com/book.php?isbn=9781615720552

www.damnationbooks.com

DAMNATION BOOKS

HORROR
DARK FANTASY
PARANORMALS
SCIENCE FICTION
THRILLERS
EROTICA

EBOOK
DIGITAL
TRADE PAPERBACK

CPSIA information can be obtained at www.ICGtesting.com
Printed in the USA
LVOW060327280512

283525LV00001B/33/P